T0284342

HITTING THE CROSSBAR

THE BAD BOY & THE TOMBOY SERIES

The Bad Boy and the Tomboy
Book One

Hitting the Crossbar
Book Two

Across the Line
Book Three - Winter 2024

A BAD BOY & THE TOMBOY ROMANCE

HITTING THE CROSSBAR

NICOLE NWOSU

wattpad books

wattpad books
An imprint of Wattpad WEBTOON Book Group

Copyright© 2023 Nicole Nwosu

All rights reserved.

No portion of this publication may be reproduced or transmitted, in any form or by any means, without the express written permission of the copyright holders.

Published in Canada by Wattpad WEBTOON Book Group, a division of Wattpad WEBTOON Studios, Inc.

36 Wellington Street E., Suite 200, Toronto, ON M5E 1C7 Canada

www.wattpad.com

First Wattpad Books edition: April 2023

ISBN 978-1-99077-866-7 (Trade Paper original)
ISBN 978-1-99077-867-4 (eBook edition)

Names, characters, places, and incidents featured in this publication are either the product of the author's imagination or are used fictitiously. Any resemblance to actual persons (living or dead), events, institutions, or locales, without satiric intent, is coincidental.

Wattpad Books, Wattpad WEBTOON Book Group, and associated logos are trademarks and/or registered trademarks of Wattpad WEBTOON Studios, Inc. and/or its affiliates. Wattpad and associated logos are trademarks and/or registered trademarks of Wattpad Corp.

Library and Archives Canada Cataloguing in Publication information is available upon request.

Printed and bound in Canada

1 3 5 7 9 10 8 6 4 2

Cover design by Lesley Worrell
Images © Kane Skennar via Getty Images

To Sarah. This would not exist without you.

1

GET A BOX OR TWO

It shouldn't have been this cold.

It was early October in Edward Bay, Canada. It was supposed to be cold, I got it. But cold like *autumn*, not the middle of Antarctica. Even in what should have been the warmth of my dorm room, I was freezing. I wrapped the comforter around me even tighter. I wanted to sleep. I *needed* to sleep.

"Hazel."

The bane of my existence had entered my dorm room. Well, okay, maybe he wasn't the bane of my existence in general . . . but he was *right now.*

"No, no, *no*. Get him out," I groaned into my pillow, shifting my head away from the voice. It was too early for this. My first class wasn't until ten thirty. I could still get a few more minutes of sleep in. I knew it wasn't even nine yet because I could hear another voice whose sociology lecture started then.

"Macy," said my roommate, Maddy, with a sigh. She was

probably tired of hearing my complaints every time I didn't have morning practice. It wasn't my fault that I favored my sleep.

"No, I don't want to see him. Not now," I muttered.

"She already brushed her teeth," Maddy told him, probably rolling her eyes. "She literally just crawled back into bed."

In a lazy drawl, the ruiner of my peace said, "I figured you of all people would be very happy to see me."

"I usually am," I said, muffled into the pillow. "Just not now."

"Okay," Maddy said. "I'm going to class before you two start doing whatever you're planning on doing. Bye, Mace!"

"Bye!" I yelled into my pillow, and the door slammed shut.

Before I knew it, one side of my bed dipped, and my comforter partially rose up before falling back down. When he wrapped his strong arms around me and pushed my hair out of the way to kiss the back of my neck, I leaned back into his presence involuntarily. Like I always did. "Morning," he said.

"What do you want?" I muttered.

"I come with food for you." That was all he needed to say. My eyes popped open, and I twisted around. But the only feast laid out for me was the smug expression spread across his face.

Samuel Henry Cahill.

There were a lot of things people used to call him. A bad boy. A player. Cocky. Egotistical. And while he was still some of those things, he was also my idiot of a boyfriend with vivid green eyes and curly hair that was currently spread around his face, some of the strands splayed out onto his forehead. He was extremely good-looking, and he knew it. He was an amazing soccer (or as he loved to say, *football*) player.

Although we had met only a few months ago after his parents had shipped him from his hometown in England to mine in

Canada, it didn't feel that short. It felt like we had known each other our whole lives.

He wasn't perfect, but he was to me. Even when he had the audacity to lie about food.

I narrowed my eyes at him. "There's no food."

"We'll get some when you're happy to see me." He grinned.

I hiked one leg over his body, straddling him while leaning forward into his warm embrace. "I *am* happy to see you. But I wanted to sleep, and when I hear you in the morning on Fridays coming to walk with me to class, that means my sleep is ruined."

Since the school year had started back in September, I was grateful every time I got to see Sam. Sam went to Hayes University, about an hour away from me in Southford, near Hamilton, while I attended Henry David Florentine University, just east of London. The two of us played for the varsity soccer teams at our schools. Both of us were constantly busy. We might not have seen each other as much as I would have liked, but I soaked in every moment I could with him.

"Well, do you want to come and stay over tomorrow night? I'll let you sleep all you want."

That sounded really good. "Is Peter going to be there?"

Sam shrugged. "He said that he might go see his girlfriend in Toronto."

Peter wasn't directly Sam's cousin, but everyone referred to him as such. While Peter wasn't a Cahill, he acted like one. He reminded me a bit of Sam's cousin Ivan. He had that mischievous sparkle in his eyes and a head full of bad ideas.

Come to think of it, he was basically sworn in as a Cahill.

"You have practice tomorrow?" Sam asked.

"In the afternoon," I said, glancing over to where my cleats were hanging out of my duffel bag on the floor. Soccer. I got to play the sport at a university pro soccer players had attended, where they had been scouted and signed, and now they were professionals. "You know, I still can't believe I made the team."

Sam's hands went up against my back, leaving tingles in their wake until he reached my ponytail. He took the hair tie out, letting my brown hair escape its confines. "Why? You deserved it."

I leaned back, my eyes roaming his expression. His green eyes showed so much sincerity that without thinking I moved forward, kissing him. He responded with equal intensity, his hands tightening around me, one moving up to my face and the other to my hip. The feeling that surged through me from this, the simplicity of this moment, always surprised me. The way I had to bite back a smile every time we kissed always shocked me. Especially when he pressed us closer to each other and I could feel his body heat even through the leather jacket he was wearing. Especially when his teeth tugged on my bottom lip as a tease. The sound he made when I combed my fingers through his hair jolted down my body.

I could have kissed him forever if that had been possible. The two of us in a little bubble. Unfortunately, bubbles were meant to be popped.

"Whoa, guys!"

I pushed myself off Sam quickly, stumbling to my feet. We met my roommate's wide eyes before she looked apologetic.

"Maddy," Sam huffed with irritation that I knew would be forgotten in a second.

Sam liked Maddy. When he'd first met her a few weeks ago, he'd said, *She's not annoying*. And unlike most of the girls who had spotted Sam whenever he was here, she didn't think of him as anything more than a friend. That was a relief—I never had to worry about coming back to the dorm and having my roommate fawn all over my boyfriend.

"Sorry," Maddy said, walking over to her desk. "I forgot my book. You two lovebirds can go back to whatever you were doing."

Maddy—Madeline, really, but she preferred the nickname—was a Filipino girl from a small town in British Columbia, with golden-brown skin and long dark hair, around five-foot-one to my six feet. Our long-distance friendship didn't matter since we'd realized we were going to get along the second we'd met.

The first time I met her wasn't even in our room. Like me, Maddy attended our university for a sport, but she played volleyball. I had been passing by one of the many gyms on campus as I was exploring and accidentally got in the way of a volleyball game where she almost hit me in the face with the ball.

Ever since then, we'd been good friends.

When she left the room and closed the door behind her, I straightened myself, turning back to Sam. "I'm going to take a shower. Wait for me?"

"Always," he murmured.

I pushed him on the shoulder, unable to keep the smile off my face. "It's too early for you to be this corny."

But my words didn't erase the smirk from his face. He got comfortable on my bed, locking his hands behind his head. Almost six months together with this guy. Wow.

"You should wear those shorts more often," he said, eyeing my legs as I went over to the closet.

"Shut up."

~

"It's freezing here," I commented as the cold seeped through my jacket, creeping up my spine and around my neck. When I spoke, a white gust of air left my mouth. Summer wasn't my favorite season, but I missed the warmth more than anything.

Sam chuckled, shoving his hands into the pockets of his leather jacket, a gust of white cloud coming out of his mouth when he said, "For a Canadian, you complain about cold weather a lot."

"It shouldn't be this cold," I said as we entered the coffee shop. I didn't remember October ever being this cold; even though Edward Bay was two hours west of Port Meadow, I felt like I had traveled north of my hometown.

Yet despite his red nose, Sam didn't complain as we sat down at a table. He had lived in Canada for over a year now, and I'd never heard the man complain about the weather. Meanwhile, my fingers were numb and my ears were starting to hurt.

I shivered involuntarily once again, not even able to take my camera out of its bag. "I feel like I've been pushed into a meat freezer. I feel like someone buried me in snow and left me there for a full day."

"Stop exaggerating." Sam took my hands in his large ones, rubbing them to provide some heat.

His accent hadn't faded. I didn't imagine it would, especially since he surrounded himself with his family, who mostly sounded the same. Over the summer, after we had graduated high school, he had gone back to England, along with the rest of the Cahills who lived in Canada. He had visited his parents, Alice and James, and his little brother, Greg, for the first time in months. And when he'd come back, his parents and brother had returned with him for a brief visit.

When I'd first met his parents, I'd had the idea that they

didn't know what to think of me. They had sent Sam to Canada about a year after the death of his twin sister, Bethany, because he had been acting out. Initially, after Bethany had passed, Sam had run away to Redmond, Ontario, where his grandmother Lucy resided, and gotten mixed up with the wrong set of people. When his father had taken him back to Bath, England, Sam had gotten involved with an even worse crowd, whose choices led to an arson incident. His parents believed a change in scenery—and getting away from certain people—would be good for him. So he was moved again, this time to his aunt Liz and uncle Vince's house in Port Meadow. After Sam had told me months ago about how his sister's death had affected him, he'd never really spoken about it again. I knew he hadn't told me the full extent of everything he had done in England that had led to developing a bad boy reputation before we'd met.

And I didn't push him.

He would tell me when he was ready.

I'd never forget the look his mother had given me when she'd met me. There was almost a look of disbelief on her face—she'd stared at me so intensely that I'd thought I had something in my teeth. After she had glanced at Sam, then back at me, she had settled for generic questions, not asking the real questions she must have wanted to.

Had Sam changed so much since she'd last seen him? Did she think Sam and I were a bad idea? It was like she knew how Sam and I had really gotten together. Sometimes thinking about it, even though everyone else seemed to have moved past it, left me feeling like a sack of shame.

Because how do you explain to your boyfriend's family that the two of you dated behind his cousin's back, while his cousin had been dating you only to get back at your boyfriend for years of resentment?

Here's how: I never did.

Sam's parents couldn't have known what had happened between me and the two Cahill boys. Sometimes I wondered if Cedric's parents, Liz and Vince, had a suspicion, but if they did, nothing was ever discussed in my presence. I had been to their house multiple times during the summer, becoming familiar with more members of the Cahill family, and no one had ever brought it up.

But I knew one day it would come out.

Today was not going to be that day.

"I'm not exaggerating," I said, shaking myself out of my thoughts as my hands absorbed his warmth.

"Really? Because you are a walking hyperbole." Suddenly, Sam's eyes searched my face with concern. "Are you okay, though? I know it's been a bit since I've seen you."

It had been only two weeks since we'd last seen each other, but that was because we were both busy. Currently, I felt like a mess. I hadn't been sleeping properly because of all the schoolwork and soccer practices. "I'm sorry," I said. "We were supposed to go out a few days ago, but then I had that essay I still had to finish writing and—"

"Hazel, it's okay. Trust me. I'm happy that I at least get to see you now. That's all that matters." He took off his hat, combing his fingers through the curls in an attempt to tame them.

"How are your practices?" I asked.

"They're good," he said with some hesitation. I shot him a look. Something was wrong. "The senior guys on the team still call us fresh meat. They tried to haze us."

Haze? Sam waved a dismissive hand at my anxious look.

"They remind me of my team from back home. They're not messing with me." He uttered those words with confidence. Not that I had any reason to worry. "Speaking of back home, we're watching the recording at my place tomorrow?"

"We're rooting for Chelsea."

"*You're* rooting for Chelsea," he corrected. "I'm rooting for Man United."

"You're not even from Manchester!"

"*You're* not even from the UK," he pointed out with a grin. "What are *you* going on about?"

Before I had the chance to answer, my phone cut me off with a loud ring. I answered the call.

"How are you doing, princess?" asked Caleb Romero Henderson, Sam's best friend. I hadn't heard from him in a little over a week. Honestly, if he had the chance to, Caleb would probably call me every hour of every day.

"I'm doing okay, Charming," I answered. Sam rolled his eyes at the nickname, getting up to get our orders.

"How is your damsel in distress?"

"Damsel in distress?" I asked with a laugh.

"Yes, my best friend is your damsel in distress. Definitely not a knight in shining armor," he said. "I feel like he's trying to avoid my calls."

"Well, how many times have you called him?"

"You mean since this morning? I don't know. Like seventy-two times, and he's not answering." *Well, if you called seventy-two times and he never picked up, maybe you should take the hint.*

Sam returned with a cup of hot chocolate for me and a coffee for himself. I covered the speaker of my phone, asking, "You aren't answering Caleb's calls?"

"No," Sam stated. "He's been on my case about another stupid theory of his."

"What theory?" Sam took a sip of his coffee, gesturing to my phone. I repeated the question to Caleb, who was quick to get excited.

"Okay, so I was with this girl the other night—"

"Hold up. *No*. I've gone through an entire summer of your theories and your stories. I think I'm good for the rest of the year. Forget I asked. Change the topic."

"Fine." I could visualize him pouting, and I cracked a smile. I already missed him. Caleb was attending college in our hometown to study creative writing. Last I heard, he was working on a story he hoped to turn into a novel. "Wow, princess. I thought that you liked hearing me talk."

"I do, but hearing you talk about your sex life is not number one on my list of conversations," I said, sipping my drink.

Across from me, Sam tensed, then gestured for me to hand the phone to him. When he pressed it against his ear, he took a very deep breath before saying, "Caleb, why the hell are you discussing sex stuff with my girlfriend?"

I didn't hear Caleb's response, but whatever it was, it irritated Sam. "You are an idiot."

That's when Caleb yelled so loud, I heard it. *"I am not an idiot!"*

"We'll talk later." Caleb clearly kept talking, and Sam began rubbing his temples. "*Yes*, I'll answer my phone." He closed his eyes. "No, I do not. I am *never* going to say that to you, you insufferable prick." The insult wasn't unfamiliar, nor was the sight of Sam struggling to suppress his amusement. "I don't care. Bye." He hung up the phone and handed it to me.

"Your relationship will never fail," I said. Sam's scowl deepened. "What did he want you to say?"

"He wanted me to tell him that I missed him."

"You do," I pointed out.

"No, I don't," Sam retorted, getting up and moving away from the subject as he put his hat on. He started walking out of the shop while I laughed in disbelief, putting on my hat and following him.

"You *do* miss Caleb," I said as I caught up with him. He certainly did. There was a picture of a younger version of Sam and Caleb that had been in his room back in Port Meadow that he'd brought with him to Southford. Deep down, he loved it when Caleb called him excessively—I was sure of it.

I would know: I was the same with Andrew and Jasmine. With all our friends from back home, really. Andrew had texted me that morning. I had sent a text to Jasmine a few days ago. She hadn't responded yet, but she was probably busy. We all were.

"No, I don't," he said, kicking at a rock as we walked down the busy sidewalk.

"Don't lie to me." I punched his shoulder lightly. "He's like your brother. Besides, in a few weeks you'll see him again."

A few more weeks and we'd see *everyone* in Port Meadow again. Sam's cousin Ivan was getting married to his girlfriend of many years, Natasha. Natasha, the redheaded violinist, was smitten with Ivan Cahill. She'd invited me to be a part of her wedding as a photographer after we had spent some time together over the summer. As dramatic and arrogant as Ivan was, it wasn't a surprise that he wanted a big wedding, resulting in him inviting all our friends to come to the wedding as well.

Sam slung an arm around me, the leather of his jacket

rubbing against my Adidas one. "I'm never going to say that to his face, though, so shut it." He ended his sentence by kissing the side of my head.

As we continued walking down the street, I spotted a couple of people around our age glancing over in our direction, speaking under their breath. When one girl—whom I vaguely recognized—decided to be the brave one of the group, she broke apart from them and approached us.

Correction: she approached *Sam.*

I wasn't surprised. Many of the business majors on campus knew about the Cahill corporation and the family's wealth, and in turn, they knew about the Cahill boys. However, that Cahill notoriety had grown over the summer when Sam's mother, Alice, who had been a popular singer in the UK when she was younger, released a comeback album, which immediately became a huge hit. After she had put herself into the limelight, Sam, his brother, and a few of their cousins had been thrown into it a bit as well, resulting in people approaching Sam more than he ever liked. People online and off started paying more and more attention to him and his family.

His mother had started touring Europe as well. With Alice rarely staying in a city for more than two days and Sam staying in Canada for university, Greg had voiced that he wanted to be closer to his brother. This had resulted in Greg now living with his uncle John and aunt Naomi in Port Meadow, while his father, James, frequently visited as he handled the Cahill corporation in England.

"You're Sam Cahill, right?" She didn't have to ask. She knew who he was. "I thought you attended Hayes?"

"And how would you know that?" Sam asked.

"Everyone knows that," she said, her eyes sparkling, and I blinked. Okay. Give her the benefit of the doubt. "So, what are you doing here?"

"Visiting," he quipped, glancing over at me.

When her eyes slid over in my direction, her smile slipped. There it was. The flicker of annoyance. Her gaze narrowed as she scrutinized me before she pursed her lips. "I think we have geography tutorial together?"

I wasn't taking geography.

Don't pretend, I wanted to say, but I focused on not crushing the hot chocolate in my hand. "I think so," I lied.

Her gaze swept over me once again in a way that made me clear my throat as something else to do. "Nice to see you." Before I had a chance to say anything, she turned her attention back to Sam, who had stiffened next to me. "Some of my friends and I were wondering if you wanted to—"

Sam shook his head. "I've got plans."

"You sure?"

"I'm positive."

But she wasn't taken aback by his steely tone. "There's no way to possibly convince you to join us?"

She wasn't backing off. And she wasn't subtle with her intentions when her hand fell on Sam's arm. *Oh*. Sam immediately shrugged her hand off with ease as he took the drink from my hand. "Don't worry about it," he said coolly. "It's fine."

Fine? His patience was running thin. And fast.

It was becoming a matter of whose patience would snap first: his or mine. But I had work to do back at my dorm. I didn't have all day for this.

I tapped him. "I need to stop at the store. You want me to get them? We ran out after last time."

I didn't miss the girl's eyes widen a fraction. Sam almost failed to hide his amusement. "Yeah, get a box or two. Maybe one."

"*One* box?" I pretended to be appalled. "That's what you said that one time, and it wasn't enough."

"Two boxes, then?" Sam suggested. "No, get three just in case. See if you can get any of the free ones they have in the bathrooms on campus."

"From the bathrooms?" I cringed.

"You're not going to be complaining when we're using them. Protection is key, Hazel." The ease of his tone—actually, the entire conversation, despite the months that we'd been together—made me flush. He was smooth with his words, and there I was, flustered by a fantasy that had no bearing in reality.

The girl didn't notice my expression as she slowly started backing away. "Um, I'll see you around, Sam."

Good. When she quickly shuffled back to her friends, I burst out laughing. Sam didn't join in my elation. Instead, he frowned. "Wait, you're not going to get them?"

"In your dreams."

Sam sighed dramatically, intertwining my fingers with his. "At least my dreams are wild."

"*You* are disgusting."

"And yet you are still in love with me."

"That's true," I murmured. The reassurance made him press a light kiss to my lips as we walked through the cold back to campus.

2
FATE IS AN EVIL SPIRIT

Sometimes, I forgot that my boyfriend was rich.

When I stepped into the penthouse Sam and Peter were living in, the reminder hit me in the face. It was so big that their bedrooms were located in different hallways. That was a good thing, seeing as Peter claimed that he liked to walk around naked.

I had taken a long bus ride over to their place immediately after my practice had finished, only to almost trip on one of Sam's Converse shoes in the hallway. After I took off my Jordans and made my way to the kitchen, I dropped my camera bag and backpack on the counter. I was ready for the game. My Chelsea jersey was underneath my sweater, and my pride was on the table . . . along with a box of Pop-Tarts.

I was tearing into a packet when Sam's voice rang throughout the apartment. "Hazel?"

"Kitchen!" I yelled back.

Sam came into the room, flipping through the back of a

calculus textbook as my gaze dipped down to his exposed torso. The only clothing on his body was a pair of blue-and-green neon socks I was certain Caleb had bought him and gray sweatpants. He looked great in gray sweatpants. Not that I would tell him to his face. "How was practice?"

"Fine," I said, my mouth filled with Pop-Tart as he put the book down, reaching into the fridge to get a bottle of water. "How was yours?"

As he was about to raise the bottle to his lips, he stopped and raised an eyebrow at me. "It was *fine*?"

"My legs feel as if they tried to run around the world at least *eight* times. I could barely keep my eyes open on the bus. So I am totally and completely *fine*." I closed my eyes and sagged against the fridge, feeling the refreshing cool steel against my back.

"My poor baby." I could clearly hear the mocking tone even as he included the stupid term of endearment.

I reached out, hitting him lightly on the chest. "Don't be a jerk."

Sam didn't retaliate. Instead, his fingers toyed with the zipper of my sweater. "I'm not being a jerk," he said quietly. Then he tugged, pulling the zipper down until it reached the bottom. "Am I being a jerk now?"

I didn't answer him. This happened more often than I'd thought it would. I glanced down at his torso, then up to his lips. He didn't change his calm expression, but I knew if I put my hand over his heart, I'd feel his pulse rapidly fluttering against my skin. When he pushed the sleeves off my shoulder, my sweater fell to the ground. Then his warm hands found their way to my hips. He broke eye contact as he pushed my jersey up by a fraction before brushing his thumb along the sliver of my skin that was exposed.

I exhaled, goose bumps manifesting where his hands resided. Sam tilted his head, getting closer to me as he asked in a low voice, "And now?"

"Honey, I'm home!"

Both Sam and I let out a breath at the intrusion. I wasn't sure if I was grateful for Peter or irritated. Definitely a mixture of both. Sam, on the other hand, was annoyed. "Shit," he whispered, not taking his hands off me as he looked over his shoulder at Peter.

Like every boy in the Cahill orbit, Peter was attractive, with wavy brown hair, brown eyes, and tanned skin. Usually, he was a great guy. Funny. But right now, the irritated side of me was taking over as I plastered a fake smile on my face. "Peter."

"Macy!" he called in a singsong, walking over to a cabinet and taking out an energy drink.

"I thought you were leaving for Toronto," Sam said, taking his hands off me as I released a breath. *Too much.*

"Nah, next weekend," Peter said, pulling himself up to sit on the counter. "I think Jenna's getting sick of me after being together for five years, but . . ." He shrugged, cracking open the can and taking a swig.

"*Five* years?" I asked. I hadn't met Peter's girlfriend yet, but Sam had told me good things. "You've been dating since you were thirteen?"

Peter nodded, reading the nutrition facts on the can in his hand. He didn't say anything for a moment, but when he looked back up, his face wore a grin. "I'll be in my room. Goodbye, *lovers*!"

When Peter left, Sam turned back to me. "Can we go back to what we were doing?"

I pushed him back gently. "No, we have food to order and a game to watch."

I flicked through food options on my phone as I made my way into their living room. Once I was lying along their comfy sofa and Sam had joined me, scrolling through channels, he asked, "What's Mads up to? She took the bus with you, right?"

"Yeah, she's going on a date with this guy who goes to school here." I pulled up his Instagram page, which Maddy and I had researched thoroughly on the bus, and Sam made a face. Oh, he really didn't like this guy.

"I've seen him in my calc class. Robert or something?" I nodded. "Yeah, he's kind of a prick. Do you think Maddy will figure that out on her own, or do we need to save her?"

"She said she'll text if she needs any saving. They're going somewhere public," I assured him. And myself. I sent a quick text to Maddy to see if she was okay.

Sam didn't seem convinced, but he didn't push. Relief went through me as Maddy sent a thumbs-up back. "Wait, so why was practice only fine today?"

Ugh. I handed him my phone to double-check our food order, struggling to contain my sudden flare of annoyance. Or anger. Yeah, it was definitely anger. "The same reason why I was annoyed at practice last week."

Sam handed me back my phone, his tongue pressed into his bottom lip as his face screwed up in thought. "Is her name, um, Miranda? Sasha? Monya?"

I snorted as his phone buzzed in his pocket. "Tanya. Defender? Sweeper? Thinks she's the absolute best at everything?"

I'd encountered my fair share of mean girls. Beatrice, back at Wellington High, was like a mean girl times ten. But I had never played a sport with Beatrice. Tanya and I were on the same team. Tanya was someone who was supposed to have my back and I hers. Instead, she was like a porcupine in a herd of soft, fluffy bunnies.

When I'd first met her in late August, I hadn't understood why she kept trying to come after me during practices. Then she began making snide remarks outside our practices, which I pushed aside for the sake of the team. That was when I learned something after overhearing a few conversations: she hated me because of the person who was currently sitting next to me.

Sam glanced down at his phone. Then it buzzed again in his hand. It must've been Caleb again. He didn't bother responding as he shoved the device into his pocket, clearing his throat uncomfortably. "Yeah, she saw me yesterday."

As I mentioned, people in business had possibly heard of Sam and his family. People in the music industry had definitely heard of Sam and his family. And because Sam's aunt Liz was a fashion designer—and Sam sometimes modeled for her—people knew his family from that industry as well. The Cahills knew famous people, and some of those famous people had daughters. Daughters like Tanya, who seemed to have a huge obsession with my boyfriend.

The only reason she even knew he had any connection to me was because he had shown up at one of our tryouts to pick me up. She'd spent the last twenty minutes of the tryouts talking about him. And then proceeded to keep talking about him—loudly enough that I could hear her—when she saw us leave together. She talked about him whenever I was within earshot. She would mention how gorgeous he was. That she didn't think he should be tied down by, and I quote, *some grungy girl from some unknown town.*

She attempted to talk to him whenever he was at one of our practices. Over the last couple of months, Sam had trying to be a little bit more polite. He would acknowledge people instead of ignoring them and walking on by. Sam kept his conversations with Tanya short and monosyllabic, which was more than I had recently been giving her.

Let's just say, we weren't friends.

"Where did you see her? What did she do?" I asked.

"Nothing out of the ordinary. Invited me to a party. Fate decided to put her in my path as I was trying to get into your building."

"Well, fate is an evil spirit," I muttered, crossing my arms.

Sam reached out and wrapped his arms around my waist, pulling me between his legs. "I said no to the party invite. Then she invited me to go to the library to study with her."

"You should file a restraining order." I shifted, grumbling my words into his neck. "Make sure she has to be be at least three hundred feet from you or else she gets arrested."

"Your possessiveness is shining rather brightly today, Hazel."

"It's not possessiveness. It's *Tanya.* I swear, she wants to kidnap you and hide you in her closet."

"If she wanted to kidnap me, she wouldn't succeed because I'm sure you'd knock her out if she even touched me," he said, cheeriness coating his tone.

"I wouldn't knock her out," I whined as I flipped to another channel before our food arrived. "You make me sound like I'm violent."

"You are."

"Hey!" I nudged him as he chuckled. The smile that came to

my face as I turned my attention to the TV faded as I realized what show was playing: *Boy Meets World.*

"Hey, you okay?" Sam asked.

Staring at the screen, I was instantly transported to another time, when Andrew, Jasmine, and I would run straight to my house after school to watch reruns. I felt a pang in my heart. I already missed Justin and my dad calling me "Sandy." I missed the gang playing video games in my basement and cackling at the dumbest stories. I missed home. It hadn't even been that long since we'd left, but time doesn't seem to matter when it comes to being away from the people you love. "Homesick," I admitted in a low voice.

He rubbed the side of my arm. "Only a couple of weeks until the wedding. You'll be seeing everyone in no time. They all said they're attending."

"I know." I said as his arms tightened around me. His words were comforting as he twirled a strand of my hair with his fingers.

"Think about it: you'll be able to argue with your brother, I'll be able to argue with the idiots I call my brothers. It'll be a great time for everyone."

"All your cousins and your brother are going to be there? All seven?"

"All *eight*," he corrected. "Nine boys in total. There's one Cahill cousin you haven't met yet. He's as much my brother as the rest of them."

Ivan. Lucas. Joey. Christian. Phillip. Cedric. And his actual brother, Greg. Plus the one I didn't know much about. The Cahill boys, his aunt would jokingly say. I had been on good terms with all of them since the summer, so I wasn't worried about getting along with this cousin of his I hadn't met yet.

"You'll see your family and the gang," Sam said, his eyes glued to the TV as he pulled up the recording of the game. "It'll be like old times."

~

After watching the game, Sam and I were walking through the streets of Southford. It was a college town, so when loud music was coming from all directions, I wasn't really surprised. But as we made our way to the main road, I took in the nice night sky as cars zipped past us and Sam sulked about the game.

"You're acting like they aren't going to beat them next time," he grouched. "Have you seen the stats—"

"You lost this time, dude." I patted his cheek as my phone buzzed in my pocket. It was probably a text from Andrew. "Andrew's going to lose his mind. We bet fifty dollars on it, and I won."

I hadn't seen Andrew since the summer. He'd gone to a university up in Northern Ontario, about fourteen hours away from our hometown. Jasmine had gone even farther away to school: British Columbia. Even though we were all apart, I liked that we all made time to speak to one another. I spoke to Andrew a lot more than Jasmine, but I figured that was because she lived in a completely different province now.

Sam didn't say anything. His eyes were focused on the ground in front of him, obviously lost in thought. There was no way he was thinking about the soccer game that intensely. I poked him with my elbow. "What's up?"

He blinked as if my voice had brought him out of his little trance. "What?"

"There's something bothering you. What is it?"

"A lot going on."

I nudged him to the point where he cracked a smile, the dent between his eyebrows disappearing. The sight left me pleased. "Midterm next Tuesday, outdoor season coming to an end soon. Offers. Indoor season coming. It's a lot. I know you get it."

Wait. "Offers?" I asked.

"This afternoon, my coach told me that he'd sent tapes of each player around to different people. Because I'm not from here, he told me that a few people from the UK are looking at me too. He said that there will be games where some of those people will come to see me. I won't know which games. All I know is that at some point, I'm being watched."

"Haven't you been given offers before?" Sam didn't talk much about his soccer days back in England, but I knew he had been good enough to be scouted on a national level.

His bottom lip pulled into his mouth as he nodded. "Calls stopped when I stopped playing."

Now he was playing again. "Do you feel stressed?"

"Don't be scared if you see a white strand in my beautiful hair." He took his hat off his head and dramatically ran his fingers through his locks.

"Cocky." But I cracked a smile at his attempt to lighten the mood.

"I know." He grinned, but then it slowly faded as he clutched the hat to his chest. "I—I don't want to mess up, you know?"

The self-doubt surprised me. Sam knew how well he played, how skillful he was when the ball was at his feet. He'd trained as much as he could once he'd decided to get back into the sport again. To have him worry over this when he was always the confident one between us made me squeeze his hand.

"You won't mess up."

"How do you know that?" he asked.

"Because you're you. Even if you mess up, it's not going to be the end of the world," I promised him. I understood him, but he needed to hear it. "I'll be right there encouraging you to keep going."

Sam's mouth twisted to the side as he bit back a smile. "You always know the right thing to say."

"What if I said something wrong?" I asked him, pulling my head back to look at his face as my phone beeped in my pocket.

He smirked. "Define 'wrong'? I didn't think you of all people could talk dirt—"

"That's not what I meant, idiot. I mean what if I said something that didn't motivate you, like 'pineapple tapioca.'"

Sam shot me a look of bafflement. "Why would you say 'pineapple tapioca'?"

"It's the first thing that popped into my mind," I said as I took a moment to check the text message I had received.

When I read the message, I stopped walking. A puzzled expression crossed Sam's face until he read the message, that dent between his eyebrows returning immediately. "C'mon."

Sam lived less than a five-minute car ride from the campus of his university. When we arrived at one of the dorm buildings, I could already hear Maddy yelling from the parking lot. Sam and I rushed out of the car, heading past other cars to see Maddy pushing away the same boy whose picture I had shown Sam earlier that day.

"Whoa, whoa! What is going on?" Sam asked, stepping in front of Maddy.

I extended my hand toward Maddy. She took it, but she

didn't need my support. Maddy had enough anger for both of us. She had texted me throughout the evening that the date had gone well, but clearly, the opposite was the case now. When she glanced at me, she gave me a thumbs-up as a sign that she was okay.

Robert only laughed, and as I took a closer look at his face, I realized his eyes were red. Maddy's eyes were not the same. "Relax, Mads. Stop playing hard to get—"

Maddy huffed. "I'm not *playing* hard to get. I *am* hard to get."

But Robert acted like he hadn't heard, and he wasn't budging from his spot. "It's not that big a deal."

"You got high and then tried to get me in the car with you!" she exclaimed. I stilled. *What?*

Sam's head whipped toward Maddy. "He what?"

"He said he wanted to go for a *joyride*," she spat, glowering at Robert. "Screw you."

Robert snickered. I hated that sound. How at ease he sounded. As if driving under the influence wasn't going to have consequences. Consequences that both Sam and I had lived through. "Maddy, *c'mon*. It's not a big deal. It's a drive."

Sam shifted, blocking Maddy from Robert's gaze. His jaw clenched as he stared down at the man. "It's not just a drive, you idiot. Go home." Sam's tone wasn't meant to be played with. If Robert hadn't been high, I figured that he would have peed his pants at Sam's intimidation.

Robert chuckled like Sam had shared an inside joke. "Move aside, man. Let's not make this serious." Sam didn't say anything, and Robert pursed his lips. "Come on, move, man."

"No."

"Bro, move."

"No."

"*Move.*"

Sam didn't take any notice of Robert's sudden irritation, and his anger level rose as he glared at him. "*Go.*"

That's when the first punch came.

3
SEE? FATE HATES ME

Sam put a hand to his jaw, staring at Robert in disbelief.

Next to me, Maddy mumbled, "Oh God" as Robert groaned, shaking his hand from the terrible punch he had just landed.

Sam scoffed, his mouth hard as he glowered at Robert. "Are you kidding me?"

Robert's nostrils flared as he attempted to swing at Sam again. This time, Sam quickly got out of the way, pushing Robert back hard. Robert stumbled as Sam hissed at him, "You thought you were okay to drive?"

Robert adjusted himself, coming for Sam again, but Sam pushed him harder. Robert almost tripped on his feet before he recovered. It didn't matter; Sam was only getting angrier, his green eyes flashing. "And you were going to put her and everyone else around you at risk?"

He shoved Robert to the ground before Robert even thought to retaliate. I winced at Robert falling onto his back with a loud slam accompanied by a deep groan. The sound started to gain attraction from the group of people on the other side of the parking lot. Sam didn't notice as he glowered down at Robert. "Are you fucking kidding me?"

The crowd of people started to move over to our area. *No, no, no.* Sam didn't cause commotions; he didn't get into fights. He didn't do what he used to do anymore. If someone took a picture or a video of what was happening and it got back to his parents, it would erase all the positive changes he had made since he'd been in his dark place.

"Sam," I warned.

Sam glanced back at me, and I tilted my head in the direction of the group of people making their way over to us. They weren't far now. Sam looked at them but then set his focus back on Robert, glaring down at him. Robert wasn't amused now. In fact, he was breathing hard and fast, waiting, wincing as if Sam was going to shove him again.

"Now leave Maddy alone," Sam said, gesturing for us to follow him to the car. Maddy and I were quick to follow before the group of people reached us. I sighed in relief as Sam glanced over at our friend. "You okay?"

"Yeah." She squeezed my hand. "Thanks for coming. Both of you."

Sam unlocked the car and was about to enter, but not before I reached out to see where Robert had punched him. He'd barely caught him, but the skin near his cheekbone was bright red. "Are you okay?"

When he locked eyes with me, he knew that was a loaded question. Nevertheless, he nodded. "You?"

"Yeah," I whispered, glancing over at the scene in the distance.

Robert was still on the ground, the people crowding him. But no one saw us.

"Mads, you staying over tonight?" he asked once we all settled in the car.

"If you don't mind?" Maddy's voice was mixed with the sudden buzzing of Sam's phone in his pocket. "I was going to sleep over at my friend's, but she's probably out right now."

Sam didn't seem bothered, but he did stare down at his phone for longer than I had expected. When he caught me looking, he shrugged. "Telemarketer."

When we entered the apartment moments later, Peter wasn't there. There was a note on the counter stating that his girlfriend wasn't sick of him after all, and he had left to visit her in Toronto a few hours earlier. Leaving Sam in his bedroom to do schoolwork, I joined Maddy in the guest room later that night. She was lying on the bed, scrolling through her phone with the laptop I had let her borrow next to her. "What are you doing?"

"Blocking that guy on everything and deleting his phone number. He can no longer look at my Instagram, Snapchat, Tumblr—"

"*Tumblr?* He had your *Tumblr*?" I asked her, lying down on the bed next to her and opening my laptop.

"Don't judge me. Anyway, this place is big. Sam's really loaded." I nodded in agreement as she put her phone down. "Wait, don't you and Sam have your something-month anniversary coming up?"

"Our six-month. If Sam was here, he would tell you how many months, days, hours, minutes, and seconds it's been since we got together."

"I always knew the guy was a freak."

I let out a laugh at that before a video call request pinged on my screen, and I grinned, accepting it. Andrew was currently eating a sandwich in his single dorm room. His blond hair had grown out a bit, and his skin still held the tan he had gotten in the summer.

"Drew!"

He gave me a sandwich-filled smile. I was glad to know that, like me, his love of food would never change.

"Sorry, this is really good," he said, taking another bite.

"Guess what?"

"What?"

"You owe me fifty bucks."

His jaw dropped, and quickly he put a hand to his mouth to keep the food he had yet to swallow from falling out. "Chelsea won?"

"Send me the money," I demanded, grinning at him.

Andrew grumbled, taking out his phone. "Have you heard from Jasmine?" he suddenly asked.

"You haven't talked to your girlfriend?" I understood me not talking to her in a while since we were both busy, but they were *dating*. The Jasmine I'd known pre-university had been stuck to Andrew like glue. Whenever they were apart, she'd constantly text him.

"I haven't heard from her since Tuesday. Do you think something is wrong?"

"I spoke to Drake on Thursday," I said, referring to Jasmine's brother. "He said she's fine, just busy. She joined some extracurriculars and got a job as a part-time lifeguard."

"I know." He rubbed the back of his neck. "It's not like her to take days to respond, though, you know?"

I know. But I was here to assure my friend, not feed him more doubts.

"Andrew, wait it out," Maddy said, moving over to show herself on the screen. "Jasmine will respond soon."

"Hey, Maddy," Andrew said, finishing his sandwich as my phone lit up with the notification of the money he'd sent. The two quickly engaged in a conversation about how her night had gone. While I still felt anger toward the guy who had attempted to take her on a *joyride*, another thought was also on my mind: What was happening with Jasmine?

~

"Let's go, go, go!" Coach Fields pressured us on Monday morning. It was going to be a week filled with lectures, labs, exams, assignments, and intense practices like this one. "Let's go. Practices should be harder than the real game. You'll get used to this in no time."

He'd been saying that since August.

By the looks of it, no one was getting used to his methods of torture.

Along with the team, I sprinted down the field and back to the other side. When he yelled, "Again!" we repeated the action. Every single one of us was panting as Coach shook his head. "Shame. You didn't make it," he said dryly, as we'd fallen short of his expected time.

That's when everyone groaned loudly in unison, and I put my hands on my head like the others to get more oxygen through my body. "I have an idea. You are going to go down the field and back in pairs. That way I can see who makes it and who doesn't each time. I can guarantee that each and every one of you will make it down and back before my timer runs out. Is that clear?"

A grumpy "Yes sir" came out of my teammates' mouths while I said, "Crystal" under my breath.

As members of my team ran up and down the field in pairs, I shuffled, trying to figure out who I'd be up against. Not that it mattered, but to some it was going to matter more than to others.

"Okay, Nesmith, Anderson, you're up next."

Tanya.

See? Fate hates me.

I dragged myself to the starting line while Tanya did the same a small distance away from me. If she beat me, she wouldn't let me live it down. If I beat her, she'd find a way to keep annoying me or call it a fluke. I wanted to make it down and back before the time was up.

"*Go!*"

I pushed off the second he said it and forced my legs to make their way speedily down the field. The grass tore up wherever my cleats dug into the dirt. Tanya was merely a hand's length away from me. When I reached the end of the field, I almost slid, reaching my right arm out to touch the line end before pushing off and turning around.

Adrenaline pumped through my veins as Tanya gained the tiniest lead. Not on my watch. I hadn't planned on making this a competition—but now I was. I forced my legs to go faster, gaining momentum as I ended up passing her. When I reached the end, I didn't slow until I breezed past Coach.

Tanya followed, scowling at me as she crossed the line a

moment behind me. Coach looked pleased. "Anderson, good one. You both made it. Kaur! Gold! You're up!"

Tanya's dirty looks didn't stop for the rest of practice that morning. By the time we were in the change room, she was complaining loudly to her little clique on the team. I didn't care much for the rest of them, but they didn't seem to care for what she said that much either. "I think he might come to the party."

"Sam Cahill is *so* not coming," said one girl, a midfielder in the same year as us. "Tanya, I saw the whole thing go down."

I almost laughed. Good, there were witnesses.

Tanya rolled her eyes. "He would, you know?" Sure. I needed the evil shrew to back off and simmer down.

Her friends exchanged a look before one of them, a right wing, murmured, "You know Macy's right there, yeah?"

The three of them glanced at me. Thank God for the earphones that contributed to the illusion that I wasn't listening. They had been blasting music from one of my favorite bands until I had turned down the volume when I saw Tanya's mouth moving.

I was putting on a T-shirt, avoiding their eyes and looking back at my locker, but I didn't miss when Tanya got sour now that I had been brought up. "He calls her *Hazel*. Like the color. Clearly she isn't even worthy enough for him to call her by her actual name."

Okay.

"Shut up, Tanya."

My eyebrows shot up as I swiveled around the room to see who had said something.

Anmol.

Defender. Wingback. She was really good on the field. She

was South Asian, with medium-brown skin and wavy black hair that she was currently running a brush through as she rolled her brown eyes at Tanya.

"No one's talking to *you*," Tanya snapped back. How was she on the team with this behavior? Jeez.

"That's because you're taking up space by running your mouth," Anmol retorted. "Do us all a favor and be quiet."

Tanya pursed her lips. Then she took Anmol's advice, grabbing her duffel bag and walking out of the room. The room filled with chatter once again and my shoulders relaxed at how positive the atmosphere seemed to get the second she left. I was here to play soccer, not give in to high school antics. Tanya thought she could say whatever she wanted behind my back, and I didn't care for it, but it was nice to see her put in her place.

In fact, Anmol moved over, sitting down on the bench in front of my locker. I pulled my earphones out. "Thanks."

"You know you could totally take her, right?"

Anmol looked up at me. Sure, with my height, everyone made that assumption. And although it was likely I could, I also didn't want to be expelled from HDF two months in. Or ever. "She's not worth it."

Anmol's smile made me grin back. "Don't let her get to you. She's also probably jealous because you beat her in the duo thing today." I scoffed. "And you're a great soccer player. No wonder she's jealous of you."

"Stop," I said, knowing she was trying to cheer me up by feeding my ego. It completely worked. I definitely still planned to train more, hoping to get starter as a rookie. Hoping to get noticed.

As Anmol and I left the building, I learned that she was originally from Toronto and ethnically she was Indian. She had one sister, and she wanted a new gym buddy if I was up for it. We already had a schedule for soccer set for the year, but I was willing to find someone to partner with at the gym. Plus, it was a good chance to get to know someone on the team better.

In high school, all of my team members were my friends. The guys were like my family. Here, the dynamic was very different even though everyone worked well together. But it wasn't the same. There was no *let's hang out after school.* There was no staying on the field and joking around together. Everything about soccer at HDF was professional and mature. It was what I'd asked for, but it made me miss everything I hadn't thought I'd miss that much.

Anmol and I parted ways with a plan to meet up the next day, and I was walking toward my dorm building when I received a phone call from my dad.

I answered the call with a large smile. "Hi, Mr. Krabs."

He chuckled. "Hi, Sandy."

That never got old.

"How's Patrick?" I asked.

"Your brother is the same as he always was," Dad grumbled. "He keeps on about wanting to move to Redmond."

"Again?" Justin was relentless. When we had gone to Redmond during spring break to visit our maternal grandmother, Justin had met Emma, and soon he was over the moon for her. We had made two more visits to Redmond since then, more than we had in years, to see our Nonna. But for Justin, he was there mostly for Emma. "Dad, you should send him to live with Nonna if he keeps saying that over and over again."

"I'm not sending my fifteen-year-old son off to Redmond," Dad said. "It's bad enough my favorite daughter isn't home."

I laughed under my breath. "I'm your *only* daughter. He really loves Emma."

"I can tell, but he's going to see her next month at the wedding. It's all he can talk about."

"I know, he told me yesterday, like, five times over the phone." I loved Emma, but the only downside to seeing her was that I was guaranteed to see her older sister, Alexis. Alexis, as in Sam's friend Alexis. She was a million times worse than Tanya when it came to Sam.

You know, considering they'd slept together two years ago.

I bristled, knowing that I might be seeing and hearing more of Alexis than only at the wedding. Turned out Alexis had been modeling on the side when she was in high school and was in talks with Sam's aunt Liz. I needed to brace myself for her name coming up more often now.

There was nothing to brace myself for or worry over. Alexis was nothing to me.

Yeah, nothing. I shook my head as my dad asked, "How's soccer?"

"I'm tired," I admitted. "The games, practices, school, it's a lot sometimes."

"You still want to go to pro?"

"I do." I paused. "Not sure if I want to finish up my degree if I do, but I'm still hopeful."

There was a moment of silence before he spoke up again. "You know . . . in case soccer doesn't work out, you do have a gift with that camera."

I perked up. I could go to my dad for anything. He understood that for years, soccer had been the one thing that had been on the forefront of my mind. Suggesting something else seemed unlike him, but he wasn't wrong. Everyone had a backup plan. However, I'd always assumed mine would involve science if soccer didn't work out—not photography. "Dad."

"You do," he said.

"I don't know about that," I confessed. "I just want to survive first year."

"You'll make it through," he promised when my phone buzzed with a message from a study group for one of my chemistry courses.

"Let's hope."

4
DAMSEL IN DISTRESS

Jasmine still hadn't responded.

Her silence pressed on my mind the following Thursday night as I lay down on the floor of Sam's bedroom. My attention was held by the cherished picture on my lock screen instead of one of my chemistry courses.

Jon Ming had taken the photo back in Sam's room in Port Meadow, in front of Sam's full-length mirror. I was making a funny face on one side of him while Stevie had her phone in her hand to take a similar photo. The rest of my friends were in the background. Caleb was hanging upside down off Sam's bed while cackling at something Austin said as the two of them shoved each other. Jasmine was showing Brandon something on her phone, and in the corner, Andrew and Sam were sitting on the couch, playing on Sam's Xbox.

My concentration was shattered when someone loomed over my body. I turned onto my back only to be hit by Sam's curls.

He kept his hands on either side of my head as he held himself up in a push-up position above me. I arched an eyebrow. "What are you doing?"

"Exercise," was all he said as he came down and kissed me for a quick second before pushing back up.

"This is a way for you to exercise? To"—he leaned forward to go down again, but I turned my face, so he kissed my cheek instead—"smother me with kisses?"

"Yes. It's a great motivation." He grinned wickedly as he leaned forward, smacking kisses across my face to make me laugh and squirm. When he tried to bend down again, I quickly crawled out from his cage of two arms, going over to his desk panting but smiling so wide. Too wide. He grinned up at me from where he was lying on his back. He was always trying to make me feel better. As I typed his password into his computer, he stood up. "You looked distracted."

"Jasmine hasn't been answering me."

Sam's brows furrowed. "Still?"

"Yeah," I said, playing around with the camera on his MacBook. There were likely a million pictures of me on here dabbling with the filters. I changed the filter, watching my head get bigger and bigger, my cheeks sinking in. I chuckled as Sam appeared next to me, purposely sitting down on my thigh and crushing all the circulation as if he wasn't a protein-based soccer player. "Get off me."

"I think I'm going to stay here," he said, adjusting himself so he sat fully on my lap. He leaned forward into the camera, changing the filters a couple more times, pausing each time he did it and making me laugh. As he started making weird faces, I realized he was trying to cheer me up. I wrapped my arms around his waist, looking at him make faces at the camera. He was still so photogenic. "No wonder you're a model."

He scoffed. "I thought you were about to call me an attention whore."

"Well, that too," I said. His jaw dropped as I dissolved into laughter. "But I'm not kidding, you're picturesque."

"Ooh, big words," he mocked. "Aunt Liz is releasing a new line."

"Really? She wants to put you in it?"

"She wants to put you in it too." I made a face, and Sam chortled, getting up. Almost every time I saw his aunt, she would tell me to go into her industry. But it wasn't for me. I was much better behind the camera. Liz didn't understand that. "You'd be good for the camera."

"Okay."

"I'm serious."

"Okay," I repeated.

"Hazel . . ."

Before he could say any more, my phone buzzed on the table.

I answered the call, and Brandon's face popped up on the screen. His long brown hair from high school was cut into a buzz cut, and while he usually gave me an easygoing smile, he had a scowl on his face. "What's wrong?" I asked, realizing this was a three-way FaceTime as Stevie popped up in another square of her own on the screen.

"You're not answering your texts, I had to call," he grumbled. Stevie, on the other hand, seemed cheerful, her blond hair up in a high ponytail. She was attending college in a small town near our hometown. She'd opened her mouth to speak when Brandon beat her to it. "Have you heard from Jas?"

Him too? "No," Stevie admitted. "Not really, to be honest."

"Not for a while," I added. "Andrew said he hasn't really heard from her either, but Drake has."

"Ugh, she knows the name of this movie we were talking about a while back, and I want to watch it. That's weird she's not answering," Brandon said, just as there was a loud bang in the background. I already knew that was his twin. "Even weirder that Drew hasn't heard from her."

"I know," I said. It's not like she was trying to avoid Drew, right? "What about Jon Ming? How is he doing? Has he heard from her?"

"I think that guy is having the time of his life." Jacob appeared on the screen, waving hi to me. Jacob, while he looked so much like his brother, had his own hairstyle, piled at the top and shaved on the sides.

"Can you expand on that?" Stevie asked.

Jacob wiggled his phone toward the camera. "He's been partying pretty heavily for the past few weekends."

He showed us a video from our friend's Snapchat story. I could see Jon Ming yelling into the camera as brightly flashing lights from a club fell upon him and the numerous people around him bounced to the energy of the music.

"That artist he's been working with has been taking off, huh?" Unlike the rest of us, Jon Ming had gone straight into working after high school. He'd been doing pretty well after sending samples of his music to a few local artists to work with them as a sound engineer. He loved creating music, and I was glad to see it was all paying off. His best friend, Austin, on the other hand, had gone to school in Quebec, where he was able to speak French, his native tongue.

Sam's eyes were stuck to the video as it continued, but I couldn't decipher his expression. Suddenly, his phone buzzed in his pocket as Jacob put his phone away. As Sam glanced down at his device, Brandon said, "We talked to Jon Ming the other day. The artist he's been working with recently got a deal, and Jon Ming got taken on. He's doing really well."

Brandon and I shared a smile at our friend's road to success. Meanwhile, Sam was frowning, but he didn't say anything, pocketing his phone. Then Jacob asked, "Hey, guys, do you know how to fix a fish tank?"

"How did we get onto the topic of fish tanks?" Stevie suddenly asked. The random question from Jacob and the frown on Stevie's face made me grin. I missed them so much.

"He bought fish," Brandon explained, giving the phone to Jacob to hold as he disappeared from my screen.

"You expect to take care of fish?" I asked. "Bro, you can barely take care of *yourself*."

Jacob glared at me while Sam snorted. Stevie put her hand over her mouth while Brandon barked laughter somewhere offscreen. "Shut up."

"Good luck with the fish," I said before Brandon took the phone from his brother's hand, "and ask Google!"

"I'll talk to you later," Jacob said. "Group call soon?"

"Hopefully," Stevie said.

"We'll have it," Brandon assured us. "Mace, answer my text if you can figure out what movie I meant. I texted you—which you would know if you responded to your messages," he taunted.

I rolled my eyes. "Bye, Brandon."

"Bye," he said, and I waved goodbye to Stevie before he ended the call. When I turned around in my swivel chair, Sam was on the ground doing push-ups with one arm. *Show-off.*

I pulled myself underneath him. He raised his eyebrows, still above me. "Hello, there. You're back in my presence. Not surprised. They always come back."

When he tried to kiss me, I put a finger on his lips to stop him. "I'm wondering who *they* are because if they keep coming back, they'll have to call you something else: single."

Sam laughed, rolling off me. "Maybe I'll settle for being called 'damsel in distress.' Caleb can't stop calling me that."

"It makes sense. He's the prince, I'm the princess, and you're the damsel in distress. It suits you. We'll come save you from towers or something."

"Actually, Caleb would because he's the prince."

"I think the right version of this twisted fairy tale is that I, the princess, would probably knock out Caleb, Prince Charming, and save my damsel in distress, aka you, from the fire-breathing dragon. I can see it now: every child's favorite bedtime story." I put my hands above my head as if envisioning it on a banner.

Sam chuckled, sitting up and stretching. "I've got to take a shower before studying. I'll be back."

"Wait." I stopped him as he was about to leave the room. "You seemed a little down after the text you got. Is everything okay?"

Sam's eyes flicked down to the ground before meeting my own. "Everything's fine, Hazel. Don't worry."

"Fine?" I asked, getting up. If anything, that word only increased my concern. "C'mon, don't lie to me."

Then he pulled out that smirk. "When have I ever lied to you?"

"You lied to me not even that long ago." Sam feigned an

innocent expression, but I wasn't letting this slip by. "When you told me you had food for me. I got out of my bed still half sleepy and *boom,* no food. Samuel Henry Cahill, if you think you can tell me that everything—"

"That was something tiny, not something that mattered," he interjected gently. "If something is bothering me, I will tell you, okay? I'll always tell you. I always have, and I always will."

Slowly, I nodded. He was right. If something was troubling him, he would tell me. I might not know what to do right away, but we could figure it out together.

"Plus, you've lied to me in a tiny way like that too."

"What? When?"

"Whenever you tell me that I just look *okay* or you completely deny that I am incredibly good-looking." *Oh God.* "What is that called? *Lying.*"

"Go take your shower," I urged, getting back up to grab my backpack to study for my next midterm coming up next week. Sam's loud laughter left the room with him. He could push the subject aside, but I knew better.

Fine was never the right word for us.

5
TIFFANY? HAILEY? YOLANDA? ERICA?

"Peter!" I put my hands over my ears on the following Tuesday night. I had been talking to Sam on FaceTime while rewriting my chemistry notes when Peter decided to enter his room and burst into song. "You are making my ears bleed."

I cringed as he continued singing, ignoring me. Sam's face was stone cold, his eyes on his cousin as Peter continued his horrible rendition of a song I couldn't recognize.

Then a miracle happened. The ugly voice stopped.

My eyes widened at Sam straddling Peter on the floor of his bedroom, one hand over his mouth. Sam huffed over his struggling body, running a hand over his face. "I question how we're related."

"By *marriage*!" Peter exclaimed before Sam moved Peter's leg into a position that made the poor guy yell into Sam's hand for him to let go.

"Sam, let him go," I chuckled.

Sam did as I asked, and Peter got up, cursing under his breath as he brushed himself off. "Shouldn't you be at a party? Not harassing me?"

"Party?" I asked Sam.

"It's not that big a deal." Sam waved a hand. "It's midway between EB and Southford. A few guys on the team are throwing a party. Said it was team bonding, but we all know what that means."

"Who throws a party on a Tuesday?" I asked.

"Drake. The artist. Not Jasmine's brother," Sam answered. Of course he would say that. Drake was one of his favorite artists.

"Every night should be a party," Peter said.

"You should go," I told Sam. "It would be a chance for them to understand you better rather than staying home and being called fresh meat."

"It would be better if you were with me," he admitted.

"I have to study, and I have practice tomorrow morning." Plus, being surrounded by people getting wasted or high wasn't something at the top of my list for a Tuesday night. I knew it wasn't on his either, but I think he needed the team-bonding aspect.

"You sure?"

I nodded.

"All right," Sam said unenthusiastically. "Peter, get out."

"I didn't get an apology for you manhandling me!" Peter exclaimed.

"And you aren't going to get one, dickhead!" Sam said, all but shoving Peter out of his room.

For a moment, I watched Sam trade his sweats and plain T-shirt for a black V-neck and jeans. He was zipping up when he looked at me over his shoulder. I quickly moved my gaze to my blue chemistry notebook. “It’s okay, Hazel. It’s completely fine if you check me out. I do it to you all the time.”

I scoffed as he pulled on his leather jacket. “I wasn’t even looking at you.” My boyfriend was hot, but I wasn’t going to tell him that. He didn’t need an additional boost to his ego.

“Really?” he teased, fixing the cuffs on his arms. “I’m sure you didn’t notice that I was wearing white boxers.”

What? “They were black, not—”

I caught myself as he smirked, taunting me with his eyes. “They were *black*? I’m glad you noticed. Now, how do I look?”

“You’ve looked better,” I mumbled. He let out a hearty laugh at my tone. “I hate you.”

Sam grinned. “I’m in love with you too.”

~

Sam didn’t last half an hour at the party.

When Maddy finished studying at the library, she returned to our small dorm room, and we sat on the floor, watching an episode of a celebrity talk show Maddy told me I *had* to watch when my phone buzzed.

Jerk <3: I’m dying here.

Me: What’s wrong?

I must’ve been smiling because Maddy looked over, reading the conversation as Sam replied. I’d seen this coming from miles away.

Jerk <3: Someone's annoying me. I wanna call the police.

"He's so dramatic," Maddy mumbled, and I snickered.

Me: Tell them off.

Jerk <3: I did. Her friend finally took her away.

Jerk <3: This is actually really boring. Can you come here? Please?

Jerk <3: I even added a heart emoji. I'll get you something from McDonald's or Tim Hortons right after.

"Not him bribing you with food," Maddy mused. "Did he forget we're all on nutritional diets?"

Jerk <3: There's another girl staring at me and I feel mentally violated.

Maddy nudged me, pausing the show. "You should go."

"I have practice and a day filled with classes tomorrow. *And* a three-hour chem lab."

"It's only eight, Mace. Plus, you finished your pre-lab, and I'll come with. You need to fight off the girls who are staring at your boyfriend."

"I'm not going to fight anyone," I murmured.

But Maddy wasn't someone I could sway. The girl was already at the door of our shared closet, picking out clothes for me to wear.

About forty minutes later, Maddy and I were in one of the few towns between Southford and Edward Bay. It wasn't uncommon for people at HDF and Hayes to end up at the same parties. In fact, many students who attended either one lived outside the college cities since the towns were usually less than an hour's commute by car. That didn't mean the Uber ride to get there was cheap. Sam sent incessant text messages promising that he was going to e-transfer me the money back.

When we arrived, Maddy and I stared up at the big house littered with other university and college students from the area. Maddy had given me a brown leather jacket, a tank top, and ripped jeans, and she was sporting a long-sleeved, low-cut top with dark jeans. Her makeup had been done the fastest I had ever seen, and it was clear once we entered the house that my friend was in her element.

Her smile lit up her face as loud music filled our ears, and we were quickly surrounded by dancing bodies. From the corner of my eye, I spotted three guys on a table in the middle of another filled room, red cups in their hands. The scene reminded me of my guys from back home. I half expected Austin to come running in my direction, trying to get me to come dance with the rest of the group.

I looked around, over the heads of most people, to find Sam. The familiar curly head of hair I was used to wasn't in the living room with the other people nor sitting on one of the many couches. I started to move over to the kitchen when I realized Maddy had run into an acquaintance. "I'll be back," I told her, and she promised she would let me know where she was.

I spotted him the second I walked into the kitchen. Sam was leaning against the counter, no leather jacket in sight. A red cup was on the counter next to his hand. It didn't worry me. He didn't really drink like he'd said he used to, and it was probably one of the reasons he'd been trying to avoid going to the party in the first place.

His attention was on his phone, and the buzzing in my jacket pocket made me smirk. But when my eyes moved to the person who was trying to grab his focus, the smirk turned into a frown. I wasn't surprised to see Tanya, of all people, put a hand on my boyfriend's arm.

She can't take a hint.

I looked down at the continuous texts that had come in from Sam, who hadn't noticed I was near him.

> Jerk <3: The girl you hate is near me. I can feel her eyes on me like lasers.
>
> Jerk <3: Is her name Tiffany? Hailey? Yolanda? Erica?

I held in my amusement, glancing up at his irritated expression as he moved his arm away from Tanya's hand. At that action, he caught my gaze over her head. The agitation on his face morphed into a small smile as he dodged Tanya. In a low voice riddled with relief and desperation, he said, "*Hazel.*"

"Hey." The word barely escaped my lips as he smushed my face against his shoulder, engulfing me in a tight hug. His scent of apples and the mint from the gum he was chewing flooded my system with a sense of home.

"Thank God you're here," he whispered. "I swear she was about to go for my belt." His lips pressed against the side of my neck in greeting.

"Don't worry." I patted his chest. "I'm here to save you, my damsel in distress."

Sam frowned, the joke not having the same impact on him as it was on a beaming me. "Ha-ha. You're so funny."

"Macy," Tanya said behind Sam. Sam kept his hands on my waist as he moved to stand behind me, gaining some distance from her.

"Tanya." A bad taste was already forming in my mouth. "Hi."

"I didn't know you would be here," she said with a tight smile on her face.

"I didn't know *you* would be here." I matched her tone, the fake smile slipping off my face.

"Behave," Sam hushed against my ear.

"Only if she does," I whispered back, bringing the smile back to my face.

"You guys are so cute together," she said. I held back the biggest eye roll of my entire life.

"Really?" I turned to look at him, hoping he could see the masked hatred in my eyes. "Sam, she says we're cute."

"Okay," he abruptly said, taking the hint. "Let's go." He grabbed my hand, pulling us into the living room.

"See you in the morning," I told Tanya as he dragged me out. "Make sure you don't drink much! You wouldn't want to do drills with a hangover."

Sam pulled us into the crowd of sweaty bodies in the other room, the two of us standing in the middle of it all. He leaned close to talk in my ear over people screaming along to the song playing. "You came."

I grinned. "I'm glad you noticed."

"You know," he said, linking our fingers together, "I kind of like seeing the jealous side of you."

"I wasn't jealous," I protested, and he rolled his eyes. "It's Tanya. There's nothing to be jealous over."

Sam nuzzled his face into the side of my neck. "I have to confess, Hazel, it's pretty hot to see you like that."

My eyes widened, and my face heated up even more than it already had due to the crowded room with the floor vibrating beneath us. My hand in his became clammy, my skin already starting to feel sticky and my heartbeat racing as Sam shot me a boyish smile. I huffed, trying to mentally brush him off me, but it wasn't working. When I opened my mouth to say something, anything, my words got caught in my throat as Sam pressed his lips against mine, and my eyes closed of their own accord.

At first it was merely lips brushing against each other, Sam taking his teasing in a whole different direction as my level of impatience rose. I wasn't one for PDA, but seeing as everyone else here was captivated by the music, I didn't really mind. The people around us faded as we continued kissing, and Sam took up my entire focus. The overwhelming taste of him filled my mouth as his tongue entered my mouth skillfully, sending shocks through me.

My heartbeat increased exponentially as we continued, my hands roaming through his curly hair and his gripping my waist, pulling me even closer to him if that was possible. Everything was always on hyperdrive when he kissed me. Every single time, I couldn't get enough. My body was on fire, and it was exhilarating. I wasn't drunk. I hadn't even taken one sip of alcohol, but I felt intoxicated by him. I couldn't even stop my hands from skimming the exposed skin below his T-shirt.

He groaned into my mouth, pulling away for not even a fraction of a moment before his lips moved to my neck. I wanted more. Holy crap I wanted more, I thought, my heart beating faster as his hands moved lower to my backside. I wanted to feel his skin against mine.

I think I would have let him do anything if someone hadn't accidentally bumped into me.

"Oh, shit. *Sorry.*" Brown eyes met my own, and I relaxed at the familiar face. "Macy."

I was flushed, sweaty, with swollen lips and a hazy mind. But there was Anmol smiling at me like she hadn't noticed anything. "Hey, Anmol."

"I'm not drinking," she assured me as if I was captain of our team. "My friend wanted to meet a guy here, and, well, I was on my way out. Anyway, I should warn you—Tanya's here."

"Yeah," Sam said, sounding annoyed. His cheeks were red. His curly hair was ruffled to the extreme. I wanted to kiss him again. "We've spoken."

Anmol gave Sam a two-fingered wave. I was going to introduce them to each other when someone else came into our conversation, clamping a hand on Sam's shoulder. The man, who looked a little older than us, had fair skin with blond hair darker than Andrew's and pale-blue eyes. At the contact, I was a little surprised Sam didn't shrug him off. "Bro, we're playing beer pong upstairs."

The guy's voice trailed off when he locked eyes with Anmol. Anmol blinked once. Twice. Three times. Her lips were parted, and she looked like she had just spotted a UFO. *Okay, so they know each other.*

A slow smile came over the guy's face as he took his hand off Sam's shoulder. "Anmol."

Anmol stared at him longer than was socially acceptable. I nudged her quickly with my hand before using it to pretend to fix my hair. She blinked, and in a small voice she said, "Hi, Derek."

Sam and I exchanged looks. Derek didn't seem bothered by her sudden shyness as he glanced over at me, sticking out a hand. How formal. "I'm Macy," I said, shaking his hand.

Derek's eyebrows went up in realization, flashing Sam a grin. "As Anmol said, I'm Derek. I'm in third year. On the team with Sam. Nice to meet you. I'm going to assume you're Sam's girlfriend since you two were mauling each other's faces off." My face turned even redder than it already was, and I cleared my throat, slightly poking Anmol once again to get her out of her surprised state.

"Um." She cleared her throat. "What are you doing here?"

"I go to Hayes. You go to HDF?"

Anmol dipped her head as a small *yes*. Someone patted Derek on the shoulder, and he held up a finger to tell them to wait before he turned back to us. "As I said, we're playing beer pong upstairs. It'd be great to have you guys join."

"Actually, we're all heading out," I said for Sam's and apparently *Anmol's* sake. "It was great meeting you."

Derek frowned, but he didn't push any further. "All right. I'll see you guys. It's good seeing you, Anmol."

"You too," she said quietly, finally looking up at him.

His eyes roamed her face, lingering on her even as he turned his head in Sam's direction. He clapped his back in goodbye before disappearing into the crowd.

"Who was that?"

I jumped at the sound of Maddy's voice, putting a hand on her shoulder. "Don't do that."

"Who's the blondie?" she asked again, turning to Sam.

"Derek," Anmol answered. She didn't sound happy about seeing him. In fact, she seemed something I hadn't thought she ever was: awkward. "He was a friend of my sister's back home. I didn't know he went to Hayes."

"History?" Maddy asked her, and I could see Sam's interest grow as he narrowed his eyes at Anmol.

"I need a drink," Anmol said under her breath.

"We have practice tomorrow morning," I reminded her.

"We came here to rescue Sam, and that mission's completed, so if you want to come with us, that's cool. I sincerely encourage you to accept." Maddy grinned, her easygoing nature allowing her to link arms with Anmol. "I want the details on the blond."

"It's nothing," Anmol said as we started to make our way out of the house. It was a little after ten p.m., and with the way Anmol and Maddy had their heads close together, I knew we weren't leaving the area anytime soon. Sam didn't seem to mind, especially as he faced Anmol. He was *so* nosy.

"So, Anmol." Anmol's eyes went wide at Sam saying her name. "You sure he didn't date you?"

"No." She sputtered the word out, brushing her dark hair out of her face. "Why would you think that?"

I knew what he was doing. He didn't even have to try. His eyes were so intense they could make anyone spill information, but this was Anmol, someone who was potentially going to be my friend. I didn't want her to say anything she didn't want to.

I pinched him on the side, and he flinched. "*What?*"

"What do you mean 'what'? Stop doing that!"

He feigned innocence. "Doing what?"

"That thing with your eyes, you jerk." Anmol raised her eyebrows when I hit him lightly in the stomach. The man was capable of saying stupid things.

His best friend was Caleb—of course he said stupid things.

"I had a thing for him back in high school," Anmol blurted out.

"Did it backfire?" Maddy asked, extending her hand in my direction and pulling me into the conversation.

"It led to me and him and awkwardness when I told him before he left." Anmol groaned, placing her head in her hands.

"So, you're embarrassed," Sam said.

"*Sam,*" I hissed.

He waited for Anmol to confirm his statement but her silence said it all. He shrugged. "I think you'll be fine."

"How do you know that?"

Sam gave her another shrug, as if to say *I just do*, before he pulled out his phone and clicked the Uber app. His lack of a verbal answer gave Maddy the go-ahead to sling her arm around Anmol's shoulder. "I'm glad I met you, not because we have relatable boy issues—"

"You don't have boy issues," I interrupted.

"Did we forget about *Robert*?" Maddy rhetorically asked me before turning back to Anmol. True. "But also, you're near my height. The skyscrapers behind us make me want to grow taller whenever I'm with them."

"Mads, I don't think you can grow anymore," Sam said.

She glared at him. "Says who?"

"Says science."

"Go back to England," she grumbled, and Anmol chuckled.

The two engaged in conversation as we waited for the Uber. As Maddy and Anmol exchanged social medias, Sam glanced at me. "Thanks."

His shoulders were relaxed, his eyes bright. He seemed

more at ease than he had been when I'd first spotted him in the kitchen. "Was the party a little too much?"

"A little bit," he admitted, squeezing my hand as a car pulled up in front of us. "I'm okay, though. I'll see you soon, okay?"

He kissed me lightly on the lips, and I nodded as we pulled apart. "I'll see you soon."

I promised Sam I'd text him when I got home, and then Maddy, Anmol, and I squished ourselves into the back of the car. As Anmol and Maddy spoke about their favorite YouTubers, one of Maddy's obsessions, I received a notification from Twitter.

I had always followed Jasmine's activity even though she hated Twitter. She had retweeted a tweet. Good to know she was still alive.

6
LIVE IN IOWA IN A RANCH HOUSE BESIDE GIGI HADID

I hated being on the bench.

Feeling the cold wood underneath me as I watched the game unfold before me irritated me a bit.

A lot, actually, but I sucked it up. I held it in because I was a rookie.

But it really sucked being on the bench, headband on, ponytail low and hanging down my back. My cleats were pressed tightly against each other as I watched the ball roll across the field, in the possession of the other team on the cold October day. I was in shorts, but I wasn't entirely freezing. My attention was focused on the movement of the ball. How it rolled under feet, was passed, intercepted, played around with, and hit so hard it soared before it was controlled under the possession of someone else's foot.

"*Anderson.*"

My head snapped up. I had a few goals down this outdoor season, not as many as I had wanted, but here was a chance. *Score, dude*, I said to myself as I waited for the next substitution, bouncing on my toes both to warm myself up from the cold and in anticipation.

When the whistle blew for the next possession, I ran to take my place. The ball headed straight toward me, and I held it down, biting back the smile from rising on my lips. *Here we go*. The wind whipped through, cutting at my flushed cheeks as I ran alongside an opponent, passing the ball closer to the center. A third-year girl, Wendy, took the ball, playing a one-two pass as the ball came right back toward me. Seeing the game, hearing the crowd, I spotted the opening. This was my game. This was my element.

Soccer was my sport.

But the girl next to me was on my toes, and the perfect shot I could have taken was out of my reach. Dribbling around her, I spotted Wendy once again, open for half a second. A half second was all I needed as I powered through, kicking the ball straight in her direction. Wendy didn't even put her foot on the ground. A perfect pass. A perfect shot. A perfect goal.

The ball hit the back of the net.

"Yes!" The whole team was bouncing up and down, shouting. Wendy ruffled my hair as the rest of the team patted her back. I could have smiled complacently at Tanya at that point. *This* was how teammates treated each other. Instead, she was probably glowering at my back from the bench, resenting my assist. Yet as the game played on and I was brought back to the bench before the last half was over, I didn't feel as much joy from the assist. Even when Coach Fields patted me on the back and said, "Good job," it didn't give me the same thrill as it would have back in late August.

Maybe it was not scoring a goal for myself. Maybe it was the midterms that were taking up all my time and attention these days. Maybe it was the thought of dealing with lectures, labs, and tutorials while trying to balance soccer practice on top of it all, along with preparation for our upcoming games.

I was thinking about that on my bus ride later that day to Southford. Tonight was our anniversary. I needed a break from anything to do with school. But I couldn't stop thinking about it as I walked toward Sam's building, and then my phone buzzed with a phone call. Caleb.

"Yellow?"

Caleb laughed at my greeting. "Blue?"

"Green?" I decided to play along.

"Orange?"

"Brown?"

"Purple?"

"Black?"

"Black isn't a color," he said smugly. "It's a shade."

"Shut up," I said with a grin, grateful that he was able to shift my mood so quickly.

"Is Sam with you?"

"No, he's probably still at his game. He had one this morning." I was waiting to hear the details of it over text.

"Or he's at home and you two were talking on the phone doing stuff, which explains why he's not picking up my calls."

Doing stuff. No, Caleb.

I changed the topic. "Why did you want to know if I'd seen Sam?"

Caleb started laughing nervously. Immediately, I was concerned. "What's wrong?" I asked as I stepped onto the elevator.

But when the laugh grew hysterical, I frowned. "What did you do?"

"I'm taking this Italian class. Did I tell you that? I probably didn't." He hadn't. "Jon Ming had been giving me lessons since the summer because he knows like ten thousand languages and he's a pretty decent teacher. Did you know that?"

"Get to the point, Caleb," I insisted.

"Anyway, I met this girl in the class. Fast-forward almost twenty-four hours later, I'm in her bed."

"Why am I hearing one of your sex stories?" I asked as I got ready to hang up the call.

"Because of what happened next: her dad caught me in her bed. I ran away before the man could beat my ass." He inhaled deeply, his voice sounding far away. "I'm getting back to my building now and wanted to tell Sam the story. Remind me to ask if the girl still lives with her parents before she invites me to her house."

There had to be more to that story. *No, there had to be more to Caleb's behavior.* "All right, but are you okay?" I inquired, using my key to enter Sam's apartment.

"Because I had a one-night stand? Mace, I'm good. I just have to run away every now and then." The lightheartedness in his tone didn't push away my worry, but I didn't press him any further.

"Only you, Charming."

"Only me, princess."

I walked into the living room only to find the man of the hour seated on the couch, looking up at me with a big grin and his hands behind his head. Realizing I was on the phone, he frowned. I handed it to him, sweetness dripping in my tone. "It's your bestie."

Sam's frown went deeper when Caleb cut the call off and was now requesting to FaceTime. Sam reluctantly answered the call as I dropped my bags and sat on the couch next to him. "Ah, there's our peasant," Caleb said, his eyes lighting up. He was walking, a hat on his head, wearing a thick jacket.

Sam pushed himself up, rubbing his tired eyes adorably. "Caleb, it's too early in the day for me to hear your ugly voice."

"It's one in the afternoon."

"Exactly."

Caleb rolled his eyes before putting on a grin. "Happy six-month anniversary, guys! We made it!"

Sam and I exchanged a glance. "We?" I asked him.

"Yes. *We!* I'm as much a part of this relationship as you both are. In fact, I am the glue that holds you two together." He placed a hand to his heart, patting it a couple times with a proud look on his face.

"You're the glue that gets sticky on everyone's hands and they wish would come off, yet I can't ever seem to get rid of you," Sam said dryly.

"Love you too, Samuel."

"Caleb, we will call you later."

"But—"

"We will call you back," Sam said, quickly ending the call, and Caleb's face disappeared from my screen.

Sam's eyes went to my cleats hanging from my duffel bag. "Win?"

"Yup, but no goals. You?"

"Win. One goal." I fist-bumped him, curling into his arm as I looked up at the screen showing highlights from a game earlier today. "Are we still going to have a lazy day?"

"And I'll take you out later tonight," Sam said as I twirled a piece of his hair around my finger.

One of Sam's eyes half closed as he looked over at me. A smile played on his lips as he kissed his way up my arms to the place where my shoulder and neck met. I let out a shaky breath as his hands gripped my waist, and he moved his kisses upward until his lips were by the corner of my mouth. "Happy six months, Hazel."

For a few hours, I spent time on the couch with Sam with no interruptions, eating popcorn and watching a movie on the channel that had been playing that we'd decided to keep on. I was in the middle of a texting conversation with Stevie, who said she had talked to Caleb earlier in the week. I frowned, and Sam noticed, asking, "What's wrong?"

I turned off my phone. "It's Caleb. I'm worried about him."

"What's there to worry about? Caleb's Caleb."

"No, no, Caleb isn't just Caleb." I shrugged, trying to find a better way to explain myself. "He's the kind of guy who hides his pain behind—"

"A smile," Sam finished off, his hand gently knocking against one of my feet in his lap. "Caleb doesn't like people looking at him as if he's the saddest person in the world."

"I know. It's the persistent calling, the one-night stands, all of us so scattered. I don't know. I feel like Caleb's . . ."

"He's what?"

I struggled to find the proper word, then frowned when I did. "Lonely. I feel like Caleb is lonely."

Sam stiffened, his gaze aimed downward at the small table.

"I mean, he has *you*. You're like his brother. He has friends. He has Leona and Tia Maria and your family. But somehow, even with all these people in his life, I think that he feels like he's missing something. He doesn't want to tell us because he hides behind jokes, smiles, and laughter."

Sam closed his eyes briefly, and I could tell his hands were in fists beneath the leftover popcorn because his arm flexed and his veins protruded under the surface of his skin. "Shit."

"What?"

"How did I not notice that? He's my best friend, and I couldn't even tell. He lost his parents at a young age, he lost the love of his life. Of course he's still going through something." Sam got up from the couch and started to pace, muttering to himself. "Fuck. Fuck. Fuck. I haven't helped him even though he helped me. I don't know how."

"Hey, hey, hey." I grabbed Sam by the arm and pulled him toward me so he'd stop moving. "Time, Sam. All Caleb needs is time. Yes, he has distractions, but he needs time. He needs us, and even if we are in different countries we will still be there for him. We will always be there for him. You'll always be there for him."

Sam didn't say anything for a couple of minutes. His eyes flickered around the room before locking on mine. He leaned in, his lips pressing against my forehead, his touch still lingering even when he pulled away. He grabbed his phone and instantly started dialing; the ringing tone came from the speaker.

"*Yes!*" Caleb yelled into the phone.

Sam couldn't repress his amusement. "Hey, Caleb."

"You called back!" He sounded surprised.

"Yeah."

"What for? You never call back; it's always me calling you back after you hang up on me."

"I wanted to tell you something."

"What is it? Is it that you're hopelessly in love with me and you're breaking up with the princess so that you can be with me forever—"

"No."

"—and we'll adopt five kids and live in Iowa in a ranch house beside Gigi Hadid?"

Sam almost started laughing. "No, you idiot. That's not what I'm going to tell—Gigi Hadid?"

"Yeah." I could hear the smile in Caleb's voice as Sam mouthed *Iowa?* in disbelief. "But what were you going to say?"

"I was going to tell you that I love you, man."

There was a pause on the other side. "Sam." Caleb cleared his throat. "I was clearly joking when I said all the stuff about love and kids and Iowa—"

"You know what I mean." Sam's voice came out gently, almost as if he was reassuring him.

"You never really tell me that voluntarily," Caleb said.

"I know I don't." Sam sighed. "But I thought I should."

There was shuffling on the other end of the line. Caleb understood Sam better than anybody else. He knew him inside and out, even though they hadn't spent as much time growing up together as most childhood friends did. They were unconventional best friends, but at the end of the day that's what they were: best friends. "Well, I love you too, man."

Sam nodded. It wasn't awkward. Nothing more had to be said. "I'll let you go now. I'll call you tonight."

"No, don't," Caleb was quick to say. "It's your anniversary. Go have fun."

"Thanks, mate."

When they hung up, Sam came toward me, pressing a kiss to my forehead. When he pulled away, I asked, "What was that for?"

"I'm in love with you," he said with so much certainty. "You know that, right?"

"I know that every day," I said.

"Felt like giving you a reminder." He smiled before clapping his hands once. "Okay, we have reservations tonight. But watch a game beforehand?"

Yes, please.

7
JUST DRIVE

A few hours later, after doing some of our favorite things—watching a recorded soccer game while arguing, dissecting, analyzing, and pulling up stats on our phones—I stood in the middle of Sam's bedroom, looking into the mirror. Maddy had helped me pick out a black dress for tonight. I pushed my hair over my shoulders, fluffing it a few times as I looked at myself in the mirror. *You look fine. You look fine.*

I ended up FaceTiming Maddy for tips on how to curl my hair. She stared at me as I almost burned myself for the hundredth time. "Have you never curled your hair before?"

"Not really."

"Relax."

"I can't relax," I groaned. "I don't know how to curl my hair. Usually Jasmine or Stevie does it for me."

"I'll teach you when you get back," Maddy promised. I heard our dorm room door open and close. A murmur drifted from the screen along with a head of red hair quickly entering and leaving our room. And that head of hair was very familiar.

When Maddy looked back at the screen, I glared at her. She flinched. "What?"

"Was that George?" George was an RA in the building. We had met him during our first week at HDF. Maddy had made a fleeting comment that she thought he was cute, but she hadn't mentioned him since, and nothing had come out of it.

Or at least I *thought* nothing had come out of it.

"Yes," she said. "I gave him some old CDs, and he was giving them back."

CDs. Really? "Uh-huh."

"What? We're just friends!"

"Uh-huh," I repeated, glancing at myself in the mirror once again. "Okay, how's this?"

"Better," she said. "Don't be nervous, Macy."

"I'm not nervous." Sam and I were comfortable. We'd been terribly comfortable with each other right from the get-go. Even when he was attempting to be intimidating. Even when I was competitive. It didn't matter. He was the first boy I had ever really felt something deep for. He was the first whom I'd considered would be my last. He was waiting for me downstairs.

And yet I couldn't stop fidgeting. I almost burned my hand again trying to move the curling iron away from myself, yanking the cord from the outlet in haste. Remembering Maddy was on the line and had watched my entire struggle, I twisted to face her. We made eye contact through the screen. "Okay, I'm a little nervous." Very. "But forget about me, what's happening with George?"

"Nothing!" she exclaimed. "Since when do you even like talking about this subject?"

"What subject?"

"Romance. Dating. Crushes. I know you're in love and everything, but we only talk about it when I bring it up."

I shrugged. I wanted to see Maddy happy, especially after the disaster of her last date. "Since now. Also, I don't ever really feel the need to talk about my relationship."

"You're very private, I get it," Maddy said. "Sam doesn't really seem like that, though."

"He is and isn't," I said. "He has his moments."

Maddy raised her eyebrows, amused. "You're smiling."

I was? I was.

"Anyway—"

"I'm happy for you, Mace."

"Thanks, Maddy." I beamed. "I'm happy for you and George."

"Nothing is happening between George and me!" I could barely hear what she said; her voice was drowned out by my laughter.

Ending the call, I threw my brown leather jacket on over my dress. Then I grabbed my camera bag, which contained my wallet, and left the apartment.

When I opened the lobby doors, I found Sam leaning against his car. The first thing I noticed was his hair. The curls that were normally tousled as if he had rolled in bed all day were defined with some product. My gaze trailed down to the light-purple buttoned shirt on top of dress pants. When I met his eyes, I found that they were wandering my body as I approached him.

"*Wow.*"

"You don't look so bad yourself," I said. There was no point in saying more. Samuel Henry Cahill was a handsome man, and he knew it.

He scoffed as he opened the door for me. "I don't look bad? That's all I get?"

"Just drive."

He shut the door, hopping into the driver's seat and taking off. Before he even left the neighborhood, he tapped me on my bare knee. The action made me linger on his hand for too long when he asked, "Am I still sexy as always?"

I made a face. "You're okay."

He let out a dramatic breath, pressing one hand against his chest. "What a generous compliment, my love."

"Stop." I grinned, the two of us sharing a smile for a second before he focused on the road. "Where did you go?"

"Derek's," he said. "He put this stuff in my hair."

"It looks good," I admitted.

"So, does that mean I look good?"

"Don't get ahead of yourself."

Delight appeared in his green eyes. "Never change, Hazel."

I took out my camera and turned my body to focus on Sam. I watched him hum under his breath and bop his head slightly to the beat of whatever he was singing in his mind. His green eyes were bright with excitement, and he took one hand off the steering wheel to run through his curlier hair.

His green eyes narrowed as we reached a stoplight, and he looked over at me, his tongue pressing against the inside of his cheek. "Are you planning on capturing another photo of me?"

I grinned, holding the camera up to my eye and taking a picture. Sam shook his head, and as some lights lit us up from a store close to our car, I immediately took a picture of him before changing to my phone camera.

He tried pushing the phone away as I got multiple pictures of him.

"Are you—the model—actually avoiding the camera?"

"Yes," he said, laughing, "because I am trying to drive, and you make it very hard to concentrate on the road, Hazel."

"Can I get a picture of you when we get there then?"

"Seriously?"

"Yeah," I urged him. "You look . . ."

"I look what?" He smirked, looking at me for a quick second before moving his eyes back to the road.

"You look interesting enough to take a picture of." He rolled his eyes before grabbing my hand and pressing a kiss to the back of it.

When we got to our destination, a place on the outskirts of the city, Sam got out of the car and walked over to my side to open the door for me.

As I got out of the car, a man who looked to be close to our age jogged over to us. Sam closed the door behind me while dropping the keys in the valet's palm. But when his eyes fell upon the man, he tensed. My eyebrows rose with confusion, but the valet hadn't looked at Sam yet to notice his strange behavior. Instead, his eyes were focused on the sleek car, and he closed his fingers around the key carefully as if it were made of glass.

Sam cleared his throat, and when he spoke his voice was hard. "Don't dent it. You dent the car, you deal with me and you deal with my father."

"Yes, I understand, sir." The valet finally took his eyes off the car. When they fell onto Sam, they filled with both recognition and surprise. "Sam? Cahill?"

Sam frowned, his posture still rigid as the valet only grinned.

"Damn, I haven't seen you for a good minute. How have you been? I thought you'd gone back home to England. What are you doing in Southford?"

"What are *you* doing in Southford?" Sam countered flatly. *Uh-oh.*

"Working. Southford's familiar. You don't remember all the trips we used to take here for parties and shit when you were in town?" The guy took their interaction a step further, jabbing Sam in the stomach jokingly. But Sam wasn't laughing along with him at the memories. "You know, Anthony was saying he saw you the other day."

I got the feeling that whoever Anthony was, he wasn't someone Sam liked even remotely because tension was rolling off him in waves at this point. "I didn't see him," Sam managed to say.

"Not surprised he didn't say anything. He was always in the shadows like that." The valet chuckled before his lightness disappeared. "I didn't know you were here. I thought you'd stay in England 'cause of all the stuff that went down with your family and Bethany."

That hit a nerve. Even I closed my eyes for a brief second.

If Sam hadn't been upset before, he was now. His jaw clenched, and I took that as a cue to grab onto his arm, forcing a smile at the valet. "It was nice meeting you, but we have to go inside. Don't want to miss our reservation."

The valet nodded. "Great seeing you again, Sam." Before he could say anything further, I started to drag Sam in the direction of the twinkly restaurant.

Once we entered the building, I analyzed the details of the beautiful waiting area. Many people occupied the floor, sitting on couches and waiting for available seating behind the big doors that led to part of the restaurant. Another section of the restaurant seemed to be upstairs, and I glanced over at Sam, who rigidly gestured for us to join the few people waiting by two elevators on the side. Luckily, I was able to slip the two of us inside the less crowded one, pushing Sam toward the back as the doors closed behind us.

He was taking deep, measured breaths, gazing down at the ground as the elevator smoothly moved upward. After the doors opened, I steered Sam to one of the two hostesses as I looked beyond to where people were seated across the floor and at the bar. This room was even twinklier than the outside of the restaurant, surrounded by windows overlooking Southford. The hostess's eyes widened at the view of Sam, but I didn't care.

"Do you have a reservation?" She smiled sweetly at Sam before glancing up and over at me, her smile dropping a bit.

I didn't have time for this.

"Cahill. It's under Cahill," I said.

I didn't miss the slight widening of her eyes at the mention of the last name as she pieced it together while typing on the computer in front of her. She directed us to our table near the back of the room next to a large window and rushed off, saying she would return. I let out a breath at how far up we were. And how rich everyone around me seemed to be. Dressed in designer clothing, people of various ages were scattered around us at their tables, and lighthearted laughter lilted around the room.

When we were finally sitting, I shook myself out of being

enamored by my surroundings, looking at him. His gaze was stuck on the marble table.

"Sam."

He looked up at me with a very strained smile. It looked as if he was being held against his will and told to raise his lips. "Hazel."

I leaned back into my chair, waiting. His troubled mood wasn't going to be sorted out until he spoke up.

Sam kept his eyes on me as I crossed my arms, signaling that I wasn't planning on going anywhere. He ran a hand over his jaw. "It's really a small world, huh? He's a person I never thought I'd have to see again." Suddenly, he groaned, putting a hand on his forehead. "I'm sorry, I don't want to ruin our night with something as stupid as this."

"It's not stupid, Sam," I said quietly.

"I'm sorry." He shook his head, his eyes falling shut. They squeezed tight as he tried to collect himself. "And when he said her name? It's not like I can't handle hearing her name. It . . . it just—"

"It caught you off guard," I finished for him.

Sam's eyebrows came together, his attention down as he stiffly bowed his head. For a minute I waited for him to do anything. Say something.

Instead, he indicated to the table, to the menus in front of us. I bit the inside of my cheek and grabbed one for his sake.

Dinner was tense. Sam looked out at the view half the time, a million thoughts rolling through his mind. I wanted to know what he was thinking, but I figured that this was a time for him to have to himself.

Soon after, we were back in the car. I, for one, was elated

beyond relief that we hadn't seen the valet again. I wasn't sure what Sam would have done, but judging by the way he was currently gripping the steering wheel, I had a good idea.

He passed his apartment building.

I tapped him on the arm. "Where are we going?"

"Somewhere," Sam murmured. "You know I'll always take you somewhere."

Somewhere. How many times had he said that to me? How many times had he done so? So many times.

"I want to take you to England," he suddenly said, warmth spreading through my chest at his words. He had said that before, in the earlier days of our relationship, during the summer while showing me pictures, during talks with his family members. It wasn't a new thing, but whenever he brought it up it felt like he was trying to tether me to his home. The idea didn't scare me in the slightest.

"I want to travel home with you," he continued. He started to get comfortable, his shoulders loosening as he gained control of the conversation and wasn't thrown off by someone else bringing it up. "See you with everyone. Greg already likes you."

And I liked Greg. When I had met Greg the first time when he had visited for our high school graduation, we had bonded quickly over video games. The twelve-year-old played a lot of them. I was certain that since he was now living in Port Meadow, he was making Phillip play a million games with him.

"And you'd get to see the house, but also the castle since we spend a lot of time there as well."

"I'll never get over you saying 'castle,'" I said. "Like, you guys own a *castle.*"

"It's kind of just a big house."

I'd seen pictures. It was a *castle*.

I leaned my head against the window as the night whipped by us. Looking over at Sam, I couldn't fight my smile. "You want to take me to your home?"

He reached for my hand. "I do. Maybe spring break?"

Ours fell on the same week. "I'd like that," I admitted.

My fingers went over his knuckles, lightly tracing the soft skin. Being with him in his home country as he was with me in mine—it was a nice thought. Yet I wasn't going to let dinner go because of a good conversation in the aftermath. "Do you want to talk when we get to where we're going?" I asked.

Sam stopped speaking then, the light atmosphere that had been between us suddenly becoming strained as he agreed. Not too long after, he slowed down the car before coming to a full stop. Looking out the window, my eyebrows went up. Twinkle lights were definitely the theme for the night. Despite the lanterns already lighting up areas of the park, there was a little bridge adorned with lights not too far from where we were with a few people standing by it and taking pictures. I quickly got out of the car, not even waiting for Sam as I made my way over to the empty swing set.

I started to kick, pushing myself up into the air as he walked over to me. "How did you find this park? It's not close to your place," I asked, gaining momentum on the swing by kicking my legs. My hair stayed behind me as I moved, and Sam took a seat on the swing next to me, watching me with careful eyes. Analytic eyes. Eyes that I loved.

"I used to hang out with a few people who lived in cities near Redmond," he said slowly. "And they lived close to Southford too, so we'd hang out in random parks."

I held tighter to the chains of the swing but stopped moving my legs until I was no longer swinging. "The valet guy was one of them? And the Anthony guy he was talking about?"

"Valet guy's name is Zach." Sam cast his gaze downward. "And Anthony . . . I did a lot of stupid things after Bethany passed. You know that."

"I know."

"A *lot*," he emphasized. "And I was involved with a lot of people here and back in England that I shouldn't have been involved with."

The coping mechanisms he had turned to after his sister had died, the unhealthy ones: drugs, sex, throwing himself into reckless situations to avoid coping with the real trauma that enveloped him. I tried to imagine the state he had been in, how recent everything still was for him.

"Tonight was a little blast from the past," I said.

"Blast from the past," Sam repeated. "Can't really escape it no matter where I go, huh?"

"You could've gone to, like, Russia for university."

Sam glanced at me. "Russia?"

"Or Fiji." I shrugged. "I don't know. You're the one who chose to go to school in Canada."

Sam let out a breathy laugh, and the sound made me fight back my need to beam. He laughed, and that was what mattered.

Then he exhaled. "I can't really escape it."

"No." Although, he was trying. He was clearly trying really hard. "And that's okay."

We sat there for a moment. One who had considered herself over a death from so long ago, and another who was still working through the grief of it all and the regrets over the aftermath.

Loss was a terrible thing, a horrible and hard feeling. Sometimes pushing through that feeling felt harder.

I'd spent years pushing through my own grief. When I was nine, I was told my mother had just died in a car accident. It took me a long time to work through the initial rawness before I could think of happy memories of Mom instead of the heartaches that followed her death. But I'd found some peace and balance in my life again. Sam was still working on it, and that was okay.

He got up from the swing, offering me a hand. "Shall we continue our date?"

He led me toward the group of people by the bridge. A few were looking down at the flowing water; others were posing for pictures that would be illuminated by the bright lights. I held on to the railing, looking down at the water to see my reflection. My hair was a little messy from the swinging. Sam's reflection joined mine as he ran a hand through his own hair. "I didn't ruin tonight, did I?"

I looked up at him. "The night's not over, is it?"

"I couldn't even hold a proper conversation with you at dinner."

"You needed to think, Sam," I said. If it had been months ago, he would've lashed out. Instead, he'd taken a moment for himself.

"I'll make it up to you."

"Just be here with me, okay?" I pressed a light kiss to his lips. When I pulled away, his eyes shone with relief, even though there was no reason for it.

I wasn't going anywhere.

Sam took my camera out of my camera bag. Then he tapped

a random person on the shoulder. "Excuse me? Can you take a picture of me and my girlfriend?"

We posed for the picture, big smiles on our faces that I would look back at later in our lives. I took other pictures—of the two of us, of the scenery, of the night. No one else was mentioned for the rest of the night—not Zach, not Anthony.

But they would be brought up again. Sam was right.

The world was a small place.

8
PILLOW TALK

Nope. No way is this girl getting the ball off me.

Tanya was pressuring me from behind, pulling at the back of my shirt, trying to kick my ankles. There was a certain level of aggressiveness to soccer, but she was pushing past my limit that Monday morning.

Eventually, I found a way out of her reach and passed the ball up, then immediately yanked her hand off my shirt. I didn't bother looking at her as we were dismissed and I trudged my way to the change room.

Anmol caught up to me as I made my way toward my locker. "She's been giving you a hard time these past couple of days."

"More so than usual," I said, reaching my hands up to tighten my ponytail. "Want to hang and study? We can go to the library and invite Maddy?"

Anmol and I had started spending a bit more time together since we had coordinated our gym schedules. On top of that,

Maddy and Anmol had learned that they shared a class, as they were both taking social sciences. "Sounds good," Anmol said.

After getting cleaned up and exiting the change room, Anmol and I walked over to Hathaway Library on the south side of campus. Maddy was sitting at a table in the middle of a room that was buzzing with quiet chatter. She was on her phone, typing like her life depended on it. I recognized that look in her eyes. It reminded me a bit of how Jasmine would text Andrew. It was the eagerness and immediate need to respond.

Now who was she texting?

Anmol came up behind her, peering over to look at our friend's phone. "Who's George?"

George? My jaw dropped. "You've been talking to George?"

Maddy rolled her eyes as if this wasn't a big deal. "Again, Mace, we're just friends."

I wasn't believing that. She knew it too because she finally put her phone down. "C'mon, Mace, you of all people know what it's like to just be friends with the guys."

Maddy reached for my phone, moving her chair next to Anmol's as she unlocked it, and they went through my photos. "You should see all of her guy friends."

Anmol's eyebrows went up with interest at whatever photo they were observing. "Who's the blond?"

When I realized who she was talking about, I gagged. "That's Andrew. Please don't call him cute in front of me."

"Why? He's cute."

At that I shivered. *Dramatically*. "He's like my brother." My big, goofball brother who liked to sit on me for fun, who would pig out on pizza with me, talking and playing video games as we yelled at each other well into the night. Andrew was family.

It was enough for Jasmine to gush about him in my presence. I didn't need Maddy to do it too.

"Has he talked to Jasmine yet?" Maddy asked.

"Who's Jasmine?" Anmol questioned.

"Her other best friend," Maddy explained. "He and Jasmine are dating."

"He spoke to her," I said, not wanting to give out much information about their relationship. At the end of the day, it was *their* relationship, not mine to share with the rest of the world. According to Andrew, she'd been very busy (which I'd figured) but also her phone was broken.

It didn't take weeks to get a broken phone repaired. I knew Jasmine; the second her phone was broken, she'd just run to the store to get a new one. Besides, she could have messaged Andrew through social media on her laptop.

I didn't really want to think too much about their relationship. Andrew had said they were okay again. That's what mattered.

"Has she talked to you?" Maddy asked.

I held in a sigh, trying not to appear dejected. "I saw her retweet something on Twitter, so I know she's alive. It's not a big deal if she doesn't talk to me. We're in university. It's hard to keep up with everyone. We're all busy."

We were. There was an essay waiting to be written staring me right in the face.

"But her boyfriend? She was ghosting him. That's weird," Maddy said. "Do you think something happened? Like she's pregnant or something?"

"*Pregnant?* I don't think so. I mean, they haven't seen each other in two months. But . . ." No. Even if that'd happened, she wouldn't cut him off. Would she?

No, she wouldn't do that.

"What if she cheated on Andrew?" Anmol asked.

Instantly, I shook my head. "No. Jasmine cheating on Andrew is something that will never ever happen. They are too invested in each other. That couldn't even cross my mind."

"You'll find out eventually," Anmol said.

"Maybe," I said. "But it's between them."

Anmol peered over at my laptop, obviously not wanting to touch any of her work this early in the morning. "What are you working on?"

"Essay," I said.

"You could call up Caleb to write it for you," Maddy suggested, now leaning back in her seat. "Remember, Sam said he'd do it."

"Who's Caleb?" Anmol inquired.

"Their friend from Port Meadow," Maddy explained.

"Sam was joking when he said that," I assured her. "And there's no way I'd ask Caleb anyway." Though I knew that if I asked Caleb, he would do it in a second.

On the table, my phone buzzed repeatedly. Speak of one of the two devils. Sam. "Yeah?"

"I got a call from the agency."

My eyes widened at what that meant. This had happened before. Sam was heading to another city to do a photo shoot. It had happened at least a couple of times a month during the summer. "Is model Sam making a comeback for good?"

"Stop."

It was so easy to tease him. "Did your aunt or mom get it for you?"

"Aunt. And yeah, I'm going to Toronto after my game on Saturday, so I won't be able to see you this week. You're going to be okay without me at your beck and call for a few days?"

"Of course I am. It's not like we're attached at the hip. Plus, you live in a different city already."

"I know, but c'mon, Hazel, you're going to miss me."

~

He was right.

I was used to Sam being away from me: when we'd first realized I'd be in Edward Bay and he'd be in Southford, the thought of living in two different cities after spending months minutes away from each other had seemed tough. But when you're about an hour away from each other by highway and could see each other more often than you'd realized (when we weren't busy with midterms), it was good. It was good when I got to sleep in a bed next to him, to wake up and feel his company instead of the texts and phone calls. It was simply nice to feel his presence. But now he was going to be a lot farther away.

On Saturday evening, I had come back from a soccer game where we'd tied and was taking a break from studying for another test later that week. I was lying in my bed with a pillow on my face when the door opened. "Mace?" Maddy asked, cautiously coming in after volleyball practice.

"Yeah," I said into the pillow.

"Why do you have a pillow on your face?"

"I can't talk to a pillow?"

She removed the pillow from my face, then whacked me over the head with it. "Enough of your pillow talk. Get up. We're going out."

"No, it's Saturday."

"Yes, it *is* Saturday. That means that it is the perfect day for you to get out of this damn room."

"No, it means this is the perfect day for me to crawl into bed and watch a show. Or read a book. Or go to the gym."

"No. What the hell? Macy, get up. We don't even have to go to a party. We could just walk through town. Meet more people. Pretend we're from England and put on fake accents."

"You do a horrible accent," I said, sitting up and watching her shuffle through our shared closet for her fall boots.

"I think I sound rather dapper if you ask me," she said in the most awful, westernized form of a British accent I had ever heard in my life. "We should go get food."

I perked my head up. "Food?"

Maddy shot me a look. We'd known each other for almost two months now. She knew how much I admired food. This shouldn't have been such a surprise. "Why didn't I say that first?" she mused, pulling her boots on.

We started to head over to meet up with Anmol at her dormitory, Farrow Hall, on the other side of the campus. But we didn't get far before we found her standing in front of another house along the street, listening to a tall blond man.

Maddy and I exchanged a look. Guy problems. As we got closer, Derek was saying, "That was a long time ago."

"But it was still—" Anmol stopped speaking, interrupting herself. "I don't want to talk about it."

"So you are embarrassed."

"I . . . well . . . wouldn't you be?" she stammered.

Derek didn't say anything for a moment, and Anmol shot him a look. "Exactly. We're in two different places now, and it doesn't matter. We can move on."

"But what if I don't want to move on?"

"Derek," she scolded.

"Anmol." There was lightheartedness in his tone. I thought he meant what he said. It only confirmed my suspicions. He was into her, and she was having a hard time believing it.

Anmol noticed us over his shoulder, and she pushed past him. She was quick to link arms with both of us. "Anmol!" he called out.

"I'll see you around!" she yelled back, dragging us in the direction of the bus stop. Maddy, being Maddy, gave Derek a big wave as we rounded the block.

Anmol huffed, crossing her arms once we were out of his view. "You guys don't think he's into me, do you?"

"Yes," Maddy and I said at the same time.

"No," Anmol whined. "There is no way. We saw each other for the first time in years not that long ago. What is his issue?"

"Sometimes it doesn't take that long to realize who you really want," Maddy told her. "And he wants you."

Anmol clearly didn't believe that, but she looked flushed by the thought of it.

"Do you want him?" I asked.

"No," she said quickly.

Maddy chuckled. "She totally wants him. You're in disbelief that he might actually like you back."

"Because it doesn't make sense. It's too soon." Anmol shook her head. "Moving on. Let's move on. What's going on with you guys? Where are we going to go eat? What's the plan?" None of her deflecting questions were answered because suddenly she had another one when she looked at my camera bag hanging around my neck. "I never really got to ask you, but what's with the camera? Are you a photographer or something?"

We made our way to the bus stop, and Maddy took a seat on the nearby bench. I tapped the side of the bag. "Memories," I said. "It's been a hobby of mine for a while."

"Can I see some pictures?"

I handed her my camera, and all three of us huddled on the bench as we flicked through the multiple pictures I had left in my camera. Millions more were saved on SD cards, USBs, and online drives, but I kept a few pictures from the summer on there to look back on.

We became immersed in the photos as I explained to Anmol who each of my friends were in each picture. Glancing at Maddy and Anmol as they laughed at a picture of Jacob and Jon Ming, I realized they would fit in well with them. It was nice to have two people that I found myself getting along with just as easily as I had done with the gang back home.

Three buses passed us by as we stayed seated, talking. Maddy spoke about some new YouTubers she was following as I took pictures of them talking, then I turned my camera to the oncoming sunset, with its blending hues of blue, red, and purple. I listened to Anmol tell us of her life back home before the two started posing for funny pictures I would add to my gallery.

By the time we were done, I couldn't stop cackling when a random lady gave the three of us looks.

And then I felt it. The first flake of snow that hit the tip of my nose. Then more flakes. The shift in the air as they fell lightly from the sky.

Winter.

It meant outdoor season was ending.

It meant indoor season was starting soon.

It meant change was coming.

In front of me, Maddy's eyes lit up, and I laughed at her glee, taking a picture as she urged Anmol to catch a snowflake with her as if they were five.

However, my attention was drawn away from them when I heard voices accompanying the snow, drifting in the wind. I looked up to see a group of people walking in our direction on the sidewalk. The group had started to walk by us when someone stopped and pointed at me. "Hey, you're Sam's girl, yeah?"

Zach.

He was staring at me quizzically, and the rest of his group paused to eavesdrop. One guy in a dark-blue sweater, his hair hidden underneath a black cap, stared at me in a way that made me feel as if I was being analyzed. His gaze trailed up and down my body, and instantly I looked away from him, a bad taste forming in my mouth. *Who was that?*

I turned back to Zach. Zach seemed friendly enough, a small smile on his face as if to assure me nothing bad was going to happen. His friend continued to leer at me from behind him in a manner that made me want to wipe that smile off his face. Ew.

"Yeah, I'm Macy. Zach, right?"

He nodded, peeking over at my friends before looking back at me. "So, Sam told you a little bit about me?"

"A little bit." I kept it short. There wasn't much really to say. The guy behind Zach looked like he might have something to add but instead kept his mouth shut.

"Say, I'm throwing a Halloween party on Friday. You, your friends"—he gestured to Anmol and Maddy—"and Sam should come. No hard feelings for the guy or anything. Just a good time. Free drinks."

"Party?" Maddy hopped to her feet.

"We're in," Anmol said.

Zach rattled off the address and time to Maddy, who eagerly took down the information. As he was kindly saying goodbye, his friend locked eyes with me. "Hope Sam comes. Miss the guy."

I didn't like the way he'd said that. As if they had history together. As if Caleb had been replaced, and this guy had been Sam's best friend through every single up and down he'd gone through.

I didn't like him.

"Anthony, fuck off." Zach pushed him forward as my eyebrows rose up. So this was Anthony. I could see why Sam didn't like him already. His presence made me hold in a shiver that wasn't caused by the cold. I didn't even want to think about all the things he and Sam had done a lifetime ago. Zach's lips formed a reassuring smile. "It's going to be a good time. Come if you can."

Without another word, the entire group moved ahead, walking down the street and rounding the block. The snow I had enjoyed a mere moment ago was suddenly rather irritating. I tensed as a hand touched my arm. Maddy. "We're not going to that party, are we?"

"You can go," I assured her, but she furrowed her brow.

"You don't seriously think I'm going to go to a party without you, do you?" she asked. The words brought a smile to my face. She was too good to me. "And you too, now that we've established we're friends," Maddy said to Anmol, bumping hips with her.

When we sat down on the bench, my stomach was growling. We were definitely going to get on the next bus to eat. Anmol peeked over at me. "You all right?"

"Yeah." I ran my fingers through my brown hair, pulling it into a low ponytail. "I'm down for a party. But I don't know if Sam will want to go."

"I'm pretty sure if you go to the Halloween party, Macy, he'll go too."

"If it was any other party, sure." There was no doubt about that. "But this one I'm not so certain about."

"Why?"

The two of them peered at me with curious expressions. This wasn't my story to tell, and I settled on saying the vaguest thing possible. "Some people at the party are likely to be connected to a part of Sam's life he's been trying to push past."

Maddy frowned, realizing I was serious. "Well, we don't have to go."

"No, no, no, you guys can go."

Maddy suddenly stood, hands on her hips. "If Anmol and I go, you have to come with us. And if you don't want to go, we won't go. But if Sam considers coming, let him know we got his back."

I chuckled. "Maddy."

She pointed a finger at me. "I mean it. He can't avoid the people he's been trying to avoid forever. They're bound to pop up one way or another."

A part of me hated that she had a very good point.

"Maybe he could own the scene if he went," Anmol added.

"Have you seen the guy? He'll own it." Maddy shot me a wink, sitting back down between Anmol and me. We settled into a comfortable silence for a while until the bus came, the snow continuing to fall. A sign of a new season coming with new changes and unexpected things. But like every year in Ontario, the first snowfall felt simultaneously like something new and unexpected and something we'd seen a million times before.

9
YOU'RE STALKING

Something thumped against the other side of Sam and Peter's apartment door. When I tried to open the door, I struggled as it was partially blocked by a pyramid of toilet paper on the ground.

Looking down the small hallway, I saw Peter standing at the end of it, holding a tennis ball in his hand. There was a stack of tennis balls on the table next to him.

He grinned at me. "Hey, Macy. You mind getting out of the way so I can get a spare?"

I didn't even question it.

Bypassing him, I glanced back to see him do an underhand swing of the tennis ball, which smashed through the toilet paper rolls, all of them falling to the floor from the impact.

He raised his arms up in victory. "Yes! Sam, your turn!" he yelled as he rushed down the hall to set up the rolls again.

Sam came out of the kitchen, the corners of his lips rising once he spotted me. Immediately, we collided since we hadn't seen each other in a week. He laughed, the sound hitting me straight down to my toes as he enveloped me in a strong and solid hug. He whispered against my hair, "Hi, Hazel."

"And the lovers are reunited," Peter mused behind me.

Sam flipped him off before pulling me to the living room.

"Wait," Peter shouted. "What about our game?"

"You can take my turn," Sam yelled back.

"Thank you!"

The second we stepped into the living room, I found myself lying on my back on the couch with Sam over me on his forearms to take most of the weight off me. "Did you have practice?"

"Yeah," I told him, not bothering to bring up the amount of homework I had managed to do on the bus ride there. "I practically ran over here."

He didn't kiss me. Not yet. He used his index finger to trace under my eyes, the curve of my top lip, my chin, and my jaw. Almost as if he was memorizing me. I smiled under the ticklish feeling and twirled a lock of his curly hair around my finger. "How was the shoot?"

"Stressful. The photographer kept yelling to the point where I got a headache. He was like 'Stand there,' 'You're doing that wrong,' 'Are you serious? Why are you making that face?' or 'You look constipated.'"

"He said that all to *you*?" I asked.

"No, he said that to other people. Definitely not me," Sam said smugly, and I rolled my eyes at his cockiness.

"Anything else? Was your aunt the only person you knew there?"

"Alexis was there too," he murmured.

Alexis.

I didn't stop my movements in his hair, noting the way his eyes shut in relaxation despite me feeling the opposite at the mention of her name. Only because the mention of her reminded me of how she treated me every time she saw me. Nothing had happened between her and Sam, I was certain of it, but I didn't want to hear anything else about her.

"Any other troubles?"

Sam's eyes moved around my face as he thought. "When I was leaving one location to get to the next one down the street, I was walking on the pavement, and suddenly I was bombarded by cameras."

Cameras? No way. "What?"

"Yeah, that was my thought as well." Sam shrugged. "I don't know. I didn't think it was going to be a big deal. There was someone following me and my aunt when we were walking as well."

"Was Liz surprised?"

"Not really. She had expected it when Mum dropped her album—the eyes and focus on the entire family, people trying to pry into what we're all doing. But I wasn't expecting the cameras right in front of my face, that's all. I guess I've been sheltered being in a smaller town. I talked to Mum, and she was a little worried. She didn't think anyone was going to bother me here in Canada. Didn't think they'd try to grab pictures of the problem child of the family."

"Sam . . ."

"I am—I mean, I was." He rubbed his eyes. "Pictures were taken in England. It's one of the reasons I was moved over here. You'd think no one would care that much about a kid from a wealthy family, but apparently they still fucking do."

"Pictures?" I asked, sitting up from my position. This was new information.

"A small paper managed to get the mug shot from that night. The arson thing and the group of people I was involved with back in England. It's one of the reasons my mum and dad shipped me here. Because they didn't think paparazzi and news outlets were as big an issue here."

Oh. "Did they ask you questions? The ones outside the photo shoot, I mean."

"They did." Sam ran a hand over his face. "I did what my mum always said: 'Keep your head down and keep walking.' I managed to get my sandwich and return without making a scene. It was still a little overwhelming. Tell me you would be a fan of flashing lights in your face."

I'd hate it and would do anything I could to get out of that situation. But the realization of Sam's position creeped up on me, the image that came with his family and his own goals. "You realize that if you become a professional soccer player, you're going to face cameras more than you'd expect."

Not only with his family name already but representing a club team. Or even an entire country if he got what he wanted, what had been envisioned for him for a long time.

"I know," he muttered, lacing our fingers together.

I leaned forward. "You'll be okay."

"I have you." His lips twitched upward. "Of course I'll be okay."

I initiated the kiss, but he somehow shifted us closer than I'd ever thought he could. Lips against lips and his hands in my hair. And just like that, everything seemed to fade away. Only he was in my head the entire time. The feel of him against me left me dizzy and overwhelmed as one of my hands wound its way into his curls and the other fell over his chest to feel his erratically pounding heart, all for me.

The faint sound of Peter yelling, "Yes!" in the hallway made the two of us pull away. The man of the hour entered the living room, tossing a toilet paper roll at us as he said in a singsong, "Guess who got a strike."

"Not you," Sam said. Peter threw another toilet paper roll at Sam. Sam dodged the hit, picking up the roll that had fallen to the floor and whipping it at Peter, who shrieked before disappearing in the direction of his room.

Toilet paper. Halloween. *Oh.*

"I have something to tell you," I said.

Sam looked at me quizzically. "Yeah?"

"I saw Zach when I was with Anmol and Maddy the other day. He invited us to a Halloween party he's throwing." Sam raised an eyebrow as I waited for him to take in what I had told him. "And I was wondering if you wanted to go?"

Sam's tongue went under his bottom lip as he contemplated my words. A series of emotions flashed over his face before he looked at me, not revealing anything. "You're going, right?"

"Maddy really wants to go to the party and said she won't go without me and Anmol. She wants you to come too."

"Maddy wants me to come?" Sam asked, as if he didn't think they were friends. He exuded an intimidating exterior, but Maddy had never cared. Whenever he glared, she smiled.

"She said she has your back if anything goes wrong."

Sam scoffed, fighting back his amusement. He really considered her a friend, and I was happy about that. "Okay, fine."

Hold on. No way was he agreeing to this. Besides, *fine* wasn't the right word. At least not the right word for us. "Fine?"

"I'll come, Hazel," he repeated. "I'll go."

"Are you sure?" I asked tentatively. I didn't want to pressure him, though I wouldn't have been surprised if Maddy messaged him a million times in a Caleb manner to get him to reconsider if he said no. "Because I know how you are when you see someone from years ago."

"I'll be prepared this time. That's the difference," he said, his tone so certain, I couldn't doubt him. And yet . . . maybe he had his own reasons for wanting to go. To prove something. Either way, I didn't think this was going to go well, but when he set his mind to something, he did it. "It'll be fine."

I had to ask again. "You sure?"

"I'm going to be okay." He squeezed my hip, a glint in his eye as he asked, "Now, what are you dressing up as for Halloween?"

~

"What did you dress up as last year?" Maddy asked me outside our bathroom door on the Friday night of Halloween. Sam was probably lying down on my bed, going through his social media while we waited for Anmol to arrive.

"What do you *think* I dressed up as?" Maddy had taught me how to curl my hair, and now I was doing it without burning myself. I think seventeen-year-old me would have scoffed that I had done it, considering I had never bothered to care before. Now, I thought I looked nice with curls.

"A soccer player," Maddy answered.

"Which one?"

"Do I watch soccer?" No. "It was pretty obvious you would dress up as one, though."

"I'm not going as that this year."

"Didn't you dress up as a soccer player for ten years straight?" Sam shouted from the other side.

"No, only in high school!" I yelled back.

"That's not what Andrew said."

"You're going to believe Andrew over me?" I asked him, poking my head through the door so he wouldn't see what I was wearing.

He looked over at me, placing his phone down on my nightstand while his long body lay stretched on my bed. "I like your hair." The compliment made my face redden. "But was it only high school?"

"It was grade eight too," I grumbled. "Jerk."

"Don't be mean, Hazel," he joked before Maddy slipped inside the bathroom, closing the door behind us.

I stifled my amusement as she tried to fix her red wig in the mirror, adjusting her hat above her hair. She was dressed as Madeline from the show and books. She had the red wig and the yellow coat and everything. She looked exactly like the character from my childhood. Maddy rolled her eyes through the mirror when she caught me staring. "Stop laughing."

"I'm not laughing." My terrible attempt to lie fell apart as I snickered, forcing myself out of the room.

"Whoa," Sam said as I turned around to face him, his eyebrows up to the ceiling. I wasn't surprised when his eyes fell to my legs. I had attempted to pull the skirt down, but being tall meant that finding a skirt (which I felt uncomfortable in considering I never wore them) that suited my height was more difficult than Anmol, Maddy, and I had imagined. When I'd sent a picture earlier to Stevie, she'd been floored. I'd imagine if Jasmine had responded she would've been confused as to how someone had managed to get me into a skirt.

But nothing else would have worked—I was going as the female version of Captain America. Hours away, Andrew was dressed up as Bucky, who was Cap's childhood best friend in the comics. It was the best thing we could think of to go for, especially considering Sam didn't bother dressing up for Halloween.

Speaking of Sam, he was still staring at my legs.

I snapped my fingers in his face. "Don't get so excited. I'm wearing shorts underneath, and I might wear tights."

"Please don't," Sam said under his breath. I slapped him upside the head. He hissed with a loud laugh, reaching out toward me. I batted his hands away, unable to hold in my laugh as Maddy came out of the bathroom.

"Doesn't she look great?" Maddy asked, handing me the blue mask that went with the outfit. I was still debating holding the plastic shield that was currently on my bed.

Sam removed his eyes from my legs, looked up at me with a small smile on his face that brought a flush to mine, and he nodded. "Then again, you always do."

"What are you supposed to be?" Maddy asked Sam.

Sam looked down at his outfit: dark jeans, his leather jacket thrown over a shirt, and Converse on his feet. He shrugged. "I'm Sam Cahill. I'd say that's a pretty good Halloween costume."

"*This* is your costume?" I asked him, crossing my arms.

"Lame," Maddy said in a singsong.

"Yes, it is. You want to find out what's underneath?" Sam

smirked, leaning closer to me, but I pushed him back lightly, a stupid grin finding its way to my face.

"She already has," Maddy quipped, looking through her phone.

No, I hadn't.

Maddy didn't know that. My other friends didn't either, though with the reputation Sam had once had, everyone assumed we had done it, and I'd never really said anything to confirm or deny their words. Sex wasn't a priority for me, and I'd never truly explored why. It was a personal choice. Besides, I wanted to be ready.

I didn't even know if Sam was ready for it. He probably was. Although the look he gave me after Maddy spoke made me settle. It was an expression that told me there was no expectation. He held so much patience in his green eyes without having to say anything. And if I hadn't known it before, I definitely knew it when he took my hand and squeezed it.

Yet the doubt didn't disappear.

I mean, after six months together? Sam wasn't the type to put pressure on me or push me, I knew that, but he was bound to be impatient.

Right?

My uncertainty was squashed by a knock on our dorm room door. Maddy opened it to reveal Anmol, who to my delight was dressed as a classic soccer player, wearing an Arsenal jersey—*ew*—with long socks up and over her shin pads and a headband pushing the baby hairs that couldn't be captured by her ponytail backward. As she stood at the threshold, she wasn't looking at us, though. Her focus was on her phone, glaring at it as she analyzed someone's Instagram.

"*Hello?* Earth to Anmol." Maddy waved her hand in front of the phone, and Anmol blinked, softening her concentration. Maddy's brow furrowed at the Instagram page she was looking at. "You're stalking Derek's account?"

"I'm not stalking!" Anmol insisted. "I was . . . researching."

"Stalking," Maddy corrected.

"Browsing," Anmol stressed, but she glanced over at Sam. "Do you know if he's going to be at this party?"

Sam shrugged. "I don't know if he's going to show up." Then he coughed into his hand, looking a bit uncomfortable. I stared at him. What the heck was he going to do? "I'm not one to give out relationship advice, but—"

"No, no, no." Anmol shut him down, strained laughter leaving her lips. "Relationship advice? Me and Derek? No. We're not even friends."

Sam put his hands up in mock surrender before shoving them into his pockets. "I think you should give the poor mate a chance."

Mate? I almost grinned, but Sam rolled his eyes at my expression before turning back to Anmol. Anmol, whose brow furrowed in annoyance as she asked, "Why?"

Sam grabbed his keys. "Why not?"

"He doesn't know me like he used to."

"Exactly," Sam said as he pushed past her and headed into the hallway, cutting the conversation short.

Anmol was already on his tail while Maddy stood next to me, fixing her yellow hat. "This is going to be an interesting party, isn't it?"

One thousand and ten percent it was going to be.

10
I'D LOVE TO EXPLORE ALL OF THAT

People were clustered outside Zach's town house. One group was smoking weed on my left and another group of guys cackled on my right as my friends and I stood at the threshold waiting for Zach to open the door. The Weeknd's voice spilled out from inside, and we could see flashing lights of red, blue, and green. Dressed as the Mad Hatter from *Alice in Wonderland*, with a bottle of beer in his hand, Zach gave us all big grins. Sam managed to give him a stiff nod as a greeting, and Zach ushered us all inside.

Anmol and Maddy were quick to follow him, but next to me, Sam became rigid. His eyes darted around the room, like he was sussing out who'd be at the party. Immediately, I laced my fingers with his, squeezing gently. "You know I'm right here, yeah?"

"I know," he said, pressing a light kiss to the side of my head before the two of us went inside.

Hot, sticky house. Yelling. People screaming the lyrics.

Someone in a witch costume making out with someone who was a hot dog in the corner. Alcohol and weed mixed together. The party itself wasn't unfamiliar to me and yet I had an underlying feeling that something was going to happen.

The first person I found was Maddy. She was in the middle of breaking a hug with . . . I gasped, grabbing Sam's arm tightly.

"What?" he asked.

"George," I breathed. The redheaded guy was dressed as a bottle of ketchup and was beaming down at Maddy, the two of them engaged in an animated conversation. "Maddy hugged George."

Sam looked over at them before staring at me. "Since when do you care about someone's romantic life?"

"Since Maddy thinks she's cursed by having a terrible track record with men. But this guy seems nice." Sam blinked once. "What? I can't be curious?" He blinked again, and I shoved him. "Stop it, you dumbegg!"

"There you are," he chuckled, but his smile disappeared as we made our way to the living room and Zach appeared with a girl next to him.

"Guys, this is my roommate, Rosaline." The girl had curly, dyed honey-brown hair, light-brown skin, and doe-like eyes, and she gave me a two-fingered wave. She was dressed as a fairy, with fake wings clipped to her tank top, extending outward and almost poking Zach in the side. When she turned to Sam, her eyebrows rose. "Holy shit, you're Sam Cahill."

Sam raised an eyebrow at the greeting. "Uh, hi."

"Sorry." She was grinning. "It's just your parents are famous, and you're kind of famous—"

"I'm definitely not famous," Sam said calmly, but it sounded as if it'd taken everything in him to respond. There was no way this girl alone was bothering him that much.

"Aren't you?" she asked, puzzled. "Your mom was trending on Twitter the other day when that interview of hers came out. Remember, Zach?"

Zach took swig of his beer. "Yeah, we watched it a bit after I saw you at the restaurant. Your mom was talking about your future and stuff. Mentioned your dad. She also mentioned you becoming a professional soccer player." Sam inhaled deeply, and then he opened his mouth, ready to speak when Zach's eyes suddenly lit up. "Oh yeah, some of our old friends are here. They wanted to see you."

Instantly, Sam shut down. All the emotion on his face—the conflict, the tiredness, the agitation—slipped away into blankness when he asked, "Friends?"

Friends? The idea of that creepy guy being here set off alarm bells in my head.

Zach remained unfazed by both of our expressions. "C'mon, man." He grabbed Sam by the crook of his arm and pulled him to the living room. Rosaline followed along with me as we made our way over to the corner of the living room where people were lounging on the couches and the carpet.

The alarm bells in my head returned immediately at one of the men in the corner snickering loudly: Anthony. When he spotted Sam, recognition lit up his face, but his smile didn't seem friendly, as if he had known Sam would come.

On the other hand, my boyfriend seemed anything but happy. The way his green eyes flashed, I knew he was pissed off as he yanked his arm out of Zach's grip.

"Sam?" A voice came from the left: a girl dressed up as a sexy police officer. "Is that actually you?"

Sam didn't acknowledge her, redirecting his glare at Zach. "Is *everybody* going to school here?" he hissed.

Next to me, Rosaline shifted, sensing the discomfort. "He doesn't look elated to be seeing old friends," she whispered.

"He isn't," I said as we kept our attention on the scene in front of us.

"Not everybody." Anthony rubbed his nose before raking his hand through his hair. He wasn't wearing anything costume-like, apart from the devil horns on his head, which seemed apt in the moment. "Some of us stuck together. It's good to see you, man. We never really got to speak last time I saw you."

"Didn't have the need to say anything," Sam said, his voice stoic.

"You haven't changed *that* much, have you?" Anthony tilted his head. "It hasn't been that long."

Sam knew how long it had been. The way his tongue dove into the corner of his bottom lip let me know he could say it out loud right now. His coping mechanism. Time. Numbers. Math. His thing. The girl next to Anthony spoke up. "Well, I didn't think it was possible, but you got hotter, Cahill. I'd love to explore all of *that* again."

Her implication didn't make me bristle. The seductive lure she was attempting to create with her eyes right at this moment didn't even bother me. And it didn't trouble Sam, whose focus was still on Anthony. Instead, Zach was the one who spoke up with an eye roll. "Lay off the man. He's taken."

Anthony and the girl—really, everyone in their circle—looked over at me. Anthony's gaze was the one I felt the most, the one that made me feel like my skin was crawling. The way he was leering at me from head to toe made me want to take my heels off and throw them in his direction. When he turned back to Sam, I exhaled.

"Sam Cahill with a *girlfriend*? That's new." The girl raised her eyebrows, assessing me. Like she was picking out new clothes and didn't like anything she was seeing. "Cute costume."

I gave her a tight smile. That definitely wasn't meant to be a compliment. "Thanks."

"How are you, man?" Anthony suddenly asked. "I haven't heard a word from you in a long time. Didn't even know you were here to stay. Are you?"

"Am I what?" Sam didn't budge. I wasn't sure if he had breathed in the past few minutes.

"Here to stay," Anthony asked slowly, patting his pockets while keeping his attention on Sam.

Sam's jaw clenched. "I'm not really here to answer ridiculous questions."

"Sam." Anthony let out a bitter laugh, shaking his head. "We were friends once. We did things together. Took joyrides. Had fun. Dove in the snow together. Don't you remember?"

"Not really," Sam said coldly, holding Anthony's eyes. This area of the room was terribly closed off by their calm stare-off. The people around us were dancing, laughing, screaming, having the time of their lives. Yet here, everyone was focused on one man or the other. Two men with a past: one who wouldn't mind going back to it all while the other hated the idea of touching the memories.

Anthony snorted. "You don't remember a few other things, do you?" He removed a few items from his pockets, holding up something. My eyes fell on a small bag with white powder inside. *Oh.* He glanced down at it with a lazy smile. "Anyway, how's your family? Still rich?"

Sam pursed his lips. "And what about it?"

Anthony narrowed his eyes. "Still go to the fancy parties you used to tell us about? Back to living your posh life? How's Ivan? Heard he's getting married. Does he still party too—"

"Okay," Sam interjected. How did Anthony know Sam's cousin? "What do you want?"

Maybe Zach understood the heightening tension by now. Maybe he understood why I had been hesitant about coming here in the first place because he said, "Okay, maybe—"

"Why?" Anthony didn't take his attention off Sam. "You look mad, Sam. Take the stress off, man. You know what? Here. On the house. I won't even add it to your tab."

He tossed the white bag in Sam's direction, and it hit him square in the chest before bouncing off and dropping down to the floor. Anthony's mouth tilted up in a smirk while Sam glowered at him. Zach stepped in between them, picking up the cocaine and handing it back to Anthony. "All right, let's relax. He clearly doesn't do that."

"*Anymore,*" Anthony added, tapping the guy behind him, who was dressed as a vampire. "Sam needs to relax."

The guy held up what was in his hand, gesturing with it in Sam's direction. A rolled-up joint, by the looks of it. The flicks of the ember on the end must have looked tempting. "You want?"

I knew Sam was used to this.

The whole party scene. The whole getting-high-and-drunk scene. Conflict arose in his eyes. When his fingers twitched and his hand rose up a bit, I wasn't that surprised.

But he put his hand down as fast as it had risen up, and I let out a breath of air I hadn't even known I'd been holding in. He turned to Zach with his voice as hard as steel. "Where's your bathroom?"

"Down that hallway on your left—"

Before Zach finished his sentence, Sam's hand wrapped around mine and he was pulling me in the other direction, away from the group of people whose amused eyes were focused on us. Finding the bathroom unlocked, he closed the door behind us. "Fucking hell."

He was going to kick the door in. His leg reared back, and for his sake and because this was someone else's house, I yanked on his arm. Sam huffed as I turned him around to face me, putting a halt to his action. "Sam. Don't kick the door."

"I'm not going to kick the door." He wasn't fooling me, and he knew I wasn't buying it either because he said, "I was just stretching."

"Stretching by *kicking*?" I said dryly. "You actually do need to relax, though. Not by weed, just . . ." If we went back out there, he was going to explode. I wasn't risking it. "Stay here."

He leaned back against the wall, tilting his head back and closing his eyes. Taking my advice. I watched him take deep breaths as I leaned against the sink of the tiny bathroom. Coming here had been such a bad idea.

Sam opened one eye. "Are you upset?"

"No," I said, standing in front of him. To reassure him and because I felt the need to touch him of my own accord, I smoothed his hair with my hand. He closed his eyes. *Oh, Sam.* "You don't have to talk about it if you don't want to."

Sam kept his eyes closed. I raked my fingers through the

curls, and his body relaxed, shoulders loosening, breaths coming out more normally. "Every summer, my entire family would visit my grandmother in Redmond, right? Ivan had gone through a party phase of his own when he was younger and knew a lot of people over the years we visited. Sometimes, when he went to meet his friends, Beth and I would tag along. We met Zach one summer."

His palms dug into his eyes as he collected himself before dragging his hands off his face. "After Bethany, I went to my grandmother's. Saw some old faces that Ivan knew and met Anthony. Things happened there. I spiraled. Went back to England. Spiraled there. Spiraled worse. Got sent to Port Meadow."

"And Anthony was your friend? Who also knows Ivan?"

"Anthony was not my friend." Sam shook his head. "You saw what just happened six minutes and twenty-three seconds ago when he tossed the coke at me. And he knew Ivan because Ivan had visited Redmond more than I had since he had lived here longer. Before Natasha, he was also a bit of a partier. Now he's grown up. He knew Anthony through mutual friends, and they'd seen each other here and there."

"Anthony seemed to know a bit about your family too."

"Unfortunately." Sam rolled his eyes. "Anthony didn't know I was rich when he met me. He didn't know Ivan was my cousin, and when he somehow found out, he attempted to make me pay for a bunch of things. He tried to take advantage of me when I was in my lowest state, and I was lucky that I was brought back to England before he got me to pay him anything."

Oh. There it was. I didn't think there was much left of Sam's story that I didn't know. But this, the knowledge of what Anthony had tried to do to him, made me suck in a long inhale.

His greasy stare had made my blood freeze before, and now it was boiling with rage.

"So, no," Sam continued, "he was never my friend. He was my connection to doing things I no longer want to do and haven't wanted to do for a while."

Okay. "But you were tempted."

Sam's tongue went under his bottom lip, poking underneath as the gears in his head turned. There was no point in him denying it. Then he opened his eyes. Vivid, forest green eyes—it had been my favorite color before I met him and was completely incomparable to any other color after he found his way into my life. "I was tempted."

I stopped my movements in his hair, only for him to pull me closer to his body. "And you didn't take the joint."

"And I didn't take the joint," he whispered against the side of my head.

I pulled back, my hands slipping from his head and falling onto his chest. My fingers, restless, played with the collar of his jacket. "I'm worried about you."

He gave me a strained smile. "You have nothing to worry about."

"Sam . . ."

"Hazel . . ." he teased, a glint in his eyes that made me feel warm inside. "I'm okay now. It bothers me, but I'll get used to it. To seeing them. To seeing Anthony around."

Anthony, with his creepy gaze and taunting expressions. I almost did a full-body shiver. What a weirdo. Sam furrowed his brow as he searched my face. "You okay?"

I nodded, and he leaned in, either for his assurance or mine—it didn't matter when I placed my hands on his face. Suddenly, the sink was digging into my back and my lips were locked on his own. His fingers deepened into my curled hair, and his tongue slicked against mine. The music outside the bathroom faded away along with my thoughts, and the only thing left in my mind was him. Just him. Just Sam.

When one of his hands dipped down to brush against my bare leg then moved against my thigh, I gasped but didn't stop him. When he brushed my hair back off my neck, broke our kiss, and traced my skin from my jaw down to the center of my throat, I didn't stop him. When his hand on my leg rose up, leaving goose bumps in its wake before settling to press on the top of my thigh, holding me, I didn't stop him.

There were no warning bells going off in my head because it felt good. This always felt good. Impulsively, I brought his head back up, his mouth meeting mine to steal my breath again.

Am I going to let it happen?

Here?

In a bathroom?

I broke the kiss first, panting. Sam's head dipped down, his hand still on the top of my thigh as he let out a slow breath. We caught our breath in silence—as much silence as anyone could expect with a Beyoncé song in the background—and then Sam laughed in a low voice. "Yeah, I wouldn't want to have my first time in a bathroom if I were you."

I joined him in laughter, adjusting myself as he fixed the T-shirt my hand had clenched. And then adjusted his jeans. I flushed, but he gave me a patient smile, fixing my curls. "All right, I think we're good."

I thought so too—at least, until I realized I had another

question. "Your mom did a recent interview? That's what Zach said, yeah?"

"On her album and her family life, since, um . . ." Sam cleared his throat. ". . . she hadn't spoken about Bethany in a while. I watched it before it aired. She did really well."

I bet she did. Sam's mother was elegant the same way his aunt Liz was. Composed and a person of few words, like his uncle Vince. Before I could say anything further, a loud knock sounded on the door. Without missing a beat, Anmol burst through. She didn't look happy. "There you guys are. Can someone explain to me why Derek actually showed up at this party?"

We both looked at Sam.

Here we go.

11
YOU FLYING LEMUR

"Why?" Anmol and I asked at the same time as she shut the door behind her.

Sam crossed his arms, his agitation clear as day. "You know what? That guy out there has been pissing me off nonstop every practice, every game, because he never stops talking about *you*."

Anmol's eyes went wide, but Sam wasn't finished, evidently fed up. "*Never*, Anmol. He's asking me about you because my girlfriend is friends with you, which means that I am now associated with you, and he knows that. And you're too shy to talk to him, to even look at him, to hold a simple conversation with him, because you're embarrassed over something that happened years ago. I honestly think you should talk to him."

"But—"

"*Talk to him*. Stand tall. Have an actual conversation between two adults."

Sam was playing matchmaker.

Wow.

Anmol's gaze fell to the ground, all three of us waiting. When her shoulders pressed back a bit, I asked, "You're going to talk to him, aren't you?"

At Anmol's nod, Sam huffed as he took his jacket off and handed it to me. It was hot out there; no wonder he wanted it off. "All right, I'm going to find him and bring the man here."

When he walked out, I shrugged his jacket on as Anmol grumbled under her breath, "I'm not shy."

"You're not," I said. "But you are around Derek."

"Because he's Derek," she moaned, shaking her head before looking at herself in the mirror. "What about you? You okay?"

"Yeah, it's just been a long night."

Anmol turned to face me, puzzled. "But we haven't even been here for half an hour."

The irony. It felt like we'd been there for hours. "Exactly."

Before Anmol could open her mouth to say anything, the door to the bathroom opened again. Sam shoved Derek through the door and closed it behind them, sighing. Derek looked down at Anmol with a smile on his face. "Hey."

Anmol slowly exhaled. "Hi."

"Okay, I think we'll give you two some space." Sam clapped his hands. "Meanwhile, Hazel and I will be outside."

"Hazel?" Derek questioned, looking confused in a way that made me want to laugh.

Sam and I made our way into the hallway, which thankfully was empty, but I couldn't help but press my ear against the door, hoping awkward silence wasn't filling the air. I could hear their muffled voices on the other side. Good.

When I pushed away, I said, "I can't believe you just did that."

Sam leaned against the wall opposite the bathroom door, sliding down to sit on the floor. "Something had to be done."

"So, you and Derek?"

Sam narrowed his eyes. "What about Derek and me?"

"I meant that you're friends with him? Like . . . you call him a mate?" This was an accomplishment. Sam barely made any friends outside of our group at home. This was good.

"He's all right." Sam leaned his head back against the wall while glancing over at me. "What? Why are you smiling like that? I love your smile, but it's getting a little creepy right now."

"Jerk," I grumbled before the same smile returned to my face as I took a seat next to him, crossing one of my legs over the other. "You rarely call someone your friend. It just reminds me how much you've changed since I met you. I barely hear you call Caleb your friend."

Sam shot me a look as people started to make their way up and down the hallway, stepping over our outstretched feet. "I can't call Caleb my friend because he's not just my friend."

"Then what is he?"

"Caleb is . . ." His expression softened. "Caleb is like a brother, but he's also *more* than a brother to me, you know? He's my best friend. See? I said it. Happy now? Wipe that smile off your face."

We shared a laugh. Like I could help it when he said something like that. Caleb meant everything to him in the same way Andrew and Jasmine meant everything to me.

"Caleb is one of the few people I know who'll stick with me through success and failure. He's crazy, he's random, and he's weird as hell, but I wouldn't change him. He's also going to be my best man at our wedding, but you knew that."

Our wedding.

That's when my heart went into overdrive. The content expression on his face—the certainty—made the organ want to burst out of my rib cage. Whenever he spoke about the future, he always included me in it. I wanted to be included in it, and I was glad he wanted me on the ride with him for as long as it would take us.

The two of us settled in silence—as much silence as we could since we could still hear the music and chatter from where we were sitting. But then the silence was broken at the sound of joint merriment from the other side of the bathroom door. "Sounds like they're having a good time."

"The good time might turn into a *real* good time if you get what I'm saying," he said. I nudged him as he chuckled. "They'll be fine. It's good they're talking."

I hummed in agreement as he shifted, pressing his arm closer to me. When I peeked over at him, I realized he was staring at me. "What?"

"You know, you've changed a bit too," Sam continued. "You only had two girls who were your friends before university, and you've managed to secure Maddy and Anmol pretty quickly."

"Girls didn't want to be my friend because of Beatrice." Sam and I both held in full-body shudders at the mention of her name. "She spread too many rumors about me being a weirdo and too much like a guy for the girls at school to consider being a close friend of mine."

Except for Jasmine and Stevie. I missed the way they would attempt to drag me shopping. The way they would try to see what makeup look worked *for me.* How we'd discuss what was happening in our lives during sleepovers at my house. I missed them both.

"But now you have them. You like them a lot."

"I do," I admitted, unable to fight back the smile. I was happy about it. Two people, two girls, who seemed to like me for me. The boys back home were going to fall on the ground in shock at me finding more female friends.

Sam and I both turned to stare at the bathroom door behind us. "You don't hear anything either, right?"

I shook my head, getting up slowly. Sam raised an eyebrow, following my lead. He pushed himself up against the door, and I watched his expression change from confusion to amusement. He slowly twisted the handle and pushed the door open.

Sam and I exchanged glances before turning back to Anmol and Derek, who were living out the expression "kiss and make up" very heavily.

Wow.

Sam cleared his throat, and the two pulled apart quickly; Anmol looked embarrassed, while Derek had the widest grin plastered on his face. "Well then." Sam looked over at me. "See? I told you they'd have a real good time."

~

Maddy, Anmol, and I sat in the common room of the residence hall two nights later, the night before our possible last game of the outdoor season. Someone had left their PlayStation hooked up to the only TV, and while there were plenty of people still sitting, lingering, I was in the middle of playing *GTA*, my fingers dapping on the controller, while Anmol, who'd just arrived two seconds ago, tried to pry anything she could get out of Maddy.

"*Maddy*," Anmol urged.

"*Anmol*," Maddy said back before gasping. "Did you see the latest upload—"

"We're not talking about YouTubers right now. What happened with George?"

"Nothing interesting happened."

Anmol wasn't buying it. She tapped me on the arm, and I whined, watching the car turn around. My friend was apparently insanely impatient because she tapped me multiple times until I had no choice but to stop playing. "Anmol, are you kidding me?"

"Did she tell you anything?"

"She did not," I said. Halloween night had gone smoothly after Sam and I had caught Anmol and Derek. We had left soon after, Anmol staying with Derek while Maddy had come back to us with no information to spare. There had also been no further encounters with Zach or Anthony, to my relief.

Sam didn't bother speaking about them, and if it was still troubling him, which I knew it likely was no matter how hard he tried to mask it, he hadn't said a word.

Anmol narrowed her eyes at Maddy, and I picked up the controller again, driving my car onto the road. I watched as it went onto a ramp, and suddenly, I was in the air.

Maddy shot back, "And you and Derek?"

"We're taking things slow."

Maddy scoffed, "Slow? Sure."

"You kiss George yet?"

Maddy's silence said enough. My concentration slipped a bit as I listened, the game suddenly feeling a bit less intriguing. Less than a week left and I could do this with Andrew and the guys right by my side. The idea of all of us gathered in my basement, chortling like idiots, made me home in on the game as my car landed.

"More?" Anmol pried again.

Anmol suddenly gasped, latching on to my arm and driving me off the road and straight into the water. I stood up, my jaw falling into the floor as the word *Wasted* appeared on the screen. "Anmol! You—"

"You what?" Maddy's tone was teasing and only made my frown deepen. The race had been going so well. "You flying lemur?"

When she burst out laughing, I rolled my eyes. "Shut up."

At Anmol's confused expression, Maddy spoke up. "When I met this giant over here—"

"Hey!" I hit her lightly on the arm, and she only laughed harder.

"When I first met this tall, beautiful, amazing friend of mine"—the glare I was giving her only seemed to fuel her laughter even further—"I may have accidentally spiked the ball at her face."

"Are you serious?" Anmol asked.

"It was an accident!" Maddy exclaimed. "Anyway, as an instant reflcx I honestly thought that she would've called me something rude or would've said something in shock. But the first words that came out of her mouth were 'holy flying lemur.'"

"What?" Anmol stared at me, amused, before she and Maddy both burst out into giggles.

I grimaced, sitting down. "I used to say that a lot, okay? You'll rarely hear me say it now."

"No, no, no," Anmol started, "I wanna hear you say it."

I scowled. "No."

"C'mon, Mace," Anmol pleaded when out of the corner of my eye I saw a familiar person walk in with a group of people. It was a big residence, plenty of first-year students coming and going. *Ugh*. I'd almost forgotten she lived here too. Tanya didn't notice me, and I wasn't planning on being found by her. Outdoor season was ending. Indoor season would start in a few months, but we still had to train together. Work together. It'd probably be hell. I planned on avoiding her at all costs outside of soccer.

"Do I get details?" Anmol asked Maddy.

"Do I get *Derek* details?"

"Of course," Anmol said in a *duh* tone before turning to me. "Mace, do you want details?"

"I will ask for the details when I finish the game," I told her with a tight smile. Priorities, people.

"Then can I ask you something in the meantime?" Anmol asked as I restarted the game. I hummed in acknowledgment, keeping my eyes on the screen. "How did you and Sam get together?"

While my character leapt out of the car and I flicked through my choice of weapons, I couldn't fight my small smile. "I first met him last February, and he was a—"

"Dick," Maddy finished for me. "The guy was a dick."

"He was a bit of a jerk," I agreed. "But eventually, he grew on me."

"Oh, so he was a jerk back then?"

"He's still kind of a jerk now," I joked. "Honestly, Sam had this bad boy image and rep. The more I got to know him, the more I realized that wasn't him. Intimidating? Yeah. A jerk? Yeah. Trouble? A little bit, but—" I shook my head; I was getting off track. "Soon after I met him for the first time, I ended up dating his cousin. And Cedric and I—"

"Whoa," Maddy intervened. "You dated *Cedric*? I didn't know that!"

"You know now," I said, feeling a little bit awkward because I'd never really talked about this out loud. She didn't know every single detail, but as I was roaming through the fake city on the screen, she was going to get them now. "Then I started to get feelings for Sam and—yada yada yada—we started dating—"

"No, that's not how it happened," Maddy interrupted. "What *really* happened?"

The two of them looked painfully curious, but they were my friends. If they didn't want to continue being friends with me after this confession, then . . . I exhaled lowly, pausing the game to face them both. "Sam and I ended up in the same place during March Break, and I was still dating his cousin. We kissed." Maddy's lips parted. Anmol's eyebrows rose. Still, neither of them interrupted me as I continued. "We had this stupid idea to get each other out of our systems by being together for the rest of that week. On the Monday, we acted as if everything would return to normal." I rolled my eyes. "We were idiots. Of course, that wouldn't happen. You don't go back to being friends after that."

My fingers rolled over the buttons on the controller, my gaze lowering to them. You don't establish a connection with someone, act on that connection, and then pretend you severed it when it had only drawn you closer together.

"I cheated on Cedric," I said quietly. "Then Cedric says, 'Oh hey, guess what? I used you too because while I did *like* you, I mostly went out with *you* because my cousin—who apparently gets everything—didn't seem to want you because you weren't like other girls. And here was my chance to be with someone he might not want and who might not want him.'"

"Oh, shit," Maddy whispered, her eyes rounded.

"Even with him confessing that, I still felt guilty," I admitted. "What I'd done with Sam wasn't a mistake, but I should have ended things with Cedric the second I knew there was something between me and Sam. That's where I went wrong."

Maddy and Anmol both had indecipherable expressions on their faces, processing my confession. Yet after I'd said all of that out loud, I released a breath weighted with relief. That had been the first time I had spoken about it in months.

"But everything's okay now, right?" Anmol asked, one leg crossed over the other. Her expression, along with Maddy's, had softened. With no judgment in their eyes, all the tension I had felt in my stomach unknotted.

"Like, you and Cedric are friends now, and you've both moved on from each other?" Maddy added.

I nodded. Along with my group back home, I was excited to catch up with Cedric as well. He was studying at another university in Ontario while playing rugby for their team. "We're good friends and have moved past it."

"What makes you think that you won't cheat on the current one?" a voice said.

I hadn't even realized that Tanya had been standing near us, her arms crossed. Then she continued speaking. Unprovoked. My fingers stilled on the controller. "You cheated. You're a cheater. Meaning you'll probably end up cheating on Sam."

No. I wouldn't. The fact that she of all people was making that assumption made me toss the controller to the other side of the couch. Maddy's eyes went rounder. "I am not going to explain myself to you," I shot at her, attempting to suppress the anger that was slowly rising at her judgmental look.

"Because you're badly defending yourself?" she taunted, her smirk pressed into her face and only irritating me further. "Sam might as well find a new girl because he knows you're going to end up che—"

Oh God. I could've punched her. Instead, I stood, hopping over the couch to approach her as I said, "Does any information get through your incredibly thick skull? I said I'm not going to explain myself to you."

Tanya narrowed her eyes into a glare, but that didn't have the impact she thought it would. It had been hard enough relaying what I had done to my friends, but to have her overhear, to have her judge me for her own advantage in the little mental game she was playing? I was sick of it. "Did you process *that* information?" I asked, noting that the common room had become incredibly quiet.

Tanya blinked. I never retaliated. I never said a word to anything she said—I'd never wanted to egg her on, to make it worse. But this? This was crossing a line. This was information she had used in the hopes of gaining an upper hand, and while I was not threatened by her in any way, she was not going to think she could belittle me any further, I decided.

Without another word, she left the common room. Chatter arose once again, and I exhaled slowly, my attention still on the door. Her retreat brought back my sanity.

I grabbed the controller, settled into my spot, and started the game again. Out of the corner of my eye, I saw Maddy open her mouth to say something, but I shut her down quickly when I said, "I'm fine."

12
SWEET CHEEKS

Henry David Florentine's women's varsity soccer team finished second in the outdoor league. My track record wasn't where I wanted it to be, with more assists than goals, so with indoor season coming up, I had something to prove.

I can do it, I told myself, rolling a soccer ball underneath my feet. I was on the empty field that night. No one else was practicing on it. The lights were still bright, illuminating the crisp grass dusted by white frost.

"Can you wait one second?" I said into the phone in my hand, taking a few steps back.

"Sure," my little brother said from the speaker.

Gripping my phone, I ran ahead to make the shot. Power reared in my leg and tightened my muscles, and my foot connected with the ball. With a swift curve, the ball hit the back of the net with a force that made me smile.

That was always going to be a top-three best feeling.

"Did you make the shot?" Justin asked.

"Obviously," I told him with a small laugh. It was so great to hear my brother's voice. I wanted to see how tall he was now. To see if in the months we'd been apart, he'd finally grown facial hair. Or if I could still put him in a headlock whenever he annoyed me. The one thing I could tell from the call was that his voice had gotten deeper. That was freaky.

"You're not saying anything," he pointed out.

"I can't get over your voice. It's absolutely crazy that that part of puberty happened to hit you when I left home."

"At least my voice isn't cracking anymore. Everyone kept mocking me the entire time during the summer," he whined.

I snorted. "I swear Emma mocked you too."

"But she *actually* apologized. None of the rest of you can say the same."

"What's going on between the two of you now?" Oh, I was so excited for the weekend. I'd get to see Justin follow her around like a lovesick puppy again.

"I mean, the distance thing is always going to be hard, but you know what they say, absence makes the heart grow fonder or whatever."

"I'm sorry, who are you and what have you done to my little brother? I don't think you're Patrick anymore," I said, using his old *SpongeBob* nickname.

Justin laughed deeply. "In case you haven't noticed, *Sandy*, I'm not stupid. Emma and I are great."

"At least you'll get to see her soon."

"Yeah, Christian won't stop reminding me about it." I grinned at the mention of the other Cahill who'd managed to make his way into our lives. Justin and Christian, another one of Sam's cousins, had become close friends as they were both in grade ten at Wellington High, my old school. "I'll let you go. Wait, can you score another one for me?"

"On it," I promised, setting up another ball. When my foot hit it, the ball soared in the air, barely skimming under the crossbar before it went in. "Gooooooal!"

"Of course it was." He chuckled. "All right, bye, Sandy."

"Bye, Patrick," I said softly, feeling a major wave of homesickness hit me as I hung up on him.

"Was that Justin?" a voice asked, and I almost jumped out of my skin.

Sam's hands were stuffed in his leather jacket as he approached me. He must've come in through the only open door, far on the other side of the field. It was good to see him, even if his presence had made me jump.

"Holy fudgenuggets, you scared me." I put a hand to my chest, looking up at Sam, who was looking back at me with amusement.

"I didn't think my presence was *that* frightening," he murmured. "Why are you here?"

"Why are *you* here? You don't even go here," I teased.

"I went by your dorm, and Mads said you were here."

"Oh," I said. "Are you okay?"

"I just wanted to see you," he said as I bent down to reach for my camera bag.

I took out my camera and watched as he took cleats out of the small bag he had brought with him and put them on. "You wanted to play?"

"Yeah," he said, tying the laces. He glanced up at me with a light smile. "I've missed playing football with you."

I'd missed it too. The game, the easy awareness of where the other was on the field, the understanding that would connect us up near the goalkeeper. Soccer was our game. "I miss playing with you too," I said.

When he finished tying his laces, I turned my camera downward, taking a picture of our shoes. I showed him the simple photo, grinning from ear to ear. He rolled his eyes. "Very aesthetic."

"Why thank you," I said, placing my camera back down on the ground and rolling the ball under my feet toward the net. Sam shuffled ahead, and I passed him the ball. The two of us went back and forth for a while in silence. There was never any communication that needed to happen in these moments, but he was clearly attempting to distract himself from something, having driven all the way here.

His team had placed first in the outdoor league, and he had been ahead in goals. He had been focused this season—I'd noticed it at his first game back in August.

I didn't resent him for the natural talent he had, given the training he had put himself through once he'd established that he was going to strive for his original goal, to turn pro. Sam was great. He had been great in high school, but he had only gotten better.

He shuffled forward, passing me the ball over my head. I angled myself, bouncing it off my chest toward the ground as I got in control. We rallied for a bit, triangle passes, passes we each attempted to control. But when Sam shot a pass toward me that was completely out of my reach, bypassing me by a mile, he burst out laughing while I glowered. "That wasn't fair!"

"Since when are things fair in football?" I left the ball where it was, rolling off to the side, my jaw agape as I stomped over to him, but his amusement only increased at my expression. "You cannot be mad. After that terrible pass you gave me two seconds ago?"

"You got the ball, you dumbegg!"

"Barely," he snapped back with a grin, and when I pushed his chest, he only grinned wider. "Hazel, you can't be losing your touch now."

"I am not."

"You sure? That shot at the net was looking a little weak."

"Shut up!"

He was beaming now. "The love of my life is a football goddess. Where did she go?"

His smirking face. His taunting words. I hit his shoulder against my own hard before I went to get the soccer ball he had brought with him. I rolled it ahead of me as he stepped in front of me. I dribbled the ball, intent on getting it toward the net, on getting it past him. Sam met my eyes with a challenge. He was going to give it his all. He never backed down from me. He never cared about gender. When we played, it was always with equality, and there was never an easy pass on who was better. When he defended, pressured, and jockeyed me, it was with every intention of securing the ball for himself.

I didn't let him.

Bringing it to my left, then rolling it back when he tried to reach out to get it once again, I saw the opening. Passing it through his legs in a fluid manner, I rounded him, getting the ball. Before he could steal it, which I knew he was fully capable of doing, I shot the ball outside the box. The two of us watched it curve beautifully, go across the goal line, and roll into the net.

When I turned to Sam, he was beaming. "You definitely still have it, Hazel."

To another person, that could have been endearing. If he hadn't been trying to mock me with his eyes.

Without another thought, I pushed him away from me. Him trying to rile me up to do exactly what he wanted only left me heated as I smacked him in the arm, and he laughed every single time, the sound hitting me right in the chest and diving straight into my stomach with a backflip. Somehow, I jumped onto his back, and suddenly we were spinning, my arms around his neck as we laughed at his stupidity, at my rise in anger, and at how the two of us functioned.

The joyful sound only faded when the sound of his phone ringing cut through the air. I jumped off his back as he walked over to his phone, and I went to retrieve both balls. When I walked back to Sam, his phone was still ringing. Still blaring. He wasn't answering, but by the way he was staring at the phone, I knew he recognized the number.

"What's wrong?" I asked him.

Sam looked up at me with a jolt, declining the call.

What the—

"Nothing."

What was he hiding? He couldn't be that bothered by a random caller, could he? "Who was it?"

He shoved his phone into his pocket, taking the ball between my feet and rolling it under his own. "No one important."

If he didn't look like someone had given him terrible news, then maybe it could have been no one important, but this? And why was he hiding it from me? The hurt must have shown because when he finally looked at me, he reached a hand in my direction. "Hazel, it's no one important."

"It might be no one important, but that's not the full story, is it?"

Sam looked down. "It's nothing you have to worry about."

"Sam—"

"Hazel, drop it. *Please.*" He sounded exasperated.

I licked my lips and stepped forward, my arms crossed. "Don't shut me out."

He kicked the ball away, dipping slightly to level his eyes with mine. "I'm not shutting you out. This isn't important at the moment, okay?"

"But whatever it is, it's upsetting you," I said. "I can tell." He didn't say anything else, his expression hidden. I wasn't going to get any more information from him until he was ready. Or until he resolved whatever the heck was happening. "You know I'm here, right?"

"I know," he said, leaning forward until his lips were pressed against the side of my head. "I'm in love with you, you know that?"

"I never doubted that for a second," I said. He didn't say it all the time; he didn't need to. Nor did he ever just say, *I love you.* And yet it hit me deeper every single time the words left his mouth. I'd never been more certain in my life than I was when it came to him, and I wasn't going to let someone like Tanya make me feel terrible over it. Why was I still thinking about what she'd said the other day?

"What's wrong?" Sam asked, keeping his hands by my neck, running his thumb over my jaw.

"Nothing," I said.

"I know it's not nothing," Sam said.

I know the person calling you wasn't nothing either.

Yet if I didn't talk about it, we were going to spend hours here. While I liked the idea of spending time on a field with a soccer ball, my camera, and Sam, I wasn't going to be there for the right reasons.

"That week over March Break. When we were trying to get each other out of our systems by being together, I guess? Which was really stupid and immature because clearly that made things worse—or better depending on how you look at it. Wait . . . no. Definitely worse, and—"

"Hazel."

"Sorry." I winced at my rambling. *Get to the point, Macy.* "And you know how I, uh, I cheated on Cedric, but then Cedric and I—"

"—had that whole discussion and words were said, but now you're friends?" His summary was good. Vague but good.

"Yeah." I kept my attention on the Nike symbol on his sweater. "Tanya overheard me talking to Anmol and Maddy about it, and then she called me a cheater."

Sam blinked, his face falling. "She what?"

My focus was still on his sweater. "She said because I cheated on Cedric that I'm probably going to cheat on you as well."

Sam didn't speak. He didn't have to as his eyes searched mine and his brow furrowed. His jaw clenched as he ran one of his hands over his face. "Seriously?"

"It's just Tanya." I tried to blow it off. "It wasn't that—"

"Hazel, don't tell me that it wasn't that serious because I know you and I know that from the time she said that till now, it's been stuck in your head."

Right.

He ran a hand through his hair, muttering under his breath. "Fucking hell. Hazel?"

"Yeah?"

"Tanya's annoying."

The bluntness of his words made me laugh out loud. His face broke out into a smile at the sound as he cupped my face in his hands, his thumbs brushing my cheeks.

"What you said was right. We made a stupid, immature decision. One that could have ended very badly. We know that. Cedric knows that. We've all moved past that and acknowledged that we were stupid."

"I know," I said, my hands covering his on my face. "But I wouldn't. Cheat on you."

"I know," he said back. "I wouldn't either. No one else has ever been in my head like you are." He pressed another kiss to my head. "Besides, if I have to have my heart broken by someone one day, it'll have to be you and only you because you are the only person I'll give my heart to," he whispered before pressing a kiss to my lips briefly.

When we broke the kiss, the cocky expression on his face made me roll my eyes. "That was pretty sentimental for me, wasn't it?"

"It was sweet," I admitted, holding a hand to my chest. That word sounded weird coming out of my mouth.

Sam noticed that too. "Did Macy Victoria Marie Anderson just say *sweet*?"

"I'm glad you find me amusing," I said wryly.

"Next thing you know you'll be calling me things like 'baby.'"

"No." I didn't mind when he called me that, but me calling him that was a no: it would be weird.

"Or 'hot.'"

No.

"Or something like 'sweet cheeks.'"

"What?" I burst out laughing, my hands lightly hitting and staying on his chest because I would never *ever* call him that.

Sam grinned, fetching the ball back and grabbing me by the hand. "C'mon, let's play football."

"Soccer," I corrected, grabbing my phone to check for any recent messages. Sam went off with the ball, dribbling it between his feet, when I saw a text message from a familiar person.

Jasmine.

I grinned. Finally. She'd responded. The messages weren't as wordy as they usually were, and they were followed by a short apology saying that she'd been busy like I'd assumed. It didn't matter. She'd replied. She was okay.

Then I saw an email. The mark from my last midterm had been released. When I checked it, I felt like I'd been hit in the gut. The number, one I had never gotten in my entire life, made my lips part in surprise.

My heart dropped.

I'd failed.

"Oh my God," I whispered.

"Hazel!" Sam yelled, getting my attention as he took the shot.

The ball went across the line, but my mind was no longer on the game. This was so often the story of my life: something good followed by something bad, repeat.

I couldn't wait to go home.

13
HE'S SO BIG

Being in a car with Peter and Sam was an experience. Sitting in sweatpants and my biggest hoodie, I was playing a video game on my phone that Thursday evening, doing everything I could to focus on my game as the two argued in the front seat.

"I'm not playing that stupid game," Sam complained, his focus on the highway.

"Why not?" Peter asked. "If Caleb was here, you would play it."

Sam grunted. "No, I wouldn't."

"Macy?"

"He wouldn't," I assured Peter.

"Well, I spy—"

"Peter, stop being a dickhead," Sam groaned.

"Shut up."

"*You* shut up."

This went on for twenty minutes while I focused on my game

in the back. Then Peter got a phone call from Aunt Liz.

"Speaker," Sam said, glancing up at the rearview mirror to me.

I perked up at the voice of Elizabeth Cahill, the connection between Peter's and Sam's families. With blue-gray eyes like her eldest son and jet-black hair, she was a person of beauty, grace, and confidence. She voiced her greetings before Sam asked a question: "Have my parents arrived?"

"This morning," she said. "They'll be staying at ours, but Greg is still over at your cousins'. When you arrive, they'll all be here. Did you speak to your mum about the interview?"

I turned to Sam. "What interview?"

He glanced at me in the mirror. "She texted me. Some paper wanted to interview me after hers came out."

"No pressure," Liz said to him. "But I was speaking to her last night, and she said it would give you more exposure."

"For football?" Peter asked. Sam nodded. "That's what you want, no? And there's been more exposure on the Cahills. Didn't Uncle Vince do something for *Forbes* the other day?"

"They're interviewing my dad next week."

"All these interviews," Peter mused. "Next thing you know you'll be offered a reality show." He put his hands out in front of him. "The next big family."

Liz chuckled. "Don't think too hard about whether you want to do it or not, Samuel. But if you do, I could come down with you?"

Sam bit his lip, not expressing anything, but I knew there was gratitude there. His uncle and aunt had been a bigger presence in his life over the past year since he had lived with them. He and Aunt Liz had had a sort of mother-son relationship while he'd been away from his own especially.

“I’d like that,” he said. “Thank you.”

“Of course. But first, we’re going to get you a much-needed haircut.”

“Aunt Liz.”

“Don’t give me attitude, Sam.”

“I’m not giving you attitude!”

“He rolled his eyes,” Peter snitched, and Sam reached over to jab him in the stomach, at which Peter groaned loudly and dramatically.

Aunt Liz laughed on the other end.

When Sam ended the call, Peter continued talking. “Your little brother told me Caleb kept asking him questions last night.”

Sam huffed, and I sat up, realizing he was getting off the highway. We were close to home. “He keeps bothering Greg and Phillip with another one of his weird questions whenever he sees them.”

“What’s the question?” I asked.

“It’s so dumb,” Sam drawled.

“It’s starting problems in the family,” Peter added.

“*What is the question?*” I repeated.

“Yeah, Ivan brought it up in the group chat last night. Lucas and Joey were on opposite sides. Cedric ended up siding with the right side. Toby too. We ended up on a call with all of us because of it. And then Caleb got into an argument with Greg over it last night, and because Greg was staying over there, they burst into Phillip’s room asking an eight-year-old kid and making a huge deal over—”

“What is the question?” I yelled.

Sam shot me a sheepish smile through the mirror, finally acknowledging me. “Caleb was asking whether you pour your milk or your cereal into the bowl first.”

"Milk," I stated.

When we reached a red light, Sam twisted to stare at me. Peter did the same, his jaw hanging agape. "You have to be joking?"

"Are you mad?" Sam asked.

"Are *you* mad?" I mocked him in his attractive accent. "I'm not mad. You pour the milk first."

"No, you *don't*," Sam said, facing ahead again.

"That's so weird." Peter looked disgusted. "You pour the cereal first."

"You're weird," I muttered.

"This is coming from the girl who likes relish," Sam said, taking a left.

I made a face. "You're the one who likes mustard."

Peter rubbed his temples. "I don't get paid enough for this."

My house was the first stop on our journey. Coming up the cul-de-sac, we saw a few people were already lingering out on the porch steps. At the sight of the car pulling up, I heard one person yell my nickname. "*Princess!*"

All eyes were on Caleb as he ran toward me before I could even close the door. He scooped me up in a hug that made me laugh with joy at seeing his face in person, not on a screen. His hair, like Sam's, had grown out. His handsome face was accompanied by scruff on his cheeks, but his brown eyes were the same as they'd always been, a mixture of mischievousness and elation no one else I knew had.

"Hey, Charming." I flashed him a smile, looking over at Jon Ming, who was walking toward us.

"Hola, princess." Caleb kept the biggest grin on his face as he hugged me again before switching to Sam, who was still getting out of the car.

The two of them stared at each other, wondering who was going to say something first. I knew Sam's pride wouldn't let him speak first, but I also knew he missed his best friend a lot.

Jon Ming reached us, and I hugged my close friend since grade nine, looking at his half-blue hair that was styled a bit differently than when I'd last seen him. He also looked a bit more muscular. Like Caleb, he had more tattoos on his arms. But he still had a pair of Beats around his neck. I flicked them, and he grinned, lightly hitting my arm before we turned to the bromance in front of us.

Peter stuck his head out the window, coughing into his hand. "Could one of you speak?"

That's when Caleb scowled, punching Sam in the arm, and my jaw dropped. Sam winced, staring at his best friend. "What the *fuck*?"

"You pour your cereal first? You weirdo. You're supposed to pour the milk first."

"Are you—It's amazing how I haven't seen you for months, and this is the greeting I get from you?"

Caleb's small smile morphed into the grin that everyone was accustomed to. The smile he had could make anyone in the world smile in return. He embraced Sam, and Sam returned the hug without hesitation.

"I missed you, damsel in distress."

"Shut up."

The front door opened, and I grinned as if it had been years instead of months since I'd last seen my family. "Hey!"

I wrapped my arms around my dad and brother. I tried not to react to the strand of gray hair showing in Dad's brown hair, but I clearly had because he grumbled, "I know, I know, I'm getting old."

I hugged him tightly before looking over at Justin. If I'd thought this kid couldn't get any taller, I'd clearly been wrong. He was probably Sam's height, an inch taller than he used to be, and he was actually starting to have muscles from what I could see through his shirt.

I reached out, squeezing his arm tightly to make sure my eyes weren't deceiving me. He swatted my hand away. "What is wrong with you? I didn't think Edward Bay would make you weirder."

My face broke out in a smile. His voice was even deeper than I'd thought. He was growing up. I couldn't help but hug him again. "I missed you, Patrick."

"I missed you too, Sandy." Justin laughed before pulling away. Then he handed me something. A box of Pop-Tarts. I reached into my bag, handing him his own delicacy: a box of Twinkies. We swapped quickly with big smiles, our dad laughing loudly. "So this is what happens when my children are reunited."

"Of course," I said, but not before putting Justin in a headlock in the middle of our driveway.

Justin groaned loudly and clasped my arm, trying to get out of my grip. Ah, I still had it. "I hate it when you do this, Macy. Get off me."

"No." I brought my fist up to give him a well-deserved noogie, my knuckles ruffling through his hair.

Some things hadn't changed.

After Sam, Peter, Jon Ming, and Caleb had left, I headed straight to my bed for much-needed sleep. The three best things on earth were my bed, my PlayStation hooked up downstairs, and the Xbox One my brother and I shared. But now, my bed was winning.

~

The following morning, I was in limbo between consciousness and sleep, burying my face in my pillow to try to eke out a few more minutes of—

A gigantic body landed on top of my own, and my lungs squeezed, fighting to absorb air. "Oh my God," I wheezed, pushing the person off me and breathing in deeply.

The thought of beating that person to death flew out of my mind when I saw the flash of blond hair and heard the bark of a dog. "Andrew," I almost whispered, seeing my best friend in front of me.

He cackled when I leapt on him, giving him a hug that sent us both tumbling to the ground. His hair was now closely cropped, showing off his bright-blue eyes and that dimple etched into his cheek. Andrew Prescott in the flesh.

I hugged him again, and his laugh rumbled through his chest. "Yeah, I missed you too, Mace."

"I doubt that," I told him as we both stood. "You were probably too busy to think of me."

"I missed my un-biological sister almost as much as my little sister," he said, reminding me of his four-year-old sister, Riley, whom I was going to see later that day. Andrew held up two packages of cinnamon rolls, and my eyes couldn't help but widen. He grinned and put a finger on his lips. "Don't tell your coach."

"I won't if you won't," I told him.

We camped out in the middle of my bed, eating and catching up. He gave me the rundown on his classes, parties, and new friends. I told him more about my own life, as if we hadn't been keeping caught up through constant updates and video calls. I didn't relay that I had failed a midterm—I didn't want to diminish his bubbly excitement at being here as he stuffed his face with each sugary piece.

I was rubbing his dog, Freddy's, belly when we turned silent. Then I asked him the question I wanted to ask: "Have you heard from her?"

"Yeah, she'll be here in a bit," Andrew said, but he didn't look troubled. The silence from her was likely an issue of miscommunication.

Through the open window of my bedroom, the sound of another car pulling up to our driveway filled the room. I already knew who it was, and it made me grab my camera. Andrew, Freddy, and I hopped off the bed to look through the window as I pointed my lens down toward the car. Down below, my brother had already bolted out the door. I could tell that in the hours since I had gone to sleep, he had cleaned himself up. His hair was wet, and he had probably brushed his teeth three to five times. He was wearing presentable clothes as well. When the girl stepped out of the car, he grinned from ear to ear.

"This is so corny," Andrew said with a smile as Emma and Justin collided with a hug. As if on cue, Andrew and I made gagging sounds that made Justin glare at us over Emma's shoulder. Andrew cupped his hands over his mouth, yelling, "Get it, Justin!"

Without letting go of Emma, my brother raised his middle finger high in the sky toward Andrew. Andrew scowled, muttering something about Andersons before he pushed off my window and made his way downstairs. Justin didn't notice Andrew's disappearance. It wasn't until Andrew barreled through the front door that my brother yelped, letting go of Emma and running off down the street. Andrew chased him as Emma looked up at me with a wave. The next person to leave the car had her graying brown hair up in a high bun. Sharp, analytic hazel eyes met mine with a witty smile.

My amazing, poker-playing grandmother, Gigi. But I called her Nonna.

Lucky for me, Emma's sister, Alexis, was nowhere to be found. I knew Alexis wouldn't be here until possibly Saturday night because of a photo shoot in New York. My shoulders slumped with relief as Justin came running back, hiding from Andrew behind my grandmother. Nonna didn't care, twisting my brother and squeezing his cheeks. A rumble of Italian words spilled from her mouth, a bunch of *bambinos* and gushing that made Justin look embarrassed, going red in the face in front of Emma.

I was about to join them downstairs after breaking off a piece of my cinnamon roll when someone called me. "Yeah?" I asked with a mouthful of food.

"You're eating, aren't you?" Stevie asked.

"Yeah," I answered, trying to chew.

"Figures."

"Shut up," I told her, the two of us laughing.

"Is Drew with you?" she asked.

"Downstairs." My smile got wider when another car pulled in to the cul-de-sac. A familiar one. Stevie. Andrew reached her the second she got out of the car, the two of them embracing, but she wasn't the only one inside. I put Freddy on his leash as we made our way downstairs. After being prodded by my grandmother and hugging Emma, I made my way over to Stevie, who bent down to greet an enthusiastic Freddy. She rubbed his face as the other two people from her car came out making cooing noises. “Did he get bigger? He’s so big.”

“That’s what she said,” Jacob chortled behind Andrew as Brandon smacked him upside the head before embracing me.

“Aw, Jacob,” I mused as I hugged him as well. “You’re still annoying.”

“So are you.” He pinched my cheek, and I slapped his hand downward. When he reached for the last cinnamon roll in the box in my hand, I pushed him again. “You can’t be serious.”

“I’m starving!”

“So am I!”

“Share!”

“When have I ever shared food with you?” I asked.

“Never,” answered his twin as I broke off a piece of the cinnamon roll and stuffed it into my mouth. Brandon only grinned. “You’re always the charmer, Macy.”

And he didn’t say that in a mocking way. Brandon was, after all, the only gentleman in my group of friends. Jacob was the jokester. Caleb the writer. Jon Ming the musically and linguistically talented. Stevie the volleyball player and show lover. Andrew, my best friend. Jasmine, my other best friend. And the person who cared about his hair way more than the average person would—

“Where’s Austin?” I asked.

“Still on the train,” Jacob answered. “He’ll be here soon, though. We should play *GTA* while we wait.”

Stevie groaned. “That’s all you guys do.”

“Not true,” Andrew said, leaning against the side of her car. “*Mario Kart* is up for grabs as well.”

“Nah.” Jacob shook his head. Out of the corner of my eye, I saw my father come out of the house to welcome my grandmother. “Macy cheats.”

"I do not!" I was quick to say as they all cracked up. I was good at *Mario Kart*. They all, except for maybe Austin, sucked at it. As the five of us chattered, I set my box on the top of the car. Jacob's hands were already in there, breaking off a piece of the cinnamon roll. "Jacob, I swear to God if you do not get your hands off my food—"

Jacob yanked his hand back, giving me a hug either to hold me down or because he really wanted to show random affection. I went with the former. "I really did miss you, Macy."

"Whatever," I said, pushing him away as another car pulled in to the cul-de-sac.

When the person got out of the back seat, my lips parted in surprise. Coming out of the car was my other best friend, Jasmine Green.

She wore jeans and a thick sweater. Her hair wasn't in box braids but instead locs, which were pushed back with a headband. She looked a little drained. But once she saw me, that fatigue faded away: a bright smile came to her face, and her brown skin seemed to suddenly glow. "Is that Macy Marie Victoria Anderson?"

The silence. The lack of response. The decline in video calls. The lack of updates. None of that mattered at the sight of her and the sound of her mangling my name again.

Suddenly, tears formed in my eyes as I dropped Freddy's leash and ran in her direction. I pushed my feet hard, and she ran as well, meeting me halfway. We collided in a tight grasp, her familiar comfort surrounding me.

"It's Victoria Marie, Jaz," I sniffed. "We've been over this a million times, I swear." She laughed and hugged me back just as tightly, and I could see the tears streaming down her cheeks when I pulled away. Then another pair of arms surrounded both of us. Jasmine gasped, twisting into Andrew's chest. I let go of them both, watching them hug the same way Justin had hugged Emma.

Andrew must have tightened his hold because Jasmine hit him lightly on the shoulder. "I can't breathe, babe."

"Shit, sorry," Andrew apologized, letting go enough so that she could inhale. "I've missed you."

Jasmine grabbed her hands in his. "I missed you too."

When they kissed, I could've pretended to gag, but I didn't. They were together. Everyone (once Austin got here) was together. Nothing else mattered right now.

Finally.

"Macy, get out of the shot. Stevie is trying to take a picture, and your big head is in the way!" Jacob yelled.

I narrowed my eyes and stomped my way toward him, making sure he was running inside the house to get away from me.

I'd *really* missed them all.

14
KEEPING UP WITH THE CAHILLS

On the early morning of Ivan and the soon-to-be Natasha Cahill's wedding day, I didn't even make it into the Cahill house before I was attacked by a hug.

Phillip almost knocked me off the stairs leading up to the front door, his thin arms tight around me and his face pressed against my stomach. I hugged him back, glancing at the corridor inside. The wedding was scheduled to start at noon, but I had to be here early to get a head start on the photos, being part of the team for the entire day.

I'd be a part of that team right now, but I didn't think Phillip would let me go. I didn't mind, though; it was great to see the Cahill ball of sunshine. I squeezed him tighter. "I missed you, Phillip. Or should I be calling you Leonardo?" I asked, referencing his favorite Teenage Mutant Ninja Turtle.

"I missed you too, and I like either!" he beamed, pulling me inside. People were weaving throughout rooms with various tools in their hands. The wedding and the reception were both taking place in the giant backyard. I knew the setup for both was going to take a lot of hands, and from the instructions Natasha had carefully given me weeks before on the phone, I was going to be capturing all of it.

Phillip took my hand in his. "I'm performing today!"

"I heard. You excited?" I asked as we moved past everyone speaking, directing, and instructing. The Cahill house, one in which I had spent half my summer, was always meant to be congested with people. If it wasn't simply full of Cahills, it was the site of networking events, parties, anything that could bring a big group of people together and put them in a large space.

"Kinda nervous, but Sydney, my teacher for the routine, is really, really good, and she makes the lessons fun and—"

Suddenly, Phillip's grasp loosened on mine as we neared the living room. In fact, he screeched when suddenly he was being held upside down, his wavy hair falling into his face.

"Toby!" he screamed, attempting to wiggle out of his grasp while giggling uncontrollably.

My attention went to the tall man holding up the kid by his legs.

Toby. The only Cahill boy I had yet to meet. Like every Cahill, he was handsome, with brown hair that waved around his face in a similar manner to Phillip's. But his eyes, although blue like Ivan's, were striking. The aura he emitted made me fight the need to straighten my back.

Toby pinned those blue eyes in my direction. "You must be the infamous Hazel."

Infamous, sure. "Macy," I said. His accent, like most of the Cahills', was strong, but his voice was deeper than I'd expected.

"Hazel to *Sammy*," Phillip joked, and then he screamed again when another hand reached out to tickle him.

Sam took hold of his little cousin from his older one, flipping him right around before pushing him into the living room. Toby kept his eyes on Phillip as the kid disappeared. "We're leaving in fifteen."

"Christian's downstairs?"

Toby nodded, fishing his phone out of the pocket of his dress pants. "Lucas is going to stay here with Phillip. Joey might come. Cedric is coming."

Sam took out his phone, and I watched the two of them type with wide eyes. Eerily organized. "All right."

Toby analyzed Sam, glancing at me one more time before he followed Phillip's footsteps into the living room. Once he disappeared, I felt my body loosen. Sam stared at me. "What's going on with you?"

"Why is he so serious?" I whispered. "Could I get some background?" I always did this for each Cahill. My head now contained the family tree. Lucas, Christian, and Joey were brothers—Lucas and Joey were twins. All three were still in high school. Greg was Sam's younger brother. Phillip, Cedric, and Ivan were brothers. Lastly, there was Toby, who, of all the cousins, was the only only child. He was the son of Audrey Cahill, CEO of a cosmetic company, and Scott Cahill, a doctor.

"You could ask him yourself."

I glared at him. "You're right here."

Sam rolled his eyes but answered anyway. "That's Toby. He's really not as serious as he looks. He's the oldest Cahill at twenty-three. Plans to oversee the marketing department of the family company and is finishing his master's back in England. It's why we don't see him often. He's busy."

The big family company that invested in hotels, media, cars, and more that I'd never paid enough attention to figure out? "That seems like a big job."

"He's good at it," Sam praised. "Any other questions you're too scared to ask him?"

"I'm not scared!" I exclaimed.

"You *sound* scared," another voice said from behind me. Lucas Cahill wore a beanie on his head and glasses over his brown eyes. I was surprised there wasn't a paintbrush in his hand. He and Joey attended the local arts school in our town. Compared to the rest of the boys in his family, Lucas was a little more awkward. However, there was a girl standing next to him; after all, he was a Cahill.

The girl was stunning, about five-foot-eight with golden-brown skin and long, dark, curly hair. There was an elegant grace in her body as she walked slightly behind Lucas, yet she also embodied some of his shy awkwardness.

Lucas opened his arms to hug me. "Hey, Mace."

I grasped Lucas in a tight hug. Months ago, he had been a bit shorter than me. "You're so much taller, dude. Why am I looking directly into your eyes now?" I said.

Lucas laughed a little, and I directed my attention to the girl standing next to him, giving her a small smile. Lucas spoke up. "Macy, this is Canada Girl."

Huh?

The girl's lips parted in surprise. Without missing a beat, she smacked him in the stomach. Okay, I liked her. "You're a doofus, Turtle."

Turtle? Canada Girl? I exchanged looks with Sam, who had his eyebrows raised. *Cringey nicknames*, he mouthed, and I hit him lightly. Who cared? It was nice to see Lucas give some attention to something other than books and art supplies. I was certain all the Cahills would be thrilled if he had a crush on someone. Were they dating?

"I, uh, I'm Sydney," she said with a small smile. Phillip's dance instructor. And she probably went to the same school as Lucas.

"We gotta go," Lucas said, gesturing for Sydney to follow. They moved together, both slightly awkward and shy. I didn't think they realized it. Even as they made their way past the living room door into another hallway, it was as a unit. The glances they gave each other at the same time? The way he held the door open for her as they entered another room? It was . . . sweet.

Sam grabbed my hand and pulled me up the staircase. A familiar face appeared at the top of the stairs. Sam resembled his father more than his mother. But even if you couldn't see the physical resemblance between Sam and his mom, you could definitely see it in the way they carried themselves.

Alice Cahill was a force.

As a musically gifted spokesperson, philanthropist, and activist, she stood tall like her son. The intimidation in Sam's green eyes was derived from the brown of hers. She looked like the kind of person who had a million thoughts going through her mind at every second and would convey those ideas via a presentation, a fifty-page thesis, a poster board, and a brochure. In a word, she was organized.

She was currently wearing a dark-green jumpsuit, her brown hair piled high in a bun as she listened to a man with a clipboard give her the rundown on the events of the day.

Sam noticed her first. He steered us away from her, but she locked in on us pretty fast. Sam cursed under his breath once he realized she'd seen us; my feet suddenly became rooted to the ground like they were part of the flooring. Her heels clicked against the floor, announcing her presence. I took a step back as she crossed her arms and raised an eyebrow. Sam's forehead furrowed. "What?"

Alice tsked. Then she shook her head, patting Sam once on the cheek. "Were you trying to avoid me?"

"No."

His lie was terrible.

"No? Good then. Because if you were, that was downright awful, Samuel. Now say hi."

He rolled his eyes, and her serious exterior instantly cracked when one corner of her lips rose. He had her smile: warm, loving, and bright. "Hi, Mum."

"Say, 'I hope you're doing well on this busy day, Mum.'"

He made a face. "I'm not a puppet."

"I know. The thirty-six hours of labor I went through is a reminder that you weren't produced in a factory," she said with some amusement. A sad smile crossed her face as she held his cheek once again. Sam's scowl softened at her attention. Immediately, I wanted to disappear, to let them have their mother-and-son moment. Then she turned her gaze to me. All the humor and sadness vanished instantly, replaced with a calmness; it was a switch in emotions that I could never understand. "Hello, Macy."

"Hi."

And that was that.

Someone called her name, and her attention was directed elsewhere, her heels signaling her departure from our conversation.

I still didn't know if she liked me. And the way she looked at me always left me more conflicted. I should have asked her how she was doing. I should have asked her how touring was going since this was her small break before she was headed back on the road. Ugh. When Sam and I entered his room, my thoughts must have been all over my face because he snapped his fingers in front of my face after he closed the door. "She likes you."

"Sure," I said, my smile weak.

Sam tilted my head up in his hands. "She does."

Maybe.

He pressed a kiss to my forehead. "She does."

"Okay."

Another kiss to my cheek. "I swear."

"All right."

He didn't like that. I was lifted into the air, my shriek bouncing off the walls of his room, off the posters of soccer players, off the TV in one corner, off the photos that formed a mosaic on his wall that I had started during the summer. He dropped me onto his bed, crawling over my body. "She does," he repeated, pressing a chaste kiss to my mouth.

I didn't respond to that as he hovered above me, resting his weight on his forearms. His parents were here. His cousins. His closest family and everyone Ivan had ever possibly encountered in this lifetime and the next, all in one space. "You happy to see them?"

"I am," he said. "But our grandfather couldn't make it. He has health problems, so he couldn't be here."

I didn't know that. Sam rarely spoke of his grandfather, but I knew he was close to him, and I knew he lived in one of their houses in England. When Sam had gone back to England during the summer, I knew one of the biggest reasons he'd gone back was for him.

"I'm sure he wanted to be here."

"He did." Sam chuckled. "Sent Ivan a long video congratulating him and everything. He and my grandmother paid for their honeymoon as a gift."

Really? "So your grandmother and him still have a good relationship?" She lived here in Canada now. They had divorced long ago.

"They still talk," Sam said. "My grandmother goes back to see him often, actually. My grandfather says that it took them a while to realize that they were better off as best friends, not lovers."

"Best friends?"

Sam nodded, a small smile creeping onto his face. "He wanted to be here badly, even though he and my dad have the worst relationship in the entire world. Worse than my uncle Vince and I had when I started living with them. But he'd be here if he could."

Sam flopped down next to me as we settled in silence. I was wondering when he'd be able to see his grandfather next when he put an arm around me. Without thinking, I locked my leg around his hip, making him go to his side with his back to me.

"Did . . . I just become little spoon?"

"You've always been little spoon," I told him, hugging him from behind.

"Hazel, this is so weird," he said, lacing his fingers with my own.

"No, it's not. I actually like this position." I grinned, pressing a kiss to his shoulder.

"You all right there, babe?" he asked me suddenly.

"Yeah," I told him, shifting him onto his back so that I was straddling him and my lips were against his neck. "Just happy."

"Because everyone's here?"

"Yeah," I said, pressing a light kiss to his jaw, and I could feel Sam tense as he tried to gain a hold of himself. "Jasmine, Andrew, Stevie, Jon Ming, Austin, the twins, and Caleb. All here. And your family too."

"Yeah," Sam said, his eyes looking up at the ceiling. I kept kissing his neck because I could. "They're here. And you're here," he said, his voice a little raspier.

My hand moved over his chest, right over where his heart was beating frantically, and I couldn't help but smile against him because I was the cause of that. "Your heart's beating fast, Sam."

"You know why," he whispered, a faint smile on his face as he kept his eyes up. I shifted forward, making sure his only view was my face.

"Why?" I asked him with a tilt of my head and narrowed eyes, waiting for the answer.

"Because of you. Only you. Now kiss me, Hazel."

"Demanding."

"You love it." He locked his arms around my waist, making me push down against him and press my lips against his.

I don't know how long we were at it, but having this guy kiss me senseless always reminded me of our first kiss. The feeling of it—everything was always like the first time, a feeling I don't think I could ever get familiar with because it was overwhelming every time.

I positioned myself more comfortably on top of his body. His hands moved past my waist, all the way down to my butt, squeezing me and pulling me closer to him.

Just when a sound came out of my throat, I heard the door fly open. "Sam—"

I pulled back, and Sam groaned and sat up quickly, pulling his legs up to his body. "Caleb."

Caleb, instead of leaving the room, proceeded to walk in and even sat down on the bed with his legs crossed. Of course.

Sam scowled, and Caleb shrugged, his eyes on his phone. "Dude, I've walked in on you guys making out so much that this has become very normal for me. I can just forget that I've seen your hands on Macy's ass and you guys practically grinding into each other."

Sam took the pillow behind his head and swatted Caleb with it. Caleb laughed, and I couldn't help but smile at the two of them. "What?" Sam asked, looking down at me.

"It's really good to see you two together again."

"Yep," Caleb said. "The two amigos. The sexy devils. C and S. S and C. Hot tamales. Man crushes every day."

I scoffed. "That's debatable."

"You're debatable," Caleb countered lamely in defense.

"I missed you, Caleb," I admitted, reaching over to slap him on the shoulder.

"I missed you too. But you'll see me on my birthday."

"What?"

"Oh yeah," Sam said. "He didn't want a party, so he's coming by later in the month to celebrate being eighteen."

"You only turn eighteen once," Caleb said. "And what better way than with your best friend?" He put his hands up and down in mock celebration until I forced his hands down, not wanting to see that and the look on his face ever again. "And your best friend's girlfriend!" he sang badly, moving his body from side to side and doing the same lame actions.

I reached over to stop him, laughing. "Caleb."

Caleb parted us with his hands so that he could lay his head in my lap and put his feet on Sam's. "Peter was telling me that you guys were talking about a reality show?"

Sam rolled his eyes when we got separated. "There's no reality show."

"You should have one," Caleb commented. "Put all the Cahills up in that castle and start filming. You could call it *Keeping Up with the Cahills.*"

Sam shot Caleb a dirty look. "No."

"I'd watch that show," I admitted.

"We should host the premiere party," Caleb said. "Right here."

"I agree."

"I hate both of you."

"No, you don't," Caleb said.

"That's right. Hazel, I don't hate you."

Caleb shot Sam his middle finger, pushing him away, and my boyfriend rolled off the bed. "Are we heading out to see Ivan soon?" Caleb asked. Ivan and Natasha had been separated since the night before. As part of my job, I was staying here to take pictures. Which I should probably have been doing already.

"Yeah." Sam glanced at me. "And you'll be here?"

I nodded, getting out of the bed along with Caleb. "So what I'm hearing is that I won't see you both until eleven thirty."

"Yes, that is exactly what Sam was saying. Princess, are you okay in the head? You're a little slow this morning." I gave Caleb a dark look, and he shrank back before giving me a hug that made me want to push him off. "I'm kidding."

"Sure you were."

Sam grabbed a sweater before he looked at me and looked at

my clothing. "Isn't that mine?" He was referring to the sweatshirt I was wearing.

"What if it is?" I asked him.

"Cute," he said before he kissed me on the mouth. I tried pulling away, but he didn't let go, dropping the sweater in his hands to pull me closer to him.

"Um . . . hello? Best friend in the room? Seriously? You're lucky I love you people." I heard Caleb sigh dramatically and exit the room.

The second he left, Sam let go and picked up the sweater from the ground. "I'm going to go after him. I'll see you later."

He kissed me once more before running out, and I could hear him yell, "Caleb!"

When I caught a glimpse of them before they reached the landing of the stairs, Sam had jumped on Caleb's back. Caleb didn't push him off, grunting as he adjusted. "You're so heavy, you dick."

"Where's your muscle, you prick?" Sam asked, not letting go anytime soon. Their laughter disappeared with them down the hallway.

~

Natasha looked beautiful. Her red hair was curled and set high on her head, partially hidden by her veil. Her white dress was perfect, with a long train against the floor. I stood at different angles, switching between my own camera and the camera someone on the team had lent me while trying to adjust to the lighting in the room. "How's that?"

She held a hand up to her mouth as she examined the pictures I had taken, resting her hand on my arm. When she looked up at me, her blue eyes were glistening. For the tenth time that morning, someone shouted, "She's crying again!"

"I'm not, I'm not," she assured us, but the tears were welling up even more than before.

Before I could find a handkerchief, Elizabeth Cahill beat me to it. Sam's other mother, as Caleb liked to call her, was wearing platforms and a long green dress. Her jet-black hair was tied back, and in her manicured fingers she held the handkerchief, dabbing under Natasha's eyes for her. "Natasha," she said softly.

Natasha laughed, fanning her face. I took a picture of that as well. Ivan was going to laugh once he saw her close to tears a million times. "I'm sorry, I'm sorry!"

"I'll calm her down," Liz whispered to me with a twinkle in her eyes. She turned to me, taking the camera and removing it from my neck. "I came in for you, Macy. Jasmine and Stevie are in one of the bathrooms upstairs. The one near Cedric's room. Go get ready."

"But I still have more pictures to take."

"We have a million photographers here today," Liz assured me with a comforting touch. "We'll be graced with your talent in a few moments, but I need you to go get ready in order for that to continue to happen. *Go.*"

Her lips curved as she pushed me out of the doorway, knowing what those two were going to do to me. Whatever they were going to do didn't matter as long as I could keep the Jordans on my feet underneath my dress. I was planning on moving a lot, and there was no way I was doing that in heels all day. But as I left the room, leaving a sniffing Natasha behind, I met Alice's eyes. She was quiet, watching me from the corner of the room before walking toward Natasha, helping Liz calm her down. I was convinced to the ends of the earth that she didn't like me.

But Sam's mother was no longer on my mind once I saw my two friends in the bathroom, already wearing their own dresses and touching up their makeup. We spoke for a while as I got dressed, and I felt pleased at the compliments, especially from Jasmine, at my new ability to curl my hair.

The mood did a 180 when Stevie came toward me with eyeliner. "If you think you're going to put that on my face, I will whack your arm off."

Stevie shook her head, pulling back. "You'll never change."

Before I could say anything to that, the door burst open. Sydney. Her curly hair was now straightened, and she was wearing a sundress with black heels. "Sorry!"

"It's okay," I told her, motioning for her to come into the large bathroom. Her hand stilled on the door, looking unsure and hesitant. Instantly, based on two short interactions with her, I wanted to find a way to make her more comfortable.

Jasmine must have sensed it because suddenly she said, "Oh, you're so gorgeous. What the hell?"

Stevie glanced over at Sydney, her lips parting. "And your dress is so pretty. I'm Stevie."

"Sydney," she said with a tiny laugh, finally letting go of the door. "Sorry for barging in, I was looking for someone."

"Lucas?" I asked.

"Which one is Lucas again?" Stevie asked.

"Wears the hat," I answered. "Draws and paints a lot. Glasses."

Stevie clapped her hands in realization. "*Glasses*. He's nice."

"Are you guys dating?" Jasmine asked, twirling the mascara tube in her hand.

Sydney opened her mouth to speak, but just as quickly, she shut it. So there was something between Sydney and Lucas. *Called it.*

"What did a Cahill do now?" Stevie asked.

Sydney's eyes drifted to the ground. I was about to open my mouth to tell her she didn't have to tell us if she didn't want to, but to my surprise, she spoke up. "He didn't really do anything."

Jasmine rolled the tube in her fingers. "He likes you?"

Sydney couldn't seem to formulate a response, her eyes bouncing between me and my friends.

"You like him?" Stevie suggested, and Sydney nodded once. Jasmine grinned next to me. Of course she loved a good story. Not going to lie, I did too. It was nice to hear that it could happen to someone I knew. "Does he know that?" Sydney nodded again. *Yes*. "But we don't know how he feels?" Sydney dipped her head once again.

"Did you see them together?" Jasmine asked me.

"They have nicknames for each other," I told them.

"Oh, he likes you," Stevie concluded.

"We're just friends," Sydney mumbled.

"You confessed to him," Jasmine told her. "You're not friends anymore. You're in limbo."

"I hate being in limbo." When she rolled her eyes, Jasmine glanced back at me with a smile. *Mission accomplished.* She was already comfortable with us.

Before Jasmine and Stevie could ask Sydney more questions, her phone beeped in her pocket. She read the message with a wince, glancing up at us. "It was great to meet you guys, but I have to go."

"We'll see you later," Jasmine promised. Stevie grinned. I reached out for a fist bump that Sydney acknowledged with her fist. Sydney seemed pleased, gracing us with a small smile before she exited the room.

As we continued to get ready and I debated putting my hair in a low ponytail or keeping it down, Stevie asked Jasmine, "So how has the Andrew and Jasmine reunion show been going?"

Jasmine tensed. The movement was so small, so minuscule, that if I had blinked, I would have missed it.

She covered it up as she untwisted the tube to add another coat of mascara. "It's been good. Really good."

I knew Stevie was about to open her mouth to ask another question, and I interrupted her. "I'm so hungry."

I wasn't lying.

"You sent a picture of your breakfast to the group chat this morning," Stevie said, looking amused.

"And Justin ate more than half of it!" I complained.

Stevie got up and walked toward the door. "I'll get you a Pop-Tart; I think I saw a box Phillip was eating from downstairs."

"Love you!" I shouted at her when she left and closed the door behind her. I put my camera on the table and stood next to Jasmine, looking at her as she applied mascara in the mirror. "Hey."

"Hey," she said quietly, putting her head down and looking at me through the mirror.

I crossed my arms. "Are you going to explain?"

She laughed, the sound low and strained. She was nervous, as if she'd expected I would ask her this question. "Explain what?"

When she turned away from me to scour through her makeup bag, I clasped my hands, holding in the beginning of my frustration. "Jasmine."

"I already told you, remember? My phone broke, and it took a while to fix it."

Yeah, her phone had broken. But I knew that wasn't the full explanation because I knew her. I knew Jasmine. She'd been one of my two best friends for most of my life. Since playing *Animal Crossing* on the DS, pretending to be pirates in her backyard, laughing until milk came out of our noses at every little thing. I knew when she wasn't telling me everything.

I hated prying, but this time, for the sake of my other best friend, I felt the need to know what was going on. "I get that. I'm fine if you don't talk to me for a couple of weeks because that's understandable, but Andrew?"

She kept her back to me. "What about him?"

"Your phone may have been broken, but you could've called him from someone else's. Or messaged him on any social network. Last time I checked, you have everything, and you have a laptop too. You could've video called."

She wasn't looking at me. Instead, she focused on herself in the mirror, untwisting a tube of lip gloss. "I was busy."

"Jasmine—"

"Mace, I was busy," she snapped. "I have school. I have a job. I volunteer. I was busy, okay?"

No. She may not have been lying, but she wasn't telling the whole truth.

"How come I don't believe you?" I said quietly, watching her turn around to face me. Her expression showed that she was full of impatience and seconds away from exploding. I was waiting for her to say it. What her real reason was.

"I don't know, Macy, why can't you believe me?"

"Because I know you."

"Well, maybe I've changed," she said, walking past me. "Maybe I'm different."

"Of course you're going to be different. You've lived in a different province for a few months. You adapted to different things and different people. It would be weird if you didn't change with a new setting. But I know *you*."

"Do you?"

"Yeah. I know you. I know you're still that weird girl that I've spent my entire life with, and I'm glad to call you my best friend. But the fact that you can't even tell me of all people what's going on with you only shows what's starting to become different between the two of us."

Jasmine pursed her lips, her eyes flickering around the room when she turned to face me again. "I just don't want you to judge me."

"You're worried that *I* of all people am going to judge you?" I scoffed. Me? "I'm not. I never would."

"*Macy*."

"*Jasmine*." I walked over to her. "What is going on?"

"There's someone else."

What?

15
SHOCKER

"What do you mean there's someone else?"

My question was spoken from a place of confusion. The ignorant part of me was hoping she meant that "someone else" was a metaphor for, I don't know, a new car, a new pet, something, anything. Anything other than exactly what she was insinuating.

Please be the former. Please be the former.

My other best friend's happy expression at seeing her just yesterday hit me like a truck in my head. *No*.

"Has . . ." For some reason, the words struggled to get out of my mouth. "Has anything physical happened—"

"No, no," she promised. "Nothing like that, but . . ."

When she trailed off, I heaved out a sigh, putting my hairbrush on the table, having to release my hands from holding on to anything. Why did I feel like I was being sucker punched in the chest as I processed what she said? Then I realized. "There was an almost, wasn't there?"

"There was an almost," she whispered, her face contorted. "See? You're going to judge me."

I was one of the last people to judge her. "I'm not *judging* you, I'm just—*what*?"

Jasmine leaned against the counter, her face in her hands. There'd been an almost. She'd had an almost with someone else. Someone that wasn't Andrew. There was someone other than Andrew.

The idea of Jasmine and Andrew, Andrew and Jasmine not being that exact structure, that syntax broken down into parts, left me muddled.

There was someone else.

I leaned against the counter as well, keeping my eyes trained on her. "Wh-who is he?"

"His name's Ace." Her eyes were cast downward, her fingers on the tube loose, the item ready to fall from her grasp. "One of my roommate's friends. We met on the first day, and we hit it off pretty fast. I don't know."

Don't say, "I don't know." Jasmine was very concrete in how she felt. If she'd known how she felt from day one, it was certain. Ace was certain. And out of respect for Andrew, I wasn't sure if I wanted to hear anything else about this Ace guy. About her life in BC. About anything, really.

Jasmine had met a new guy. There was someone else. That meant that Andrew's place in her life, one that had shifted from friend to lover, was—

Realization hit me once again, and it came with knitted eyebrows and a hushed voice as I said, "You didn't just come back for the wedding. You came back because it was time to end things with Andrew before you did something you'd regret."

Her silence was my answer.

My exhalation was rough when I pushed off the counter. What was Andrew going to say? How was he going to react? He loved her. The guy had been so happy to see her again and be with her that he'd practically ignored that she hadn't talked to him for weeks and had left him on edge.

She was emotionally cheating on him, leaving him with no explanation, not answering him. Meanwhile there was Justin, little Justin who was like a puppy gravitating toward his phone just to speak to Emma through their own long-distance relationship. But Andrew. Jasmine. *Oh God.*

"Macy," she said with wide eyes, pushing off the counter.

I stopped in front of her, looking her in the eye. "Do you love this—this Ace guy?"

She licked her lips nervously, closing her eyes for a brief moment before letting out a breath. "I think I do."

"Do you still love Andrew?"

"Of course I do," she assured me. "I just felt so guilty all the time because I kept thinking about Ace, and I held it off for so long." How long? Even the times when Andrew would call asking if I had heard from his own girlfriend? "I didn't want to imagine his face if I told him everything."

"If? *If?* You're going to tell him, right?" By now I had a hand on her shoulder, hoping she was thinking this through, because there should be no *if.* She should tell him. His relationship with the girl he loved was falling apart, and he didn't even know it.

"I don't know," Jasmine said, putting a hand over her eyes. "I don't think I should mention Ace."

"Jasmine," I said quietly. "You have to tell him."

"I don't want to let him go by saying he's been replaced by someone. He's been there for me forever. I still love him."

"I know that. And he's not being replaced." This Ace guy didn't have the history that came with Andrew. No one did. He was not a replaceable person.

"And if I tell him, it's going to break his heart, and I don't want to destroy our friendship over this." She put her face in her hands. "But it's already done. Ace is just . . ."

I winced. I loved both of my friends, and the part that loved Andrew was cringing every time the other guy's name was mentioned.

Before I could say anything, Stevie entered the room, a Pop-Tart in one hand and her attention on her phone in the other. When I took the Pop-Tart from her, putting on a smile, she must have sensed the tension because her eyes flicked from me to Jasmine. "Everything okay here?"

"Yup," I answered. Jasmine silently went back to putting on her lip gloss. "It's fine."

~

As I watched the men, a mixture of Ivan's friends and Cahills, pile out of a limo in front of the Cahill house, I didn't think I looked *that* nervous as I snapped pictures. But I fidgeted in between shots. My fingers played with each other, skimmed along the material of the long blue dress I was wearing, which managed to cover most of my Jordans. Although when Sam reached me, his expression was one of instant concern. "What's wrong?"

I looked him up and down. He wore black Converse—I knew when Liz saw him, she might have a meltdown at what she would see as a tragic combination of clothing. My gaze trailed upward to the dark-blue tuxedo he was sporting with a black bow tie like every other guy close by.

"Hazel," he repeated, not even bothering to acknowledge how I was outright ogling him.

"Nothing," I immediately responded while a random man tried to gather some of the boys to take pictures. Guests filtered around the front yard, soon making their way to the backyard where the ceremony would be taking place.

My answer didn't do any good. Sam looked right through me. His hands went up to my arms, moving up and down in a calming gesture. "You sure? You look bothered by something," he said quietly.

I was about to push the subject away when I saw Andrew in my peripheral vision wearing a dress shirt and pants. There was a bright smile on my best friend's face. Sam followed my gaze. "It's something about him and Jasmine, isn't it?"

I didn't question how he understood. Either my emotions were on my sleeve or he knew me too well. Both, I guessed. Sam continued to speak. "She did something. Something that he's probably not aware of, didn't she?"

I didn't speak, keeping my eyes on Andrew as he joined Caleb, Austin, Jon Ming, and the twins, who were calling for me to take pictures. Sam kept talking. "She's not going to tell him, is she? The whole story of whatever happened."

I moved my gaze to Sam's piercing one. "I don't know," I admitted before giving him a smile. It was weak, it was pathetic, but I was going to push the conversation forward. I didn't want to think about it any longer or I was going to be nauseated. "Go pose with your friends, you model."

He wasn't moving. I reached up to his collar, pulling him closer to me.

He appeared puzzled. "What?"

"I'm trying to avoid a situation that does not involve me. It involves my two best friends who I hoped would have a day like this for themselves. But I don't think that's going to happen anymore. So, because today is a sad and a good day, I'm going to give you something good. Now, I'm only going to say this once, you ready?"

Sam blinked, taking in what I had said before nodding quickly. "What is it?"

"You look really hot right now." The words sounded strange coming out of my mouth, but it felt good to give Sam a well-deserved compliment. He knew it. I hoped he had saved that in his memory along with his numbers and love of soccer.

"I look what?"

"You—*nuh-uh*. I'm not saying that again."

"I look hot." He tested the words slowly, pulling me in closer. "Did my girlfriend, Hazel, the love of my life, Macy Anderson, say that?"

He wasn't ever going to let this go.

"And not even hot. She said *really* hot. I don't think I'm in the right world if my girlfriend said that and looks as beautiful as she does every day. I think I'm dreaming. I don't want to wake up. Or maybe I'm in heaven," he breathed out, running his hands through his curls.

I couldn't help but snicker at his dramatics when someone cut in. "Okay, you two, separate, would you?" Austin yelled. The sun bounced off his golden-brown skin, and I couldn't help but grin. It was great to see him. "We need a picture."

We took picture after picture. Too many pictures where they tried acting serious only to end up laughing. One where Jacob kept trying to copy every move Jon Ming was doing. One where Stevie had to abandon her classic peace sign pose after Brandon pointed out that she did it in every single picture. For a few seconds, they made me forget what had happened moments ago.

Faces after faces of people I recognized, people I didn't. People I'd once seen at the grocery store, at parties from high school, filled the seats in the backyard. Ivan hadn't been kidding when he'd said he'd invited everyone. That included Jasmine's brother, Drake, who I gave much-needed hug. "Hi!"

"Your hair," he said, eyebrows high. "You barely curl your hair. University's changed you, hasn't it?"

"Only been a few months," I said, but he shrugged.

"Doesn't matter. You realize the change when you least expect it." He surveyed the surroundings. "Where's my sister?"

"Right here." Jasmine stepped up next to me. But her eyes were on Andrew, who was standing at a distance speaking to one of Ivan's friends.

"You good?" Drake asked her. "Why do you look out of place?"

She put on a good front. If I didn't know her so well, I'd believe that she was fine. "I'm good."

Drake looked at her with narrowed eyes. "C'mon, let's go sit. Catch you later, Mace."

I waved goodbye. More and more people found their way to the back as the ceremony was about to start. Caleb fell into step with me as I took pictures of those following the path to find their seats on the other side of the house. "Word through the grapevine is that you called a certain damsel in distress *hot*?"

"Oh my God," I groaned. "Stop eavesdropping."

"If I hadn't heard it, I would've known something had happened from Sam's face. He's in too good a mood," Caleb pointed out. We looked over at where Sam was standing with the rest of the Cahills near the back patio. He was wearing a bright grin, his hands on Greg's shoulders as his brother explained something to the rest of the group.

"I'm never giving him a compliment ever again," I decided.

"*Liar*," Caleb chuckled. "You'd probably do it again to see him smile like that. You get all hot and bothered looking at him and want to jump his bones." The dry look I shot Caleb didn't do any good as he laughed louder. "Kidding. But it's good to see him happy."

"It is," I admitted. The two of us watched the entire group of Cahill boys laugh. Sam reached toward Phillip, adjusting the kid's suit jacket as Christian bent down to fix his hair. No one was going to ruin one of their own's day.

"And you too," Caleb said, squeezing my arm gently. "It's good to see you both happy."

Before I could say anything further, he bid me goodbye as people were asked to be seated. I continued to do my job, coordinating with various people before the ceremony started.

The path led to where all the people were sitting and waiting for the ceremony to start. I looked at the large audience of people in the chairs, spotting my father's face near the middle with Justin on his other side as I took pictures. I froze when I realized my father wasn't speaking to Justin, who was sitting next to Emma. He was turned around, speaking to a woman who looked strangely familiar. Before I could even question it, music started playing from the quartet and piano by the makeshift altar. One by one, Cahills made their way down the aisle in their matching tuxes. I stood near the altar taking photos from the side as they walked down. When Sam had walked down and stood in his position near me, he whispered, "At our wedding, are you going to wear Jordans?"

There it was again. *Our* wedding.

"Is that going to be a problem?" I mumbled, fighting a smile.

"Can I wear Converse?"

"Of course."

"Then it would never be a problem," he chuckled, before glancing at Ivan. "Holy shit, I never thought I'd see the day Ivan would look like he's about to piss his pants."

I'd known Ivan for almost a year, and he didn't get nervous. Ever. But now I could see the sweat breaking out on his forehead. When he made it to the altar, murmurs were being exchanged between his groomsmen as the music changed and the person playing the piano was replaced with Joey Cahill. Eyes were focused on the women making their way down the path toward the altar, all in lavender dresses. But then the real star of the show, in her white dress with her white train, her arm linked with that of her father, who had the same red hair, came into view.

The crowd rose to their feet, the wedding march playing as the bride began walking toward the altar. The attention was all on her. All cameras pointed in her direction, for her day. She looked beautiful. Her dress, her hair, herself. Everything. I swear she was glowing.

I took multiple photos of her as her eyes were locked on Ivan's. When I turned to take pictures of Ivan, he was staring right back at her, but what he was doing made me almost drop my camera.

Ivan Cahill was crying.

That was the most unexpected thing. Tears streamed down his face. By the time Natasha's dad had handed her over to Ivan, he was laughing and smiling at her through the tears, and I took multiple pictures of them through it all, along with the other photographer.

If anyone had managed *not* to cry, by the time they got to the vows there wasn't a dry eye in the house. "Natasha, I've loved you for the longest time. And I'm grateful that I've had the chance to call you the girl next door every summer, then call you my friend, then my girlfriend, then my fiancé, and after today my wife because I don't want to spend another second of my life without you in it. I love you so much."

Natasha was crying so much at that point, Ivan was laughing quietly, trying to wipe the tears from her face, but she couldn't stop crying and smiling even when she was trying to get to her own vows.

Then they exchanged the rings. "Do you, Ivanovo Peter, take—"

Ivanovo?

The minister stopped at the sound of Sam and his family struggling to contain their laughter. I shot Sam my best *what?* look, and he whispered, "Named after a great-uncle."

Ivanovo?

I didn't ask any further questions, taking pictures of the boys in their elation; even Toby's seriousness cracked.

I heard Ivan say to Natasha, loud enough for the crowd to hear, "You did promise to never leave me because of my name, remember?"

By now I'd started laughing along with everyone else, and

Natasha only had joy shining through her tears. "I did."

"Okay." Ivan exhaled dramatically, turning back to the minister. "You can continue."

"Do you, Ivanovo Peter, take Natasha Rose to be your wife?"

He beamed, proud. "I do."

"Do you, Natasha Rose, take Ivanovo Peter to be your husband?"

"I do," she said, her eyes welling once again. *Click.*

"Then, without further ado, I now pronounce you husband and wife." The minister had his hands out. "You may now kiss the bride."

Then Ivan took Natasha in his arms and kissed her, and because it was Ivan, he proceeded to dip her. I took pictures of the minute-long kiss, which was accompanied by shouts of encouragement from the groomsmen and I'm pretty sure a whistle from either Jon Ming or Caleb.

When they broke apart, I couldn't stop the smile that came to my face. *Click.*

That smile slipped quickly when a voice—familiar, creepy, and disgusting—suddenly broke through the cheers. "Well, well, well. Ivan Cahill finally settled down?" The laugh that came with the voice made my whole body go cold. "Shocker."

I didn't look toward the source. From where I was bent, close to the middle of the front row to take photos, I twisted to Sam. Sam, who was staring straight ahead at where the voice had come from. At the person in the middle of the aisle.

Anthony.

16
OH MY GOD

"What?" Anthony taunted. "You're not going to say hello to an old friend?"

"Shit." The harsh whisper came from Caleb, who was sitting close to where I was crouched. This couldn't be happening. Not now. Not today.

I stood, looking directly at Anthony. He wore a tux jacket, which had probably gotten him past security. Even in the outfit, he still looked the way he had the first time I'd met him. Unsettled. *Off.*

"No words, Ivan? Sam?"

"Leave," Sam said in a quiet but firm voice, his fingers curled into fists.

"Security!" Vincent Cahill stood up from his seat. "Young man—"

"What? I can't wish another old friend a happy wedding that I wasn't even invited to?" Anthony sneered. "Ivan, I can't believe you invited everyone in the world but me."

Ivan didn't say anything; his eyes were on the group of men who were marching in Anthony's direction. Anthony stepped forward, unfazed by them. But the second he moved, Sam moved toward him. *No.*

Anthony tsked, shaking his head. "Sam, you know why I'm here."

"Leave, Anthony," he demanded again.

"You can't just ignore my calls, man. You know what you've done. You need to pay me back for it."

What?

"That was two years ago."

"Two years in *debt.* You're lucky I don't charge interest." Anthony looked around at the backyard, at the covered pool, the pool house, the acres of land. The money. "You can certainly afford it. All you have to do is pay me back and we can go right back to being old friends."

"I'm not your friend," Sam said stoically. "I was never your friend, Anthony."

"C'mon, man, I was your friend." One security guard put a hand on Anthony, starting to drag him up the aisle. Anthony was undeterred, keeping his gaze trained on Sam without missing a beat. "Remember the good old days when we went to party after party? Getting so wasted and so high and so fucked up? Remember you telling me all the shit that happened, man? With your family? You running off to Grandmother's house because you couldn't stand to be in England anymore because of your sister?"

Oh, that did it.

I think every single Cahill homed in on Anthony in that moment as he was being dragged away, but he was grinning because he knew he was going to make Sam snap. And there wasn't anything anyone could do to stop it.

"Don't you dare talk about my sister." Sam stepped forward. Toby reached ahead to grab him by the arm, but Sam yanked his arm out of his cousin's hold.

"Control your anger, Sam. I always knew you had issues," Anthony taunted, a leering smile on his face even as he struggled against the guard. His slim frame was able to slip through his grasp, and he moved quickly back toward Sam. Provoking, unrelenting. And then his attention fell on to me. I almost shivered with disgust. "I can't believe you found someone who's putting up with all your shit. Or did she stay by your side while you did the drugs and drank the alcohol and found a new girl every night—"

"I was *sixteen*," Sam interrupted.

"And we were *friends*," Anthony taunted, stopping meters from Sam as security attempted to drag him away once again. But he didn't stop talking. "We were *always* friends. I think Bethany and I would have been great friends, don't you think? Considering she already knew who I was."

Sam stilled. The security guard had Anthony on lock, but Sam held a hand out. "Stop talking. Stop!" The guard holding Anthony glanced over at Vince Cahill, who had made his way to Sam along with Sam's father.

"Sam," James urged.

Vince didn't say anything, his attention on Sam without touching him. Without making him lash out. "Get him off my property," Vince demanded.

Anthony only let out a dark laugh, even as he was being pulled away. "You came around to Redmond every summer, remember? I didn't know you then, but Bethany? People *saw* Bethany. Daughter of a multimillionaire, and you think people didn't talk? You think people didn't get to know her? That I never met her? I remember people throwing themselves at her in the summer of ninth grade. One of the hottest girls I'd ever seen."

Then suddenly, as he was a good distance away, his laugh cut through the silence. And then he said, "Too bad she was a fucking bitch."

That's when all hell broke loose.

Sam got out of his father and uncle's bubble, out of his cousin's grasp as he ran in Anthony's direction. Toby and Cedric were hot on his heels, but neither was fast enough when Sam surprised the security guard and everyone else by launching himself at Anthony.

A blur of twists, turns, fists, and legs mixed together the second the two fell to the ground. Near me, Ivan pushed Natasha behind him, hiding her away from the scene that was ruining her wedding. The audience closer to the brawl moved away, gasps and shocked expressions spreading throughout the area along with one scream. Toby was the first to reach the chaos as he and security tried tearing the two apart.

I could see Sam from where I was standing. His eyes were ablaze, his face set in stone as he socked a punch across Anthony's face. Cedric pulled him back by the waist, but Sam wriggled out of his hold, reaching for Anthony, whose lip was busted open, blood spilling down into his mouth and between his teeth. Even from where I was standing, frozen in place, I saw the grin on Anthony's face as he continued to taunt Sam. "You're never going to be over it. Look at you."

Sam thrashed against his dad and cousin's hold, his face

flushed with exertion. Words didn't leave his mouth, but his face contorted with pure rage.

"Pathetic." Anthony spat in Sam's direction as he was lugged away. "You're still the same broken, angry kid from two years ago."

No.

Anthony's words had cut too deep. In a voice filled with hatred that made my heart squeeze, Sam yelled, "*Fuck you!*"

Those two words seemed to exhaust him. The second they were released, he continued to thrash against the hold of his family, but the fight was gone. Anthony's fading laughter echoed in the air as he was finally lugged off the property.

Sam. His face, so tired, was red and blotchy, his eyes bleary, and his fists bloody and peeling. I willed my feet to move from where they'd been rooted in place and rushed over to him. I grabbed the handkerchief I'd been using to dab at my happy tears and wiped the blood underneath his mouth as his heavy breaths made his chest lift up and down. It was like he didn't even see me there. His father and Toby were trying to speak to him.

"Samuel," James whispered as people stared, and I wanted to glare at everyone until they turned away from him.

When Sam finally turned and made eye contact with his father, his hard expression slipped. He came back to himself, realizing what exactly had just happened, how he had reacted, and how he hadn't controlled himself. And when his gaze found mine, the exhaustion morphed into disappointment. In himself. For having allowed his anger to take over. For letting Anthony get to him.

He knew that his anger was one of his worst traits. I remembered that night in my mom's bedroom months ago in Redmond.

I had forgiven him even when he had gotten into a fight with Drake.

If there was something that had scared me then, it was definitely Sam getting into a physical fight with someone. But this one had been different. He knew that, didn't he? Anthony had come here to get whatever debt he believed Sam owed him. And when he didn't, he had triggered him.

That was not Sam's fault.

But Sam didn't get that. One second he was looking at me, and the next he shook himself out of his family's hold, bolting toward the forest bordering the backyard.

Without a second thought, I hiked up my dress to follow him when someone placed a hand on my arm. Calm brown eyes met my hazel ones. Alice. "Let him breathe," she said.

Immediately, I unclenched my hands from my outfit. Sam wasn't going to do anything that would worry me. I wouldn't find him on the edge of a cliff with a bottle of liquor in his hands. He might have lost control a minute ago, but he deserved a chance to calm himself down and show us that wasn't who he was anymore.

He just needed a moment to breathe.

But the commotion wasn't over. Between everyone chattering, whispering, and wondering, no one realized that something else was happening.

"*Lucas!*" a voice whispered in anguish. Sydney. By the time I turned my head, she was already on the ground next to him on the makeshift steps. Lucas had one hand to his chest. His face was red. When he opened his mouth, a high-pitched squeak came out, as if he couldn't get any air into his lungs.

He was struggling to breathe.

The crowd next to him didn't process what was happening,

but the Cahills did. Joey dropped down next to him, assessing him. "He's having an asthma attack."

His stepmother, Naomi, a tall Black woman in a long dress with a sleek ponytail, immediately rushed to Lucas's side, cradling his face. "Someone call 911. Now! We need his inhaler!"

Christian pulled out his phone and dialed 911 while Cedric and Toby pushed back the crowd to give Lucas space. Another man, sharply dressed like the rest of the family, turned to Joey. "Where does he keep it?"

"I—I don't know where it is. Probably back at the house," Joey admitted. "He hasn't needed it in years."

"I know where it is." Sydney shot up. She quickly ran, disappearing through the back doors. Greg and Phillip were right behind her.

"Lucas." Joey kneeled down in front of him. "C'mon, buddy. I need you to breathe for me."

Christian spoke to the dispatcher on the phone as Joey continued speaking to his twin. "I'm here for you, but I need you to calm down. You know you need to calm down. Clear your mind. It's me, c'mon. It's me."

Lucas's gaze shifted over to his brother, and under his glasses, his eyes looked frantic as he tried to gasp for air. His face was starting to turn purple. I could feel genuine fear start to move through me.

Joey took off Lucas's glasses and sat in front of his brother. "C'mon, L, it's me, Joey. It's me. Breathe. You can do it. Relax." Lucas couldn't calm down; he was clearly panicking, no doubt making it worse. Just then, Sydney rushed down the steps, inhaler in hand. "I got it, I got it!"

She quickly ran over to Lucas as Joey moved to the other side of him. She grabbed Lucas's hand, bringing it up to his mouth and pressing the inhaler. The puff of the inhaler broke through the apprehensive silence.

For a few seconds, everyone waited. Then another second passed as Lucas moved the inhaler away from his mouth, his breaths shallow but there. I felt everyone, including myself, exhale in relief.

"Oh my God," he whispered loud enough for us to hear before leaning his head against Sydney's shoulder.

Christian hung up the phone. "An ambulance is coming." He looked down at his older brother. "You haven't had an asthma attack since we were kids. What the hell?"

Lucas opened his mouth to speak, but his stepmother silenced him with a hand, the concern on her face never dropping. "Do not say a word. We're going to make sure you're okay in a second."

Lucas dropped the inhaler on the ground as Joey handed him his glasses to put on. "Overwhelmed?"

Lucas nodded, exhaustion evident in his features.

The rest of the family likely had the same expression. A lot of terrible things had just happened at once on what was supposed to be a happy day. When I glanced over at Alice and James, they were speaking to Greg quietly, James's hand on his son's shoulder.

Vincent Cahill cleared his throat. "Lucas, I suggest you go inside. The paramedics will meet you there."

Lucas stood up slowly. With Sydney's hand in his own, he shuffled along as they went inside the house. His parents went with them, his father holding him up on one side. Liz exhaled lowly, moving over to Natasha and Ivan, who seemed a little shellshocked by the events that had just transpired. She whispered a couple of words to them before saying something to the minister.

The minister cleared his throat, still, like many of the other people, looking shocked. "Once again, the new Mr. and Mrs. Cahill."

Everyone applauded, and Ivan put an arm around Natasha's waist as they walked down the aisle toward the inside of the house.

Eventually, everyone started to follow suit.

I remained standing near the spot where Lucas had fallen, my focus on the high trees in the distance. Oh, Sam.

Someone grabbed my hand, and little fingers gave me a tight, confident squeeze. Phillip. I looked down at him with a soft smile that he returned, but the worry in his eyes gave away his true feelings. He loved Sam so much, *too* much—they were practically brothers. "He's going to be okay."

"You sure?" Phillip asked.

"Yeah," Toby answered. Although he wasn't looking at the youngest Cahill. He was looking at me. "Give him at least ten minutes, and if he isn't in the house, then you go after him, okay?"

I nodded once. Without another word, Toby grabbed Phillip, letting the kid climb onto his back. Andrew stepped up next to me, reminding me of the other bad thing that had happened that morning. This day was turning out to be a lot less joyful than I'd hoped it would be.

"You okay?" My best friend tilted his head. "You're looking a little pale."

"Just a lot to take in" were the only words I could muster.

Andrew offered me his arm, extending his elbow in my direction. I hooked mine through his as we made our way inside. Yet I couldn't help but glance at the trees once again.

17
DUMBEGG

"What if he left?" Caleb asked.

Ten minutes were coming to an end. We were standing by the door leading to the backyard. I had a ginger ale in my hand. Caleb had a glass of wine he had managed to sneak off a waiter's tray, swirling it around like he was plotting something, but in reality, I knew he was trying to avoid freaking out. If someone thought I would be the person most worried about Sam, then they probably hadn't met Caleb.

"Security would tell us," Toby answered.

"Well, security has been doing a horrible job considering they let that psycho in," Caleb said with hostility.

"Caleb," Cedric said, "he had them convinced that he was on the list."

"Of course he had them convinced he was on the list," Caleb hissed, the veins popping out of his neck. "I've met that guy. He changed my best friend. You think I don't know how manipulative he can be? Don't these so-called security men get paid hundreds to not make that kind of mistake?"

A hand fell onto my shoulder. My dad looked almost as worried as Caleb. "Did you talk to him?"

I shook my head. "We're letting him breathe a little."

Out of the corner of my eye, Austin appeared. In his hand was a cupcake that he held out in my direction with a soft smile. "I'm sure he's okay."

Caleb's eyes narrowed, and I sighed, biting into the cupcake. *Here we go*. "Okay?" Caleb exclaimed. "What do you mean by *okay*? Did you hear what that sick prick said?"

Suddenly, Toby lightly pushed Caleb back with a hand on his chest, moving him away from Austin. "Don't yell at him."

Huh? I glanced at Cedric, who seemed as confused as I was. How did Toby know Austin? However, the look on Austin's face told me he didn't know Toby. Although when they locked eyes, Toby seemed calm as Caleb fixed his suit, and Austin seemed confused. I was intrigued and puzzled, but now was not the time to wonder.

Caleb huffed. "Sorry. I'm just worried."

"You and me both," I said. Toby was still looking at Austin, who cleared his throat, leaning next to me by the wall.

Dad patted Caleb on the shoulder. "He'll be okay, son."

Caleb shook his head. "I don't know."

I looked over his shoulder to see James Cahill move through a crowd of people in the living room, identical in almost every way to Vince Cahill except for his haircut. When he stopped before us, he looked at Cedric and Toby. "The medics are with Lucas, Uncle John, and Aunt Naomi. Elizabeth's assistant is going to the police station to give a report."

"I'll go with her," Toby offered.

"Is Lucas okay?" my dad asked.

"He's a little shaken up," James said. "He'll be okay. Just needs to take it easy."

"Thank God," Cedric muttered, sitting down on the couch.

James turned to me, anxiety swimming in his gaze. "How about Samuel?"

"Macy's about to check the backyard to see if he's there," Caleb said.

"What about you?" I asked as he dropped next to Austin. "Aren't you coming with me?"

He shooed me away. "Princess, go check on him. He'll be okay when he sees you."

"I'll be back," I told James, handing Austin my camera before exiting the room. Pushing past people lingering, whispering, and gossiping agitated the life out of me. Ivan had invited a ton of people, people who would spread the information of what had happened today online. Sam and his family were always in the spotlight, but this was attention that none of them would want.

By the time I made it down the backyard, looking at the ruined pathway from the fight, Sam was nowhere in sight.

Then I smelled cigarette smoke.

My teeth dug into my bottom lip as I made my way around the large house. Sam was sitting against the wall, his attention on a pack of cigarettes he was flipping in his hand. His cheek already had a bruise forming, but he didn't look like he was in any pain. Casting my eyes downward, I noted the remnants of a crushed cigarette on the ground next to his feet.

"I was told to give you ten minutes," I said.

"It was nine minutes and forty-two seconds." Sam stopped flipping the package. "Ask the question you want to ask."

Fine. "Did you drink? Did you do anything?"

"I smoked. That's it." Relief flooded my system as I moved myself toward him, fighting the need to wrap my arms around his neck in a tight hug. Instead, I took the spot next to him as he yanked his bow tie off. Our legs stretched out next to each other, feet close but not close enough to be touching. "I wasn't going to do anything. I found the cigs in the pool house. I think Christian must have stuffed them there or something."

"What makes you think that?" I asked.

"Yesterday we were all in there talking. He was bringing up some things he had been doing. Toby smokes, but it's not this brand. Ivan doesn't anymore. Lucas stays away from smoke for obvious reasons. Joey doesn't like it, and neither does Cedric. Greg wouldn't, and Phillip is Phillip. All signs point to Christian. Justin will probably bring him out of it. Or else I'll probably have to knock some sense into the lad."

"Why did you smoke?" I asked. Sure, I was concerned about Christian, seeing as he was my little brother's good friend, but I really wanted to know what was going through Sam's mind at the moment.

"I was upset," he said slowly, rubbing his face with his hands before leaning his head against the wall and letting out a long breath. "Are you mad?"

"No," I admitted. I'd never been confronted like that; I didn't know how I would have reacted if it had happened to me, but I probably would have felt the same anger. I took his hand in mine. "Are you okay?"

Sam's other hand moved up to touch my neck. His fingers

touched the pendant on the necklace that he had given me all those months ago. He twisted the glittering soccer ball between his thumb and index finger. The light reflecting off it shimmered across the wound on his face. "I didn't think I'd see him again. Or anyone from that time."

"Would it not have been the same in England?"

"It would have; it just would have been a different group of people," he confessed. "Anthony, that dick. He saw me weeks before Zach's Halloween party. I never thought I'd see him of all people ever again." Sam scoffed, and the short laugh that came from him wasn't humorous in the slightest. "They're going to find drugs on him. He'll be arrested for drug possession, and he'll never again be able to take advantage of a fucking broken kid like me—"

"Sam." I stopped him, not liking the glint in his eyes.

He ran another hand across his face. "Sorry. If there's one person in the world I really hate, it's him. It's definitely him." Sam reached up, pressing the heels of his hands into his eyes. We sat there in silence. A long stretch of silence as I waited for him to speak. I waited for him to find the words to say anything.

"God," Sam said quietly, so quietly I wasn't sure I'd heard him right until he continued. "He was right. I was pathetic."

"You're not—"

"I know." He cut me off, moving his hands from his face. He looked so dejected my heart squeezed in my chest. "But I *was*. That's how Anthony found me. When I ran away from England and came straight to Redmond. That's how he found me: angry, pathetic, weak, and vulnerable. Angry because my sister was gone. Angry because she'd been here one day and gone the next. Pathetic because I wanted to escape the pain any way that I could. Vulnerable because the second he realized I came from money, he decided to extort me and blackmail me for it. He manipulated me into thinking he was my friend and then tried to use me to his advantage and still thought he could do it again."

At that moment, Sam heaved a downhearted sigh, his gaze focused on the grass a distance away. "I'm so tired of being angry, Hazel."

"I know," I said, my hand finding its way to his hair. When my fingers tangled into his curls the way I knew he liked, he closed his eyes.

"He wouldn't stop calling. I don't know how the hell he got my number, but he kept calling. Kept using different numbers, different phones."

The unknown caller ID from the other night. The call weeks before that. Maybe some of the calls I had assumed were Caleb had been Anthony instead.

"I didn't want you to worry," Sam continued. "You have enough going on with football and school yourself. I didn't want to bother you. I didn't want to bother anyone with him."

"You're not bothering me," I whispered. "Sam, you didn't need to bear these burdens alone. You have me. You have all of us."

He did. If I hadn't known it before today, it was obvious the second Anthony had stepped in. His cousins, his brother, his parents, uncles, and aunts—none of them had judged Sam's behavior. Not even our friends. Everyone was only concerned.

If there was a problem, he had support. But I didn't think he thought he deserved us all when he really did.

Sam squeezed our hands together. "I'm sorry." Then he whispered, "I'm sorry I broke my promise."

"You didn't break anything," I assured him.

"I told you I wouldn't fight anyone anymore, months ago. That I wouldn't let my anger take me over."

"He egged you on. He expected you to do it." My defense for him didn't do anything. Sam seemed more distraught, Anthony and his words running through his head, everything likely moving through his brain in a way he had yet to process or did not want to at all. Running my hand through his curls one more time, I said gently, "And I don't see you any differently. I'm not scared of you. I'm not scared of the way you lashed out either. I'm just worried, and I want to know if you're okay. That's all I want to know."

"I want to know that too," another voice said. Caleb joined us, and, similarly, he ruined his nice clothes by sitting down on the asphalt with careful eyes on his best friend.

Sam brought his knees up to his chest, putting his chin on top of them as his eyes flicked between Caleb and me. "You know? I'm really lucky to have you two."

"We know," Caleb immediately said. He didn't say that as a boost to his ego. He said it seriously because it was true. He said it because he knew we'd be there for Sam through anything. "Are you okay? After all that he said? About you? About her?"

Sam kept his eyes on the ground, but after a moment, he moved his head up and looked at Caleb and me with more confidence than I'd ever seen him have. And he had a lot of confidence. "I'm okay."

A small smile appeared on my face. Caleb clapped his hands together, grinning like a lunatic. "All right. Now, let's get going. You have to talk to Ivan and Natasha. And then we have to take pictures, and I'm pretty sure even though we aren't sitting on grass, we might have dirt on our asses, meaning Mama Cahill is going to kill us."

"Which Mama Cahill?" I asked. Four women with the Cahill last name were here today.

Caleb didn't seem to think about it when he said, "All of them. But mostly Liz."

Sam and Caleb both got up, dusting themselves off, and I beamed up at them, stretching my arms out. Caleb dramatically rolled his eyes. "Lazy ass."

They reached out to take one arm each, and I yanked hard with the arm Caleb was holding. His momentum moved forward, and he put his arms out to hold himself as he smacked into the wall, groaning loudly.

"Dumbegg," I said, smiling as Sam helped me up and I dusted myself off.

Caleb stayed there on the wall, still groaning. "Still violent as ever, princess."

"Well, when you call me things like that, it's kind of hard not to be," I told him as he detached himself from the wall.

Sam chuckled, looking a lot better even when Caleb shoved him lightly. At the sight of him with a smile on his face, I leaned over to kiss him on the cheek. As we walked to the gazebo in the backyard where the groomsmen and bridesmaids and a few others were speaking, Sam wordlessly helped me brush the rest of the dirt off my dress. I gave him a thumbs-up, asking if I was good, and he replied by pressing a kiss to my cheek, as if to say thank you. I didn't have time to say a word to him because my attention shifted to where Andrew and Jasmine were speaking.

Andrew still had a bright smile on his face. She hadn't told him anything yet.

Caleb must've detected my gaze because he groaned. "Oh no."

"What?" I asked.

"Something happened, didn't it?" His eyes flicked between Andrew and Jasmine and me.

I fixed my stare on both Caleb and Sam. How the heck were they able to figure that out? "You two are—"

"Aware? Observant? Perceptive? Watchful? Keen? What about—"

"Okay, *thesaurus*." I stopped Caleb, slapping him on the chest. "I get it. I was going to say freaky."

"Because we noticed something was wrong by the way you were looking over at your two best friends?" Sam said dryly. "That's how we're freaky?"

I shoved him in the stomach, not appreciating his attitude even though it came with lightheartedness. "Yes."

Caleb shrugged. "I've been called a freak once or twice . . ." He trailed off. *Wait for it.* "In bed."

He winked as he walked off, and I couldn't help but laugh. "He's an idiot."

All Sam did was shake his head, letting out a small laugh. "Yeah, I'm really lucky to have that idiot around."

18
AN ALMOST

Wow.

That was the only way I could describe the reception.

Since it was early November, the weather dipping below ten degrees, patio heaters dotted the interior of the massive tent where the reception was being held, trapping the heat inside. Tables upon tables were arranged amidst the blue-and-white decorations, the large wedding cake, and the food that lit up my spirits as my friends and I grabbed a little bit of everything we could. While table service was provided as servers strolled in and out of the tent, a grand buffet had been placed off to the side, and everyone took advantage of the best of both worlds. A makeshift dance floor was in the middle as people walked and talked, pushing the incidents from earlier today out of their minds. Ivan and Natasha were currently at the head table with their families, talking and laughing as if the events of this afternoon hadn't happened. Natasha had a big smile that hadn't slipped since Sam had spoken to her and Ivan. Neither resented or blamed him for anything, with Ivan clapping his cousin on the back, telling him to move past the entire ordeal.

As people ate, an orchestra played in the background. I was still doing my job, taking pictures in the moonlight and the generous lighting set up around the area. I was in the middle of looking through the pictures on one of the cameras when a wad of fabric hit me in the forehead.

I glared at Jacob, who was grinning at me, and began crumpling my napkin to hit him back. The ball swatted him on the cheek. Brandon was quick to stop him from throwing another napkin ball in my direction, and Austin reached over to me to hold down my arm. Stevie huffed, "I did not miss the two of you doing that."

"Yes, you did." I beamed at her, putting my camera down.

The crowd was silenced when Natasha came to the center of the room, a violin in her hand. Immediately, she positioned the violin under her chin. When she started to play, the quartet nearby joined her.

Stuffing a forkful of carrots into my mouth, I jumped up with the rest of the photo crew, capturing the moment as she continued to play. The story of Ivan and Natasha—she was a violinist who had lived next door while Ivan listened to her play in the summers before she flew down to New York to attend Juilliard. He watched her with a proud smile.

During the speeches, everyone listened to Natasha's maid of honor, Ivan's best man, their friends, and eventually their families speak. Everyone had said their piece one by one, but when it came to the Cahill side of the family, all the Cahill boys came up in a straight line. I stood at a distance, crouching to get a picture of them facing Ivan and Natasha.

Phillip had the microphone first. "Um, Ivan is really cool. He taught me how to skate back home." Ivan smiled. "He also gives me help, and he's funny. But Sam told me that when I was five, he almost hit me with an ATV? Right, Sam?"

Ivan groaned, glaring at my boyfriend, and even though he didn't have the microphone, his voice was clear across the tent. "Why did you tell him that?"

"Why wouldn't I?" Sam shot back.

"Oh," Phillip piped up again. "And he's weird. Greg always talks about how you used to collect Barbies."

"*Greg!*" Ivan exclaimed, and the crowd laughed lightly.

Greg smiled at his cousin unapologetically as Phillip continued. "Even though you did all those things, you're great. Natasha, you're awesome. You give really good presents. You're pretty, and I like that you make Ivan happy. There. I'm done. Can I eat now?"

Laughter broke out through the crowd as Greg took the microphone next. The speeches went on as the microphone was passed down the line. I kept my eyes on Sam when Cedric passed the microphone to him. "Ivan, I think the first memory I have of you was when you pinned me to the ground at the house and you thought you were able to wrestle me."

Toby chuckled. His seriousness broke with his smile. "I remember that. Ivan ended up with a broken arm."

I snorted as Ivan grumbled to Natasha, obviously displeased. "Yeah," Sam said. "Out of all of us, with every story to be told, you are definitely the weirdest. But you're also the one that no one thought would settle down. Then Natasha appeared in your life. She made you better, and everyone saw that. I remember meeting Natasha the same day Ivan met her." Sam turned to Natasha. "I was about twelve back then, visiting you guys here for the summer. And although I didn't have a proper conversation with you that day, Natasha, I was certain that you would be the girl for him. Bethany thought so too."

At the mention of his sister, everyone stiffened. But I didn't, even though it was unexpected. He was able to speak about her to a few people. Yet in front of a huge crowd? I glanced at Caleb, who was frozen: the fork in his hand piled with salad had stopped in midair, his mouth hanging open.

Sam took a deep breath. "She was probably rooting for the two of you before you realized how you felt about one another. I remember her coming into my room here constantly and gushing about you two all the time whenever Natasha was over. If she was here right now, I know she would be really happy for both of you. She'd probably be sobbing right now, unable to process that you're married. And if she was speaking into the mic, she'd be blubbering." Sam chuckled. "But she'd end it off by saying that she loves you and that she wishes you nothing but a lifetime of happiness." Sam grinned, his joy for his cousin bright in his green eyes. "And so do I, Ivan. So do we."

Ivan got up from his seat, hopping over the large table. When he made it to Sam, he knocked into him, grabbing him in a loving hug. I watched the Cahill boys get into one really huge hug, Phillip disappearing in the midst of it.

When that was over and everyone had returned to their seats, I sat back down, taking Sam's hand in mine. He flashed me a small smile and reached for his glass of water just as Natasha and Ivan stood in the center again, one of Ivan's hands on her waist and his other hand on the microphone. "We have a special announcement."

The crowd settled down, and I glanced at Sam in confusion; his facial expression mirrored mine as he took a sip of water. "Now, we were going to say this after we cut the cake, near the end, but seeing as all of our friends and families are still here, we wanted to tell you all together."

Ivan looked over at his parents before turning to everyone. "Not only are we married but . . . we're pregnant."

I heard a glass drop, and the shatter echoed around the room.

There were many gasps and hushed words at each table.

Sam started choking on his water, and Caleb and Cedric started choking on their food.

Liz screamed with joy and ran up to congratulate them, hitting Ivan on the arm. I was patting Sam's back when Caleb, once he recovered, got up and started snickering. "They really couldn't wait until their honeymoon, could they?"

Although there were mixed reactions throughout the crowd, Cedric gulped before he looked down at Phillip, who was staring back at him with wide eyes. "We're going to be uncles."

"We're *all* basically going to be uncles." Christian's words were muffled by his hand over his mouth.

Toby tensed as well, looking at the other boys. "Not only that. Ivan's going to be a *dad*."

Everyone in the vicinity of this table had the same exact reaction: shock.

Joey started to laugh, and everyone stared at him weirdly. "What? We all should've seen that coming. I mean, it's Ivan; of course he wouldn't wait for the honeymoon."

People got up to congratulate the newlywed couple, and I

was about to as well when I noticed Jasmine and how hard she was staring at the tablecloth. I tapped her, and she blinked several times, shooting me an uneasy smile. "Can you believe it?" she said nervously. "Natasha's pregnant?"

"Yeah, I can," I said before leaning in to her and asking gently, "When?"

The shift in conversation brought confusion to her face, as if she hadn't dropped a bomb earlier that day. As if on top of Sam, it wasn't the only other thing I had been constantly thinking about. "When what?"

"When are you going to tell him?"

Jasmine opened her mouth and then closed it: she was second-guessing herself. Was she even going to tell him that there was someone else? That she had fallen out of love with him or whatever the heck had happened?

Andrew came back to our table, Sam trailing right behind him. Sam's green eyes flicked between Jasmine and me while Andrew looked confused by the uneasiness.

"What's going on?" Andrew asked slowly.

Tell him, my eyes urged her. After all, our friendship, spanning a decade, told me that if I could read her that well, she should be able to read me back.

She did. When she turned to face Andrew, apprehension took over her face. "We need to talk."

Andrew's brow furrowed, but he put on a small smile, his own way of bracing himself. I think a part of him knew. There was nothing good that could come from those four words. "Okay, talk."

She shifted uncomfortably as she stood. "Not here."

"Inside?" Sam suggested, digging into his pocket to hand Andrew a key. "You can talk in my room."

When they slipped out of the tent, Sam looked down at me. An understanding passed between us that made him take my hand seconds later, pulling me outside just as we caught a glimpse of my best friends entering the house. When a cool breeze brushed by us, I instinctively crossed my arms to hug myself. Wordlessly, Sam removed his suit jacket, placing it around my shoulders. "So she did do something."

"You guessed it," I huffed, holding on to his jacket with one hand as he took my other with his own. The music vibrated from the tent behind us, but the dim lighting emitting from Vincent and Elizabeth Cahill's home was a dull contrast in the moment.

"There's someone else?" he asked as we started moving toward the back doors. The home was mostly empty save for the few people lingering in the kitchen.

As we moved past the kitchen into the hallway, I said, "There was an almost."

I hated that word. I hated speaking about this in general. I mostly hated knowing what was happening right now. What was happening at this second, and how my two best friends were going to be torn apart over it.

I needed to crawl into my bed and sleep the entire day off, but I also knew I needed to be there for both of them.

"You're basically going to be an uncle. How about that?"

Sam shrugged. "It's great, but don't change the subject." We had made it to the staircase, lingering by the foyer. When I glanced up to the steps, Sam moved toward me, rubbing my arms in a comforting motion. "You good?"

"No," I admitted. "I hope Jasmine can break up with him in a—"

The sound of footsteps, of someone on a mission to escape, cut me off.

Andrew was storming down the stairs. His expression was as hard as stone, and my heart dropped into my stomach. He yanked his tie off, ready to burst out of the house, when he realized Sam and I were in his proximity.

When he approached me, I kept my face impassive even as he looked me dead in the eyes. Even as he looked at me with a level of hurt that I'd never seen on him. "Did you know?"

Jasmine rushed down the stairs. "Andrew—"

He put a hand up, silencing her, and kept his eyes on me. "Did you know?" he repeated.

My mouth opened to speak, but no words came out. Oh God. Oh God. His nostrils flared. "When did she tell you? Because I know that she told you. I can tell."

"This morning," I said. I'd seen Andrew upset. I'd seen him at his happiest. I'd seen him cry and struggle for the tears to stop. But I definitely did not like seeing my best friend mad. That was a rarity.

"And?"

"And what?"

"What's his name?"

"Ace." Jasmine was the one who answered. "His name is Ace."

"Cool," he scoffed, and his voice, which had been hard as steel, was suddenly dry with sarcasm. "His name starts with an *A* too."

"Andrew . . ." Jasmine trailed off, not knowing what to say.

There was a heavy moment of silence. I watched Andrew carefully—watched the hurt turn to puzzlement then to something I couldn't decipher. Suddenly, Sam cleared his throat, grabbing my hand. "I think we're going to leave—"

"No," Andrew suddenly said, his tone unreadable. "Stay. You have no reason to leave. You live here." Then Andrew turned around, facing Jasmine. I was surprised that he was staring her right in the eyes. "I—I don't blame you."

She blinked. "What?"

"I don't blame you." He placed his hands on his face, dragging his fingers down and down until he interlocked them, looking defeated. "I mean I—*we* should've seen it coming, Jazzy."

We waited for him to continue. Andrew let out a laugh, one that definitely wasn't a happy one. "It wouldn't have worked out. There was a point where I felt it and you felt it, and yet we went through with it. What were we thinking? That long-distance would actually work?"

Jasmine looked hurt. "We did think that."

Andrew laughed that same laugh again. "Obviously, it didn't work. Let's face it. We should've known it wouldn't have worked out. We're not like Sam and Macy."

Sam and I glanced at each other, obviously not wanting our relationship to be brought into this.

"What do you mean by that?" Jasmine asked, stepping forward cautiously.

Andrew shook his head, keeping his eyes on the ground. "Jasmine, our love isn't—wasn't—like theirs. Not contacting each other for long periods of time? Being okay with it even when we're changing? I'm pretty sure that if those two were on opposite sides of the country, hell if they were on different continents, they would still be together and not let anyone get between them."

When he stopped talking, there was silence in the room, and I couldn't even hear the people who had been chattering in the kitchen. It was so quiet, and I patiently waited for someone to say something, placing my hands on my camera and putting my fingers over its covered lens like it was a child watching its parents fight.

Jasmine's eyes fell shut. "Andrew, I'm—"

"You're sorry? I know you are."

Jasmine's eyes closed tightly, and her fingers rested in the space between her eyebrows. "I've turned into my own dad." She said it so quietly to herself, I don't think she knew we'd heard.

Sam might not have understood what that meant to Jasmine, but Andrew and I did. I froze. Andrew tensed. This time, even amidst his hurt, he stepped toward her. "You—you cannot say that."

"Why not? I hurt you, didn't I? It's the truth."

"No, it's not." I spoke up. "Don't compare yourself to your dad."

"Don't," Andrew agreed. "Look, did you just so happen to break up a family, cheat with someone half your age, and then knock them up?"

"Why are you defending me?" she asked. "You should be angry at me. Not trying to make me feel better."

"Maybe because I'm still in love with you. Even after you told me that, I am still in love with you. You may have fallen out of love with me—"

"I didn't."

"Do you love him? The other guy?" Andrew asked, moving to look down at Jasmine.

Jasmine didn't answer, and Andrew continued. "Does he make you feel a certain way whenever you're around him?"

She didn't answer.

Andrew, dejected beyond words, rubbed his hands on his face before he asked the last question, locking his fingers against his lips. "Jasmine, does he make you happy? Much happier than I've ever been able to over the past months? Over our summer together?"

Jasmine moved her eyes to the ground. "I don't want to lose you, Andrew."

"Jasmine, we were friends for years before we started dating." The smile he gave her was a sad one. "I don't exactly think you're ever truly going to lose me."

"But—"

Andrew pushed off the railing, and although his eyes were becoming glossy, he didn't shed a tear. "Jazzy, I just need some time, all right? I'm not angry at you."

"Andrew." He didn't listen to her, leaving the room, leaving the house.

Instantly, I shot out of there, pushing through the front door behind him and rushing down the steps. I managed to grab his arm, to spin him around, but he avoided my gaze, keeping his head up. "Drew . . ." I trailed off, not even knowing what to say.

He gave me a tight smile. "I'll see you tomorrow, right?"

He didn't want to talk. He didn't want to speak about it until he was ready, and I had to be okay with that. Suddenly, he held out his fist. I bumped it back reluctantly. He walked off, down the long driveway and out of my view.

A comforting presence approached me from behind. Sam wrapped his arms around my waist, putting his chin on my shoulder. "Jasmine?" I asked, turning in his arms to look past him to the door. No one was there.

"She was going to find her brother. Said she would speak to you when you wanted to speak to her."

"I'm not angry with her," I admitted. I wasn't. What she had just done had been hard. I knew that it had taken everything in her to do.

"I know," Sam said. "She knows that. But she probably knows how torn you are between the two of them, Hazel."

God. "Today was so stressful," I breathed out, dropping my head onto his shoulder.

Sam rested his locked fingers on my back as he supported my weight. "You can say that again."

"Sam?"

Just when I thought this long day couldn't get any longer.

We broke apart and twisted to face the girl standing on top of the front staircase.

Tall, with fair skin and brown hair in waves down to the middle of her back. Pretty features that had graced billboards and runways. Features that typically scowled once she spotted me now brightened at the sight of the person holding me. "Sam."

She breathed his name in a way that would have sounded like glee, but apparently only I could see the loving delight in her eyes. Ugh.

"Lexi!" Surprise coated Sam's voice as she bounced down the stairs with open arms. My boyfriend hugged her back, a respectable amount of time that she attempted to make last. Because of course she was still in love with him even after he had told her that nothing would ever happen between them. Sam didn't seem to notice that. "I didn't think I would see you tonight."

"I managed to get an early flight back, but I still missed most of it. I just got bombarded by questions from your mom and aunt." I wasn't sure if Sam's mom even liked me, but of course she'd bonded with Alexis. I had to shake that off, but the irritation was rising.

Alexis's eyes drifted to me, down to where Sam's hand was linked with mine then back up to my eyes. She covered up her distaste well enough, but I still saw it. "It's nice seeing you again, Mabel."

Before I even had a chance to respond, she walked back inside. "She's kidding me, right? She's still calling me Mabel?"

"Baby, ignore her. She's just playing around," Sam said. I huffed. Forget her.

My gaze went to where Andrew had walked off in the distance then back to the house where Jasmine was probably asking Drake if they could leave.

Sam broke my attention with a brush of his hand. "Do you want to stay outside for a bit?"

I gave him a once-over. That dress shirt alone was not warm enough to be outside for this long. "You're going to get cold."

"That's okay," he reassured me, enveloping me in his arms and completely shutting out any of the freezing chill from reaching me. "It's all going to be okay."

"How do you know?" I said, muffled against his shoulder.

He didn't answer me.

19
CALEB IS A GOD

Getting my period after having the longest day ever was a terrible, unwelcome addition.

I was camped in my bed the following morning, mentally fighting the discomfort in my lower abdomen. The blinds of my window were closed, blocking any light from entering. The only brightness came from the screen of my phone as I stared at the delivered messages I had sent Jasmine since last night. She had disappeared afterward like I'd expected, along with her brother, who must have taken her home. Although the radio silence sucked, I knew she wanted to be alone, and I just hoped that she'd seen my messages of support, that she knew I wasn't angry with her.

Either way, I was going to see her before she left. That was a promise.

Suddenly, my door opened, and when light flooded my room, I almost hissed like a snake, pulling the covers over my head.

I could hear Sam set his helmet on the table along with something else. His footsteps were light as he walked over and placed his hand on my head over the covers. "You okay?"

I pushed my head up over the covers with a frown as he crouched next to my bed. "I hate periods."

"I know," he said in a gentle tone. His hair was extra bedhead today, and dark circles were present beneath his eyes. He had probably gone for a run this morning, but he'd still come all the way over here when he could have slept in despite being tired.

I pulled myself down to the ground with him, my carpet feeling extra prickly today as I leaned into his hug, closing my eyes. "I see you brought the helmet."

"Oh yeah, I really missed BS."

"You should have just taken her with you to university."

"Mum said it was the car or the motorcycle. The car was more convenient. I was lucky enough that the bike was able to be shipped over here when I first moved anyway." Sam shifted me in his arms once again.

"Nonna said she's hoping you come over for card night tonight."

"I'll be there," he promised. "I need to beat her at poker."

I chuckled against his chest, loosening myself from his hold. I still had to get on with my day. "Good luck with that. I'll be back."

By the time I returned from the shower, Sam was lying on my bed, twisting a soccer ball in his hands while Emma and Justin sat on my bedroom floor, all three of them talking. "Are we having a secret meeting?"

Emma gasped excitedly at my presence. "Hi!"

"Hi!" I grinned at her as I put my stuff back. "I've barely had a chance to talk to you. My brother keeps hogging you all to himself."

Justin was about to launch a pillow at my head when Sam quickly took it from him, tucking it behind his own. "We playing on the Xbox later?" Justin asked.

I nodded, and he flashed me a smile before Emma spoke up. "Mace, you know my sister is here, right?"

Ugh. "Yeah, I saw her last night."

Justin started chuckling. "You still don't like her."

"She doesn't like *me*," I clarified.

"Why can't you guys just get along?"

The question came from Sam.

And that specific question made me bristle from where I was standing. Maybe it was the words themselves. Maybe it was the nonchalant way he had said them.

"They will never get along," Justin added. "Some people don't click. Macy and Alexis haven't since day one."

"And that will continue for the rest of our lives." I glanced at Sam. "We're been over this a hundred times."

"Especially during the summer." Justin made a face because he knew how much Alexis annoyed me whenever it came to Sam. "And we all know why."

"What do you mean 'we all know why'?" Sam sat up, his eyes narrowing at my little brother. "She's over me."

"She's over you?" Emma scoffed. I mentally high-fived her. Cheered, actually—had a whole poster for her and everything. "She probably spent the whole plane ride over here talking about you to the person next to her."

"She's over me," Sam repeated, flicking the ball in Justin's direction. My brother caught the ball as Sam fell back against the pillows of my bed once again. He crossed one leg over the other in complete peace. I was not a fan of his peace at the moment.

"You sure?" I couldn't help but bite back.

Sam didn't comment on my attitude, his tone light as he said, "Hey, I'm Sam Cahill, and although I completely understand why she *wouldn't* be over me—"

"Continue that sentence," I snapped. Sam's smirk disappeared when he realized I was serious. Emma and Justin exchanged a glance that made me take a deep breath. I wasn't going to start something with him while other people were in the room. But this was not a day to joke with me. This was not a day for him to boost his ego, especially in a way that was starting to make me more agitated than I ever wanted to be.

Sam's expression softened, an apology in his eyes. "Hazel, even if she *was* still into me, I wouldn't care because she's not you."

Because she's not you.

Any other day, I would have felt myself let go of any pent-up irritation.

Today was not that day, even though I was less annoyed than a second ago. I knew I wasn't like her. I didn't doubt what Sam felt for me. But I didn't doubt the lengths Alexis would go to in order to be with Sam either.

In my hand, my phone buzzed with a message, one that had come through from one of the two people I really wanted to see.

Stiffly, I walked over to Sam and pressed a kiss to his cheek. "I'm going to Andrew's."

"What about breakfast? I got you some." He gestured to the

backpack next to his helmet and gave me a breathtaking smile I averted my eyes from seeing.

I grabbed the bag he had come in with and took a sweater—one of his—pulling it on. "I'll see you later."

"Hazel, are you mad?" he yelled once I had left the room.

At how you are when it comes to Alexis? That I actually know Alexis is still obsessed with you and that we will never get along because she probably thinks I took you away from her?

"No, I'm not mad," I shouted back.

I was mad.

But I had a best friend to talk to first.

~

I almost collided with Andrew's little sister, Riley, when I made my way into the Prescott household. Waving at Andrew's parents, who were used to me barging into their house, I stomped my way up the stairs to their son's room. I opened the door to find Andrew lying down on his bed, facing the ceiling, throwing a tiny football up in the air.

As I closed the door behind me, he let out a sigh, shuffling over on the bed. I lay down next to him. The familiarity of his room—the blue walls, the posters of football players and soccer players, the gaming chair in the corner—brought back too many memories from over the years.

"You know what I thought that day we all went our separate ways?" he asked, still throwing the football up in the air before catching it.

"What?" I questioned, watching the football.

"I thought that there was actually a chance that none of

us would truly talk to one another like we used to do in high school. I thought eventually we'd be like, 'Yeah, that was just my friend from when I was younger.'"

"Do you still think it's going to happen?" I inquired.

"I definitely don't think that's going to happen between us. I mean, we took baths together when we were like two. You're the sister I'll never let go of no matter how hard I try, Mace."

"I don't think that'll happen between us either," I agreed with a snort. "We've never really had a rough patch with each other."

"Outside video games."

"True," I said. "We never really had terrible arguments or awkward conversations. We've always had a really good bond."

"I thought I would have the same with Jasmine," he said lowly.

He caught the football before turning to me, cradling it to his chest. "Yeah," I concurred with a whisper. "I thought you would too."

"You know, I thought about it a lot. That this whole long-distance thing wouldn't work." Andrew turned his head toward the ceiling again. "That something would come between us."

I stayed silent as he threw the football up in the air and caught it and then repeated the action. He continued talking. "It was noticeable. The first week, every day, we would talk. She would tell me about what was happening and all the people she'd met. She mentioned the other guy too. Then, as weeks went by, the conversations grew shorter and different. And then it seemed like we weren't talking. But I was trying to talk. And when we did eventually talk, it was like two different conversations that had nothing to do with each other."

"But you told me you were fine."

"I was just happy she'd called me," he confessed. "I thought we'd be fine."

Andrew caught the ball and threw it to the other side of his room. We watched it hit the lamp, and the lamp fell to the carpet with a heavy thump. Andrew didn't even bother picking it up when he sat up, bringing his knees up to his chest. "Don't pick sides."

"What?"

"Don't pick a side," he repeated. "Between her and me."

"I wasn't going to pick a side," I told him. "I came here because I knew you needed someone to talk to and were probably going to shut everyone else out. I'm going to be here for you both no matter the situation."

"Okay," Andrew mumbled. Side by side, we settled into silence as I gave him my presence and a shoulder to lean on if he wanted.

"Change is weird," he suddenly said.

My brain brought me back to the mark I'd received before I'd arrived home. "Tell me about it."

"No, I mean compare this day to last year. In November." Andrew and Jasmine hadn't been dating. She probably would have been trying to drag us to watch another *Star Wars* movie with her. Andrew would have tried to get us to play a game instead, and I would have wanted us to go to the rec center to play soccer. And then we'd have gone to school and repeat.

"We'd probably be at the rec center right now," Andrew said, as if reading my mind. "And then you would have been trying to kick my balls whenever I pissed you off."

"The only time I did that was an accident," I declared.

"An accident that has probably happened a hundred times since we were five. You're so lucky I can still—"

"Nope. Nope. I do not want to hear the last words of that sentence," I told him, putting my hands over my ears.

Andrew took my hands off my ears, laughing. "On that note, I'm guessing you and Sam haven't exactly . . ."

"No," I said.

"Can I ask why?" Andrew asked. "Is it the whole Catholic and celibacy thing, because last I checked, you weren't religious. I mean, you're in love with him, right? And if you think he's the right person—"

"He is," I said without any doubt. Andrew's eyebrows rose at my certainty. "I don't know how to explain it. It's just . . . for me and Sam, I feel like sex has never really been a priority. For me, specifically. But I know when the time is right, it'll happen. I haven't given it much thought, I guess. Does that make sense?"

"Kind of," Andrew agreed. "Well, do what you want. As long as he isn't pressuring you into anything."

"He isn't," I assured him.

"Good," Andrew said before laughing a little.

"What? What's funny?"

"It's just I know that you're on your thing . . ." He trailed off, that stupid smile on his face. "And we're talking about *sex*. And I know girls are supposedly really horn—"

"We are *not* discussing this." My face was flaming up. "I don't care how close we are, I'm not discussing this with you. Not now. Not ever."

Andrew's shoulders shook with laughter at how uncomfortable I suddenly was at the topic. I cracked a smile because he seemed a little bit happier than he'd been when I'd walked in here. "Sorry."

"Shut up," I mumbled. When he eventually stopped laughing,

a shaky breath left him. I glanced up at him. "Are you going to be okay? I'm just asking because I know you, and you're taking it a little differently than I thought you would."

He looked at me. His eyes zoned out for a second, but they focused back on me. "I don't know, Mace," he admitted. "I haven't really processed it yet. I really don't know."

Understandable. Andrew's attention was now on the bag that was lying on the foot of his bed. "What's that?"

"Sam brought me food or something," I muttered.

Andrew grabbed it, looking at me skeptically. "You sound like you're mad at him."

"I kind of am."

"Why?"

"I don't think he understands how much Alexis likes him and hates me."

"The observant Samuel Cahill is oblivious to one girl's feelings for him? Like how it was when she came to visit during the summer?"

"Yes." A bitter taste suddenly filled my mouth. "What an idiot. Samuel Henry Cahill, that is."

"Go talk to him."

"No," I said seriously, grabbing a muffin from the bag. Apple cinnamon. He really knew me. "No matter how good these muffins are, I am not going to talk to him until he understands the problem at hand."

~

"Those muffins were really good and cramp-relieving," I said to Sam as we walked into the living room of the Cahill house.

"Really?" he asked me a little cautiously.

"Okay." I put a hand up. "I'm not a ticking time bomb, Sam. I'm not going to explode."

"I'm sorry for whatever I did wrong, but I still don't understand why you're mad at me."

"Sam, conciliate your girlfriend before someone loses their baby maker machine." Caleb spoke up from the couch, his feet on the pillow on Jacob's lap.

"What does that mean?" Jacob asked as Jon Ming entered the room with a Red Bull in his hands.

"Baby maker machine?" Caleb asked. "Jacob, I know you're *slow* but—"

"Not *that*, asshole. I meant *conciliate*."

"You know, when you stop someone from being mad or angry."

"Well, sorry for not knowing what that meant, Mister Dictionary," Jacob grumbled, opting to scroll through his phone.

Caleb rolled his eyes, and Brandon looked at us from the other couch, muting the TV. "What's going on?"

"So." I sat up. "You saw how the she-devil was here, right?"

Stevie perked up, putting her phone, on which she had definitely been watching a random show, in her pocket. "Wait, is it that bitch that makes moves on your boyfriend even when you're there?"

Sam shot Stevie a dry look. "She's not a bitch, and she's just a family friend."

Brandon said, "Yeah, she's not a bitch and—"

"And Caleb isn't sexy." Caleb chuckled. "No offense, Sam."

Andrew took a seat on the ground in front of Brandon, his knees up against his chest. "Man, if she's your friend, then she's your friend. Macy's not going to stop a friendship, but you should really understand Alexis's possible intentions and that she and Macy are just never going to get along."

Sam did not say anything for a couple of seconds, and I noticed he was staring at Andrew and had probably noticed the tone in his voice. "What are her intentions?"

"That she wants you!" Stevie and I both exclaimed at him.

"Okay, okay, you can be right about her wanting me even though she told me she didn't see me like that anymore," Sam said, but those words only made me bristle. He had to have deluded himself into believing Alexis was not in love with him. That was the only explanation. "We're friends, and she knows that. Practically family."

As if my thoughts were telepathic, Caleb glanced at me. Of course he did. We both knew something no one else in this room knew about.

It didn't bother me as much as it could have bothered a lot of people, but I knew you wouldn't normally have your first time with someone you considered *family*.

"But why does that make you mad?" Sam asked as Caleb got up, entering the kitchen. "Because I asked why you guys won't get along?"

Stevie and Brandon let out simultaneous groans at Sam. I didn't even say anything. I walked over to an empty couch, leaning my head back. The muffins hadn't been as effective as I'd hoped they would be. "I hate periods," I said under my breath.

Jacob overheard me, his eyes rounding as if an alarm was sounding as he turned to Sam. "Shit, man, you need to apologize right now."

"Sam," Brandon said as I put a pillow over my face to block out everything and everyone, "Macy and Alexis will possibly never be friends."

"Never," I said loudly into the pillow.

"And she's been your girlfriend for what now?"

"Almost seven months," I said again into the pillow.

"As your girlfriend of seven months who's in love with you, she's not exactly ever going to be friends with the girl you call a friend, because she—"

"—absolutely does not like me," I said, not even stopping myself because of how irritated I was with the situation and with my body.

"Now, Macy doesn't want to ruin any friendships. She's not going to be that girlfriend that gets in the way of any of your friendships, considering you wouldn't do that to her."

"Keep telling him." I started snapping my fingers. "Say it for the people in the back."

"Whether you think Alexis is into you is one thing, but questioning why they won't get along after it was obvious over the summer that they simply don't click is another. It's annoying to Macy because she's told you that time and time again, she's made an effort to get along with Alexis, but it has backfired. You just need to understand that."

"Someone give this man an award," I told them, mentally clapping for Brandon for saying what was going through my brain.

The pillow got taken away from me, and I squinted my eyes due to the change in the light. I noticed Caleb handing me a container of unopened strawberry ice cream with a small, sympathetic smile on his face. I felt like giving him a hug when he sat beside me but forgot about it when he handed me the spoon and I opened the ice cream, instantly digging in.

On the other hand, Sam placed himself at my other side. He put an arm around me, and I didn't even bother to pull away from him at the moment because of the ice cream and his body heat. "I'm sorry," he whispered, kissing my forehead.

"I know," I said into his shirt.

"There's a reason why I don't care or do anything to stop Alexis. It's like I told you before, there's only you, and if she's into me then she's into me. It doesn't affect my life because I'm only in love with you."

"Aw, the happy couple," Caleb said on the other side of me.

"It's not like it was a fight," I said.

Caleb rolled his eyes. "Oh, I think we all know a Sam and Macy fight when we see one, especially when it's small and pointless."

"Remember when you guys got mad at each other over painting Sam's room and the type of blue it should be?" Stevie reminded us.

"You guys didn't talk to each other for three days over that stupid argument," Brandon said.

"What about that time you had that dumb argument when we went bowling once? Never going again because of you two," Jon Ming said.

"It wasn't *that* bad," I protested.

"I had to change my shirt three times because of your and Sam's unhealthy competitiveness." *Yeah . . . our arguments have often involved food fights.*

"I wanted to win," I said.

"And I wasn't going to let you," Sam said.

"Well, neither of you losers won, because last I checked *I* did," Caleb said proudly. "Meanwhile, Caleb here is waiting for a well-deserved thank-you for bringing the princess the ice cream that the damsel in distress failed to."

"I bought her muffins," Sam said defensively.

"And? Do you know your girlfriend? Ice cream, man. It's always ice cream. I bought it for her and stuck it in your freezer when I got here."

"It's not like I could give her ice cream for breakfast." Sam scowled.

Stevie glanced down at me with a grin. "Your coach is going to kill you."

"What my coach doesn't know won't hurt him." I beamed back.

Caleb turned to Sam. "So your publicity is increasing."

Sam whipped his head to look at his best friend. "Have you been stalking me, or did you go into my Instagram account again?"

"*Both*. Putting 'Caleb Is a God' in your bio really boosted my self-esteem."

Sam took his phone out of his pocket as Calcb put his own phone back in his. "I haven't seen you get this much attention since you stuck pads all over Ivan's room back in England. I don't think I've ever seen your mom so mad before in my life."

Sam made a face. "She wasn't that mad."

Caleb glanced at all of us. "She was *furious*. Told him he shouldn't be wasting sanitary products like that."

"He broke my PSP," Sam explained. "I was pissed."

"How did she find out it was you?" Stevie asked.

Sam started explaining the story when Jacob looked around. "Wait, where's Jasmine? She's the only one missing."

"She's with her brother," I lied. She had yet to answer my messages, so I didn't know, but it was my best guess. My attention trailed over to Andrew, who was changing the channel on the remote really aggressively at the mention of her name. He'd said he wasn't angry, but clearly that remote was feeling it right now.

"What?" Austin asked. "I thought she would spend the day with you, Andrew. At least until we all leave."

Andrew grunted, getting up and heading toward the kitchen. "We all thought a lot of things."

"What happened?" Jon Ming asked, blocking his way out of the room.

"Guys, leave him alone," Caleb said beside me in a serious tone.

"Nah," Jacob cut in. "Obviously something's bothering him, so we want to know."

"Can I go microwave popcorn in peace?" Andrew asked in a monotone voice.

"No, what's going on? You've been looking down ever since you stepped into the house."

Andrew's eyes flicked to the ceiling before they moved on to Jacob. He was getting more annoyed by the second. "Jacob, leave me alone."

"No, we—"

"Okay, you want to know what's going on?" Andrew snapped. Oh God.

Jacob put his hands out. "Drew, chill."

"I can't just 'chill.' My girlfriend almost cheated on me and broke up with me, okay? That's what's happening. So excuse me if I don't exactly want to talk about it. Now, can I go microwave popcorn? Thanks." He stomped out of the room.

The entire room was silenced, and I got up, handing the ice cream back to Caleb as I entered the kitchen. "Andrew—"

I stopped myself. Liz was sitting at the island on a stool staring at Andrew with a perfectly raised eyebrow before glancing at me with a smile.

I gave her a hug, taking a seat next to her as she nudged me. "Alice likes you, you know."

"Did Sam talk to you about it?" I groaned, placing my face in my hands. "Please don't tell her."

"I won't," Liz chuckled. "She does like you, she just doesn't show it."

"She doesn't show it because she doesn't talk to me, Liz." Before Liz could respond, the sound of Andrew shoving the popcorn bag into the microwave caught our attention. Then he proceeded to hit a couple of the buttons really, really hard.

"I love how you all treat my home as yours, but Andrew, try not to abuse it."

Andrew gave Liz an embarrassed smile. "Sorry, just having a rough time. How's life going, Mrs. Cahill, since your eldest is married?"

She pushed her black hair over her shoulder. "Ivan is married."

"Weird, isn't it?" I teased, and she poked me again.

"Agreed, but he's grown up," she said fondly. "If only the rest of the boys could do the same. Every time they're all together, it's chaos like no other. Phillip was so happy to have all of his favorite people back together in the same place, he wouldn't stop bouncing around and broke a vase the other day. Then he tried to blame it on Gregory, who is probably the only calm one in my vicinity when they are all together."

I laughed, and I could hear Andrew chuckle by the microwave as well. Liz closed her eyes for a second, rubbing her temple before she opened them and peered at Andrew. "But my problems don't seem to be affecting me as much as your own are affecting you, Andrew."

Andrew didn't face her; he kept his focus on the microwave, watching the timer before the ding sounded. He opened the little door, shaking his head. "My problem isn't that serious, Mrs. Cahill."

"I've told you kids a thousand times to call me Liz."

"Sorry." He smiled sheepishly. "My problem isn't that serious, Liz."

"It's serious if you were harassing my microwave."

I held in a snort as Andrew rubbed the back of his neck. "It's a relationship thing. It's not a big deal."

Liz immediately rolled her eyes while I scoffed. I was certain she was ready to give him whatever motherly advice was up her sleeve when someone walked into the kitchen.

Correction: *clicked* their way into the kitchen.

"Liz—" Alexis stopped herself from talking when she realized Andrew and I were in the room. The smile that formed for Andrew was pleasant, but in my stomach a pit was beginning to form. "Andrew, right?"

Andrew hummed in acknowledgment, and Alexis turned to me. There it was. There was the smile I was always given. If she weren't terrible at hiding how horrible it was giving me a friendly expression, it might have been nice. I should probably feel special, though. It was reserved only for me. "Mabel, good to see you again."

The feeling wasn't mutual.

20
BEGGING

In my eighteen years of life, I had met a few people that I'd disliked.

There was Michael, the sexist pig I had to see every year on account of us living in the same town and playing soccer. I hoped he'd moved.

There was Beatrice. And, well, she was Beatrice—a bully, a mean girl, and, given some of the things she'd said to Jasmine, a racist. I hoped she'd moved away from Port Meadow too.

Now there was Tanya, who was like Michael and Beatrice combined: a soccer rival (despite us being on the same team) and a queen bee bully.

But there was also Alexis.

Alexis, at whom I said fake witchcraft spells in my head every time she rolled her eyes at something I said, cut me off, or managed to actually divert Sam's attention from me. She was the girl who could never get my name right even though she knew it.

When she'd come to Port Meadow over the summer, I'd tried to be nice to her. Everyone could vouch for me, but my attempts to be nice clearly didn't work.

I got out of the kitchen, Andrew right behind me as Alexis started talking to Liz, probably trying to finagle her way into another photo shoot or something. But while walking out of the room, I almost bumped into someone. "Lucy."

"Macy," Sam's grandmother replied, giving me a hug.

Her gray hair was in a bun on her head. Her green eyes glowed as she looked at me. "Could you tell Samuel to talk to me later today?"

"Of course," I said before she moved past Andrew and me into the kitchen.

We walked back into the living room, noticing that everyone was silent the second they saw Andrew. Jacob spoke up. "Sorry, Andrew. We should've left you alone."

Andrew shrugged, sitting back down on the ground, facing the TV. "I understand."

I sat down on the ground in front of Sam, who had the spoon in his mouth and my ice cream in his hand as he eyed Andrew carefully. I took it from him, passing on his grandmother's message as Alexis came into the room. She had magazines in her hands as she stepped over me, scraping her heels over my knee and sitting next to Sam.

Then Toby entered, standing tall at the entrance, not wearing a suit today and instead opting for a T-shirt and jeans. He surveyed the room, granting me a nod of acknowledgment. Then he made his way over to me.

Why was he walking in my direction? Why was he taking a seat near me on the armrest? Why was he looking down at me?

Even Sam couldn't save me; he was too busy being in conversation with the she-devil.

"Um, hi," I said.

"Hi," Toby responded. "You're driving back tonight?"

Keep it together. He's just Sam's cousin. You like Sam's family. The boys liked you back. Win over this one too. Maybe. I don't know. "We both have practice tomorrow morning."

Toby's eyebrows went up. "How long have you played football?"

Soccer. "Since I was three."

"Competitively too?" I nodded. "You were scouted for your university team?" I nodded again. "Damn."

Everyone had teetered off to their own conversations, but Toby, with the way he spoke, the way he held himself, kept you inside his own little bubble. His voice dropped to a whisper. "I know I don't know you very well, but thank you."

I blinked. "For what?"

He stared at me for a beat longer. He didn't have to say the words out loud, but I got the gist, peeking over at Sam. "He told me you're scared of me," Toby suddenly said.

"I'm not!" I exclaimed. "I swear."

"Don't lie."

"I'm not lying!" I insisted. "You're just very serious."

"You'll get used to it." The curve of his lip made me roll my eyes. "Oh yeah, we're definitely going to get along."

"You think so? Do you play soccer?"

"Football," he corrected with a familiar smirk. "And no, I did rugby." Toby was about to say more when Jacob suddenly groaned, his voice obnoxiously loud.

"I don't want go back to school. Exams are coming up, and I feel like I'm going to fail."

"You're not going to," Austin assured him.

"Don't lie to him," Jon Ming said, half laughing.

"I'm sorry, who had the sixth-highest average in grade twelve?" Jacob snapped.

"Someone who didn't even make it to the top five," Jon Ming retorted.

Jacob waved a hand. "Who cares? School doesn't test your intelligence."

The Jacob and Jon Ming banter continued as Toby leaned toward me again. "What's his name?"

"Who?"

He raised his chin over in the direction of Austin, who was currently laughing at something Jon Ming had said. "Him."

"That's Austin," I answered. "He goes to university in Quebec."

"He speaks French?" Toby's eyes lingered on Austin. They didn't look like they were going to be pulling away anytime soon. "Interesting."

"Jon Ming speaks several languages," I noted. "He's a polyglot."

"Hmm."

He totally wasn't interested in Jon Ming.

I tuned out their conversation, trying to focus on whatever show was on the TV when I heard Sam ask Alexis a question. "Wait, so you're going to be in London eventually?"

"Yeah," she answered a little too eagerly. "I accepted the offer today. Twenty-four models from all around the world, and I'm one of three from Canada. And we're going to Milan, Paris—I can't wait. It's insane."

"That's great."

"I swear your name was mentioned too, but they said you turned them down. Why? I didn't get the chance to ask you on the phone the other day."

All the eyes in the room turned to Sam, and I tried to ignore what they were thinking. He was just talking to a friend. A friend. It wasn't that serious. Yes, Alexis was bothersome, but . . . friends talked on the phone.

"School. Football. You're going to be doing this for a month and will become a full-time model once you finish the semester. It's what you've been wanting since you were five, remember?"

Alexis laughed, the sound distracting me even further from trying to figure out the show on the television. "Yeah, I remember."

Caleb snickered, and I turned to him, confused. "What are you laughing at?"

"I'm trying to picture *you* as a model." He laughed even louder.

I closed my eyes, trying to imagine myself walking down a runway, flashing cameras trying to take pictures of me.

Nope.

"I think I would fall off the runway," I said, opening my eyes.

Andrew joined in Caleb's amusement, and I hit him in the back with my foot lightly, rolling my eyes. "Shut up."

"I'm sorry," Andrew said, chuckling, and Jacob and Jon Ming joined in. "I can imagine you falling right off the side or falling flat on your face. Thank God you play soccer."

"You're so funny," I said sarcastically.

"Do you actually want to be a model?"

Alexis's question was directed at me.

I turned around to look at her. "No. Nope. Never. Right, Liz?" I asked her as she passed by, her phone to her ear.

"The offer still stands," she said as she left the room.

"She wants you to be one?" Alexis asked in disbelief.

"Shockingly, she does," I mocked in the same tone Alexis had used. Alexis gave me a dirty look for imitating her, and I smiled in response.

"But what if you didn't play soccer? What's your plan B again?" Caleb asked.

"Anything in the chemistry field. I'm not sure yet, just a type of chemist."

"At least you don't want to be a doctor," Andrew mumbled. "You realized that instead of saving people you put people like your best friend at risk of losing the chance to ever have children and you of ever being a godmother."

I narrowed my eyes at Andrew as Sam gestured for the ice cream in my hand. I moved it out of his reach. "Caleb bought it for *me*. Not you, last time I checked."

Sam gave me a dry look, and Caleb groaned. "Just give the man the ice cream. He's begging. You don't see that often."

Sam shoved his sock-covered foot in Caleb's face, hitting him right in the cheek. "Shut up."

"Shut can't go up, prices do."

"How am I going to bear more days with you?" Sam groaned, but I could hear that smile in his voice as I handed him the tub.

"You already spent seven summers with me. Vacations too. You'll be fine with a few more days, *beggar*," Caleb taunted.

"Fuck you," Sam said before shoving the spoon in his mouth.

Caleb sighed dramatically. "I do miss our playful banter."

Alexis asked Sam another of her endless questions as I grabbed the ice cream from Sam's hand, moving over to Andrew. "Hey," I whispered.

"Hey." He had a hand to his temple. When he took it off, I realized how exhausted he seemed, judging by his heavy eyes. He probably hadn't slept much the night before. "I think I'm gonna go home."

Good idea.

"Go home. Go sleep."

He gave me a side hug. "I'll see you before I leave."

I nodded quickly when he stood up and said his goodbyes. Once we heard the front door slam, Jacob immediately joined me on the floor. "What did he mean that Jasmine almost cheated on him?"

Jon Ming, Caleb, even Stevie joined me on the ground, curious looks on their faces. "Exactly what he said. No more information on my side. Find out from them yourselves."

"I—I just don't get it," Jon Ming said. "I don't understand that kind of love. I probably never will, but isn't their type of love supposed to last in this world?"

"People fall out of love, JM. It happens," Caleb answered.

"And if they're meant to be, they'll find each other in the end, right?" Brandon asked.

"Right," Caleb confirmed. "Most relationships don't last from high school. That's why some people think dating in high school is completely unnecessary. What's the percentage? Sam?"

Sam looked down at Caleb as if he'd just asked the dumbest question on earth. "Why the hell would I know the percentage?" His eyes flicked over to me before looking at Caleb with an annoyed expression.

"You do well with numbers, I figured you would know!" Caleb defended very loudly.

"Well, do the math yourself, idiot, or how about you look it up?"

"Fine," Caleb quipped, but I could see he was too lazy to look it up. "It's probably a low percentage of people anyway."

A sudden silence, an awkward one, fell over the room. Jasmine had done something that had affected another one of our friends. I felt like all of them were going to take sides or distance themselves from her because of it. The thought made me queasy.

Stevie broke the quiet first, walking over to Caleb to crouch and run a hand through his hair. "You need a haircut."

"No, I don't," he whined. "This is what happens when you go to beauty school? You just give free makeovers?"

"No." She rolled her eyes. "It takes work, and it's more than just that, and if someone could hold Caleb still and get me scissors and a razor that would help."

"What?" he almost yelled, scrambling away from her. "I don't want a haircut!"

"I don't care. You need it."

Caleb practically screamed as Stevie pulled him up—which was impressive since she was short compared to him—and dragged him over to a bathroom. Half the room followed to watch the show, and I looked back at Sam, a hand on my camera.

I didn't change my blank expression as I watched Alexis put a hand on his bicep, talking to him and leaning a little bit closer to give him her full attention. Sam's eyes went down to the hand as she was talking, and he wordlessly took her hand off him. She looked a little bit rejected when he did that, and he stood up with confidence, moving over to help me stand up.

"You okay?" he asked me.

"Yeah," I told him, letting him take the last of the ice cream. "Let's go see Caleb freak out that his precious hair is all over the floor." Sam laughed, and we walked out as a high-pitched scream sounded from the next room.

~

"You didn't answer my messages," I said after I opened my bedroom door. My duffel bag was already slung over my shoulder, but there was no need to leave with it yet.

Jasmine stood at the threshold of my room.

"I wanted to speak face-to-face," she said, her gaze flicking down to my bag. "You're leaving."

"Yeah." I gestured for her to come in, and she closed the door behind her. "Practice in the morning. What about you?"

"It's my Reading Week, remember?" She had told me that in the summer. Sam and I's schools only had a Reading *Day* back in October. "He left, didn't he? I didn't really expect him to say goodbye anyway."

"It's Andrew, Jasmine. He may not want to talk to you now, but he'll speak to you eventually."

"I know." She rubbed her face, sitting down on my bed. God, I'd known it would be hard for her to tell him. And I realized a part of me had been angry in the moment, not at her but at her hesitation.

"I'm sorry if I put pressure on you—"

"You didn't."

"I did," I said plainly. "But he needed to know, and I was getting worried when you looked like you didn't want to tell him. I didn't really think about how difficult it would be for you. Really."

She kept her face down in her hands. "It was so hard, Mace. God, we were in the middle of Sam's room, and the way he looked at me, like he'd already seen it coming. He looked shattered. The *definition* of shattered. I hated doing that. I never wanted to do that to him of all people. But . . ."

It was inevitable, I wanted to say out loud.

And for a moment, I replayed how I'd felt when she told me: how I knew this was going to tear apart our friendship, our trio in the midst of our friends. How it would never be the same as it had once been.

Jasmine had broken up with Andrew. It would take a long time for Andrew to even speak to her again, let alone be friends with her again.

But I knew Andrew. He would one day.

Before I could reply, my dad's voice traveled up from downstairs. "Mace! They're here!"

I exhaled, grabbing my luggage in one hand as I looked at my other best friend. "Knowing Andrew as well as I do, I know he'll get past this. He'll be ready to speak to you again. And I know that you love him even if it's not in that way anymore. And he loves you back."

"Yeah?"

"Yeah," I said. "I'll let you know how he's doing. And let me know how you're doing a little more often, okay?"

"Okay," she promised. I moved my duffel bag to my back so

I could hug her tightly. She inhaled sharply, almost as if she was crying. But when she let go, there were no tears. "I'll see you soon."

"Christmas?" I asked. "And summer?"

"For sure." She squeezed my arms, trying to give me an upbeat smile. "We can do road trips like we said we should do over the summer."

"I like the sound of that," I told her.

The drive back with Peter and Sam was surprisingly quiet. As we drove through the night, no one spoke more than a couple of words. The silence was comforting, but it was also deafening as I pondered everything that had happened over the weekend. Ivan and Natasha were married *and* pregnant. Anthony had crashed the wedding, had a full-on fight with Sam, and gotten arrested. My best friends had broken up. I had been forced to see Alexis again.

Now I had to face the reality of university—and that failing grade that I had managed to push out of my brain for the weekend hit me like a flood.

If the winter break coming up would be anything like my weekend had been, I was in for one hell of a ride.

21
LOOK AT THE SIZE OF THAT THING

When Maddy and I walked into Anmol's room the following Wednesday, I was greeted by motivational words on her desk and walls, her books organized on the shelves, photos of her friends and family back home, and a dirty look. From Anmol.

I froze, standing at the threshold. "Now what did I do?"

"She hasn't told you what happened over the weekend, has she?" Maddy asked her, plopping down on Anmol's bed. Anmol scowled in confirmation as they both turned back to me. "Join the club. She said she wasn't going to say anything until we were all together."

"It had better be good," Anmol muttered, closing the door behind me as her phone went off in her pocket.

Glancing at it, I watched her scowl soften as she read the message. When she started smiling as she texted the person—no doubt a tall blond third-year who played on the Hayes soccer team—Maddy launched one of her pillows in her direction. It struck Anmol on her side, and she flinched. "What?"

"Did you not go on a date this weekend?" Maddy asked.

"Didn't *you*?"

Huh? I gasped, turning to Maddy. "You did *what*?"

Maddy closed her eyes patiently before she glared at Anmol from the bed. "Anmol."

"You did!" Anmol pointed at her, looking at me. "She did! And guess who it was with?"

My jaw fell open as I approached Maddy, grabbing the fallen pillow on the way. "You went on a date with George, and you didn't tell me?"

She screamed as I started batting her lightly with the pillow. "You don't even *like* talking about romance! Besides, I was going to say something *after* you told us about your weekend. Anmol ruined it."

We both turned to Anmol, who threw her hands up in the air. "How did this turn back on me?"

"Just tell us about your date, and then I'll tell you about mine." We gathered on Anmol's bed as she shared every single detail of her skating date with Derek. Anmol looked more flushed than after soccer practice.

"You really like him," Maddy noticed. "Or *still* like him."

"We're taking things slow," she said, beaming at this point before moving it over to Maddy, who'd had a volleyball tournament over the weekend that included George, who was covering the game as a photographer for the school newspaper.

"It was just coffee," Maddy said. "We're talking."

"*Talking*." Anmol snorted. "Okay."

Maddy didn't argue. The two of them were sitting across

from me, Maddy's head on Anmol's shoulder as they brought their attention to me. "And *your* weekend?"

My two nosy friends wanted all the details, but I stuck to the most important one. I told them about Andrew and Jasmine—despite all the excitement of the weekend, to me that was the most life-altering part. When I broke the news, Maddy's jaw fell to the floor and Anmol's eyebrows rose high to the ceiling. Their expressions stuck until I finished, and they seemed to have a hard time processing what I'd said.

Somehow, Maddy recovered first. "Are you okay?"

Me? "Forget *me.*"

"You're their best friend," Anmol said.

Good point. Neither had reached out since Sunday, but I was giving them both space to do what they wanted.

"I don't think I'm ready to talk about it," I admitted.

The two of them nodded. Easy as that. No further prying, simply waiting until I was ready. Anmol cleared her throat. "Okay, moving on, anything else happen?"

I relayed all the information they wanted, but when I mentioned Anthony, Maddy gasped. "That greasy-looking guy from the party? Oh God, I knew he was bad news. Is Sam okay?"

"Yeah, he's all right," I said.

"You've had an eventful weekend," Anmol mumbled. "Any good news?"

"One of Macy's hot friends is going to come over in a couple weeks for his birthday and will be staying with Sam," Maddy said.

Anmol's eyebrows rose with interest while I rolled my eyes. "It's just Caleb."

"And he's hot." Maddy was already pulling out her phone.

"It's Caleb."

She handed her phone to Anmol. "He's sexy."

"Again, it's Caleb."

Anmol glanced at me with an apologetic face. "Sorry, Mace, I'm going to have to agree with Maddy on this one."

"Ew." I shuddered.

"Is he staying for a while?"

"Yeah, for about a week," I said. "He wants to spend his birthday here."

"Doesn't he have school?" Maddy asked.

"Yeah." But from the conversations I'd had with Caleb, none involving school, I didn't really think that was going to last long. Most of what I had seen him do all weekend, or whenever we video called, was write. Typing on his laptop, writing in his notebook, no textbooks in sight.

Was he even doing any schoolwork?

"I miss one lecture and I'm lost," Anmol stated. "He can afford to miss a whole week?"

Now, that was a *really* good question.

~

The opportunity to ask Caleb came about two weeks later on his birthday, November 27. I bounced my way out of the elevator that Thursday evening, looking down at my phone in my hands. I had recently received another midterm grade. This one was a good one—not the sort of grades I'd gotten in high school, but not a fail either.

Sam's Converse shoes and Caleb's sneakers were out on the carpet, dusted with snow, letting me know they had recently returned. Quietly walking into the kitchen, I pulled out what I'd brought from my duffel bag and placed it in the fridge. Laughter echoed from down the hallway.

I followed the sound to outside Sam's room, where he and Caleb were seated on the bed. Sam wore a thick sweater, and from what I could see Caleb wasn't wearing a shirt. I didn't question it and decided to hang back, realizing they hadn't seen me. "That guy didn't see it coming," Caleb gasped, he and Sam laughing even harder, making a smile come to my face.

Caleb wiped under his eyes. "This has been such a great day. I mean, I got to spend the day with you, man."

"Not to mention you almost fell off the bridge."

"I got thirty bucks, didn't I?" He waved the money in Sam's face. "No, seriously, it's been a great day. Thanks."

"Any time."

Caleb's face was thoughtful, and he rubbed a hand over his jaw. "It's November, and the last time I saw you before the wedding was in August. We haven't been apart that long for a while.

"Yeah," Sam agreed. "Even during the summer back in Port Meadow, my parents couldn't keep the three of us apart."

Caleb chuckled. "I remember visiting you and Beth every time there was a break. Even though we went to different high schools, we still managed to talk to each other every single day."

"When you'd come over to Aunt Liz and Uncle Vince's house. And you would walk into the house, screaming my name and—"

"Beth would jump on my back, thinking she could surprise me every time." Caleb's face scrunched up, eyes drifting off a bit. "She never did. But I would end up carrying her up the stairs on my back anyway."

"And you two would barge into my room, most of the time

laughing about something. And I would try to improve my math skills even during summer break—"

"You were the smartest guy I knew. Still are. You studied quadratics when most were learning the importance of a line in math, thinking it was stupid."

"What about you in English? Or your writing in general? You have an insane way with words. You would always be writing whether we were all talking or eating or brushing our teeth."

"Did you just compliment me?" Caleb gasped dramatically, and Sam reached over, smacking him upside the head.

"It's your birthday; I figured you should get at least one compliment from me today."

A small smile sat on Caleb's face. "*Three months.* Three months without my best friend. I really did miss you."

I figured Sam would crack a joke, brush it off, or roll his eyes. But he didn't. "I missed you too," he said, and as if it couldn't get any more shocking, Sam leaned forward, giving Caleb a hug.

Caleb hugged him back, and I put my hands over my mouth and nose, unable to keep from smiling at the sight. Quickly taking my camera and holding it up, I took multiple pictures of the two hugging.

Sam glanced at me over Caleb's shoulder. "Hazel."

"Sorry to interrupt your budding bromance," I said, putting my camera down and stepping into the room. "Happy birthday, Caleb."

He grinned, letting go of Sam to give me one of his lung-squashing hugs. "Thank you."

When I pulled away, I realized Caleb was not only not wearing a shirt—he also wasn't wearing pants. As he sat back down on the bed, reclining so his back was on the comforter, I realized his boxers were blue . . . with ducks. I couldn't believe I recognized them. "Really? You're still wearing those?"

"My ass looks great in these," he said. "They show my pronounced buttocks."

"You did not just say *buttocks*," I said deadpan, staring at the idiot in front of me.

"What would you prefer, gluteus ma—" I stopped him by taking my duffel bag and dropping it on top of his body, making him whine.

"So," I asked once he stopped groaning, "how does it feel to be eighteen?"

Caleb tilted his head to the side, pushing my duffel bag to the floor. "I feel the same as I did yesterday. Although, there is something I want to do that will make me feel like I'm a legal adult."

"Buy a lottery ticket?"

He made a face. "No. But wait, did you get me a cake?"

It didn't matter if I answered; Caleb had already bolted out of the room without me responding to his question.

"Caleb!"

"I'm going to give you two five minutes alone, and then I want me time!" he yelled, running down the hallway and into the kitchen.

All Sam did was chuckle as he lay down on the bed, extending a hand in my direction.

I took it easily after closing the door. "Today was good?"

"Today was great. You?"

"I have a paper due next Friday and I'm almost done, so that's fine."

"When was the paper assigned?"

"Like four hours ago."

"And you're almost done?"

"One of my classes was canceled. I got lucky and felt really productive," I said as I walked over to him. Caleb was probably going to be devouring the cupcakes I'd brought. I didn't expect anything less from the guy.

He reached his arms out, and I gladly stepped into them. He pulled me into a position where my legs were by his sides. "You ready for exams?"

"No," I told him without hesitation.

He laughed, his hands coming up and holding my face. "You'll be okay. If you weren't stressing out, that's when I think there'd be a problem." Me stressing and him acting like an exam was nothing. Maybe that's why I hadn't told him about the bad grade.

Forget the bad grade, you're okay. You're doing better.

Until I was contemplating when I could schedule a breakdown but couldn't between practices, the gym, training more and training harder while studying, and then repeat. While stressing about my friends who still hadn't spoken to each other.

"Hey." His fingers brushed my cheek, gaining my attention with ease. "You okay?"

"Stressed."

Sam cupped my face with his hands. "You're going to do great, Hazel. I know it."

Did he, though? Or did he think I was the same student I had been in high school, the one who only got good grades? Who had never received a failing grade in her entire life? Who balanced both soccer and school with ease because it had once been second nature? Now it didn't feel that way.

The more I thought about it, the more he was going to want

to bring up what was going on in my head. I didn't want him to do that. Instead, I leaned forward, pressing my lips against his.

Sam reciprocated by kissing me back slowly, but that's not what I wanted. I kissed him hard and felt his grip on me tighten as my hands roamed over his shirt. I needed to feel something, anything, and his shirt was getting in the way. I ignored how eager I seemed considering we had been in this position many times, but today I was antsy.

I tugged at his shirt, and he complied. Sam made me get off him, removing his shirt and throwing it to the other side of the room. Before I could see his torso, he stood, kissing me with full force. My breath was knocked out of me, but I didn't care; I was enveloped by the sensation of his lips against mine. Before I knew it, my back was against the bed and he was crawling over me, his hands bringing the zipper of my sweater down.

When my sweater was thrown aside, he pulled away, both of us panting with him above me, his weight balanced on his forearms. "Hazel."

"What?" I asked quickly.

He moved himself off me, staring at me. "What's wrong?"

"Nothing," I assured him.

"You . . ." Sam ran his fingers through his hair, blinking several times. "All right, Hazel. We don't really talk about this, but I need you to answer me, yeah?"

"What?"

"On a scale of one to ten, how ready do you think you are to have sex with me?"

He was right: we really didn't talk about it. I felt like we had an understanding, but we didn't really speak about it out loud. Part of the problem was, I was confused about my thoughts, so

I couldn't put them into words; if I couldn't explain my feelings to myself, how could I explain them to him? "It's not that I don't want to—"

"That's not the question," he said, looking at me with those intense eyes of his. "How ready would you be? Answer honestly."

I tried to look somewhere else in the room—which was suddenly hot—but Sam gently turned my face back to his. I swallowed, wondering if he would be offended by my answer.

"Six," I blurted out.

Sam analyzed me for a beat before he chuckled. He *laughed.* Irritation surged within me, causing me to use his pillow to get him to stop. Instead, he laughed even harder, pushing the pillow down. "Did you think I would be mad at that answer?"

"No, but I thought I'd get a different reaction than that."

"It's not like I don't understand. I really do. I've told you before, and I'll say it again. If you want to wait, then I want to wait, even if it's until the day we're married or on our honeymoon in the Bahamas."

I couldn't help it when the corners of my lips quirked. "Who said I wanted our honeymoon to be in the Bahamas?"

"Okay, wherever the hell you want it to be; I don't care as long as you're there." He squeezed my hip, and I pulled myself up, taking his bottom lip between my teeth, a move he loved. I could hear him groan in frustration, pulling away so his lips trailed down the side of my neck.

I could feel his teeth graze against the juncture of my neck and shoulder, making me push myself closer to him, if that was even possible. I could feel my fingertips burn where my hands were touching his skin. He pressed a kiss to a spot under my ear, and I sucked in a sharp breath, feeling him smile against my skin.

He looked up at me under his eyelashes, and that stupid smirk was on his face. I stared at him, feeling a little light-headed. "What?"

"Nothing," he said, but he held my eyes with his gaze, which sent a shiver down my spine.

After a moment, he leaned forward, continuing his kisses along my neck and making me tilt my head back. I knew someone would interrupt us. Trust me, I knew. I enjoyed the moment while it lasted, but I knew someone would interrupt us.

So when Caleb came into the room, I expected Sam to instantly pull off me as his best friend stilled at the threshold, staring at us. "Did I interrupt something?" His eyes flickered around the room innocently.

My face, which was already flushed, got even hotter when Sam moved his lips off my neck, a loud *pop* sounding through the room.

Sam ran his thumb over his slightly swollen bottom lip as he got off me. "What do you need, Caleb?"

"I was wondering if you would like to give me my early present now or later."

"What early present?" I asked, trying to regain my breath as best I could, sitting up.

"We always give one small present early before the real one on the day," Caleb explained. "But Sam had a busy day filled with classes and studying yesterday, so he said he'd give it to me earlier today."

Sam nodded, observing Caleb. "I got you a new set of boxers."

"Really?" Caleb asked wide-eyed, and I couldn't help but laugh at his excitement.

There was even a smile playing on Sam's lips. "Wait." Sam

reached over into his nightstand and pulled out a wrapped gift, which he tossed to Caleb.

Caleb flipped the package over in his hands, looking at the note on top. "'Because you have the worst underpants taste, Sam.' Awwww," Caleb said, making me laugh harder.

Caleb tore open the package and sat down next to me on the bed. "Oh my God, Macy, look. These ones have cows on them. These ones have a frog. These ones have frogs *and* ducks. Sam?"

"What?" Sam asked, glancing at him from the other side of me.

"You really love me." Caleb sniffed dramatically.

Sam rolled his eyes when Caleb leapt over me to give him a hug. I got out of the bed, trying to put my hair in place. "I need some water."

"I bet you do," said Caleb as Sam punched him.

I leaned over to kiss Sam before heading out of the room. I wished I had waited a couple of seconds before doing so because what I saw probably traumatized me for life.

"Oh my God!" I held my hand up to my eyes, wishing I could unsee what I'd just seen.

"What?" Concern filled Sam's tone. "What happened?"

When Caleb laughed loudly, I held my hand away to block my view of Peter as I turned to face Sam. Sam looked annoyed, his eyes up at the ceiling as he tried not to take in his cousin's lack of clothing. "Why the hell are you naked?"

"I was just going to go to the balcony and—"

"Wait, were you going to do the thing where you want to feel all free and shit?" Sam asked, shaking his head, his eyes closed by now. So this was what Sam had meant when he'd explained that Peter liked walking around naked.

"You do that too?" Caleb asked, and it was then I realized that Peter and Caleb were alike in more ways than I'd noticed.

"Yeah!" Peter said. I could hear the slap of a high five, and I groaned, wanting Peter to leave.

"Wow, Macy."

"What?" I asked, making sure not to look at Peter.

"That sure is a dark hickey on your neck. Look at the *size* of that thing."

"Sam, were you trying to brand her, or were you a bite away from making your girlfriend a vampire?" Caleb said, and I glanced over at him, rolling my eyes while swatting his hands away from my neck.

"Shut up," I told him before turning back to Peter and remembering that he was naked. Putting my hands on my eyes, I asked him, "You realize how cold it is outside, right?"

"Yeah, but the outdoor Jacuzzi was just installed. Life is good," Peter said, and I could hear the sound of retreating footsteps. I took my hands off my eyes too quickly because the view of Peter's butt greeted me as he walked farther down the hall.

"Why do I come here?" I muttered.

"Definitely not to see Peter's dick, that's for sure." Caleb grinned, walking in the opposite direction as Peter.

Sam and I exchanged glances. My boyfriend crossed his arms and followed Caleb down the hall. "So, Caleb, what exactly do you have in mind for tonight?"

"It's not like it's something I've never done before."

"That scares me," I admitted.

Caleb waved a hand, grinning widely. "Now that I'm eighteen, I want to go to a pub and drink legally for the first time."

"But you have to be nineteen to get in—we're in Ontario, not Quebec."

Caleb threw himself dramatically onto the couch. "Great. I turned eighteen in the wrong province."

Sam rubbed the back of his neck, glancing at Caleb, whose smile widened as he saw the look on his best friend's face. "There's one place downtown we can go."

22
PINKY

"You really want to go to a bar?" I asked again that night. The guys had spent the afternoon out doing things while I'd tried to finish up assignments. We'd had dinner and watched a movie, and now we were walking through the snowy streets of Southford.

Caleb walked ahead of us, having no idea where he was going. He grabbed a pole and swung himself around it, nearly getting hit by a car in the process. Idiot. "Yeah. Why not?"

"You sure you don't want to go to a club, mate?" Peter asked from behind me and Sam. "I'm definitely all for getting drunk, but I figured you would want to get—"

"Laid," Sam finished, fixing the hat on his head as the light snow fell down around us.

"I was thinking that too, right? I could probably get with three—"

"I don't want to hear about your possible adventures," I said, cringing.

Caleb grinned, rolling his eyes. "I could get laid any night, but this is the first time I can actually drink, legally. Think about that!"

"You keep saying *legally*, but last I checked you had to be nineteen to be served alcohol in a bar in Ontario. So, while you're legal to vote, you're not legal to drink." Peter shook his head. "What the hell is wrong with this country?"

Peter stepped in front of us just as we approached the building. A quaint bar, buzzing with people chatting by the windows with screens full of various sports showing inside.

But the big, scary bouncer at the front asking people for IDs gave off a completely opposite vibe.

Peter cleared his throat, running a hand over his face. "Everyone get out your IDs."

Sam rolled his eyes. "We've done this before."

"Macy hasn't," said Peter. I opened my mouth to ask how he would know that, but Peter cut me off. "You give off an energy that you don't like to break the rules, to be honest."

"I do not," I grumbled.

"Yes, you do." Caleb chuckled as he took out his driver's license.

Peter turned to us. "Each of you got a twenty? Slip it under your ID when he checks it."

"I can't believe we're doing this."

But then Caleb cleared his throat. The action was followed by a neck crack and a challenge in his eyes. "Let me go first."

With Sam's choice of building and Caleb's charm, somehow we ended up not having to bribe the bouncer after all. Sam had shuffled me inside as Caleb somehow made the bouncer beam with a story before he slipped in himself.

"I'm not even going to ask how you did that," I whispered to Caleb.

He winked before putting his hands on my shoulders and steering me toward an empty seat. "Being attractive and funny helps in this world."

Caleb sat down at the counter, and I took the seat next to him, Peter on my other side. The girl at the counter immediately turned her attention to the three boys that surrounded me. The girl took her lingering eyes off Sam the moment he put his arms around my shoulders from behind, and she instead focused on Caleb.

"Hi there."

"Hello." Caleb's eyes lit up with intrigue. Behind me, Sam sighed at the same time as I did.

"What can I get you?" She leaned over the counter, her turtle-neck crop top rising up even farther.

Caleb's grin grew wide. "It's my birthday today."

"Congratulations, birthday boy!" The girl grinned at him. "You can have anything you want. On the house."

"Actually . . ." He used his index finger to lure her in closer to him, and he whispered something in her ear.

"One sec." She winked, walking away.

"What did you say?" Peter asked.

Caleb looked over at Sam behind me. "Just wait. Macy, hand me your camera, would you?" I shot him a look, and he pouted, batting his eyelashes at me. "*Please*. I won't break it. I promise."

Reluctantly, I took the strap off my neck, and handed it over to him once the girl came back. She held two shot glasses filled with a blue liquid in her hands, and she pushed them over to me. I glanced down at the drinks before looking up at her, then at Caleb. "Why do I have this?"

"Because you're going to drink it."

"What? No." If Caleb thought I would be doing this, he thought wrong. I didn't really drink; if I ever did, it was nothing more than a cooler in the safety of my friends' living rooms.

"C'mon, Macy. I've never ever seen you drink before. Neither has Sam. Two shots. Just two."

"No."

He turned my camera on. "Please, Mace. Do it for me. Do it for Charming."

I frowned. "No."

"C'mon, Mace." He jutted his lip out, and it was then that the accent he always hid, a mixture of Salvadoran Spanish and Scottish, decided to come out. It reminded me, even more than his tan skin and his features, that Caleb had not grown up in Canada. As a kid, he had lived in Scotland and El Salvador before coming here. After all, he and Sam had bonded over their non-Canadian accents. "It's my birthday. Please, *princesa*."

The princess card from Caleb Romero Henderson was a terrible play, I decided. I inhaled sharply, reaching for the first small glass. "I can't believe I'm doing this."

"Holy shit." Sam stood beside Caleb, eyes moving down to the screen on my camera before glancing at my face.

"Ma-cy, Ma-cy, Ma-cy, Ma-cy!" Peter started chanting, and Caleb eventually joined him, banging on the counter. I rolled my eyes when Sam started chanting with them, getting louder and attracting attention. It got even worse when some strangers started chanting my name as well, banging on their tables like maniacs.

It reminded me of the past, and a laugh bubbled its way out of my body as I said, "Oh my God. It's just a shot. Calm down."

I took the first shot quickly, immediately cringing as it went down my throat. The burn that accompanied it forced a few coughs out of me as I reached for the second drink, causing the people lingering nearby to laugh and clap for me, Caleb whooping with joy.

By the time I had downed the second shot, I was fighting the need to scrape my tongue with my finger. Sam pushed a Coke in my direction. I took a large swig of the drink. "Never, never again," I managed to rasp out. "What the heck was in that? So I know how to avoid it for next time? Ugh." Caleb laughed, and Peter joined him, the two mocking my drinking innocence. I leaned back on Sam, who wrapped his arms around my shoulders.

He chuckled. "Honestly, I didn't think you had it in you."

"It's this idiot's birthday, plus life's all risks, right?"

"That was not a risk," Peter commented as we made our way to a booth.

"So, I'm guessing you aren't drinking with us tonight?" Caleb asked me, handing me back my camera.

"Nope. What part of 'never again' do you not understand?" I said.

"I'm not either," Sam announced.

Caleb frowned, analyzing him. "It's okay, you know?"

Sam shrugged just as the girl came over with a tray full of cocktails, setting it down on our table. Caleb grabbed an orange-colored one, taking a sip. "Not to be all into peer pressure, Sam, but I think you'll be good. It's us. But if you don't want to drink, that's good too. I just want you to have a good time with people you trust."

Sam kept his eyes on his best friend. Caleb took another sip of his drink as we all watched Sam take his jacket off and place it behind his. His tongue poked inside his bottom lip as he continued to contemplate his choices. "Is it good?"

Caleb pushed the cocktail in his hand over to Sam. "It's nice and fruity."

Sam took a sip, his eyebrows going up in pleased delight. Caleb beamed at him, encouraging him to try the second cocktail he had ordered when the waitress suddenly came back. She flashed me a small smile as she handed me a glass with a clear liquid. Caleb stared at the cup. "That seems like a lot for vodka."

The girl laughed. "It's *water.*" She turned to face me. "Figured you'd need it while the rest of them are drinking."

"Thanks," I said to her, returning the smile as she walked away.

Caleb held his orange cocktail up. "I want to make a toast. Thank you all for coming, but a toast to Macy taking a shot. To Macy!"

"To Macy," the boys said, and I shook my head, clinking my glass of water against their alcohol-filled ones.

The rest of the night was fun. Although I didn't touch any more alcohol, it was hilarious to see the rest of them get drunk over the course of the night. This food in this place wasn't bad either.

I was eating a salad while waiting for my burger when Caleb shoved more shots in front of my face. I pushed them back in his direction. "Nope."

As Caleb brought a couple of people over to our table, allowing them to sit and share the drinks he was willing to give out, I realized the types of drunks my boyfriend, his cousin, and his best friend were.

Caleb was overly happy. And much chattier than usual too. He told constant stories about things that had happened to him while giggling at parts that normally wouldn't be funny, but his joy at the retelling made us all laugh with him.

Peter was emotional. "It's just, I want to be there for her, right? But she's not letting me in anymore." Tears welled up in his eyes as he told us about him and his girlfriend of five years. "We've been together since we were thirteen. Thirteen! And I went to university here because she was going to school in Toronto, and we'd be close, you know? But I feel like she's going to end it even though she keeps assuring me that she still loves me."

When he looked up at us, there were tears welling in his eyes. Oh dear. "What if—what if I'm not good enough for her anymore?"

"You just have to talk to her, Peter," I told him. "I think it'll be best if you tell her everything you're telling us. Work up a good conversation."

When he sniffed, I patted his hand in comfort.

"Thanks, Mace. You're a good friend." He then proceeded to take out his phone, tears still in his eyes, which suddenly lit up when the person on the other end answered. "Jenna?"

Now, Sam, he was just more of himself. That meant that he was cockier, flirtier, more confident, just *more*.

For instance, I caught him staring at me as everyone around us was listening to another one of Caleb's stories. "What?" I asked.

"Have I told you how beautiful you are?"

"Um . . ." My lips twisted to the side to stop myself from smiling. "Yes. Many times."

"I should be telling you every single second of every single day." He leaned closer, and at that point, my face was getting heated. "You're beautiful. You're beautiful. You're beautiful—"

"Sam!" I laughed, shoving him away.

"I mean it, you know?" he said quietly. "To me, no one else compares to you. None. At all." Sam grinned at me almost childishly, and I couldn't help but grin back.

"Thank you."

"Just speaking my mind," he murmured, his fingers trailing along the palm of my hand, tingles zinging with each brush of his skin. "I think about us a lot, you know?" His voice was low enough for no one else but me to pick up on. He stared at our hands, at his fingers unable to disconnect from my own as he continued. "I think about our future. Both of us playing football, representing our countries whether it be the national team or a club team. I think about us getting married. I think about us having kids—you want kids, yeah?"

He spoke quickly, rambling faster to keep up with his thoughts. His words, his perception of the future—our future—made my heart rise within my chest. It wasn't hard to imagine a smaller version of us, a mixture of me and him, in the world one day.

"Yeah," I admitted. "If we had a boy, he would have your curly hair."

"He would probably have your nose," he added, smiling as he took a fry off my plate.

"He'd have your eyes too."

"And if we had a girl, she would have your eyes," he said as he ate. "And both would be tall, maybe taller than us. Maybe they'll follow in our footsteps and become football players." *Soccer.* "What would we name them?"

I glanced over at Caleb, who was speaking animatedly to a group of girls. "I have a feeling that when that time happens, Caleb would do anything to make sure that the boy would be named after him. Or at least that he'd be the godfather."

Sam chuckled at that, and I grinned as his head burrowed its way into my neck. The action was comforting as I threaded my fingers through his hair. "But if we had a girl," I continued, "maybe we could name her Annabeth."

"Annabeth?" he asked, puzzled.

I took a fry from my plate. I didn't have to think hard about my next words. "Yeah, Annabeth Lauren Cahill. After Bethany and my mom."

Sam moved his head from my neck to look up at me. The smile he granted me was so bright, my heart squeezed, especially as his green eyes shone. "I'd like that."

Me too.

We sat there quietly for a few moments, the chatter around us loud as people came in and out of our bubble to listen to Caleb's stories.

Then Sam broke the silence, the alcohol very much still in his system as he said, "Can you call me sexy?"

I burst out laughing. "Absolutely not."

"You don't think I am?"

Yes, I do. I wasn't going to say it to boost his ego. That's why we played this game every time.

I shrugged. "Whatever you want to think."

He put on an exaggerated smile that I hadn't seen when he was sober. "You're always putting me down, Hazel."

"You make it so hard not to," I teased.

"You make another thing hard, but I'm not complaining."

"*Oh my God.*" If the energy tonight had been any different, I probably would have cringed, but I couldn't help my amusement, putting a hand over my eyes as he joined me in loud laughter.

A content smile fell upon his lips. "You know, this is great."

"What is?"

"This night. My cousin. My best friend. You wearing another one of my sweaters you are probably not going to give back to me—"

"Probably not."

"It's good. It's great. I feel happy," he confessed, and I shared a smile with him. That was all I really wanted for him.

"Sam, you idiot." Peter suddenly spoke up, finally off the phone. "Someone can't make you happy. Jenna makes me happy. But even when I wasn't with her, I was still happy. I'm just happier *with* her."

Sam squinted at Peter, as confused as I was about the direction this conversation had taken. "And . . . ?"

"He means that Macy doesn't make you happy," Caleb interjected from where he was leaning against the side of the booth. "She only enhances your happiness."

"Exactly." Peter clapped his hands once as if Caleb had just solved all of life's mysteries. "Jenna *enhances* my happiness. *Exactly*. Caleb, you always understand me."

What?

Sam glanced at me. "I think Peter could use some water."

"I agree," I said as I got out of my chair. "I'll get some for all of you." But Sam didn't like the idea of me moving away from him because he reached for my hand again. "I'll be right back," I promised. Reluctantly, he let go as Peter attempted to get his attention with another story about his girlfriend.

After asking for four water bottles at the busy bar, I sat down at the counter, and someone sitting next to me spoke up. "You're Macy, right?"

I turned to face the person. The guy seemed familiar—tanned skin with wavy dark hair close to his shoulders. Currently he was sitting, but I had an idea that he was much taller than me. And I had no idea who he was. "Yes. Sorry, do I know you?"

The bartender handed him two bottled beers.

"I'm in your intro analytical—"

"—chemistry class!" I interjected. We were in the same lab section. That's why he looked familiar. He might possibly be in some of my other classes as well if he was also a chemistry major.

He nodded enthusiastically. "I'm Dante."

"Macy, but you already know that." He grinned at my response, hopping off the stool. My eyes widened when I craned my neck. Oh, he was tall.

"What are you? Six-five?" I asked.

"Six-four, but there're other guys on the team who make me look like a toddler." He chuckled as a server returned with my bottles of water.

"You play basketball?" I asked.

He nodded. "On the varsity team."

When I got off my stool, standing to my full height, his eyebrows rose. I laughed. "Yeah, I get that face a lot."

"I'm guessing you play basketball too?"

I shook my head. "Soccer. Varsity."

"No way," he said, evidently intrigued. He gestured over to a group of people sitting at a table a distance away, "I'm here with some Hayes friends if you want to join. You're here with people too?"

"Yeah," I said. "My boyfriend, his cousin, and our friend. We're celebrating the friend's birthday."

Dante's expression turned thoughtful as he surveyed the booth I pointed out. "Sam Cahill."

The recognition in his tone didn't surprise me. "That's my boyfriend."

"How's that?"

"What do you mean?" I asked.

"His family is wealthy beyond belief. I mean, his mom dropped that album recently, no?" he asked. "I'd figure dating him would be interesting considering how much attention he's been getting from many people—he's kind of recognizable, yeah?"

"I guess so," I responded, hearing the faint sound of the person of interest laughing. "Well, I'm going to head back, but it was nice to meet you."

"You too," Dante said with a soft smile. "See you in class, Macy."

Without another glance, Dante headed toward his group of friends, easily settling in with the crowd. When I returned to the booth, Caleb had stopped entertaining strangers and was currently helping himself to the fries on my plate. Then I realized Peter and Sam were missing.

"They went to the bathroom," Caleb informed me with a mouthful of fries. "Peter was complaining how he would've pissed into a cup if Sam didn't take him." He gestured to the burger on my plate. I guess he was hungry. I was about to encourage him to take it, but he was already pulling my plate over to himself across the table. Then he took the cutlery that had been placed by the side and start cutting the burger into smaller pieces. "Can I say something?"

"What?" I asked, eyes on the plate as he massacred my burger.

"Promise you won't tell Macy or Sam," he said with a grin. I rolled my eyes. He wasn't that gone, was he?

With all the cocktails and the shots, I wouldn't have been surprised.

"I promise."

"Pinky." He held his pinky up, and I locked mine with his.

"You see, Sam and Macy? I kind of like what they have." I stared at Caleb, wondering where his mind was going with this. "I realize that they are not as intimate as some would think they should be, but I think it's good."

I froze. I wasn't mad that Caleb was aware that Sam and I weren't intimate in that way, but I still wasn't entirely certain if he was aware of who he was discussing this topic with. "Elaborate."

Caleb paused, taking a bite of the burger and shifting in his seat weirdly, one foot resting on the edge of the chair beside him. "Don't tell Sam I said this, but my homeboy kind of thought with everything *down there* years ago." For emphasis, Caleb gestured below the table. "Now he finally thinks with the head above his shoulders."

I opened my mouth to speak, but Caleb leaned across the table, pressing a finger to my lips. "Shh, let me talk."

I fought back my irritation at being silenced, shoving a water bottle in his direction instead. He ignored the bottle, continuing his slurred speech. "Sam needs this. Abstinence. Think about it. He used to go around sleeping with random girls for a distraction from reality. I mean, the man hasn't gotten laid in so long."

"Is that a problem?" I blurted out the question without thinking. But unconsciously, even though Sam had vocalized that it was not, what he was telling me could be so different from what he told Caleb.

Caleb shook his head very quickly. "No, no, it's, like, what's that thing they give you in school?"

"A test?"

"Yeah, a test!" Caleb dropped the cutlery to clap his hands. "See, I believe that Sam loves her. He's *so* in love with her. I believe that. Him not having sex with her will be a good thing. They'll build a relationship based on emotional intimacy instead of physical. You know what I mean?"

A part of me wanted to ask another question, but I didn't get the chance before Caleb suddenly hiccupped. I raised my eyebrows, and he held a hand out. "Macy, I'm good. Princess, I'm okay." So he *was* aware of who he was talking to. Relief flooded my system, until he murmured, "I'm not as think as you drunk, you know?"

He hiccupped again, this time letting out a little giggle. "Oh shit. I think I am."

By the time we were making our way back to the boys' penthouse, Peter and Caleb had an arm thrown around each other, trying to help the other one up while giggling like idiots.

"Why is this so amusing?" I asked Sam as he took a sip of water. His eyes were a little more focused than they had been a half hour ago. He had been staying hydrated since he and Peter had come back from the bathroom and had made sure Peter and Caleb were doing the same.

"Because those two are absolute twats," he answered.

"I heard that!" they both yelled at the same time.

Sam stifled his laughter as Caleb tried jumping on Peter's back, only for the two of them to end up collapsing on the snow-covered sidewalk. "I think I broke my wrist!" Caleb yelled between chortling as he struggled to get back up. The pair slipped and slid against each other, and Sam stood in front of the struggling duo, giving me a smile with a thumbs-up. I quickly took a picture before Caleb and Peter had a chance to recover.

"Can I get a picture of all of you stable now?" I asked them, eyeing the busy streets of Southford behind them: the night sky, the lights of the lampposts, the laughter and chatter coming from up and down the street as the townspeople moved about on this snowy night.

"Do I get something for allowing another picture?" Sam asked as he approached me.

"What would that be?" I retorted, holding on to my camera to make sure it didn't slip from my grasp at his sudden proximity.

"You know . . ." He moved to the side of my face, pressing a kiss to the side of my neck, and I felt my face heat up. When he took my earlobe in his teeth and pulled slightly at it, he said, "Just call me sexy."

I was about to shove him away when Caleb shouted, "Sam, get over here for the picture. You can swallow your girlfriend when you get home."

I flushed as Sam chuckled, the three of them posing for picture after picture. This was a night I was going to look back on with love.

When we approached the building, Peter and Caleb walked ahead into the lobby. However, I held on to Sam's arm, dodging his lips as he pressed light kisses to my face at the same time. "We have to go upstairs." I laughed, tugging him along.

When he leaned forward again, I gave him a light kiss on the lips. Even as I pulled away, he groaned. No, he pleaded. "One more, please?"

"One more," I said, repeating the action again as he squeezed my hips. Caleb and Peter laughed at something in the distance.

Under his breath, Sam murmured, "I'm so in love with you, Hazel."

"The feeling is very mutual," I confessed, and the smile we shared, although a little under the influence, was bright and alight, warmth spreading through my chest at how happy he looked. At how much happier he made me.

"Whipped," Peter sang in our direction from where he and Caleb were standing in the elevator. By the time we made it upstairs, I glanced at the time, taking my shoes off. "It's 11:43."

Sam grabbed my jacket, tossing it on a couch in the living room as Caleb sat down on the other one, wondering what was going on when Sam went into the kitchen.

"What's happening?" he asked just when Sam came back into the room. He held the chocolate cake he had made—the real cake, not the decoy cupcakes I'd put in the fridge for Caleb to find earlier. Once he placed it on the glass table, he took a seat next to Caleb as I took my camera out, setting it to the side before handing Caleb a present. He'd gotten Sam's joke gift a while ago, but because Caleb loved to snoop, the real one had been with me. I handed Caleb my own gift first, urging him to take it, and he did, unwrapping the paper.

Underneath the paper was a dark-blue leather notebook with a feather pen by its side. On the front, engraved, were the words *Caleb Romero Henderson* in neat calligraphy. Underneath the words was a picture I had taken of Caleb back home. One where he was laughing with his old notebook on his lap as the summer breeze ruffled his hair. One where he was completely and utterly happy.

"It's for another story you might plan on writing."

"And I plan to write a lot. Thank you, Macy," he said softly with gratitude before he looked at Sam. "Okay, she didn't have to get me a present, but *you* definitely did."

Sam rolled his eyes as Caleb giddily accepted the other present I handed him: a box with a white bow. "Are you proposing?" Caleb joked.

"Just open it," Sam muttered.

Caleb took off the ribbon and opened the box. "*Oh*," he whispered, the gift laid out in his palm. In the center was a pendant, the outline of a boy; his hand formed what looked like half a lock.

"Where's the other half?" Caleb asked, still staring down at the pendant.

"Right here." Sam fished out the necklace he always wore with the small golden *B*. The new addition dangled next to it: an outline of a boy whose hand was the other half of the lock.

Caleb, who appeared dumbfounded, looked down at the pendant in his palm. When he let out a little laugh, there was an underlying fondness that made my heart warm. "Hey, he has curly hair like you."

"Yeah," Sam said, moving his own pendant with his index finger and thumb. Caleb clutched his in his palm, making his way toward his best friend. When they hugged, I didn't take another picture. This was a moment for themselves.

But when they let go, with the atmosphere happy and light, Sam did something I didn't expect him to do. I had done something similar to Andrew on his birthdays, but usually after people had had their share of cake. Sam had no mercy.

He grabbed the back of Caleb's neck and dunked his head into the cake, making him groan loudly. My jaw fell to the floor when Caleb came back up, chocolate and vanilla smeared all over his face. He wiped the cake from his eyes, laughing along with the rest of us. "Fuck you, man."

Sam laughed even louder as Caleb took two fingers and swiped the cake across Sam's face. My boyfriend didn't retaliate. He welcomed the attack with open arms and a beaming smile. Peter wouldn't want to miss this. I looked around, but he was nowhere to be found. "Where's Peter?"

We found him on the ground behind the couch, snoring and mumbling as he hugged a boot to his chest.

And we laughed again.

23
DAY BY DAY

"Someone had a fun night," Anmol said when I yawned for the hundredth time the following afternoon as we entered the change room postpractice.

"Sure," I said, rubbing my eyes. When Peter and Caleb had woken up this morning, they couldn't stop complaining. Even when you made the slightest movement, they would complain about how loud your footsteps were.

Then there was Sam, who was calmer. The first thing he'd said when he'd woken up was, "Hangovers are the reason I don't miss drinking."

Shaking my head at the memory of yesterday, I zipped my sweater over my shirt. "Peter was throwing up in a boot he was holding all night, and Caleb was so cranky and throwing up in the toilet. I've never been so annoyed in my life."

"It was that bad?"

"It was so bad that I couldn't even stay there for five more seconds. Sam drove me back to my dorm room in the morning so I could do homework and shower without hearing the constant yelling and moaning. I'm still tired."

"Damn."

I rubbed my eyes as we made our way out of the indoor field, quickly putting my jacket over my sweater. "How's Derek?"

Anmol smiled at the sound of his name. "He's good. A team has been watching him for a while, and he thinks he might get a chance to be on it."

"Really?" I shouldn't have been surprised. The Hayes men's soccer team was one of the best in Canada; their players, like the ones on our team, were known to be invited to trials for professional teams.

"Yeah," Anmol said. "He's been waiting for this for a really long time. Also, don't you have class in like five minutes?"

I quickly took my phone out, glancing at the time. "Oh fudge."

"Fudge?" Anmol asked.

"Don't ask," I told her, already running. "I'll see you later!"

By the time I entered the lecture hall on the other side of campus, the class had already started. I glanced at the mostly full auditorium from above as the professor talked about chemical equations. My usual seat was already taken. Ugh.

"Macy," a voice whispered. I looked in the direction of the voice. Dante. He was already shifting his bag from the chair next to him to make space for me.

I smiled, putting my jacket behind the chair and taking out my laptop. "Thanks."

"Not a problem," he said with a crooked smile, his pen in hand as he listened to whatever the professor was saying.

An hour later, at the end of class, Dante put his textbook in his bag. "Did you have practice?"

"Yeah," I answered, slinging my backpack on and following him out. I was looking up at him. I rarely ever looked up at people, but Dante managed to make me crane my neck a bit. "Can I ask you a question?"

"Sure." We turned a corner, and I put my hood up as the cold wind hit me in the face. The brief snowfall was gone. All the snow that had been on the ground was gone. I knew that back at home, the snow would be piling up, and I could already imagine my dad complaining about shoveling the driveway.

"It's just your name," I said. "Dante. I'm just assuming that—"

"I'm Italian," he confirmed.

"Thought so."

"What about you?" He stopped in front of a coffee kiosk, where I was certain the guy standing behind the counter was freezing due to wearing only a sweater.

"I'm half," I answered after he placed his order. "My mom's side."

"You speak it?"

"I used to, but I forgot a lot of it."

He said a couple of words in Italian, and I took a moment to realize what he'd said before starting to laugh. "Did you just call me an apple?"

He snickered along with me as he paid for his drink. "Have you recovered from last night?"

"Yeah, but I'm not sure my friends have yet. I didn't drink much."

"Me neither. I'm just too busy right now to deal with a hangover."

"Tell me about it. I'm probably going to spend the rest of today finishing more assignments and an essay. Plus, I have games tomorrow and Sunday. They're exhibition matches before indoor season starts next semester."

"That sounds intense." Dante blew out a breath, the white air exhaling from his mouth. "The transition to university was more stressful than I imagined."

I could relate on so many levels. In high school, all I did was play soccer and stay up-to-date on my classes. It had seemed stressful at the time, but now that I thought about it, those problems weren't anything compared to what I felt coming here.

High school was like a playground compared to university.

"The first week I got here, I was freaking out," I said. It was so weird being away from home, not waking up and pushing Justin out of the bathroom in the morning. Not having Andrew pick me up with Jasmine already in the passenger seat.

"I know how you feel," he said, taking his coffee. "Did you want anything?" I shook my head, and we continued walking. "I didn't really know how to cope with school and basketball."

"It was the same thing with soccer for me. And I thought I would have time to do assignments or look over my notes during that first month of school, and then I realized that—"

"—twenty-four hours in a day isn't enough." Dante ended my sentence exactly the way I had been going to.

"Exactly," I agreed. "With training and soccer seasons and early and late classes and practices it's—"

"Intense."

I nodded, my hands flicking against the strap of my camera bag. I took out the device, crouching to capture a photo of the frost-covered tree in front of us. "Three months in and it's still stressful, even when we think everything is calm and we're used to it."

"True. Nice camera, by the way," he said as I stood back up. "But it's day-by-day stress for everyone here, isn't it?"

"Pretty much," I said, the white fog expelling from my mouth.

Dante pushed his hair back, taking a band from his wrist and tying his shoulder-length hair into a low ponytail. "Welcome to real life."

~

When I walked out of the library that evening, I received a phone call from someone who truly didn't call me that often.

"What's wrong?" I asked.

"Why would something be wrong?" Austin asked. "What kind of greeting is that?"

"You don't call me." Whenever there was a crisis, he would go to Jon Ming first and then the rest of us. "So for you to call me, something must be wrong."

"Nothing's wrong," he promised. "I mean, not wrong in the way that's like 'something terrible happened.' I need advice from someone who's dating a Cahill."

What? Why would he need—

A light bulb turned on in my head. "Toby."

"What the hell?" he exclaimed. "How did you—"

"He was looking at you for most of the wedding day and night. And he asked me about you the day after."

"He *what*?" Austin yelled, and I winced. My friends were loud people. "Why didn't you tell me?"

Wait, why am I being attacked? "Because I forgot!"

"Macy!"

"I'm sorry!"

"Jesus," he muttered. "If you'd told me, I wouldn't have been so caught off guard by his flirting."

"*Off guard?* I thought he made it obvious he was interested," I said. "What happened?"

"I saw him today." My eyebrows rose. "He was attending a conference at my university."

"And?"

"And? You actually care? Who are you and what have you done to Macy Anderson?"

Had I really not cared that much about everyone's romantic life before? Maybe Anmol and Maddy constantly talking about their dates had had an impact on me. "What happened?"

"Nothing," he said. "But he's going to be here again next week for another conference, and he said I should come. Mace, I don't know if I should put myself out there again."

Austin had been in a relationship that had ended in the middle of the summer. He hadn't said much about it, but from the long nights of playing video games and the way he had tried to stretch out the time we all spent together back then, I didn't think it had ended well.

"I think you should do what feels right," I said.

"Do what feels right," he repeated to himself. "We'll see."

Before I could respond to that, my phone buzzed with a notification. An email. Without thinking, I opened it up. Reading the words across the page, I couldn't control the gasp that left my mouth.

"Mace? Macy?" Austin asked. "You good?"

"Um." I blinked, feeling my stomach sink farther and farther into itself. Another bad test score. This time I'd passed, but barely. *Barely*. The number was staring me straight in the face. "I received a mark."

Austin paused before his faint voice spoke up from the speaker. "Bad?"

"Bad," I confirmed in a shaky voice.

There was silence on the line again as I stood still, staring at the screen. It had started to snow again, and the flakes were falling down upon me, but it didn't seem to matter. The wind was chilling as I took in the number. "Mace?" Austin asked again, his tone almost sympathetic as I sniffed.

I walked off the sidewalk, shuffling over to the park benches. I parked my butt on the cold seat without a care in the world. "I'm tired of bad marks."

"University can be hard." Austin's words were meant to reassure me, but I only felt myself get more frustrated as tears pricked in my eyes. And then the tears got me more frustrated.

"I'm tired of chemistry," I confessed. "And I think I'm becoming tired of soccer."

"*Whoa!*" Austin cried out. "Mace!"

"I am," I huffed. "I'm not doing well in school. I'm sort of doing okay, but I'm not getting As. I'm not really liking what I'm studying. I'm not even where I should be for soccer, Austin. I'm not a starter. I'm starting to think I won't be able to go pro." That word, *pro*, broke as I spoke. I took a deep breath to restructure myself, but my shoulders stayed hunched with defeat. "I don't know what to do."

Austin cleared his throat. "Have you talked to Sam or Andrew or Jasmine about it?"

"Andrew and Jasmine? I don't wanna bother them when they're still shaky over their breakup. And Sam has enough on his plate. Between interviews because his mom is getting popular again and school and his own soccer games—I don't want to bother him."

"But you're not going to if you just talk to him," Austin said, his voice soothing. "Why aren't you letting him in?"

I sniffed, hastily wiping my eyes with the back of my hand. "I think if I talk to him about it, he's going to think that I'm jealous of how he's doing."

"He's not like that."

"But I don't want him to think that," I confessed.

"You know him, Mace," Austin said. "He's not going to think that of you. You can't push him out of your head like that. You can't let that happen."

He was right, I couldn't.

"Also, for school and soccer, I think you should just do your best. Work hard and smart. I know you can do it." His tone was assertive, not allowing for any argument. Yet when I glanced back at the email and the mark glaring back at me, I didn't share his optimism.

24
LIKE A FRICKIN' HAWK

In soccer, a hat trick is when you get three goals within one game. On this early December night before final exams, in this exhibition match against a team from a few hours away, I knew I wasn't going to get a hat trick. But I was determined to score.

My feet took me down the field, dribbling the ball as I completed a triangle pass into the box. When another player, Alana, passed me the shot, I didn't hesitate.

The ball connected with my foot, sailing past the goalie's hands and hitting the back of the net with a clean sweep. "Yes!" My hands shot straight up as my teammates cheered me on, crowding me, before the game reset.

Exhibition games were being held intermittently during off-season before indoor season started next semester. The exhibition matches were a chance to showcase our skills beyond practice, beyond the outdoor season. I was ready to use these games to my advantage.

After the game ended (we won) and I was seated in the change room, I glanced over at Anmol. "Gym tomorrow morning?"

"Shit, I can't. I'm leaving tonight to head back home for my sister's birthday tomorrow." She turned to me with a cautious expression. "Are you okay?"

"Yeah, why?"

"You've been grinding pretty hard," she commented. "Maddy said yesterday that you've been studying nonstop when you aren't at practice."

"It's finals." Final exams were just over a week away, and I was determined to do the best I could, even if it meant not getting the grades I wanted. After I'd spoken to Austin, his advice had stayed in my head like a mantra.

I'd even asked Dante about studying chemistry together and had a copy of his notes to look over—his were far more meticulous than mine. It was nice to find someone in the same major as me, especially someone who found it hard to juggle school with a sport at the same time. We had a few moments before our intro analytical chemistry class when we'd go over things together to make sure we both understood every single aspect of the content.

Dante helped. Actually, Dante had managed to help me out a ton.

"Also, Dante was asking if he could join in on our gym sessions if that's okay with you?"

"Yeah, for sure," she said. "You and Dante have been spending a lot of time together, huh?"

"Just because of exams coming up," I said, putting on a shirt over my sports bra. It wasn't an issue, was it? I saw him the way I saw the gang back home. "Other than sports and chemistry, we don't have that much in common. He doesn't even like video games."

"Someone doesn't like video games, call 911!" Anmol mock-shouted. "Macy just had a heart attack!"

"Shut up." I laughed. "He's cool, though. I think Maddy would like him. He brought up YouTubers the other day."

"Oh, she'll love him, then," Anmol said, hiking her bag over her shoulder. "If you end up going to the gym with him, bring Maddy for sure."

~

Maddy wasn't the only one who accompanied me one afternoon to the gym when I was going to meet Dante.

"Hurry up," I ordered Sam, pulling him by the hand down the stairs toward the indoor track and gym where we were supposed to have met Maddy ten minutes earlier. We'd have gotten there a lot faster if he hadn't kept looking down at his phone.

"Hazel, give me one second," he said, fingers tapping on the screen frantically. Because of the hectic energy exams seemed to bring everyone on both of our campuses, including ourselves, we hadn't seen each other much since Caleb's birthday, mostly interacting through brief phone calls on study breaks or while walking to practice.

I'd yet to tell him about the conversation I'd had with Austin, but then again I really hadn't had a chance.

No, you're deflecting.

Right now, my energy was focused on wanting to exercise. "You've said that like five times," I whined. "I want to work on cardio."

Sam put a hand on the bottom of my back, looking back down at the screen. "At least running can take your mind off exams for a while."

I groaned out loud, slumping against him as we walked through the doors to the track. "Why did you remind me?"

Sam patted my back. "Baby, let's go."

We walked through the track, where some people were working on agility techniques in the middle, some were on yoga mats by the side, and some were waiting in a line to enter the adjacent gym. Suddenly, out of the corner of my eye, I saw Sam's lips part as we stopped at the back of the line. I nudged him with my water bottle. "What?"

"The designer that Aunt Liz knows, the one I've been texting, he's been trying to get me to be in one of his photo shoots."

"Really?" I gave him a smile. "That's great, Sam."

Sam turned his phone off, obviously not answering the text message. By the way he rubbed the back of his neck and the awkward look on his face, I knew there was something else. "What is it?" I asked.

"Remember Ivan and Natasha's wedding?" How could I forget? "When Lexi and I were talking? She mentioned how she'd gotten that offer to travel around the world and be a part of twenty-four models in these shows?"

Getting a tiny bit irritated not only by the nickname but by where I knew this was going, I asked, "Were you given an offer?"

"No, but the same designer wants me to do some shoots, and she's going to be there. See, I know that Alexis and you—"

"Sam. It's fi—Don't worry about it." I barely caught myself on my wording. This was good for Sam. Alexis knew it would be good for Sam. And with him worrying about showing his family in a negative light, especially considering how lucky he was that nothing had gone public about what had happened at Ivan's wedding, I knew he was trying to put on a good front. "This is good for you. It's great publicity. And even if Alexis and I don't get along, it's okay. I know she's your friend."

"You really don't mind?" Sam asked as we moved up in the line.

I shook my head. "I don't. Please accept the offer. Now." I took his phone out of his pocket, opening it up myself and handing it back to him for him to say yes.

"You sure?" he asked again, his fingers hovering over the screen very hesitantly.

I grabbed him by the forearms, jerking him closer to me. "I'm sure. Now call and tell him you're going to accept. I'll find Maddy; she said for me to grab her once we got in line." I kissed him on the cheek quickly before leaving him to his call. As I strolled down the track, I found Maddy near the group of people on the yoga mats.

She looked a little agitated when I approached her. She reached up to fix her ponytail and yanked it a lot harder than one normally would. "What's wrong?" I asked.

She tilted her head over to the side where there was a window that faced the gym. I spotted George, the RA I thought Maddy was seeing, lifting weights and talking to a girl very closely. The boyish charm he had turned on was clearly working since her hand was on his chest and she was throwing her head back in laughter.

"*Oh.*" I winced as Maddy and I watched the scene in front of us.

"Trust me when I say I'm saying more than just *oh* in my

head right now," she grunted. "I'm not going to make a scene."

I swallowed—the way she was glaring at him right now seemed like she was about to snap at any moment. "Okay."

"I'm not going to act like we've been seeing each other for a month. I'm going to contain myself."

Her words were not matching the way her fingers were curled into fists. "Okay," I said, watching her closely.

"When we get in there, we're going to ignore him," she announced.

"All right."

"And then we're going to go to the punching bags on the third floor, and you're going to hold one while I punch it." An effective way to release anger. That was good. The controlled and calm way she said the words, though, still worried me.

"We'll do that," I promised. She was still glowering. Oh God.

"Victoria," a voice said behind me. I swiveled around, narrowing my eyes at Dante, who seemed to think he had permission to call me by my middle name instead of my actual name.

"Stop calling me that," I demanded.

"It suits you." He flashed me a toothy smile. "You look more like a Victoria than a Macy."

I glanced over at Maddy, sticking my thumb in Dante's direction, "Dante, this is my roommate, Maddy. Maddy, this is Dante; he's a chemistry major."

"Hi," she said, her gaze still fixed on George.

Dante's eyes flicked over to me. "Is she okay?"

"She's having boy issues," I said, putting a hand on my friend's shoulder to grab her attention. She blinked, turning to me when Sam joined us.

"You're supposed to be in line," I said.

"The line's short now, and you guys were taking too long with whatever you were doing."

Maddy snorted. "He got lonely."

Sam shot her a glare that was immediately cut off when he noticed the man looming over the two of us. Dante didn't waver under his intimidating stare, instead offering his hand. "Dante."

Sam looked down at Dante's outstretched hand. For a moment I worried he might embarrass me by not taking the proffered hand, but he did. "Sam."

"I heard. Nice meeting you."

Sam absentmindedly nodded, his eyes wandering around the track. Not looking at Dante. Not holding him in any importance. Immediately, I frowned.

Sam was being a jerk.

I didn't even get the chance to bother him about it before he looked at me. "I might do a lap before heading inside. Want to come?"

I opened my mouth to speak, but Maddy let out an exasperated breath, making it seem like she was tired even though I already knew she hadn't done much. "I'm going to get some water. Mace, come with me."

She dragged me away from the odd tension with a hand on my arm. When she pulled me over to the water fountain, she took the shortest sip of water I had ever seen in my life before she glanced behind me. "So, Dante."

"What about him?" I asked.

"He's cute." She leaned against the wall.

"I hadn't noticed." It's not like I would've pointed it out. Yes, Dante was attractive with his thick head of dark hair and Italian features, but it didn't affect me the same way it was likely affecting Maddy.

"Really?"

"Really."

Maddy kept her eyes on the scene behind me. "I don't think Sam likes Dante."

"I *did* notice that," I mumbled, turning around to see what Maddy was talking about. I spotted Sam at the end of the hundred-meter mark of the track, and I knew he had just sprinted down there. Dante was a little bit ahead of him.

No way.

Maddy and I watched Dante and Sam sprint. I got the impression that due to Sam's natural need to win, he was thinking about beating Dante even though they were only working on running.

"Is he kidding me?" I muttered.

"I think he's jealous of Dante," Maddy whispered.

I let out a long breath, and Maddy and I walked over to the start just as the boys came back over to us. Sam was panting as he walked over to me. "You ready?"

I opened my mouth to answer him, but he swooped in like a frickin' hawk, pressing an intoxicating kiss to my mouth. Before I even had the chance to recover, he pulled away, leaving me light-headed as he sprinted back down the track. I glared at his back, knowing he'd done that for only one reason. However, Dante didn't seem fazed by it. "Interesting guy," Dante said before sprinting to catch up to Sam.

~

About an hour and a half later, Dante bid us goodbye, and Maddy left for our dorm, leaving Sam and me alone in the gym.

I sat on the floor in front of Sam, who was currently shirtless and using the rowing machine. His muscles tightened as he pulled the cord toward him by the handle, his body moving back and forth due to the stretch and retraction of his arms. I wasn't the only one watching. Some girls that lingered near the track glanced through the window from time to time.

When he slowed down eventually, I tossed him his water bottle. While he drank, I stared at him, waiting for him to speak. He pulled the drink away from his mouth. "I don't like him."

Already knowing who he was talking about, I sighed, leaning back on my hands. "Why?"

"I have to have a reason?" he asked, dropping down in front of me with his knees up and against his broad chest.

I shot him a look. "Makes sense for you to have a reason if you dislike someone you literally just met. Especially when they've done nothing to you."

"It's his energy," Sam said, reaching over to grab my hand.

He traced my palm with his index finger, and while that tickled and I knew he was trying to distract me, I pulled it away. "His energy?"

"I don't get along with his energy." He shrugged. "You know what I mean."

"We're going with *that* reason as to why you don't like him?" I got up, and Sam followed suit.

"It's not like I said you couldn't be friends with him." He brushed me off, grabbing his sweater to head to the men's locker room.

I grabbed him by the arm before he could open the door. I was irritated by the boredom crossing his face, as if this conversation meant nothing, as if it wasn't bothering him as much as it was bothering me. "I don't know if this is some type of jealousy or—"

Sam chuckled, glancing down at the ground. "Is it that obvious?" It was, but this was odd.

"You have nothing to worry about," I assured him. "Even though you acted like a jerk toward him—"

"That's your name for me," he teased. "Don't wear it out."

I pretended he hadn't spoken. "And even though you kissed me like you had something to prove, I can look past it." I lightly knocked his temple with my knuckles. "It's me and you, jerk."

A slow smile came to his lips. "Me and you, Hazel."

I gave him a brief kiss, and he smiled into it. "That sure warded off all the girls by the window," he mumbled against my lips.

I glanced at the window, where some of the girls on the other side had been watching Sam, and noticed that some of them had gone back to what they had been doing, some with irritation clear on their faces. "Sure did."

Sam's expression showed amusement as I patted his cheek. "I'll see you in a bit."

I turned around to head to the women's locker room when a hand swiftly swatted my butt. I twisted to face Sam as he looked around the room as if he were lost. "What?" He widened his green eyes, making me think that he'd probably gotten away with so many things as a kid because he could pull off that innocent look even though he was far from it.

"You're not slick, jerk," I told him as a smirk took over his face. "But that definitely warded off everyone."

"Never meant to be, Hazel." He winked before pushing through to the locker room.

Anmol was right.

Maddy and Dante got along very well, but as well as they got along, they were just as quick to argue.

For instance, Dante and I had two days left until our last final exam (three for Maddy), and the second Dante entered one of the study rooms in our dorm, she shot up from her seat, dropping her stylus. “The video you sent in the group chat was *not* funny.”

The group chat between Maddy, Dante, and me had started when Maddy found a video and decided she needed to send it to both of us. It had quickly turned into a group chat where they did most of the talking or sending memes and videos to each other while I stayed quiet.

“Yes, it was,” Dante said as he took off his headphones, plopping onto the couch next to me.

“No, it wasn’t.” Maddy made a face. “Your humor sucks.”

“And your humor is dead. Revive it,” he said with an eye roll. They were always like this. “Besides, the one *you* sent was terrible.”

“It wasn’t terrible!” Maddy exclaimed. “Macy liked it. I even heard her laugh.”

“Her laugh was out of pity,” Dante said deadpan, taking his textbooks out of his backpack.

It had been.

“Leave me out of this conversation,” I said as a text came in from Sam.

Jerk <3: I hate math.

I scoffed. No, he didn’t. I knew he was at home in his apartment. Studying alone worked best for him these days, but he visited my campus whenever he could. His math exam was later tonight, and all I really wanted was to be there with him. Yet as I glanced at my textbook, I knew my next couple of days would involve chemistry concepts instead. Honestly, the misery I was starting to feel around chemistry was rising every day.

Me: No, you don't.

Jerk <3: Break in 20 minutes?

Me: Can it be after Dante and I go over a chapter? He just got to the study room with me and Maddy.

For a few moments, Sam didn't respond.

I stared down at my phone as the two in the room continued to bicker, their topic a random YouTuber I wasn't familiar with but whom they both watched. Why wasn't he answering?

"It was funny!" Maddy was saying as I stood. "Where are you going?"

"Away from this conversation," I declared lightly, forcing myself into the hallway.

I didn't hesitate to hit the Call button. Sam picked up within one ring. "Hey," he said in a deep voice.

"Are you okay?" I asked. "What's wrong?"

"Nothing," he automatically said.

"I know something's wrong." I knew *him*.

"I was just a little caught off guard by the mention of Dante," he confessed. "You've been studying with him a lot."

"He's been making me feel better going over concepts, that's all." There was no reason for him to dislike Dante. Dante was only a friend. He was someone who shared my stress at being caught between sports and chemistry formulas. Sam had to understand that, didn't he? Then again, Austin's voice came into my head. He didn't entirely know how I had been feeling over the past weeks. "I've been kind of having a hard time."

"Hard time?" he asked, puzzled. "You all right, Hazel?"

"Yeah," I admitted. "I'm doing better now."

"Promise?"

The corners of my lips rose. "I promise. I'll call you in a bit, before you go to your exam."

"Okay," he said lightly. "Don't miss me too much."

"Shut up."

When I returned, Dante had pulled out three drinks—all bubble teas. He greeted me with a mischievous grin. "Victoria, I think you'll like the pink one. Maddy, the green one is yours."

"Stop calling me that," I grumbled as Maddy took one of the drinks happily.

"You know what?" Maddy said. "When Anmol comes by after her exam we'll have a tiebreaker. She'll agree with me that it was *funny*."

"You can't just bring in one of your friends to this argument," Dante protested. "We need a neutral party."

I flipped open my textbook and then grabbed one of the straws on the table. Then I stabbed my straw into the top of my drink before sipping it. Dante was right. This was good.

The pair looked at me with hopeful eyes. How lucky and annoyed I was to have them to survive with me for the first semester of university. I gave them both a tight smile. "No."

25
KINKY

Holidays were a good time to bring everyone together. For instance, all the Cahills had plans to be under one roof, spending their Christmas break here in Canada rather than wherever the Cahills usually went to spend it. So Sam was at his aunt Liz and uncle Vince's house. I lay down in his room, free from soccer and school for a while, flipping through his camera alongside Phillip, who was lying down beside me.

My life was at ease for a moment, and I didn't think anything could ruin my break, especially since I was with Phillip again.

Phillip let out a little giggle as he flicked through the different filters, the joyful sound making me crack up. "This one," he said, pointing at the screen eagerly. I did as he asked, the two of us watching our faces change once again.

Sam entered the room, staring down at us with a raised eyebrow. "What are you doing?"

"Taking pictures," Phillip answered, and like the kid he was, he leaned into the camera, parting his lips to take pictures of the inside of his mouth. As he tried to lean in to capture pictures of his tongue, Sam squeezed between me and his little cousin. He pushed Phillip out of the frame to get into the shot with me.

"Hey!" Phillip yelled just as he jumped onto Sam's back.

Sam let out a loud grunt. "Phil, I don't think you realize how much older you're getting. If you keep jumping on me like that, you're going to break my back one day."

"Then don't steal my Macy time." Phillip wiggled his way between me and Sam.

"Macy time?"

"Yeah, you get her all the time. My turn now." He tried shoving Sam, who didn't budge, and whined when he couldn't get Sam to move.

"You realize she's *my* girlfriend, right?"

Phillip looked up at his cousin without a care in the world. "And? What does that have to do with me?"

I rolled out of the frame once Sam started to wrestle his cousin, who was laughing like crazy when Sam picked him up. "Have you seen Greg, by the way?" Sam asked.

"He's at the ice rink," Phillip said, dropping to his feet once Sam let him go. "He's really liking ice dancing."

"Ice dancing?" I asked. "I thought Greg played tennis."

"He does!" Phillip said. "But he's thinking about ice dancing a lot. Aunt Naomi has been speaking to him about it since she did it when she was younger."

"And you?"

"Wait!" Suddenly, Phillip bolted out of the room. I glanced at Sam, who shrugged.

"Have you spent time with Greg?"

"Yeah, a lot of time. I don't know, it's so weird talking to him now, seeing him grow up," he confessed. "We're going out for dinner later, though. I'm taking him and Phillip to an arcade."

Aw.

"Greg was telling me Phillip's been a little lonely since Ivan went on his honeymoon and has been in New York. And Cedric and I aren't here, so he's latched on to Greg, I guess. He's been over at the twins and Christian's place a lot."

"Are you worried about him?"

Sam shook his head. "Greg's a great brother. He'll be a good one to Phillip as well, I know it."

Phillip returned before I could say anything else, holding a silver trophy in his hands. Sam's eyebrows went up as he read the plaque while Phillip turned to me with excitement. "That's from my dance competition from two weeks ago. I won."

Sam's lips parted in surprise. "Wow. First place."

But Phillip didn't seem excited about his win. He grabbed the Leonardo Ninja Turtle action figure that was on Sam's nightstand and held it in his hands. He blew a raspberry with his lips, taking the trophy from Sam's hand; it looked like it weighed him down. "I talked to Greg about this, but I don't want to do dance anymore."

Sam and I exchanged a look. "What? Why not?"

Phillip shrugged. "I don't know. I just don't want to do it."

"There's got to be a better reason than that."

Phillip's eyes lit up, "I want to go back to the tumbling classes and gymnastics I did before I got into dance and before I played football."

"Are you certain?" Sam asked. Phillip nodded quickly, his

fingers moving the arms of the action figure. "All right. I'll tell your mum."

Phillip's jaw fell open as he yelled, "Really?"

"Yeah." Sam's voice softened in a way he used only for Greg and Phillip. "Why would you think she wouldn't say yes?"

"It's not her," Phillip said miserably. "It's Dad. I thought he'd be mad if I wanted to go back to gymnastics after quitting."

"I think Uncle Vince will understand, considering Cedric played multiple sports before he chose rugby."

Phillip's lips parted in surprise. "Did he really?"

Sam nodded, a short laugh escaping him. "I'm pretty sure Ivan did gymnastics back home as well. I think he'll be okay with you going back to gymnastics, okay, Phil?"

Phillip grinned. "Thanks. I'm going to join the guys outside." He ran out of the room, and I glanced at Sam.

"Greg's doing ice dancing?"

"Mm-hmm," Sam said as we headed out of the room. "Lucas sent me a couple of videos. He's actually good. I'm pretty sure—"

The sound of the large door closing cut Sam off as he looked over the railing to see Liz, Joey, and Lucas making their way inside. I rushed down and over to the twins, who were taking off their jackets. "Happy birthday, guys!"

They hugged me back, and even with their identical grins, I could sense some weird tension between them. "Thanks," they both said at the same time.

"How are you celebrating it?" I asked.

"Apparently, Joseph is kicking everyone out of their house to throw a party," Liz said, walking up the stairs past Sam.

"I'm still wondering how you managed to convince your parents to do that," Sam said. "I know you threw shit before, but not to the point where you practically kick everyone out of the house."

"I'm not kicking out everyone," Joey said, crossing his arms. "You guys can come if you want."

"Going back to a high school party when I went to my last one months ago? Even if it's your birthday, sorry, Joey." I patted him on the back, and he laughed, clearly expecting that answer from me. Joey disappeared down the hallway to the backyard, where the majority of the Cahill boys were, leaving his twin behind.

"What about you?" Sam asked Lucas.

Lucas shrugged. "I'm not doing anything."

"Oh yeah?" Sam asked, and there was something in his tone that let me know that he was trying to get Lucas to admit something out loud.

"I'm probably going to go to a friend's house or something."

"Or something?"

"Yeah," Lucas mumbled.

"Really? Nothing? No special friends to be with?"

Lucas's cheeks turned a light-pink color. *Oh.* "Wait, who is it?" I teased him, poking him in the stomach multiple times to the point where he swatted my hand away.

"Do you remember Sydney?" Lucas took the beanie off his head, running his hands through hair that was not gelled, which to me was a rare sight to see.

"From the wedding?" I asked, my lips parting with surprise and a huge grin appearing on my face. "Are you guys dating now?"

Lucas rolled his eyes, and Sam grabbed his cousin, putting him in a headlock. "Tell her what you told me. How she—"

"Shut up." Lucas elbowed Sam in the stomach, making him let go with a grunt. Lucas fixed his shirt, grumbling, "You talk like you weren't rambling about Macy when you guys started dating."

I looked at Sam, feeling surprised. "That's news to me."

He pointed a finger toward me. "Mute."

"Excuse me? Did you just tell me to mute? I—" I glanced at Lucas, changing the topic and composing myself. "So you guys are dating now?"

Lucas's cheeks were now a rosy red and he twisted the ring on his finger. "Yeah."

"I'm glad you finally got the balls to tell her how you feel," Sam jested.

"Don't listen to him," I said with a pat on Lucas's shoulder. "Hope you have a great day."

"Thanks," he said with a sheepish smile. "I'll see you later."

He walked away from us, going up the stairs, and it was then that I shoved Sam. "What is wrong with you?"

"What?" Sam asked as I walked over to the front door to put on my shoes and jacket. He quickly followed my lead but remained perplexed. "What did I do?"

We made our way out the door and to the back of the large house, nearing the group of people near the trees in front of the pool house. "Why do you have to bother Lucas like that?"

"Because it's his first girlfriend," Sam said, in a *duh* tone. "And it's fun."

I picked up snow as Sam continued walking, cupping it tightly with my hands before I threw it in his direction. It hit him in the middle of his back, and he stilled, turning around to face me. "What was that for?"

I couldn't help the smile that came to my face. "You were being a jerk."

"I was being a jerk? Really? That's why?" He reached down and gathered snow in his gloved hands. "C'mere, Hazel, let me show you what a jerk really is."

He walked over to me, and I ran. I ran so quickly that the first snowball flew right past my shoulder. Sam laughed when I stumbled, and I quickly reached down to gather more snow, throwing it back at him. He dodged it easily. "Look who can't throw," he taunted.

With the adrenaline pumping through my body, I ran over to him. He tried getting out of the way, but I quickly jumped on his back, making him spin in a circle.

Without his knowing, I shoved the snow down the back of his neck. "Holy shit! What the hell?" He shook the snow out of his clothing, and laughter rang through the backyard as the Cahill boys walked toward us. "What are you guys doing?" Christian asked.

I grabbed more snow, packing it in my hand before flinging it at Christian. It hit him in the chest, exploding against his jacket, and he fell back dramatically.

"Really?" Ivan asked as Sam got him in the shoulder.

"Fight!" Phillip ran in my direction with snow in his hand.

I backed up as the Cahill boys ran: Christian had shoved snow down Joey's back, and in retaliation Joey pushed him down to the ground. Close to the brothers, Phillip was giggling hard as Lucas helped Ivan pelt Sam with snowballs. Cedric, next to Sam, said something to him before the pair started throwing snow at Ivan and Lucas. Cedric yelled, charging toward his little brother and lifting him in the air to use as a shield. Sam helped Cedric hold Phillip up to block the attack from Lucas and Christian.

The other two Cahill boys were off to the side amid the yelling. Greg, his brown hair now wavy and curling around his ears, was in the process of making a snowman. Next to him, Toby simply stood and watched the progress. When Sam burst out laughing, the sound clear as day, Greg stopped patting the snow to look over at the scene. "It's nice to hear him laugh like that."

"Yeah," Toby agreed, his eyes on his little cousin as he made the snowball for the base of the snowman bigger and bigger in the middle of the large backyard.

Toby glanced over at me. For a second I stilled, but then mentally shook myself out of it. It was just Toby. He was just another Cahill. Glancing at the boys now, I realized there was absolutely no reason to be intimidated by him.

"Macy," he said.

"Toby," I said back.

"His real name is Tobias," Greg offered in a snarky manner.

"Tobias," I corrected, flashing Greg a smile. "What's going on with you and Austin?"

Toby settled his serious gaze onto me. His lips curved into a hidden smile. "I'm still deciding."

Still deciding? That wasn't enough information to take back to my friend, and knowing Austin, he was going to be pissed if I relayed those words to him.

Before I could say anything, I was forced to the ground. I groaned, rolling onto my back as Sam laughed above me. There was snow in his hand. With my eyes wide, I was already warning him, "Don't you dare."

He threw it down, and I shrieked loudly when the snow hit my cheek. In retaliation, I grabbed snow from the pile next to

Greg and shoved it in his face. "You suck," I yelled as I stood back on my feet, wiping snow off me.

"Baby, don't be like that, c'mon," he yelled back when I ran away from him, straight toward the group throwing snowballs at each other. Behind me, Greg laughed as Sam pushed his little brother to the ground.

Greg was right. It was nice to hear him laugh like that. It was nice to hear everyone laugh in the same way under the light snowfall.

~

"Ugh, why can't you ever let me win this game?" Andrew grumbled in frustration, tossing the controller onto one side of the couch.

I stopped the game, turning off the PlayStation. "Because you suck."

Andrew and I had been downstairs for a long while. Justin was with Emma at the movies. I didn't question where Alexis was, but I knew she was going to be here closer to Christmas. My father had taken Nonna to see Lucy and was probably speaking to the Cahills at this moment. I had texted my friends to swing by later regardless of where the conversation was going to go tonight.

Andrew had barely spoken to me over the past weeks since everything had happened, but he had assured me that when he was ready to talk, he'd do it.

Clearly the time was now. He glanced at me, shifting uncomfortably. I spoke up first. "How is everything?"

"You mean how is everything without Jasmine?"

Okay, then. "I honestly didn't want to force you to talk about it."

"You're not," he said. "Um, it's been a rough few weeks." I waited patiently, both of our eyes on the controller in my hand. "First week was weird. Wasn't really myself. Everyone kept saying how down I felt about it. How depressed I was acting."

He leaned back, running a hand through his hair. "Week two consisted of me deleting almost everything I had of her, but I couldn't just delete all of them because she's a big part of my life, you know?"

He ran a hand through his blond hair. Andrew's voice was low when he said, "Week three came, and I think I broke down." He glanced at me. "I knew you were there. Like I said, I just needed to be alone for a while. I didn't want to speak to anyone. I don't know. I couldn't wrap my head around her being with someone else. Falling out of love with me for someone else. I didn't get it. Even with our distance, I didn't think it would ever happen, you know? But it did."

"But it did," I whispered.

"And I was angry for a while after." Andrew sat up. "Then I found something that kind of made everything a little bit better."

Better? I sat up too. That was good. Progress was really good. "What?"

"Boxing."

"Really?" I was a little bit surprised.

"I like it," he said with a light smile, and the sight had me grinning back. "It helps me clear my head. *You* should definitely try it sometime."

I narrowed my gaze. "Dude, I hit the gym. I'm okay."

Andrew chuckled. "Well, now we're on week six since the

breakup, and I'm starting to slowly get by. I kind of wish I still had exams. It was a good distraction."

My phone pinged. Great timing. "I'm sure we can find you something to do."

"We?"

Right on cue, the door to the basement opened, and boys hurried their way through the threshold. "*Prescott!*" Jacob yelled as he ran down the stairs, tackling Andrew in a much-needed hug.

Brandon and Jon Ming ran to the air hockey table. Austin grabbed the controller from my hand and tossed the other one to Jacob. "Let's play, man."

"Hey, princess? You have to ask your dad to buy some more chips. He's out." Caleb held up two bags of chips as he sat down in front of my legs, eyes on the screen as the game played.

"You called them?" Andrew glanced at me with a little more ease than he'd had then when he'd gotten here.

"Texted."

"We figured you needed some type of guys' night," Jacob said, as he flicked through levels. "Stevie's at a relative's, so it's just us."

"Yeah, it's a regular guys' night," Austin said, lying down sideways on the couch. He softly punched me on the arm, giving me a light smile. "All of us and Macy."

26
RIPPING HIS SHIRT OFF

My father was very chill when it came to parenting. As a lawyer, he was stern when he had to be, but Justin and I rarely caused problems; we almost never fought unless it was over a game we were playing. I'd like to think we were angel children for him growing up.

When I began dating Sam and my father realized how serious our relationship was, he didn't give me a talk, but there were clear expectations. Whenever Sam was over, let it be known to everyone in the household. If Sam was eating dinner here, let it be known. If he was staying over, let it be known. Sam typically woke up before I did, and whenever he slept over, I'd go down to the kitchen or the living room to find them talking, which they could do for hours. However, when my Nonna was there, my father's lenient parenting style went straight out the window.

On the morning of Christmas Eve, I woke up to loud knocking. I groaned in agitation, keeping my eyes tightly shut.

Whoever it was needed to take the hint and stop trying to break down my door.

The knocking became more persistent, and eventually I leaned back into Sam, who had a tight grip around my waist. He was still asleep; I could tell by the way he was breathing against the back of my neck.

When I realized the knocking wasn't going to slow down, it hit me who was likely on the other side. I sat up. "Sam! Sam!" I whisper-yelled at him, but he didn't wake up. Instead, he shifted to lie on his stomach, his head buried in the pillow.

I grabbed another pillow and used it to whack him on the head several times before he groaned loudly, snatching it from me. "What?" he asked in a low voice, sending a quick thrill through me. Morning voice was so evil when it came to him.

"Nonna is outside. Hide!" I hit him again with the pillow as he sat up; he wasn't processing my words. It was when he was in the middle of stretching that what I'd said hit him, and he quickly dove out of my bed and crawled underneath it.

Nonna didn't like the idea of Sam sleeping over. The few times she had caught him, she'd made him go home even though she and my dad knew we wouldn't do anything under his roof.

When I opened the door to reveal my lovely grandmother on the other side, I pretended to yawn. "Morning."

She stepped into my room, her eyes looking around skeptically like she already knew he was here. Fudge.

"Morning, bella," she said, moving her gaze back to me. "We're going over plans for tonight's little dinner with family. You're in charge of pasta, remember?"

"I remember," I said. "I'll see you guys downstairs in a second. Let me just get ready."

I was practically pushing my grandmother out of my room at that point, and she was about to cross the threshold when she turned around. Both of our gazes went down to the foot peeking out from underneath my bed. I groaned internally. He could've at least *tried* to hide a little bit better.

She moved past me and reached down, grabbing Sam's foot and, with all her might, pulling my boyfriend out from under my bed. He yelped, smiling at my grandmother sheepishly. "Hi."

"Samuel," she warned. "I'm going to have a word with your grandmother and mother about this."

"You could've just said my mother; we don't need to involve Grandmother in this."

"Your grandmother and I see things the same way—she'll do something about it. Now go home, Samuel." Nonna grabbed his shirt from the floor and tossed it to him as he stood up.

Sam threw his shirt on, grabbing his jacket, which was on the desk. He kissed me on the cheek, smiling. "I'll see you tonight."

After Sam was gone and I'd cleaned up, I walked into the kitchen and spotted Justin lying down on the kitchen counter and my dad opening and closing cabinets in the kitchen. Nonna was doing the same beside him, going through a list and muttering harshly in Italian under her breath. "I cannot believe you, Nicholas."

"I forgot, okay?" My dad tried to reassure her, walking over to kiss my forehead before sitting on a chair. "Justin, get off the counter."

Justin did as he asked while I stared at the other two people in the room, specifically my grandmother, who looked like she was going to lose it. "What did Dad forget?" I asked.

"A whole bunch of things to buy for our small Christmas Eve dinner tonight." Nonna pinned my dad with a look that immediately softened at the apologetic expression on his face.

"Justin and I can get them." I turned to my brother. "You have anything to do before tonight?"

He shook his head, the two of us sharing a smile. Always time for sibling bonding.

~

"I need something else," Justin said after tossing aluminum foil into the cart I was pushing and running down the aisle to another one. When he came back, he threw in one thing that definitely wasn't on our list of items we needed. "No," I told him, handing him back the box.

"It's Christmas!" he argued, holding the package of Twinkies against his chest.

"I don't care," I said, looking at my brother and wondering how he was approaching sixteen. The thought of him growing up bewildered me every time. What if there came a day when he no longer liked Twinkies? "You know what? Put it in." He grinned and threw it in again.

"We're grabbing food after this, right?" he asked me as I was reading off the next item on the list. Our jackets were both unzipped to reveal me in a Chelsea jersey and Justin in a basketball jersey. Yeah, nothing had really changed with us.

I nodded. "How is everything?" I asked him as we bagged tomatoes.

"Everything? Like *everything* everything?"

"I'm pretty sure that's what *everything* means, yes."

He surveyed the onions nearby for a moment before saying, "I don't want Emma to go back to Redmond."

Oh. "Well, it's not that simple, Justin. It's not like she can pack up her entire family and move here." I made a face. "Also, I wouldn't exactly appreciate it if Alexis moved all the way to where I was born and raised, thanks."

"Alexis is traveling all over the world after Christmas anyway. She's irrelevant in this," Justin said. "Emma and I aren't even together, though. Like, when she's here, we have a label, but when we're not together it's like, oh, we're just friends, but at the same time not really."

"Yeah, I know," I said, grabbing a bag of potatoes. "But isn't that only because of distance? Because every time she comes here, you guys are all boyfriend and girlfriend either way."

"Yeah, but before the break, this girl in my history class asked me out, and I didn't really give her a clear answer because of Emma."

Really? "Did you tell Emma about that?"

"She told me to go out with her," he spat out like he had something horrible in his mouth. "She encouraged me to be with someone else, Mace."

I opened my mouth to speak, but my little brother was ready to rant. Our dad would talk endlessly whenever he got excited about something; Justin was the opposite and he only ranted when he was upset about something . . . which was what he was doing now. "I didn't understand it. I love Emma, and I thought she knew that. But she thinks I don't really love her. That I'm caught up in this whole high school idea of loving someone. She started talking about how we're probably too young to understand what love is and all this other stuff. I don't want her to push me onto someone else just because we're not really together."

"But if someone else asked Emma out and she asked you about it, would you stop her from going out with him?"

"I don't know," he grunted, putting his hands on the handle of the cart. "I guess I'm looking for some advice."

I could offer that. "I think she's only telling you to go out with the other girl because she doesn't want to be this kind of roadblock stopping you from going on with your everyday life," I said, taking the cart from him and moving us away from the vegetable area. "Maybe you would do the same thing. I think you need to understand that because of your situation and the distance, she doesn't want to prevent you from having something with someone else. Does that make sense?"

"Yeah, it does," he said.

"You should talk to her tonight," I suggested, my mind going to Jasmine and Andrew. "Try to establish what would be best for you two before it blows up in some way."

"I probably should. Thanks." He flashed me a tight smile as we passed through an aisle. Then my little brother did a double take. "Wait, isn't that Jasmine?"

Speak of the devil.

"Have you guys talked since the breakup?"

"Um . . ." How could I explain that there had been radio silence on her end since even before the breakup? How could I explain that I'd reached out and it made me feel terrible because it was likely she had seen the messages and hadn't bothered replying? Yet now, as she picked out a sauce from one of the shelves, she was speaking to someone on the phone with a light smile on her face. "Not really."

"Go talk to her." Justin put both hands on the cart, steering it in a different direction and grabbing the list from my hand. "I'll finish getting everything."

He disappeared before I could say another word. Down the

aisle, Jasmine had noticed me already, and as I approached her, she was saying, "I'll talk to you later. Bye." There was a pause, and suddenly she was struggling to fight the smile creeping up on her face. "Yeah, I love you too."

She hung up the phone, sliding it into her pocket as she shot me an apologetic face. There was nothing for her to be sorry for. I had to get used to her saying that to someone who wasn't Andrew.

Things change, I had to remind myself.

"Let me guess," I said, "that was Ace?" She nodded. "How is he?"

"Do you really want to know?"

I didn't even know his last name. I didn't know what he was studying at her university. I didn't even know if he liked soccer. "It seems like the polite thing to ask since we haven't spoken since November. I only knew you were coming home for the break because Drake told me."

Jasmine's apologetic expression grew tenfold. Her phone wasn't broken this time. But when Andrew had needed space, he'd told me. He hadn't implied it. He hadn't ignored me.

A year ago, Jasmine wouldn't have ignored me.

I decided to give her the benefit of the doubt. "You okay?"

"I'm okay," she said. "I needed space. From everyone."

"I figured," I said. "But I thought you could tell me that considering you promised to give me updates the last time we spoke."

And for the first time in the years of our friendship, there was a moment of awkward silence between us. There had *never* been silence between us. Jasmine and I were the type of friends who could stare at each other for one second before bursting into laughter.

How we were acting right now wasn't normal. How we were acting right now was something I didn't like. I wanted to move past it. I wasn't planning on throwing away a decade of friendship because of a few months of no communication.

"How are you?" I ended up asking.

She shrugged. "I'm okay. It's him I'm wondering about. How is Drew?"

"He's getting by." The conversation we'd had about him taking up boxing had given me the impression that eventually he would be okay. The concern on Jasmine's face let me know how terrible she felt, but it wasn't her fault. Besides, sometimes things just happened because they happened. "It's not like your relationship was a waste. Sure, the terms you ended it on weren't the best ones, but at least you learned from it."

Jasmine tilted her head. "Did you just make dating seem like a class lesson? Like we were back in high school?"

A memory hit me. "Remember our history teacher in grade ten? He turned every single lesson into a story about his dating life."

"At least from him we learned not to give out your bank card to people you think you're completely in love with."

"And how to use Match.com properly."

"Or Tinder."

"Or all the other dating sites and apps."

Jasmine and I laughed. That was nice. That was a good moment.

"I wonder if he's married now," she contemplated.

"One could only hope with his dating record." I grinned, and just like we'd done since we were nine, we looked at each other and started laughing again. "Are you coming to the Cahills'

Christmas party tomorrow night?" Liz had extended an invitation to our friends to join them at their house tomorrow.

She shook her head. "I'm going to spend it with my mom and Drake instead."

"And . . . and your dad?"

"Spending it with his other family." She shrugged as if it wasn't a big deal, but I knew otherwise. This was going to be her first Christmas without him. For her sake, I switched gears. "We're definitely going to hang out this week, right?"

"You and me?"

"Yeah. Stevie too. It can be like old times."

Jasmine smiled, and I realized she needed this. Despite how it had ended with Andrew and how her relationship with her dad had changed, I figured she needed a bit of the old normalcy. She had us regardless of the distance she was putting between herself and our friends. She had me. I had to think of her not as my best friend who'd broken our other best friend's heart. Instead, she was the girl I had met back in grade three with her long box braids, bright smile, and love of *Star Wars*. "Thanks, Mace."

"You're still one of my best friends," I said. "You know that, right?"

She blinked once. Then several times. When she started exaggeratedly fanning her eyes with her hands, I rolled my eyes as I lightly shoved her. "Stop being dramatic and hug me, you dumbegg."

We embraced tightly, and against my shoulder, she mumbled, "We're so stupid. We're actually hugging in a grocery store."

I couldn't help but grin. Normalcy. At least for a little while.

27
MERRY CHRISTMAS

"*Buon Natale*!" Nonna's words cut my little brother off midsentence.

"Merry Christmas!" my brother and I chimed.

Justin had been in the middle of raving about the video game I had gotten for him. He showed Nonna, who clearly didn't know what the heck he was talking about. The table still held remnants of the night before: random poker chips and cards along with a pile of snacks placed nearby.

From the threshold, Dad entered in his pajamas, holding my camera in his hands. "Hey, why didn't Grandpa and Grandma come over this year?" I asked him. Last night's dinner had consisted of only us this year. My mother didn't have siblings, and the rest of my maternal family was in Italy. My dad had one brother, and he and his family lived on the other side of Canada in BC and had spent the holiday there this year. However, my paternal grandparents didn't live far from Port Meadow and typically visited.

"They went on a cruise," Dad said. "Something about not wanting to experience snow this year. They'll call later today."

"Smart move," Justin said distractedly, looking outside at the snow falling. "It's really coming down."

"At least it's not a green Christmas like last year," I pointed out, glancing outside.

"That's because global warming—"

"Justin, I really don't want to have a lesson when I'm going back to school in a week. I would love to refrain from learning, please and thank you. Now, let me beat you in this game before we go to the Cahills'."

"Actually . . ." My father cleared his throat. "Mace, can I speak to you for a bit?"

I glanced at Justin, who was still marveling over the game. My grandma had decided to preoccupy herself with cleaning up from last night. Okay, I was left in the dark here.

I followed my dad to his office cautiously. When I closed the door behind me, I swiveled to face him. "Did you commit a crime?"

My dad shot me a look. "Macy."

"Did you do something illegal?"

"Are you serious?"

"Notice how you didn't answer any of my questions," I pointed out. The dry look he sent me made me realize this was actually a serious conversation. I sat down on his couch. "Sorry."

He took a seat next to me, looking apprehensive. "I've been trying to have this conversation with you for a while, really."

I frowned, twisting to face him. My dad and I talked about a lot of things; we'd rarely kept things from each other, even when I was a kid. But right now, he looked like he was struggling.

That's when I grew concerned, sitting up. "Are you okay?"

"I'm okay, Mace," he promised. "I've spoken to Justin about this, but I also needed to have this conversation with you."

I stared at him. "And what's the conversation about?"

"Dating."

I blinked. "Huh? You like Sam! You literally took him to his first baseball game over the summer. You've kept him in the garage for hours. He's like your third kid in this—"

"*Me*," he cut in. "Me dating."

Oh.

Oh, that was new.

My mom had died almost ten years ago, and since then my dad had never so much as looked at another woman. That was probably a little strange, but I'd just assumed he was okay.

My dad stared at me. "How do you feel about that?"

I felt like if my dad wanted to explore that route, that he should be able to do so. If he wanted to find—no, *enhance*—happiness again, then he should be able to do it. But if he was dating, then who?

"Is there someone in particular?"

"Not yet, but it's something I wanted to talk to you about before there *was* someone in particular."

"Whatever you say," I said, a little bit suspicious but patting him on the shoulder. This was good, I decided. It was good for him to find someone again. "I'm okay with it. If you want us to set you up a dating profile, my friends and I—"

He shot me a stern look as I laughed. "Just kidding."

~

Hours later, we had made our way into the decorated Cahill household. The large house was filled with various people, a lot more people than only the Cahill clan. There was Dad, Justin, and me; Emma, Alexis, and their parents; Caleb, Tia Maria, and Caleb's older sister, Leona. Every year, Andrew's family had come over to our house, so Liz had extended an invitation to them as well. That made for over thirty people having Christmas dinner that night.

I had barely made my way inside when Phillip bombarded me at the front door. The rest of the Andersons and the Prescott family made their way inside as Phillip talked my ear off while I removed my shoes. I was wearing a fitted brown dress that Stevie and Jasmine had coerced me into buying over the summer, with a black jacket on top. I didn't feel uncomfortable; in fact, when I had video called Maddy earlier before I left, she'd given the outfit an A-plus, which Anmol had seconded when we'd added her to the call.

Phillip was showing me the new Teenage Mutant Ninja Turtle game he had gotten where he was able to be Leonardo when someone slipped through the door behind me: Sydney, Lucas's girlfriend. I still couldn't believe that Lucas, probably the only Cahill who had no real social skills, had a girlfriend.

Cutting through the group of people, a pregnant Natasha made her way over to Sydney and her mom, whom Sydney introduced as Danielle.

Danielle bid her daughter goodbye just as Sam's aunt Naomi caught her attention from a distance. Phillip cut through Natasha and Sydney's hug with a question for Sydney. "Did you get me something?"

"Phillip," Natasha said sternly, and I was trying to hide my smile when my phone buzzed in my pocket.

Dante: What do you call a person afraid of Santa Claus?

Dante: CLAUStrophobic LOL

Maddy: That was horrible.

I laughed inwardly at the dumb joke. "It's great, but I know you don't care, PJ," I heard Sydney say.

"PJ?" Phillip asked, his eyes bright. "I've been called Philly, Leonardo, Phil, even Little Cahill, but not PJ."

"Yeah, PJ," Sydney said. "For Phillip John."

"I like it," I commented, approaching them.

"I like it too. I'm PJ from now on," Phillip declared, rushing out of the room. He was definitely going to spread the news of his new nickname.

"So . . . I heard," Natasha said to Sydney, and I linked my fingers together, leaning over slightly to hear more about the interesting topic of Lucas and his now-girlfriend.

"Heard?"

"You and Lucas," Natasha confirmed.

Sydney let out an awkward laugh, looking anywhere but at Natasha. "Oh."

"Yeah, oh." Natasha wiggled her eyebrows, but now I felt kind of bad for teasing Sydney. Kind of.

"Hey, Sydney," I said to her, and she gave me a grateful smile as she said hi back. One that seemed to indicate she wanted a change in conversation. Unluckily for her, Natasha wasn't budging.

"So . . . details."

Sydney rolled her lips into her mouth like she was embarrassed about the topic and wasn't comfortable speaking about it. In fact, her eyes glanced over at where her mom was talking to Naomi.

Wait a second. "She doesn't know, does she?" I asked.

Natasha followed my gaze. "Your mom? She doesn't know about you and Lucas?" Sydney shook her head, worry arising in her gaze. Oh no. "You'd better tell her soon. Moms find out things when you least expect it."

"I'm planning on it," Sydney answered as we looked at Lucas's stepmother talking to her mom. Then someone else joined their conversation—my dad. It took less than five seconds for my father to get Sydney's mom laughing at something he'd said. That's when I recognized Sydney's mom: she'd been the woman my dad had been talking to at the wedding. *Sure* there was no one in particular, Dad.

"I think we might be seeing each other more often," I whispered to Sydney. "That's my dad, Nick Anderson."

"Your dad?" Sydney's eyes widened. "And my mom. Oh, wow."

"Yup," I said, glancing at Sydney. She could be my stepsister one day.

Surprisingly, the thought didn't scare me. Looking at my dad right now, as he beamed at something Danielle had said, I realized it didn't scare me at all.

A few moments later, everyone was crowding into the dining room. Instead of the typical single long table, there were now three, with adults at the center and the younger people on the ends. Waiters moved in and out, handing out appetizers, entrees, and desserts when needed. The entire feast was incredible, along with the Christmas decorations around the room. Cedric nudged me with his foot under the table. "Stop staring," he whispered.

"There's just so much going on," I whispered back as someone set mini burgers in front of me. My eyes widened as Cedric laughed again. We had caught up a bit more over the break. He was doing well and seeing someone new. Currently, he looked great, happy being with his family.

"She's so annoying," Andrew said to Cedric, and Cedric chuckled as I glared at the two of them. Idiots.

Andrew picked at the broccoli on his plate, handing some over to Riley, who made a disgruntled face next to him. "You can't give it to her. You should eat it," I insisted, almost choking when I felt Sam's foot nudge my own. "It's good for you."

I glanced up at him as he was chatting with Alexis, and the slight smile on his face let me know he was trying to distract me on purpose.

"Says the girl who treats food like her first love," Andrew grumbled.

"I'm right here," Sam announced, and I rolled my eyes, pushing his foot down with my own under the table.

"You're a close second," I commented.

He put a hand to his chest and pouted. "I'm hurt."

I turned away from him as Andrew kept piling broccoli on my plate. He turned to his little sister. "Riley, you like the broccoli?"

She made a face, and everyone laughed. Sam looked at her over the table. "Riley, just finish *one* for me." Riley crossed her arms. "Please?"

Hesitantly, she took her fork, stabbing the vegetable with it, then slowly put a small piece of it inside her mouth. I couldn't help but start cackling when she made an even worse face than before, struggling to chew and eventually swallow it. "I did it!" she exclaimed.

"Good, now you can give the rest to Andrew."

"Who will give it to Macy!" Andrew proclaimed, adding more broccoli to the pile on my plate.

I shot my best friend a look. "You do realize that this happens every single year, right?"

"You realize that I will still hate broccoli every single year, right?"

"Andrew, eat it," Nonna said, turning from where she was sitting at the middle table with all the older adults. "You're a grown boy. You should know that you should eat your vegetables."

Andrew huffed, taking a piece of broccoli off my plate to eat it himself. "I hate every single second of this."

Nonna's eyes went straight to me and Sam. "And you two. Don't disappear. This is Christmas. Be with family."

Sam and I exchanged a glance. Even if we'd planned to escape this house tonight, I didn't think that we could. Caleb chuckled once Nonna turned back around. "She thinks you guys are going to go outside and do kinky things."

My face went up in flames. If there was an award for turning everything into a sexual innuendo, Caleb would take first place. Sam rolled his eyes, but Ivan—who would take second—entertained the conversation as he made his way over to us, placing his hands on Sam's shoulders. "Only need one of us to be a father right now, you hear?"

Sam batted his cousin's hands away. "Fuck off."

"Macy is seconds away from ripping your shirt off, Sam. Watch out." Caleb continued joking, and next to me Andrew snorted.

I shot him a glare as Ivan continued his teasing. "Macy, you've got to remember, there are people around."

"Oh my God." The people around us at the table, even Toby, laughed while I put my face in my hands.

Yet underneath the table, Sam's foot pressed against my own. I caught his eye over the glass of water he was taking a sip from. Comfort shone from his gaze. No pressure ever came from him. None at all.

~

After dinner was over, people lingered downstairs in every room. I sat on the staircase between Caleb and Andrew. Caleb was typing something frantically on his phone. "What are you doing?" Andrew asked him.

"I've got an idea," Caleb responded without breaking concentration. "I need to write it down."

"How do you balance school and writing?" Andrew asked. "Every time I talk to you, you're always writing."

"Easy," Caleb answered, pocketing his phone. "I don't do the schoolwork."

I blinked. "You're kidding, right?"

Caleb shot me a wink, getting up. That didn't answer my question.

He walked over to Sam's mother, who was speaking to Sam's aunt Naomi. Both women wore long dresses and held themselves with a confidence that made me uneasy just watching them from a distance as they conversed. However, Caleb cut through their conversation with his charming self, and before I knew it, Naomi excused herself as Alice and Caleb seemed to get into a very deep conversation, Alice pulling out her phone at one point and showing him something.

"You know what that's about?" Andrew asked.

I shook my head.

Andrew's voice was low when he asked me another question. "How do you feel about seeing Alexis?"

The name alone had me making a face. "She hasn't done anything," I said. *Yet.* She'd spent most of dinner engaged in conversation with Sam.

"You know, when Ivan and Caleb brought up the kinky thing at the table, she looked at you."

"In what way?"

"I don't know, she just looked at you," Andrew said. "Is she aware that . . . ?"

"That Sam and I haven't had sex?" I shrugged. "I don't know. It's not her business."

It wasn't. But when I was engaged in a conversation with Liz later, suddenly it was.

28
YOU RUINED THE CAROLS

Later that night, Liz was in the middle of trying to convince me to be a model once again as we spoke in the kitchen. I was piling some pigs in a blanket on a napkin as she tried to persuade me for the hundredth time when Alice and Alexis entered the room.

I had food in my mouth when I saw them enter. I almost choked.

They got along so well. In fact, Alice was laughing at something Alexis had said to her, her hand on her arm as they approached us. When's Alice's smooth gaze came to me, her laughter faded, her expression now a stony calm that made my stomach dive. "Macy."

"Hi," I said.

Liz, on the other hand, nudged me once again as she pushed her long black hair over her shoulders. "Alice, tell Macy she should be a model."

Liz didn't care about the look I shot her at that moment,

instead looking at Alice with hopeful eyes. I didn't know much about their history, but I had a feeling from the interactions I had seen over the summer that they were very good friends, even outside their Cahill connection. Alice glanced at me, then back at Liz. "Elizabeth, she's told you a million times she doesn't want to be a model."

"But look at her height!"

We all see my height, Liz. Then a rare thing occurred. A faint smile dawned on Alice's lips. "She's going to be a football player, Elizabeth. There's nothing else you can do about that."

Liz looked displeased, but she didn't push any further, settling for giving me a warm and comforting squeeze as if to apologize for constantly asking me. I didn't mind. She'd always been so kind to me, through any circumstances. Alexis didn't pay the scene any attention, texting on her phone while Alice watched us with indecipherable eyes. Liz promised she would find me later, taking Alice by the hand, and the pair of successful women left the empty room to head back into civilization.

Which left me with the she-devil.

Oh God, someone save me. All I wanted was to eat my pigs in a blanket.

Alexis put her phone down, glancing at the food piled up in my napkin before looking at me. "You don't talk to Alice much, do you?"

She knew the answer to that. Instead of responding, I shoved another pig in a blanket into my mouth.

The corners of Alexis's lips quirked up as she crossed her arms. "She's not an easy nut to crack. She's always liked me, though."

That would have been a simple comment if it didn't have snark in it. I fought the urge to roll my eyes. "Good to know."

"And Liz wants you to be a model?" Her eyes went back over to my pile of food. Her gaze scanned my seated posture from head to toe, and I fought to not squirm under her analysis. *Don't let her get to you. Don't let her get to you. Don't let her get to you.*

"I mean, you're tall," she said. "That's all you really have going for you. Do you really want to get into the industry? I'm not certain they'd take on girls like you."

I froze. "What is that supposed to mean?"

She feigned an innocent expression. "It's your features. They might not be suited for the cover of a magazine or walking down the runway. You don't scream *Vogue*. You don't really have fashion taste, either, considering you mostly wear sweats and sportswear."

"Hold on—"

"Plus, like Alice said, you're a soccer player." The smile on her face was cunning at this point. "You're aggressive, and it shows. On the field and off, apparently. Even Alice knew there was no hope for you outside of that, which is why she shut Liz down."

That's when I stood up. I had about two inches on her, and I made sure it showed when I glared at her. "What do you get out of trying to put me down?"

She blinked, and I wanted to wipe the fake good girl expression off her face. "Who said I was putting you down?"

I took a deep breath. I couldn't take this, but I wasn't going to cause a scene on what was supposed to be a good night. "You know, I try to stay out of your way and be polite to you when I have to be—for your sister's sake because she's kind and she's with my brother, and for Sam's sake because he doesn't have many friends of his own and for some reason, he seems to think you are one. I respect it because he's known you longer than he's known me."

That didn't faze her. She seemed a little smug at my last sentence as she reaffirmed it by saying, "Yes, we have a history."

I paused, knowing what she was implying, but brushed it aside for my own sake. "I've tried to be nice, but clearly, you can't do the same."

"I can be nice."

"Not to me," I pointed out with an eye roll and decided to finally say it out in the open. "Alexis, I know you dislike me so much because I'm with someone you want."

For a second, I didn't think she was going to say anything. Tension sizzled in the air as she stared at me, her innocent expression no longer apparent. Dislike was heavy in her gaze as she peered at me. That dislike shifted into satisfaction when she said, "From what I've heard, you haven't been with him the same way I have."

She must have eavesdropped on my conversation with Andrew. How she'd done that, I didn't know or care. That wasn't any of her business. My sex life, whether it was active or inactive, was none of her business.

I didn't break the eye contact, willed myself not to. It didn't matter. Sam's past, who he had been with, didn't bother me. It wasn't going to be a factor in our relationship whether it had been Alexis or someone else. I didn't care.

I didn't care.

Get out of the room. Get out of the room. "Have a good night, Alexis." I shifted my way past her, my footsteps trudging as I left the room. The second I was out of there, a long breath of relief left my body as I made my way through the corridor.

I placed my napkin on a random shelf, turning away from anyone else who was lingering in the hallway to run a hand over my face. She was so annoying. The way she'd looked at me like she knew her words were going to affect me, like she wanted to make sure I crumbled, like she was willing to do anything she could to—

My phone buzzed in the pocket of my jacket.

Maddy and Dante's group chat. I closed my eyes, looking up at the ceiling as a silent prayer for those two before looking down at the conversation that was named—wait for it—"TwoM1D." Meaning two *M*s and one *D. Groan*.

Maddy: You make me cringe.

Dante: How?

Maddy: If you're going to love a YouTuber love a good one.

Dante: Just because he doesn't have a lot of subscribers doesn't mean he isn't good.

Maddy: I've watched his videos. And half his followers hate him. He sucks.

Dante: Just because he isn't talking about makeup shit doesn't mean he's bad.

Maddy: I don't just watch makeup shit. He's trying to be funny when he's not. WAKE UP DANIEL HE'S NOT FUNNY.

Dante: CALL ME DANIEL AGAIN. I DARE YOU.

Then the start of a meme war, random pictures and gifs making my phone ping constantly.

Me: Dante, Maddy, go be with your families. If I see another picture, I'm leaving this group chat.

Me: Merry Christmas again :)

I rolled my eyes, tucking my phone in my pocket as a faint rendition of "Feliz Navidad" came from Phillip and Caleb in the living room. Someone tapped me on the shoulder, and I tilted my head back to look at Sam, who leaned forward to press a kiss to my forehead. "Get ready."

I relaxed even further, linking my hands with his. "Where are we going?"

"Quarry. Cliff," he said, glancing down the now-empty hallway to quickly pull me along to the corridor near the front door. We grabbed our things—him slinging his jacket on as I grabbed my jacket, boots, mittens, hat, and scarf. He raised an eyebrow at my getup, and I spun dramatically in a circle for him to show him how bundled up I was.

"It's freezing outside," I stated. That leather jacket was not going to give him any warmth at all.

Just as Lucas was passing by, Sam plucked the hat off his head and put it on his own, then took gloves from another person's jacket. He shot me a smile. "Now let's go."

"No, no, no." I grabbed Justin's scarf off his coat and tossed it to him. "Sam," I said as he opened the door and pulled me out of the house, "are you just going to take me out and not even tell anyone?"

"I told my dad. He's okay with it. I told your dad. He's okay with it."

"What about Nonna?" I asked him.

He paused before pulling me along to one of the cars parked in the driveway. "She'll be okay with us being gone for a bit."

"Will she?" We both knew Nonna. She loved Christmas more than anyone I knew. "Will she really?"

"No, so we should leave before she comes. Let's go." We got

into the car, and he drove off as fast as he could in the weather.

"It's so weird celebrating Christmas here," he commented when we were a good distance from the house.

"What do you guys usually do?"

"My parents aren't really holiday people," he admitted. "But they like the aspect of giving people gifts. Bethany was the person who decorated the house to get us all into the season. One time, Caleb came over for the holidays, and even though he wasn't spending Christmas with us, she dragged us around to do Christmas things."

I loved when he talked about her. "Like what?"

"Like open presents under the Christmas tree," he reminisced, his hand shifting on the steering wheel.

Of course, Sam would find something I thought was completely normal weird. "That's *normal.*"

"Not for my family." He chuckled. "Bethany made me and Caleb join in on this carol singing thing happening in a different area. We ended up walking from house to house with the group of people, making our own renditions."

"You ruined the carols?"

"I think we made it better," he insisted. "Besides, Bethany could sing well. The spotlight was on her the second she opened her mouth."

"Surely you too." He didn't sing often, but it was evident his mother's musical talent had been passed down to him and his sister.

Sam let out a long breath before a little laugh left him. "But it shut down the second Caleb opened his mouth. He can't sing for shit."

"Oh, what did Caleb get you as a present?" I asked.

"He got me socks."

He wasn't fazed by the gift. Those two and their inside jokes. "Socks?"

"Yeah. They have a weird pattern on them, but they say Italy on the bottom."

I didn't press on the choice of country. "What did you get him?"

"Socks that have a weird pattern and say England on the bottom." Sam laughed, and the sound went right down to my toes. "We planned it out and everything. He found them online. We're both wearing them right now. Because according to him, we have to do everything as best friends or some shit like that." He said that last part in a really high voice that faded out when a rendition of "Last Christmas" came on the radio.

"You guys are so weird."

Sam grinned, slowing down to park. "He doesn't usually get me anything anyway. It's not like I want him to."

"Is it because your birthday is coming up?"

For a moment, Sam paused before he took the key out of the ignition. "It's because I've never been into the 'It's Christmas, let's give each other presents' thing. I'm more into the whole 'Let's prank Ivan when he's sleeping' or 'Let's dump a bucket of cold water on Toby's head' kind of thing."

I snorted. "So . . . family bonding?"

"If you want to be formal, then I guess so." We got out of the car, and Sam grabbed a bundle of blankets, as if that was going to stop the cold from hitting us in the face. As if he'd read my mind, he shot me an exasperated look. "You'll be warm."

"If you say so," I said as we made our way along the snow-covered path through the quarry toward our spot.

When we reached our place, he spread one blanket on the

ground, making sure not to be too close to the edge of the cliff, and handed me a blanket to put on my legs. "You may not like giving presents, but I do," I said.

"Hazel . . ." He trailed off, looking down at me.

"You don't understand how hard it is to buy a present for someone who can easily go out and get it himself. It's a long process trying to find out what to give you for Christmas and your birthday, so you're going to take it whether you want to or not. Are we clear?"

He cracked a smile, sitting down next to me. "Okay, what is it?"

I took the gift out of my pocket and handed it to him. "I already knew that you weren't into the whole Christmas thing, so I settled on something simple. Simple but useful. It's kind of cheap, but honestly remember that your real present is coming for your birthday."

He stared at the makeshift book in his hands, flipping through the pages and taking the time to read each word. "A coupon book," he murmured. "One for two hugs? One for ten kisses at any time during the day; I already do that—"

"Just appreciate the gift," I demanded. "The real one is coming on your birthday."

Sam smiled as he flicked through the many pages before stumbling on one that I knew wasn't in my handwriting. *Oh my God.* "A coupon to give Sam—"

I grabbed the small book out of his hand, tearing that piece of paper out. I crumpled it in my hand and threw it over the cliff. A sigh left my throat when I realized I'd littered. "Caleb probably wrote that one. He was helping me out. Well, not really helping me out after that, I guess."

Sam's fingers thumbed the book when he took it back. "I know it doesn't seem like a lot," I said. If he'd given me this, there was a big chance I would have been confused.

"Hazel, you took time to create this. I have a feeling that you started making this during exam season—"

"I did. And there's a hundred different coupons in that thing, by the way."

When he looked at me, I felt his expression course its way through my body. The way Samuel Cahill showed his gratitude made me want to see that expression as often as I could. "You didn't have to do this."

"But I did, so—"

My sentence was cut off by the short but sweet kiss he placed on my lips. "I'm trying to say thank you," he murmured against my skin, kissing me again.

I pulled back. "You just cashed in a coupon, didn't you?"

Sam ripped the paper out and handed it to me. "Here you go."

I took it from him before I scanned the tiny print at the bottom of the paper. "It says free hug for Caleb as well."

Sam scoffed, shifting himself closer to me as he put an arm around my waist. "I have a Christmas present for you too, but it's not here." *Oh?* I took a moment to realize what he'd just said. "What?"

Sam cleared his throat, his glove-covered hand taking my mitten-covered one. "I wasn't able to bring it here. It's back in Southford."

He couldn't say that. He couldn't leave me on a cliffhanger—ironic, considering we were sitting on the edge of a literal cliff. "What is it?"

"You'll figure out what it is once we get back."

No. I didn't like that. "That makes me want to know what it is even more."

"Hazel."

"Sam, tell me."

"I can't."

"You can," I pressured him.

"I really can't."

"Sam, c'mon."

"Hazel?"

Seeing defeat in my near future, I scowled. "Yeah?"

"Merry Christmas."

He pulled me closer. Once he wrapped his arms around me, the cold of the winter season and all my complaining easily disappeared. "Merry Christmas."

In the comfortable silence, there were no problems. There was no school. There was no drama. There was no stress outside the sport we loved. No one else. It was me and him in our spot on the cliff, and that was enough.

Then he said, "I could tell you one thing, but it's not really much of a present. It's kind of a clarification of something I once said, really."

He let out a long exhale, digging into his jacket pocket. When he pulled out his wallet, he dug around until he handed me his driver's license. I stared at him, then down at the picture of him, then back at him.

"Why am I looking at a picture of you?"

"Not the picture." He seemed a little distraught. "The birthday."

Why would I need to look at his birthday? Sam was born on January—

His license said January 1.

It said January 1. Not January 3 like he had told me close to a year ago when we were driving to this cliff. When we had barely known each other but had spent time together day after day. January 3 was the date I knew.

At that moment, I realized I could be annoyed that he'd lied to me despite there only being a two-day difference—but I was his girlfriend. And I had been his friend before that. With Sam there was always an explanation. There was also a reason to hear him out before I reacted.

I took a deep breath, staring at the number. "Why did you tell me your birthday was on the third?"

"Because that's what Beth and I would tell people when they would ask." His answer made me look at him. "I didn't mean to lie to you. It was an impulse when you asked me that."

I handed him his ID back as he explained further. "When we were kids, we never celebrated our birthday on the first because our other friends would be with their families. The third was our day until we grew older. The third became an inside joke, an answer to avoid the surprised gasp of 'Oh, you're a New Year's baby.'"

"You're a New Year's baby," I whispered.

"Yeah. I am." He pocketed his wallet, his green eyes dim. "I'm sorry, I didn't mean to lie to you."

"It's okay," I said, placing my hand over his. Sam was born on January 1. Crazy. "Does that mean I can annoy you by calling you a New Year's baby every year since you kept that from me?"

"Will that make up for it?"

"Yes."

He grinned. "Then do it proudly."

I pressed a kiss to his cheek. "Good. Now, as much as I love this place, I am freezing my butt off. Can we please leave?"

"Aaand moment over." Sam got up, laughing, taking the blankets with him as we walked back to the car.

"What do you think about Caleb writing so much?" I asked him when we started driving again.

"He's been inspired a lot lately," Sam said.

"But you know something."

"I know that he has something in the works, but he doesn't want to tell anyone or have me telling anyone until it's confirmed," Sam said. "Especially you; he specifically told me not to tell you until he was ready."

And Sam was going to respect Caleb's wish, the way Caleb would do for him. I understood that completely, even if it annoyed me to be left in the dark. "Is it a good thing, though?"

Sam smiled. "It is."

"Then good." I leaned back into my seat. "Whatever it is, I'm happy for him."

In the silence, I caught Sam glancing at me.

"What?"

He let out a soft laugh, shaking his head as he focused on the road. "I just love how you always want the best for people."

I blew a raspberry before shrugging. "It'll be good for him."

My phone buzzed in my pocket for the hundredth time that night, and I looked down at the screen.

Maddy: DANIEL SHUT UP

Dante: MADELYN SHUT UP

Maddy: IT'S MADELINE

Dante: Who cares?? I'm right and you know it.

Maddy was going to explode at that response. I could picture her bent over her phone, typing a long and explicit paragraph. When I left the chat, I saw I had an individual text message from Dante.

> Dante: Victoria, just agree with me so we can end this please?
>
> Dante: My name isn't Daniel.

The name, despite being close to Dante, didn't suit him at all. A laugh escaped my lips, and Sam glanced at me as we pulled in to the driveway of the house. "Why are you laughing?"

"Dante," I said. "He and Maddy are in an argument over some YouTuber."

Sam stopped the car, taking the key out of the ignition, and even though it was kind of dark, the light outside the house illuminated the frown etched on his face. "Dante?"

"The one you met at the indoor track before exams? Remember?" I asked as we got out of the car and came back to the winter chill.

"You still talk to him?"

What? He knew that. Dante was one of the only reasons I'd had a chance to pull up some of my chemistry course marks with the final exams. "Yeah." I narrowed my eyes at Sam when we opened the door to the buzzing house. Caleb was belting out "All I Want For Christmas Is You" off-key. "We're friends."

He didn't like that, judging by his frown. His visible displeasure made me fight back an eye roll. It was just Dante. There was nothing unlikable about the guy to begin with, nothing to worry over. So why was Sam upset?

Sam opened his mouth to speak but was cut off when we heard another voice. "Where were you two?"

"Shit," Sam uttered as we turned to face the wrath of my Nonna.

29
RAT

"Are you serious?" I asked Jasmine as she rolled onto her stomach on my bed.

"Why not?" Jasmine laughed. She, Stevie, and I were crowded in my room, having a much-needed girls' night. Currently, the three of us had on facial masks; Stevie had found a recipe for them online. My skin felt strange underneath, but I didn't argue over it. I was happy that this was happening. "Swimming with animals sounds amazing. I figured you would want to try it."

"Are you crazy? I'm not about to jump into water that could lead to my death," I exclaimed. "Give me a pool with no animals and we can talk then."

Stevie let out a sound that was half laugh, half snort from where she was lying next to Jasmine, the action film I had brought to watch on my laptop suddenly forgotten. "I'll go with you if she won't."

"Good!" Jasmine's brown eyes lit up. "I was thinking of trying it out during the summer. There's this place connected to campus where people sign up to do it."

"You're planning on staying in BC for the summer?" Stevie asked.

I stopped swiveling in my chair. Had she forgotten we had plans for the summer? Ones that we'd spoken about in November? Jasmine shrugged. "Likely. I've been trying to see if I could get a job and volunteer over there. If I do, then I'll likely stay there."

Oh.

Before I could respond, my phone buzzed in my pocket.

Dante: Another pun of the day?

Me: Sure, why not?

Dante: I'd tell you a chemistry joke, but I don't think I'd get a reaction.

I clamped my hand over my mouth.

Me: That was bad.

Dante: On the other hand, you have different fingers.

"Oh my God," I mumbled as Jasmine peered over my shoulder.

"Who's that?"

"Dante."

"A university friend?"

"Yeah, who has a ridiculous love for bubble tea."

"Bubble tea sounds so good right now," Stevie mused, running a hand through her blond hair as she peered over my shoulder at my phone. "Wow, Dante sounds very punny."

I stared at her blankly as she laughed at her own joke. Then Jasmine joined in, their laughter getting louder. "You guys have the worst sense of humor."

"Macy, get on our level," Stevie said.

Jasmine barely got the words out as she giggled harder: "I don't think her elevator can reach that high."

They both started hollering from that lame excuse of a diss, making me roll my eyes. "Why am I being insulted?"

"We're not insulting you," Stevie said as she got up. "It's advanced humor."

"Don't make some kind of advancement joke," I demanded, and she chuckled at me, excusing herself to the bathroom.

"It was funny," Jasmine said.

Maybe. Though her sudden change in plans was not. "So you're planning on staying in BC?" I asked quietly.

Jasmine tugged her bottom lip into her mouth, possibly sensing the shift in the atmosphere considering I hadn't been looking at her when I'd asked the question. My attention was on the screen as she said, "Yeah. I found a place with some floormates. The lease starts in May, so I may as well make the most of it."

I reached forward to pause the movie before glancing at her. "What happened to road trips in the summer?"

"Mace." She hopped off the bed. "We can still do the road trips."

Why did a part of me not believe that?

"And all of it, really. I'll visit for sure. I mean, *you're* here,

Mace, of course I'll visit. You, Stevie, and the guys."

"You haven't really seen the guys, though."

"I hung out with some of them: the twins last week, Jon Ming this morning, and Austin last night with Caleb," she told me. "I think all of us together would remind us of old times, so I've been avoiding it until this all calms down."

Until Andrew started speaking to her again.

"Okay," I said.

"But we're okay?"

I hoped we would be. "Yeah," I said. "We're okay."

When Stevie entered the room again, she plopped down between us, all of us finally starting to watch the movie. But then as I ate some popcorn, Jasmine said, "You know what someone would call a bad popcorn joke? Corny."

And they proceeded to burst out laughing while I closed my eyes and prayed for the sweet release of death.

~

Natasha grimaced from where she was standing in the kitchen of the Cahill home. We were going through pictures on this late snowy night. Stevie, Jon Ming, Brandon, Jacob, Austin, Andrew, Caleb, and my boyfriend were currently in the living room of the house. Meanwhile, I was seated next to Natasha at the island, flicking through the photos on her laptop. She had a glow on her now-tanned skin from her honeymoon. Yet that glow dimmed every time she shifted uncomfortably and put a hand to her baby bump.

"You still have the sickness?" I asked.

"I feel like I'm going to vomit on you right this second." She held a hand to her mouth, and we both waited, willing it not to happen.

When she relaxed, she moved her hand from her mouth, and I exhaled dramatically.

"Okay, we're good. Like I said before, the pictures are amazing, Mace."

"Thanks." I beamed. "I can't believe you guys are moving."

Natasha shook her head in disbelief. "No more Port Meadow. It's so weird. We'll have a house to ourselves close to New York." They were relocating to where Natasha could perform and Ivan could do his duties at the American branch of the Cahill corporation.

Natasha's hand went to her stomach. "I just want her to be happy."

"How do you guys even know it's going to be a girl?" I questioned, shoving popcorn into my mouth.

"Ivan's certain. He bet five hundred dollars with one of his friends on what the sex of our child is going to be. There's something in his head saying that it's going to be a girl, and for his sake, I'm going along with it."

"Wife of the year," I drawled. Ivan and Natasha being married was still something I wasn't used to. Natasha being pregnant was even stranger. I couldn't possibly imagine that this time next year, she would be a mother.

Natasha's eyes suddenly widened, and it was then I noticed that she looked slightly pale. Oh no. "I need to go to the bathroom." She got up quickly and left, passing by Greg, who'd entered the kitchen. Sam's little brother did a double take, his brown eyes wide.

"Is she okay?" he asked, staring at the door.

"She's pregnant."

"Oh." He scratched his head. "Then she's fine."

I laughed as he sat next to me, gesturing toward the popcorn. I handed the bowl to him as we flicked through the photos in silence.

"You know I like you, right?" *Huh?* I turned to him, and he put his hands up in self-defense. "For my *brother*. Not in *that* way. You know what I mean."

"I know what you mean," I assured him gently.

"Okay, good." He nodded to himself. "Good."

We fell into a calm silence as he clicked picture after picture. Photos with Ivan's friends. Photos with his brother and cousins. A picture of him and Sam side by side in their matching suits, Greg beaming at the camera. Next to him, with an arm around him, Sam wore a pure grin, genuine and filled with joy. Their smiles were identical, their hair the same shade of dark brown. "He didn't smile like that for a long time," Greg suddenly mumbled, his attention fixed on the photo, "after Bethany."

I didn't know how to respond. But as I sat there, I realized I didn't need to speak much. Greg, at twelve years old, had enough to say. "I think Canada did him some good. That's why I wanted to come here. It's good seeing him more often too."

My heart warmed. It was good that he had his brother close by again. I couldn't imagine being apart from Justin for such a long time. "How are you finding it?" I asked.

Greg twisted his mouth to the side. "I like it. I've made some friends and gotten closer to people. But I miss home sometimes," he confessed, flipping through the different photographs. "I miss how things used to be."

A pang hit me straight in the chest at his voice. I'd known

loss as a child. I knew how odd it felt in the aftermath, wondering where to go and how to live in the after. It was a dreadful feeling, one that lingered for a long while then occasionally appeared out of nowhere before settling back into a dark part of the mind.

Greg continued to flick through the pictures when another person entered the room. His father, the spitting image of an older version of my boyfriend. James nodded in my direction before looking at his son. "You want to head to Aunt Naomi and Uncle John's?"

Greg shook his head, hopping off the stool. "I think I'm going to head to the game room with Phillip."

Greg waved goodbye, moving past his father, who ruffled his hair on his way out. Then it was only James Cahill and me in a room. That had never happened before.

He was polite, a lot more friendly-looking than his wife. His brown-eyed gaze was a lot more like Greg's when his attention drifted to the pictures on the laptop. "You took these?"

I blinked as he took the seat Greg had previously occupied. "Yes, I did."

He flicked through the photos, his eyebrows raised. "Sam said you had a talent with the camera. Elizabeth and Natasha said so too, but . . ."

James Cahill looked impressed.

I had impressed Sam's dad.

For some reason, that left me dumbfounded, staring at the screen as picture after picture flipped by. "Photography had better be your calling alongside football, Macy," he said, and I felt my face flame up at the compliment.

"Thank you."

When he finished sifting through the pictures, he returned to the first one: a photo of Ivan and Natasha smiling at each other. "I'm sure you heard what's happening with Anthony."

I nodded. He was going to trial. For other charges. Not for trespassing at the wedding, which Ivan had said he didn't care about, but for other things, specifically drug-related.

Anthony wasn't going to be bothering Sam ever again, and that's all that mattered to me.

James continued looking at the photograph in the midst of our silence. "When my son brought you up in a call all those months ago, I have to admit, I was wary."

I stilled.

"Wary for him and for you," he continued. "I didn't think he was in the right headspace for a relationship, nor did I want him to be taken advantage of by the people he'd met, such as Anthony. But then I saw you two when we visited. At graduation and throughout the summer," he murmured. "I wanted to let you know that I am no longer wary."

My shoulders relaxed. That assurance was so nice considering how much my dad liked Sam. It was good to have that hospitality reciprocated on the other side.

Then James let out a sigh. "I also heard that you're worried that Alice doesn't like you." I bit back a curse. *Sam.* "Alice has always taken a little longer to come around. Don't worry."

That was the third time someone had told me that.

We'd see.

Then he spun the conversation, surprising me when he asked, "Also, you support Chelsea, right?"

"Yup."

"All my brothers support Man U." James shot me a wink that

reminded me of Ivan. "My son clearly fell in love with the right person."

I let out a laugh as he shot me a familiar smile before exiting the room.

When I entered the living room, all of my friends were gathered. I frowned, knowing that if possible, Jasmine would have been here with us as well.

Caleb held a bag of marshmallows, and there was music playing from Jon Ming's phone. He was showing Jacob a song he had been working on with an artist recently.

"Time to act like we're kids in the woods!" Caleb handed each person their own skewer before making a face. "When people have a bonfire and they roast marshmallows, you know how the stick they attach the marshmallow to is from the ground?"

"Yeah," Jacob grumbled, shutting off the song. "What's your point?"

"Isn't that atrocious? You're eating a melted marshmallow. That's great and everything, but the stick has so much bacteria on it. It just spreads everywhere and goes into your body and into your system and—"

Andrew grabbed the bag of marshmallows out of Caleb's hand. "More for us. None for Caleb."

"Half of that bag is *mine*," Caleb demanded, snatching the bag back. "What's a good campfire song to sing?"

"You realize that we're not outside, right?" Sam asked.

"God, Sam, you're such a downer." Caleb glared at him. "Use your imagination, will you?"

"I imagine that we're not outside," Sam said deadpan. "Instead, we're in the living room toasting marshmallows in the fireplace."

"Your imagination sounds very realistic to me," Caleb muttered.

I turned myself upside down on the couch, taking a marshmallow from Caleb and putting it in my mouth. As my feet hung over the back of the couch, Andrew joined me in the same position. "Mace," Andrew said, "remember how much we used to fight over food?"

A short laugh escaped my lips at the memories.

"We used to turn everything into a competition. Who could eat the fastest?" he continued.

"And remember who always won?"

"Yeah . . . me."

I snorted. "You *wish* you won. You lost five times in a row that one month back in like seventh grade. Loser."

"Donkey."

"Horse."

"Rat."

"You're just mad because just like with everything else, I beat you."

Before Andrew could respond, Caleb yelled, "Sam, get the chocolate!"

Sam leapt up and was to the kitchen and back in about ten seconds. "Here."

"Okay." Caleb grinned like a madman, hovering over the fireplace to make his s'mores.

"What if we went camping?" Stevie asked, pulling her feet up as she tried watching something on her large phone.

"Like real camping? Outdoors? Tents? Bugs?" Jon Ming asked tentatively.

"Okay, so . . . Jon Ming won't be coming," Austin mumbled.

"It's not that. It's just, what if there are bears in the woods? Don't you guys ever think about that?"

"We'll just give them Caleb as a sacrifice," Jacob answered.

Caleb whipped his head toward Jacob faster than I could have imagined. "What? I mean—I'm sure I'd taste amazing, but no. Give them Brandon, the nice ones probably die first."

"What?" Brandon shot up. "No. Jacob is the better candidate."

"No, definitely Caleb," Sam insisted.

"We went camping once," Caleb said. "When we were like fourteen. One of the worst experiences of my life."

Sam started snickering, dropping down on one of the empty couches. "You screamed one night because you thought a snake was in our tent."

"What was it really?" Stevie asked.

"It was Ivan tickling his foot with a stick." Sam laughed even harder, and Caleb shoved him.

"Shut up, or I'm going to throw you into the fire."

"What are you guys doing?" Jon Ming asked Andrew and me, pushing us so he could sit between us.

The blood was definitely flowing to my head when Andrew answered, "We're just, you know, hanging."

Jon Ming laughed, and I groaned, bringing my legs down so I could sit on the couch properly. "Why is everyone making puns? First Dante sends me a pun every single day and then yesterday—"

"Dante?" Jon Ming repeated, loud enough to catch everyone's attention. I didn't miss the way Sam frowned. "Who's that?"

"He's a friend of mine. He's majoring in chemistry like me," I said, watching Caleb look over at Sam, who was tapping his foot against the ground. They'd clearly talked about Dante.

Andrew leaned over to me. "I'm guessing he doesn't like your newfound friendship with the Dante guy," he whispered, seeing the agitation on Sam's face.

"Very insightful of you, my friend," I hushed back, standing up and walking over to Sam. Thankfully, Caleb immediately began talking more loudly to redirect the room's attention back to him so Sam and I could have a little more privacy.

I sat down next to Sam, who rolled his lips into his mouth, eyes flickering across the ground as he struggled to get his point across. "Look, Daniel, or whatever his name is, is okay. All right?" He must've seen the look on my face because I did not believe what he was saying one bit. "I don't trust him."

"You don't trust him with me?" I asked, the two of us speaking low enough for only us to hear. "You think he's going to make a move on me or something?"

"I don't think he will. I *know* he will."

"First, he's not into me that way at all. And let's say he was, do you honestly think I would reciprocate?"

Sam opened his mouth to speak, but he bit his bottom lip to hold back whatever he had been going to say. He shook his head. "No, I know you wouldn't."

"Exactly. He's just a friend. That's all he'll ever be to me."

The exact same way you claim Alexis is your friend, and that's all she'll ever be.

Sam sank into the couch, looking annoyed. "He probably doesn't know that."

Okay, but neither does Alexis.

"Then I'll let him know. Sam, between soccer and school, I don't have time to make many friends on campus. You know this and I know this. It's surprising I managed to make a friend like Dante anyway."

"What about Maddy and Anmol?"

What about them? "I'm not going to limit my friends on campus to girls to make you feel better. Look around this room: you know I tend to surround myself with guys, and it's never been a problem for you. Dante is no different."

Sam exhaled slowly as our friends' voices somehow grew louder outside of our bubble. "I don't want you to limit who you become friends with, Hazel. I didn't—I'm sorry," His apology was further strengthened when he reached down, intertwining our fingers. "I don't know why I get this weird feeling around the guy."

"If something happens, I'll tell you," I promised. "Then we can deal with it together."

An understanding that I hoped would last dawned upon his face. He squeezed my hand once, his silent *I'm in love with you* as clear as day.

"Okay." Caleb's voice cut into everyone's conversations from where he stood in the middle of the room. He placed his melting marshmallow and a piece of chocolate between graham crackers, his eyes wide with childlike excitement, all eyes on him as he started handing out s'mores. "Another question. Which of you pour your milk first and which of you pour the cereal first? And before you respond, there *is* a wrong answer."

~

"Happy New Year, hon." Liz ushered me inside her home. New Year's Day marked both a new beginning and a bittersweet day: I now knew it was Sam's birthday . . . and Bethany's.

The Christmas decorations within the household had been

removed. Chatter spilled from the living room as I removed my shoes, glancing up as Caleb came toward me. He must have come over only a few moments ago.

The Cahills had spent the day out together. A part of me was wondering what place had accommodated all of them, but another question held more importance. Before I could ask, Caleb answered my unspoken inquiry. "He's doing okay. Better than I thought he'd be doing, really."

"Yeah?" Caleb gestured for me to follow him, but I stopped him. "And *you*?"

Caleb's smile slipped a little bit. He didn't bother recovering it. After all, he hadn't just known Bethany; he had been in love with her. He settled for giving me a squeeze on the arm as if to say *I'm getting there* before pulling me over to the living room.

Cahills spilled from corner to corner. The first Cahill I spotted was Alice, who was seated on a sofa next to her youngest, a hand on Greg's hair as he told something to the entire group. When Caleb and I entered the room, she caught my eye.

I couldn't imagine what she was going through on this day. But whatever the emotions were internally, they were not visible in her expression. Standing behind her was James, with comforting hands on her shoulders. She greeted me with a calm nod as everyone in the room broke out into sudden laughter—including the man of the hour, sitting on the armrest of the sofa next to Cedric. Although his chuckle was evidently quieter than normal, Caleb hadn't been wrong. He looked okay.

The attention on Greg's story was halted when Phillip barreled into me with a cheerful hello. Greetings came from my left and right, Cahill after Cahill, as Caleb and I were moved in Sam's direction. It was then I noticed the small strawberry ice cream container in Sam's hand as Caleb plopped down next to Cedric, who gave me a fist bump.

"Is the ice cream any good for a cheat day?"

Are you actually doing okay? Or is this all a front?

"The ice cream's good," he said softly, and relief flooded my system. My gaze flicked down to the golden *B* pendant that he usually kept under his shirt but that today was out in the open, dangling over his chest. "Could be better, but it's good."

That was good to hear.

"We're telling stories," Cedric told me, making space for me to sit.

Stories?

"Sam." Christian spoke up. "What about your sixteenth birthday?"

Sam's focus was on the ice cream in his hand. That had been his last birthday with her. With patience and understanding, they waited for him to speak. "I think that was one of the best days in my life."

"You got your motorcycle that day," Toby added from where he was seated between Lucas and Joey.

The corners of Sam's lips rose as he raised his head. "I didn't even expect it. I think I had only mentioned wanting one someday once, but she'd heard me. Then again, Beth always heard me." He suddenly chuckled. "She kept trying to force me and Caleb to have a spa day with her. My nails have never looked shinier."

Laughter scattered across the room as more questions were brought his way. They continued speaking for the next hour about their past. About his sister. The process of grief always varied for people. For me, I looked at pictures and videos of my mom and asked my dad for stories. For Sam, he relayed the stories in a way where there was passion, nostalgia, happiness, and pain. Memories held it all, but as each Cahill added on to whatever story he told, I knew he was grateful to have them even amidst all this emotion.

~

As the Cahills were settling in for a family birthday dinner, Caleb decided to test Sam's last nerve by trying to get him to wear a party hat.

"No," Sam answered.

"Sam, you need to do this."

"I'm nineteen, official drinking age, unlike you. I don't think I have to do anything you say." Sam smirked as he rolled up the sleeves of his button-up shirt. "Then again, I've never really bothered listening to you."

"Is it just me," Caleb started, trying to put the hat on Sam's head, "or does anyone else think turning nineteen has to be one of the ugliest birthdays ever?"

"I can assure you, it's just you," Sam said in a dry tone.

"I think I would want to go from turning nineteen to turning twenty in an instant. Nineteen is such an ugly number. You're not in your twenties, but you feel like you should be. You're still the same category as a thirteen-year-old. Who decided that turning nineteen was a good thing?"

"Caleb," Sam stressed, "I want you to shut up for five minutes. Only five minutes. That's all I ask for today, okay?"

Caleb got the hint, zipping the imaginary zipper on his lips and tossing the imaginary key away. I handed my camera to

Lucas, looking at Sam. "Caleb and I, while making you that dumb coupon book—"

"It wasn't dumb," Sam interrupted.

"Anyway, we decided to make you something else. Boys, can you bring it out?"

I turned my eyes to where a few of the Cahill boys were carrying a huge frame toward Sam, laying it down on the dining table in front of him. I glanced at Caleb before looking back at my boyfriend. "I hope you like it."

We had made a collage of photos of Sam throughout his nineteen years. I'd managed to get a hold of his laptop months ago and took all the pictures I could find to go along with the ones I had gotten from everyone else. Even though the pictures were all over the place inside the frame, they were organized so that the center photos would be of him, Greg, and Bethany.

His lips parted in shock as he zeroed in on the one in the very middle. His brow furrowed as he stared at the photo, of him, his brother, and his sister in dressy clothes, smiling at the camera. I watched him stare at that picture, then move around to the others, a million emotions flickering across his face the longer we waited for his reaction.

"When was this picture taken?" Sam whispered, pointing at a picture of him and Bethany laughing under a huge fake silver Christmas tree.

"When we all met up in Aruba a couple years ago," Toby answered, his hands on Sam's shoulders. "Neither of you noticed when I took the photo."

That look on Sam's face appeared again, the one that remained phlegmatic, yet his eyes shone looking at the images. He blinked several times as Lucas handed the camera to me so I could record his reaction.

But I didn't get a chance to start recording. Sam twisted in my direction, pulling me close enough to briefly kiss me on the lips. "Thank you," he whispered, and he glanced at Caleb as well. "Both of you."

"Of course," I responded while Caleb gave him an uplifting smile.

Sam glanced at another photograph, starting to laugh. "Oh my God, Ivan dropped to the ground right after this picture was taken."

The Cahill boys crowded around him, convulsing as a scowl grew prominent on Ivan's face.

That was the mood for the rest of the night as Sam went through most of the pictures and the memories. When the cake was brought out, Sam was finally wearing the funny party hat. The cake was placed in front of him, and his forest green eyes were alight from the reflection of the candles as his family and friends badly sang "Happy Birthday" to him. He caught my eye in the middle of Caleb shaking him as they sang his name, his happiness peeking through the sadness once they finished.

"Happy birthday, Beth," he whispered. He blew at the flames, and the brightness snuffed out.

30
MONTANA

"It's in your apartment?" I asked Sam for the hundredth time, the two of us walking into the elevator of his building. My foot tapped against the ground impatiently, but Sam looked amused the entire time at my slight irritation.

"Yes. Have some patience, would you?"

"Have you met me?" I exclaimed. "That word is not in my vocabulary."

A half smile appeared on Sam's face at my aggravation. I'd waited many days since we'd returned to our university towns. He'd reminded me the entire time that he had my Christmas present waiting for me at his place. The anticipation was killing me. "Why is this elevator ride so fricking long?"

"Maybe because I live on the top floor?"

I shot Sam the dirtiest look I could muster at his sarcasm, but the look fell when the elevator doors opened. *Finally*. I ran to the door, almost tripping over my feet. Opening the lock with my key, I asked impatiently, "Where is it?"

Sam put his hands on my shoulders from behind. "Wait for it," he whispered.

I heard it before I could see it.

The sound of Peter groaning in frustration as he made his way over to us. "Take it. *Take it.* I *hate* this thing. It's too happy. I couldn't stand being with it for three hours. Take it *now.*"

My jaw fell to the floor. There was a black bundle in his hands, an adorable puppy that was yapping happily. "Oh . . . my . . . God."

"Take it. Take it *now.*" Peter shoved the puppy into my arms, and I grasped him gently, his little nose pushing against my hand. He reminded me of Andrew's dog, Freddy, but this one was a flat-coated retriever, his fur a solid black.

I turned around to face Sam, who gazed down at the puppy with a soft smile. "I know how much you love Andrew's dog, and I figured you would want one of your own. Believe it or not, I can tell when you're missing your best friends when you're here, and I thought this would at least remind you of him and all of them."

I'm not a crier.

But between leaving my best friends after the break and the joy and trepidation I felt at the start of a new semester, I was completely overwhelmed in the moment. Tears pricked at my eyes. I rapidly blinked them away as the puppy nudged its head against my chest. Leaning over, I kissed Sam, only to pull back when the puppy continued yapping between us. "Thank you."

Sam and I looked down at the happy little dog.

"I'm going to call you Soccer," I said to him.

"What?" Sam and Peter exclaimed.

Peter looked at me like I was insane. "This thing is going to be like your first child. For both of you. And you want to name it *Soccer*?"

"Soccer. You like that?" I directed the question to the puppy, and he squirmed in my arms. I put him down, watching him run around our feet happily. "See? He likes it."

"He didn't say anything," Peter said, eyeing Soccer carefully.

"Soccer," Sam repeated, his eyes on our dog too. *Our* dog.

"It's perfect," I told both of them.

Peter looked bewildered. "I can't believe you people. Your next kid might as well be named Basketball or any other god-forsaken sport."

I ignored Peter, kneeling to pet Soccer as he approached me. He rubbed his head against my hand, and I smiled before standing back up. "Um, Sam, thank you so much, but . . . you know that the residence doesn't allow pets."

"Soccer will stay here for the most part," he assured me. "That's why Peter's a little snide today. I've got it covered. He's all yours."

"Nope." I linked my arms around Sam's neck, hugging him tightly. "You heard Peter. He's ours. And if we get another dog, then we can call him Football."

Sam stared at me almost the same way Peter had. "Babe, no."

"I thought you would like that. This one can have the proper name for our favorite sport, and the other one can have the wrong one."

"Oh, you're *funny*." I laughed at his sarcastic tone, looking down at Soccer.

He ran around our legs twice happily before running over to the kitchen. I laughed at the profanities coming from Peter, hearing him tell Soccer to stop following him. I turned back to Sam, my chin on his shoulder. "Thank you."

"You really love him?"

"You got me a dog that reminds me of home *and* he annoys Peter." I could have clapped with glee. "Of course I love him."

"I'm glad," Sam said, kissing me again, longer than expected. "Now I'm going to get Soccer before Peter does anything he might regret in five minutes."

Peter loudly cursed from the living room. "Someone take this little fucker! He's chasing me!"

~

"Crap," I whispered to myself, bolting down the field at the long pass headed straight toward me. I caught it, swerving around the opponent.

I felt like I was done with exhibition games. But exhibition games were a way to study the competition. Indoor, outdoor, it didn't matter. At the end of the day, soccer was soccer. And I was loving the sport again even as we played Hayes University's women's soccer team.

They were good. We were currently tied 1–1. I had managed to gain more play time as the games progressed this early January. And school? A new semester meant a new start. Dante was in most of my classes, and we'd managed to come up with a study schedule for the near future. I was prepared to do better this semester compared to last.

I was *going* to do better.

I sent the ball off to another player, Andrea, the other striker on my team. Squirming out of an illegal hold from one of their defenders, I made myself noticeable as I hustled closer in front of another one of their defenders as Andrea kept the ball with her before passing it off to a midfielder. The midfielder found me, sending me the ball, and I pressed myself forward, ignoring the screams from the bench and off in the stands. *Go, go, go!*

I took the shot from outside the box.

The ball soared straight through the air, over the head of another defender near the goalie. Whenever you take a wild shot in soccer, chances are you'll hit the crossbar. Only if absolutely every condition is perfect will you get it straight into the net. Hitting the crossbar doesn't mean you don't get the goal, though; it's only an obstacle in the way.

In this case, the ball went down off the angle of the crossbar . . . and then crossed the line for a goal.

My arms went up in victory. The winning goal. My team surrounded me, jumping up and down even though it was just an exhibition match. Anmol came flying toward me from down the field, yelling my name as she barreled into me with a hug.

This was soccer, and this was my game.

My confidence was strengthened further when Coach Fields approached me as my teammates started to head over to the change room. "You're doing well, Anderson."

I had to make sure I didn't smile too widely, but I couldn't help it. For a moment, I felt like I was back to my old self. The praise was entering my head and making it bigger already because I believed it. "Thank you."

Coach Fields patted me on the back as he headed toward his office. "Keep up the good work."

Afterward, in the change room, Anmol and I were still buzzing from the high of the win, chatting along with the team, when Andrea entered the room. "There were CS scouts in the stands."

CS. I froze. Canada Soccer. The women's national team. *Whoa.* It was expected, but though I knew they had watched our season games to pick people for trials, I didn't know they came to exhibitions as well.

"At an exhibition?" someone asked. "I thought they just came to season games."

"Coach said they might start showing up at more," Andrea informed us, leaving us all to our chatter.

I closed my locker, adjusting my T-shirt as I surveyed the room, when I accidentally caught someone's eye. Tanya.

What does she want now?

She approached me. "Good game, Macy."

I stared at her with caution. Who knew what was going through her mind right now? "Thanks. Same to you." I wasn't kidding. Tanya was a solid defender.

"Anyway, tell Sam that my dad wants to talk to him sometime." *Here we go.* "He wants to discuss a deal with him. He may have to meet with me for more details about it."

She said that kind of smugly, like it was supposed to faze me. Sam was in Toronto for the photo shoot with the designer who had contacted him before the break. "Cool. I'll let him know."

Tanya seemed taken aback. "You're not bothered by this?"

"Why would I be? Because he's going to spend time with you?" I strapped my duffel bag over my shoulder, giving her a tight smile for trying so hard to get to me. "I mean, he still hasn't gotten your name right. Last time I checked, he called you Montana."

Next to me, Anmol snorted, and I hid my laugh behind my hand at the sound. Bad timing. Tanya started fuming, her tanned face flushed with anger. “You’re never going to get on the starting lineup. Coach isn’t stupid.”

I remained unbothered. Her jealousy followed her as she marched back to her locker. Anmol scoffed, “She’s just jealous that you actually have a chance at making starter as a rookie.”

I glanced down at Anmol. “You really think so?”

Anmol shook her head in astonishment at my naiveté. “You’re scoring. You’re doing the work. Every time you’re at practice, you’re killing it. What did you do? Work out constantly over the break?” I had gone to the rec center and the gym several times back home, but I’d also pigged out on snacks, so I hadn’t realized my efforts would show.

Anmol squeezed my arm. “You have a shot.”

A shot at the national team. This was what I’d wanted. A shot to represent my country. It could still happen. I just needed to work harder and not give up.

That still came with a lot of pressure.

31
ONE MILLION DOLLARS

"I still can't believe you named your dog *Soccer*," Maddy mumbled. The winter break without Maddy had sucked. I was already so used to having her in my life—talking endlessly about YouTubers and interrupting me whenever I tried to play a video game—that I'd missed her terribly, despite knowing her for only four months.

We were in our room looking through videos I had taken of the puppy when I'd gone over to Sam's on the weekend. Between practices and the new school semester, Maddy and I had barely seen each other, and now we were finally catching up. "You named your dog after a sport that you play."

"Yes," I said. "Why is this such a problem for everyone?"

"You're one of the weirdest people I know, I swear. He's so cute," Maddy murmured, flicking through the multiple photos. "So did I miss anything else from your break? Wait." Maddy held my arm. "Didn't you see Alexis?"

Ugh. Suddenly, there was a bad taste in my mouth. "Yes. There's this runway show she's going to be a part of, and from what I know, Sam is going."

Maddy's face screwed up. "Ew, why?"

"Because they're friends, and friends support each other. Liz spent a good part of the break trying to convince me to go as well." Maddy shot me a confused look. "She's bugging me again to model for her." I loved Sam's aunt, but boy, was she persistent.

"You really should do it," Maddy said, crossing her legs on her bed.

"No." Before she could join in the pressuring, I decided to change the topic. "Also, remember how you noticed that Sam didn't like Dante? When they first met? Sam doesn't trust Dante around me."

"Because he's jealous?" Maddy stated.

"Yup," I agreed begrudgingly.

"I can see why. Dante's attractive," she said, still going through the photos. "The shoulder-length hair thing really works for him. Also, his personality is attractive. It is definitely one of those you can't let go—"

"Maddy, just date him already," I said, for her sake and mine. I would be happy if both my friends got together and she'd end her "boy issues" streak. I would be even happier if it demonstrated that Dante could give someone his full attention.

"Absolutely not," she said. "We're not even friends until he apologizes."

"Anyway, I'm thinking of getting Sam and Dante to hang out together . . . with us."

Maddy gave me her best *what the heck are you doing* face. "Really? You realize that Sam is still going to be jealous of this guy, right? Maybe even more so after hanging out with him?"

"But it doesn't make sense that he should be. Dante's not going to try anything. We're just friends. And even if he did, I would tell him to back off, and Sam would be informed instantly."

Maddy patted my knee. "Think about it. Dante is in your major. He's taking most of the same classes as you. He's going to be spending more time with you than Sam will get to since you both already have busy schedules. When you don't understand something chemistry-related, who are you going to call? Sam? No. Dante."

The thought of doing my chemistry work right now made me bristle. Maddy took that as a sign to do more reassuring, patting my knee. "Sam's just worried. He has insecurities, Macy. Do you forget that even though he seems invincible, he's still human?"

I took a moment to think about that. I'd seen Sam at his most vulnerable. I'd seen him cry in front of me, and Caleb had seen even worse. Sam was human; he had feelings like everyone, and although he liked to hide them for the sake of others, he couldn't hide them from me. He could get stressed but wouldn't bother showing it. Stressed about soccer and school and possibly his future. Now with Dante, he might be even more stressed for the sake of our relationship.

"It's hard to remember that little things can bother him," I admitted.

"Well, now you remember," Maddy said promptly. "Also, I'm sorry. Sam and Dante hanging out? *This* is the kind of decision you make when you're away from me for two minutes?"

She continued reprimanding me while looking at the pictures

of Soccer on my camera. I went through my phone, responding to Andrew's latest message before clicking on my message thread with Jasmine. Once again, the last messages were from me. No response. No effort.

Nothing had changed.

~

"Stop!" Maddy exclaimed hours later at Dante.

"Why? It's fun annoying you."

"I didn't sign up for this." Maddy fell back in step with me. "Does he have to make a pun every single day?"

"You get used to it over text but never in person," I agreed when we entered the pub. Sam was behind us all, saying few words since we'd met up on campus.

The lounge was buzzing. People left and right of us were chatting and laughing in corners as they ate their food and watched the sports broadcasts on the TV. "You okay?" I asked Sam.

"I'm all right," he answered. "You didn't tell me he was *this* annoying."

"You already thought he was."

"I said I didn't trust him, not that he's annoying. He's not only annoying, he's insufferable," Sam muttered. "I don't understand how you think this night is going to end well."

"Hopefully it will end with you not hating him anymore."

"I'd rather be at the flat with Soccer than staring at his face."

"Well, you're here to stare at his face for *me*, Sam," I said with a smirk.

"Yes, I am," he grumbled.

I turned to Dante. "All right, Daniel, it's time to lose."

"My name isn't Daniel, Victoria."

"My name isn't Victoria, Daniel." Sam rolled his eyes so hard I thought they'd roll back in his head. Dante racked up the balls into a perfect triangle in the center. "Just for that, I'm going first."

"Who do you think is going to win?" Maddy asked Sam as they sat down on nearby stools.

"One million dollars on my girlfriend." He glanced my way, and I gave him a heartwarming smile while preparing for my shot.

"Okay, how about instead of one million dollars, we bet five." Just as she said that, a familiar face, a face I hadn't seen in a while, passed by us.

Zach.

His eyes lit up with recognition when he spotted me. "Hey."

"Hi," I said cautiously. "Haven't seen you since the Halloween party."

Maddy let out a low whistle. "That feels like a lifetime ago." True.

Zach caught Sam's eye, the two of them observing each other with careful gazes. "Sam," Zach said.

"Zach," Sam responded, his face hard and stoic.

"Heard about Anthony." Zach shook his head. "I'm sorry he tried to screw you over. He's getting what he deserves."

"I know," Sam agreed. "I'll see you around, Zach."

Zach's eyebrows rose slightly, then fell back down. "I'll see you around, man."

When Zach left our view, Dante cleared his throat, cutting through the silence of Zach's departure. "Don't know who that was or who Anthony is, but all right. Let's play."

"So, Sam's betting on Macy, and I'm betting on Dante," Maddy announced, starting to search her pockets. "I needed a good reason to get rid of loose change."

"Get rid of . . . ?" Dante looked at Maddy with disbelief. "Do you really think I'm going to lose to *her*?"

Maddy and Sam exchanged a look. I couldn't help but grin, closing my left eye to focus and line up my shot correctly. "Yes."

"Wow, Maddy, no faith in me?"

"None."

Dante chuckled. "We'll see."

I took the shot and watched the balls roll in different directions across the table. My eyes scanned the pool table. Decent. I made sure to knock Dante's shoulder with mine as I moved around.

Fifteen minutes later, Sam was hovering over the table with crossed arms. "Well, this is rather interesting."

I had one solid ball left to get my chance to get the black one, in while Dante had two stripes. Dante looked rather confident, getting ready to take the shot with his cue. I had seen the opening he had before he probably had. He killed two birds with one stone, knocking the lined-up balls into one pocket.

Sam's eyebrows rose in surprise, and I held my cue against me, gripping the wooden rod tightly. Dante smirked. "You ready to lose now, Macy?"

"Not yet. It's still your turn. Just get the black ball into a pocket, then you win. You know how to play, right?"

"I'm beating your ass right now. I think I know how to play." He whispered that last part, bumping his shoulder lightly against mine and humming under his breath. *Dumbegg*.

He was confident. *Really* confident that he had this in the bag.

I spotted Maddy already recording this entire thing. Dante lined himself up with the easiest angle he could see to pocket the black ball. When he shot it, I didn't even react. The end of his cue hit the ball softly, and the ball rolled toward the pocket only to stop right at the edge.

Yes.

"*Shit.*" I bit back a smile at his profanity.

"That's what happens when you get too cocky," I sang, hearing Sam chuckle behind me.

I pushed Dante away from the table, and ten seconds later I had won the game with a proud grin on my face. Sam walked over to Maddy. "Pay up."

"You're the rich boy here," she complained. "Why do I have to pay you?"

"Pay up," Sam repeated, a snarky grin on his face.

"Good game, Victoria." Dante lightly hip-checked me.

"Why am I not surprised that you lost?" I asked sarcastically. "Now, since I won, it means you have to do something."

"Like what?"

"Buy me food."

"You're kidding."

"Just a future heads-up," Maddy said, slapping the money into Sam's hand, "Macy never jokes about food. *Ever.*"

Dante huffed. "Fine."

Sam cleared his throat loudly, holding a cue in his hands. He pushed his fingers through his hair. He didn't make eye contact when we gave him our attention. "So . . . Dante, is it?"

"Yeah, man," Dante said.

Sam took off his leather jacket, folding it over his arm and exposing the black shirt underneath. "How about you go get *my girl* a salad, and then we can play a round? We can do darts after, seeing that you like a challenge?"

"Sure." Dante disappeared to get me my food.

When he left, Sam started to rack the balls up, and I sat next to Maddy. "What did he say when he was sitting with you?" I whispered.

"He thinks Dante's shirt is way too tight and that he—and I quote—'needs to wake the fuck up and realize that my girlfriend is going to kick his ass.' End quote."

I licked my lips, leaning my elbow against the counter behind us. "What I am hearing is—"

"He's . . . going to take a while to come around," Maddy stated. Knew it. "So . . ." Maddy directed her next comment at Sam. "'Get my girl a salad?' I see we're playing *possessive* boyfriend today."

"Sure, Mads, we can go with possessive boyfriend today." Sam smirked, moving over to us and putting his leather jacket behind me. While doing that, he leaned in, pressing a hard kiss to my mouth.

I cleared my throat, regaining my composure. "You really think you can beat him in pool?"

Sam leaned his face closer. "I'll admit this once. He can beat me in pool. I don't really care. But he can't beat me in a game where I am the winner every time."

"Darts?" Maddy said somewhere distantly. I wasn't paying attention as I tried to pull myself out of the haze of his smoldering green eyes.

Sam didn't break the contact, brushing his lips against my cheek. "Sure. Darts."

"Sam," I warned him, grabbing the hand that didn't have the cue in it.

"Hazel. I'm only here tonight with him because of you," he reminded me. "I can't stand him. I don't like the way he calls you Victoria, but I am bearing it because of you, all right?"

I grinned. "Thank you."

Dante came back with a bowl filled with salad in one hand and a fork in the other. "All right, Daniel," said Sam. "Let's play."

"It's Dante," he said defensively, looking down at my boyfriend. Sam ignored him and finished racking up the balls.

Maddy leaned toward me. "So, who do you think is going to win this game?"

"Honestly?" Maddy nodded, waiting for my response, and I smiled, stabbing my fork into a lettuce leaf and putting it into my mouth. After swallowing, I answered with a bit more confidence. "Sam."

32
WHIPPED CREAM

"Wait, so they broke up?" Austin asked over the phone. I was currently in the elevator, making my way up to the penthouse. Our calls were becoming a little more frequent than I had initially expected. Not that Austin wasn't a close friend, but I'd thought when we entered this stage of our lives that we'd end up speaking less, not more. It was a pleasant surprise that the opposite had happened.

"Uh-huh," I said. It had been a couple of days since Peter's girlfriend—well, now *ex*-girlfriend—had broken up with him. "Sam said he's been a complete wreck. He was already really emotional when he was worrying over their relationship; I can't imagine how he'll be now."

"No way," Austin said, sympathy coating his voice. "Poor Peter."

"Yeah. They've dated for a long time." The doors of the elevator opened. "I'm not sure how he's going to get over this. I feel like everyone around me is breaking up."

"First Jasmine and Andrew. Now Peter and his girlfriend. Not to mention me with my—"

"Cahill issues," we both said at the same time. "Have you spoken to him?"

"No, there's been no contact since Christmas break. Clearly, he's 'still deciding.' Whatever that means." When I'd told Austin what Toby had said in December, he hadn't exactly taken it well.

"You've gone through all of his socials, haven't you?"

"Jon Ming did weeks ago," Austin said with a low laugh. "Found his Facebook and everything, but before you say it, I am not reaching out to him first."

"Austin."

"No. He came up to *me*. He sought *me* out; therefore, I will not be the one doing the chasing."

"But he hasn't done anything," I pointed out.

Austin let out a huff, muttering, "I hate men."

"Amen."

"A *woman*," he corrected, and we laughed. "Well, how are you and Sam? Please tell me you're good. Please tell me there are no problems and I can attend your wedding in the future."

I walked toward the door slowly, amused by his dramatics. "I haven't exactly had time to see him as often as I'd like. We're both kind of busy too."

"No more Alexis drama, right?"

I scowled at the thought of Alexis. "In a couple of weeks I'm seeing her again, remember? But she's not an issue right now. Right now, it's just Tanya."

"Tanya?" Austin let out a long groan. "Relax. She's nothing to worry about."

"She's just really annoying. I mean, she'll do anything to—"

"To get into Sam's pants?" Austin suggested.

"Yeah," I grumbled. "I can deal with her during soccer. Except when she doesn't bother passing the ball to me when she knows I'm open. I hate being on her team when we have to scrimmage. She sucks."

"She sounds like she does," Austin agreed. "You ever need help in telling her off, I'll get Jon Ming to do it for you."

"Not you?"

"Macy, I do what I have to do and mind my business."

I rolled my eyes and laughed. "It's fine. I'll just have the satisfaction of winning when I get by her every time we have a little game."

"You are so competitive," he said. "You probably race her in your head to prove that you can beat her."

"I don't have to prove anything," I said. "I already know I'm faster than her."

"Sounds like you're bragging."

"I'm not bragging. I'm stating facts."

I could picture Austin rolling his eyes at my declaration. "I gotta go. Tell Sam I say hi."

"Will do." We exchanged our goodbyes as I opened the door of the apartment. Taking off my shoes, I headed over to the kitchen, where long legs were sticking out of the cupboard under the sink.

"What the heck are you doing?" I asked Sam, dropping my backpack on the counter.

"Hazel, can you hand me that wrench on the counter?" he asked from under the sink.

I handed Sam the wrench. "Thanks, baby, and hi," Sam said,

distracted as he tried fixing the pipe while holding the flashlight between his teeth.

Before I could ask what was going on, Peter walked into the room. Correction: he trudged slowly into the room, moving as if his feet were cement blocks. A blanket was wrapped around him, and he squinted at the light in the kitchen as if it burned his retinas.

He looked miserable.

"Why don't you just call a real plumber to fix it instead?" he said in a dry, dull tone.

"Because I know how to fix it." Sam's voice echoed within the small chamber. "With a cousin and a little brother like mine, a lot of stuff goes down a sink. You need to stop shoving food down here, jackass. You're going to blow it all up one day. The sink is already clogged to the top."

"Excuse me for wanting to pig out for once in my life. It's not my fault that I decided to drown my sorrow in food," Peter muttered.

"Is that the only reason you came into the kitchen?" Sam inquired.

"Do we still have whipped cream?" Peter asked—sort of answering the question with a question.

"Really?" I questioned.

"And do we have strawberries?" Peter winked at me as he made his way to the fridge. "Just because I'm eating a lot doesn't mean that I'm going to eat unhealthy, babe."

"Stop flirting with my girlfriend," Sam demanded. "Take the strawberries and put the whipped cream back where you found it."

"But you don't even use it! Why is it still in the house then?"

"Because if I have a cheat day, the whipped cream is the first thing I'm going to go to."

Peter pouted, closing the fridge and opening cabinets. His eyebrows went up with intrigue as he reached toward the box of Pop-Tarts. "Ooh, I'm gonna have one of—"

"No!" I exclaimed, snatching the box out of his hands. "You can have anything in this place and you go for *my* thing?"

"It's in *my* flat!"

"I don't care!"

"Both of you, stop it!" Sam groaned, pulling himself out. "Peter, just take the damn whipped cream and don't touch the Pop-Tarts. They're hers."

"The box doesn't have her name on it," Peter whined like a child, pulling the blanket around himself even tighter.

"Actually," I said, turning over the box and showing Peter the sticky note on the side, "it literally does."

Peter huffed, taking the whipped cream and closing the fridge with his foot before walking out of the kitchen. "Don't finish it all," Sam warned him.

"No promises!" Peter yelled back.

Sam turned to me and gave me a light kiss in greeting before getting back under the sink. I glanced around the large kitchen, not hearing a single bark. "Where's Soccer? It's strangely quiet."

"Living room," Sam said, creaks and groans tumbling from whatever he was doing under there.

When I entered the living room, I found Peter on the couch, spraying the whipped cream into his mouth. To my surprise, Soccer was lying on Peter's stomach, his eyes on the TV as Peter flicked through the channels. Peter pulled his head back once I walked in, shaking the can and holding it in my direction. "You want some?"

"I'm good." I sat next to his head on the armrest. He looked absolutely terrible. "What's going to happen with you?"

He offered me a grim smile, "Mace, I know you give advice and stuff, but I'm not really asking for it right now."

"I wasn't going to give you advice," I said. "I wanted to know what you were going to do."

"If I'm still lying on this couch drowning myself in food next Saturday, then you have permission to not only give me advice, but you can drag me off this couch yourself, all right?"

"All right, deal," I said, patting his head.

"Don't pat my hair like that, I'm not a dog," he whined. "The dog in the house is currently lying on me like I'm its bed."

I took the can out of his hand and pulled his jaw down, spraying his mouth full of cream. "Peter?"

"Mm-hmm?" His voice was muffled behind the cream.

"Shut up."

He gave me a frothy grin, and I chuckled, handing the can back to him. I walked back to the kitchen, where Sam was still under the sink, just when his phone dinged. "Can you get my phone and read the text out loud? It's probably from Lexi or something."

I took his phone, reading the message on the screen. "She asked, 'Is next week the meeting?'"

"Can you tell her yeah?"

I typed it in, and before I knew it the three dots were floating on the screen. When her message appeared, my eyebrows rose to my hairline, and the phone almost fumbled out of my hand. "She says, 'Good luck.'"

With a red heart emoji.

I narrowed my gaze, pulling my bottom lip between my teeth.

"Can you ask her to send me details about the thing?" Sam asked.

Thing? There's a thing now?

"Um," I mumbled. "Okay."

I sent her exactly what Sam had said as he pulled himself out from under the sink. He placed the wrench and flashlight aside, and he stared at me. "What does that mean?"

My brows pulled together. "What does what mean?"

"The way you said 'um.'"

Since when was there an issue with verbal fillers? "I say 'um' all the time. It's not a big deal."

"Hazel, I'm just asking her details about the fashion show," he said cautiously. "The one in Toronto a couple of weeks from now."

"Like I said, not a big deal." I couldn't handle the intensity in his gaze, and my attention shifted to the white island in the center of the room.

Yet his focus on me didn't waver. "It sounds like it's becoming a big deal."

"It's *not*," I snapped, yet the second I released the words, I instantly regretted it with a wince. "I'm sorry, I—"

"It's okay." Sam moved toward me with concern, putting the gloves down. When he wrapped his arms around me, I dropped my head onto his shoulder, inhaling his apple and minty scent. "Did Alexis say something to you, or am I missing something?"

"She's your friend," I stated, my fingers playing with the hem of his sleeveless shirt. I didn't want to burden him with something that didn't bother me anyway. Alexis could say a million things to me about how I shouldn't be with Sam. About how I wasn't fit to be with him.

Nothing she said would ever bother me.

Right.

"That didn't answer my question."

"We had a tiny, insignificant conversation at Christmas." And I couldn't help but think about every single conversation she'd had with me where she'd basically said I wasn't good enough for him.

His brow furrowed. "What did she say? I'll talk to her."

No. "Can we forget this conversation?"

"Hazel—"

"I don't want to talk about her," I interrupted, glancing at the counter. "By the way, I know how to fix a clogged sink too. Hand me the tools, and I'll get started on what you've been inspecting for like twenty minutes."

Sam let out a half laugh as he handed me the gloves. But not before squeezing my hands lightly and kissing the side of my temple. Then he hopped on the table, reached for his phone, and started texting.

Don't let her get inside your head.

I slid under the sink, my attention on the trap of the drain underneath.

They would look good together. Alexis wore makeup, and she wore it well. She modeled. She seemed to have a good relationship with Sam's mom, whereas I wasn't even sure where I stood with Alice. Alexis fit into the Cahill world and would continue to with her modeling career, designer outfits, publicity, and money. She was the type of person who liked being in front of the camera, not behind it. And they had history. They had been together in that way before. Maybe—

Ugh. Stop it.

Then I cleared my throat to speak loudly. "Sam, we need to get a bucket before we start anything. Also, get a plunger just in case."

"I knew we had to have a bucket," Sam said. No, he didn't. "I'll be right back," he said, and I heard his footsteps as he walked away.

When I got out from under the sink, Peter had poked his head into the kitchen. "Hey, can I give you advice?"

I leaned my hip against the table. "What is it?"

"Alexis? She's a bit of a bitch to everyone when she can be. She can be nice to those that she doesn't feel threatened by, and she's threatened by you because you're with him." Peter crossed his arms. "But in Sam's eyes, she doesn't compare. He loves you. You have nothing to be worried about."

I let out a breathless laugh, wiping my hands on my sweats. Peter's tone was so certain, I almost forgot who I was speaking to for a second. However, his reassurance somehow lightened a bit of the weight on my mind. "Thanks, Peter."

"I felt like you needed it," he said, reaching out to squeeze my arm. "Just because you're the advisor doesn't mean you can't ever use some advice, no?" His gaze drifted to the sink. "Also, Sam is an idiot if he thinks that he'll be able to fix that. The guy has this need to prove his manliness."

My lips quirked. He wasn't wrong. Who was Sam without his pride?

Sam came back with a bucket and a plunger, shooting his cousin a displeased look. "I don't need to prove anything and—did you finish the whipped cream?"

Peter snickered, shaking the can before spraying the last of it into his mouth. "Now I did."

~

A couple of days later, I was rolling a soccer ball in one of the indoor fields, getting some reps in outside of practice. Which I also had the next day.

The scouts from the exhibition tournament made me uneasy. I knew they were looking, constantly watching for university players to recruit for trials.

I needed to train harder.

I also needed to push myself to study redox reactions back at the dorm, which was the last thing I wanted to do.

Instead, I focused on the five soccer balls lined up in front of me. I ran toward one, booting it with ease. When it hit the back of the net, a voice from the speaker of my phone down on the ground spoke up. "In?"

"In. Of course."

"Don't be cocky," Andrew said. "There's no goalie in the net."

"You think I don't know that?" I grumbled, shooting the next four balls. Each of them hit the back of the net. As I ran over to retrieve all of them, putting them back in the space I was currently using, another voice murmured into the phone.

A higher voice.

A girl.

My eyebrows rose when Andrew's laugh accompanied the voice. "Gianna, stop." His laughter came through once again, and so did hers as she said something I couldn't decipher. "Yeah, I'll see you in a bit," Andrew said. There was faint chatter before he started talking to me again. "Sorry about that."

"Who . . . was that?" I asked, dribbling the ball in the direction of my phone.

"Gianna? She's a friend."

"A friend like me and Stevie or a *different* type of friend?"

"What is your definition of a different type of friend?"

"You know what I'm talking about."

I could imagine him grinning, blue eyes bright as he said, "No, I think I need to know your definition of a different—"

"Andrew."

Andrew chuckled. "We're friends. Definitely just friends. It's not like that."

"Really?"

"Really," he promised. "If something new is happening, then you'll be the first to know. Plus, we only have one thing in common, so I don't really think we would work out anyway."

"What's that?"

"Boxing," he said. "She boxes at the same gym my roommate and I go to, but that's pretty much it. That's all we have in common."

A thought fluttered across my mind. "Can I be honest with you?"

There was faint shuffling in the background. "What is it?"

"You didn't have that much in common with Jasmine either."

He fell silent, and I grimaced. I shouldn't have brought her up. It was true, but it probably wasn't necessary.

"You're right."

"What?"

"I mean, the biggest thing we had in common over our years of friendship and dating was you."

"Me?" That wasn't true. That couldn't be true. *Was it?*

"Yeah," Andrew confirmed. "If it weren't for you, I'm pretty sure I wouldn't have met Jasmine."

I paused, unsure what to say next. "And that's good, right?" I asked tentatively.

"It's a good thing, Mace," he assured me, and relief went through me like a calm wave. "I think I'll be able to speak to her again one day, and we could be friends. But for now, well, I like boxing. When we see each other again, I'm going to show you so many things. You will never be able to take me down again."

I laughed this time. "Don't overestimate yourself."

"Have you talked to her lately?" he asked.

"Um . . ." I picked up my phone. The last time we had contacted each other was two weeks ago. We were supposed to have a FaceTime call, but our schedules didn't work out properly.

The last message was from me, asking her when she could talk again. She hadn't responded.

"Haven't spoken to her in a while." Saying that out loud made me feel sick considering that this time last year she'd have been at my house at all hours, telling me everything that had happened to her in the four seconds since I'd last seen her. She'd texted me two dozen times a day. We'd been inseparable at school.

I missed her. I missed her so much.

"I'm going to take another shot."

I set the phone down and took the shot, watching it soar through the air, cutting through powerfully, turning and curving. But instead of entering the empty net, the shot ricocheted off the top bar. The ball came straight back in my direction, and I caught it, controlling it with my thigh down to the ground.

"Did you get it in?" Andrew asked.

I exhaled as I bent down to grab my phone, making sure the ball was still under my control. No goal. No chance of Alexis finding her way out of my head. No message from Jasmine.

I hated this. Right after Christmas, I'd felt so rejuvenated, so full of hope, and suddenly everything was starting to feel as hopeless as it had in the fall.

Andrew's voice came from the speaker. "Mace?"

"No, I didn't get it in," I answered, trying to bite back my irritation. "I hit the crossbar."

33
YOU WERE MOANING

"Your coordination is terrible," I said after Dante almost fell off Maddy's bed one afternoon. He hissed from where he'd caught the tennis ball I had thrown at him—okay, more like whipped at him—from the opposite side of the room.

He shot me a glare. "At least give me a warning first."

"Stop playing catch," Maddy demanded with her laptop in her hands. She moved from her desk to sit down on the rug between our two beds. "If you break my lamp, you are buying me a new one."

"Where do I have the money to buy you a new lamp?" Dante asked, handing me the tennis ball and sitting down next to me on my bed.

Maddy twisted to face us. "You'll find the money if you break it."

"Something tells me that she actually wants us to break the lamp," Dante murmured.

I looked at the lamp. "It's pretty ugly, actually. Let me get at the right angle and I'll break it my—"

"Stop yourself right now, Macy Anderson," Maddy warned.

I laughed. "I wasn't actually going to do it."

"Sure," Dante said.

"*Macy*," Maddy suddenly said, her eyes wide.

"Yeah?" Dante and I turned our attention toward her, but she wasn't even looking at us. Her gaze was on the screen of her laptop.

"You might want to see this." She settled between Dante and me.

I looked down at the screen and froze.

Unbelievable.

"I'm sure it's not what it looks like." Maddy laughed nervously.

"That sounds exactly like a line out of every cliché novel I've bored myself to death reading." Dante leaned forward toward the screen, looking down at the girl with confusion. "Wait, isn't that—"

A loud, quick knock on the door interrupted that sentence. Maddy handed her laptop to me and opened the door to reveal Sam.

With wide eyes, he looked at me, starting off his sentence with: "I don—" He glanced at Dante over my shoulder, and his features hardened. "What is *he* doing here?"

"We're studying, so I told him to come by here since I didn't want to go outside and face the cold and rain," I said to Sam easily, waiting for him to react.

There was no reason for him to say anything rude. Especially not after what we'd just seen.

When his attention came back to me, he relaxed, focusing on the topic at hand. "Okay, you have to believe—"

"I know it wasn't in that context." I shoved my hands into my sweater. "But if you want to explain, go ahead. Explain why it looked like your arm was around Tanya Nesmith in that picture on Dante and Maddy's favorite gossip website. You're as famous as your parents right now."

"I wasn't even—" Sam huffed, glancing at the laptop. Without another word, he grabbed my hand and pulled me out into the small hallway.

I leaned against a wall, my arms crossed and myself ready. Although Sam and I had been having small conflicts, it wasn't like I didn't believe him. I did.

"So I was walking over to her dad's building," he started. "You know how he has a connection to the fashion world and stuff and how your frenemy—"

"Enemy is fine."

"—got me a meeting with him?"

I continued to stare. After he'd made me explain Dante a thousand times, I was going to let him sweat this one out for a while.

"Yeah, so, my mum told me to go over there this afternoon. I was walking, and *she*—only God knows how—ended up walking beside me. She came out of nowhere."

As I'd expected. "And?"

"She didn't leave me alone when I went into a store to grab some water and sit on a bench in front of the building, right? Because I had some time before my appointment with her dad, and she sat down with me. Then, suddenly, she had my water in her hand. Put it on the other side of her, and I was reaching over her shoulder to get it and—"

"They made it seem like you had an arm around her."

"Yes. Then the other picture is of her basically holding on to my arm. I yanked it out of her grasp. How convenient they didn't take a photo of that."

"Yes." I blinked. "Convenient."

He ran his fingers through the curls on top of his head.

"What did you do?" I asked slowly.

"Nothing bad," he murmured, fixing his sleeves. "I told her to leave me alone."

I almost laughed in disbelief. "Okay, now give me the exact words you said to her."

"I said, 'Fuck off, Mandy. I've been trying to be nice and give you the hint, but I'm not in the mood for your bullshit today.'"

I let my hands rest on his chest before clenching his leather jacket in my fists and pulling him against me. He tensed up but eased when I pressed a kiss to his lips. "You know, you could've been a little bit nicer."

"Admit it—you didn't really want me to be nicer." He winked, and I grinned. "Now give me a kiss. I've had a long day."

I dissolved into laughter, wrapping my arms around his neck and kissing him. He kissed me back, one hand on my jaw and the other on my hip, and my laughter quickly stopped. Before he could even manage to coax my lips open, I moved my fingers up to his curly hair, tilting his head back far enough to separate us by a fraction. Sam groaned. "That wasn't a long enough kiss. Again."

"You're making this funnier than it should be," I said, not helping myself by laughing again.

"You laugh at *everything*, that's why." Sam gently pushed me against the wall, pressing his lips against mine once again.

It was always so easy to get lost in him. In his touch, in his arms, in his scent. When his tongue brushed against my own, our breath mixing and becoming one, the hallway disappeared. Everyone disappeared, and it was only us. That's the effect he'd had on me since the beginning.

I didn't know how into it we got, but it got to a point where Maddy opened the door and poked her head out, making us pull away. "Okay, lovebirds. I get that you like shoving your tongues down each other's throats, but I think everyone on the floor can hear you moaning."

"Maddy, you're very exaggerative," Sam said.

"Nice to see you too, Cahill. Would you guys like to come inside before everyone thinks you're making a sex tape right here?" She went back inside before we could answer, and I took that moment to try to smooth down my hair.

"Your friend is very interesting," Sam mumbled.

"She's your friend too." I grabbed his hand, pulling him through the door and closing it behind us.

Maddy and Dante were both still staring at the screen. Maddy tied her hair into a bun, shaking her head at something. "Southern Ontario Twitter is going crazy over you, Sam. I didn't think you were that popular. No offense."

"None taken." Sam took off his leather jacket, putting it on the chair. "The fever since Mum dropped her album hasn't really died down, and some people began to focus on my family more."

"Which is why they think you're cheating on Macy with Montana," Maddy said.

"Montana?" Dante asked, looking.

"Sam never gets Tanya's name right, so he calls her Montana," Maddy informed him.

"Today, he called her Mandy." Maddy and I cracked up.

Dante glanced at his phone, getting up and putting on his jacket. "I've got to go. See you guys tomorrow. Bye, buddy." He directed that last part to Sam and hit him lightly on the back as he left the room.

Sam stilled before he looked at me and Maddy, pointing his thumb toward the closed door. "Did he call me buddy?"

"Oh, brother," Maddy said under her breath.

"He knows I don't like him, right?" Sam asked.

"We both know you don't like him, *buddy*," Maddy said to Sam, lying down on her bed.

"But he specifically needs to know that I don't like him."

"How about you don't wait for him to figure it out and you actually tell him," I suggested. "I'm surprised he hasn't noticed your constant rudeness or how mean you were to him that time he beat you at pool."

"*One* time, Hazel. One out of the multiple rounds of pool that I, for some stupid reason, decided to play with him. I allowed him to win."

"Sure," Maddy said deadpan. "Then explain why you looked so pissed when he finally beat you."

"I wasn't pi—" Sam tried to say, but I cut him off, grabbing my camera.

"There's proof that you were seething. I can play it right now."

Sam's eyes flicked between Maddy and me. "Where's Anmol? I think she's the only girl in this city who doesn't annoy me right now."

"You're such a . . ." I shoved him, and he laughed, pulling me down on my bed with him.

"No, but seriously, where is she?" he asked, and I laid my

head on his chest, wrapping my arms around him like he was a teddy bear.

"With Derek. Derek, whom you consider a friend? Derek, whom you were with yesterday? He doesn't tell you these things?" I asked him.

"We're not like you guys, telling each other what we're doing at every second. Like, for instance, what are Anmol and Derek doing right now?"

"Movies," Maddy and I answered.

"See? I didn't care enough to ask Derek yesterday if he was even going to see Anmol today."

"That's because you're you," Maddy declared.

"What does that mean?"

"You have this 'I don't care' attitude around you."

"That's true," I agreed.

"Is that a bad thing?"

"No. It can be annoying, but it's definitely not a bad thing."

"Don't boost his ego, Maddy."

"With the way you were moaning outside the room, I don't think I'm the one boosting his ego." I took the pillow and threw it at her from across the room. "I'm *kidding.* I didn't hear a thing."

She handed the pillow back to me as she made her way to the bathroom, but not before she exaggeratedly made the nastiest sound I had ever heard since the boys came back home. "Maddy!" I hit her with the pillow again while she and Sam laughed loudly.

~

"This is exactly where I want to be in my life, watching university boys play soccer," Maddy said sarcastically. We were sitting on the bleachers of the indoor field of Hayes University for Sam's first indoor season game.

"I thought you would be more into basketball boys. Sorry . . . basketball *men*," Anmol joked while she kept her eyes on the field, waiting for Derek to show up.

"For the last time, Dante is forever going to be just my *friend*. Besides, he's too tall for me."

"Yeah, because height is a reasonable excuse," I said over the sound of people chatting and walking to take their seats for the game.

"It is a reasonable excuse since I can barely hug the guy. He lifts me up sometimes like I'm a child. Plus, isn't he seeing that girl he met at the club the other night right now?"

"Nah, he's at practice," I said, keeping my eyes on the field.

"Thanks for the invite here, by the way," Anmol said.

"Sam and Macy always go to each other's first games of the season," Maddy informed her.

Even back in August, I had dragged Maddy with me to Southford because I had yet to figure out the bus system, and we'd watched Sam's first game together. And in return, he came to mine. It was a good feeling to know he was in the stands. To see the joy on his face, whether he was playing or watching me in the sport that we loved.

"That's cute," Anmol gushed. "Oh, wait, don't you have that runway show you're attending in Toronto tomorrow?"

I nodded and then nudged Maddy to hand me the water she was holding. "And Maddy is coming with me."

Anmol frowned. "How come I didn't get invited?"

"Because you specifically told us weeks ago that this weekend you had a wedding to go to and that your cousin is going to be helping you put on 'bomb-ass makeup.'"

Anmol flipped her hair over her shoulder and fixed the Nike hat on her head. "Okay, but an invite would have been nice anyway. A fashion show would be far more amazing to go to than a wedding."

"Your wedding will probably be more fun," I said.

"What makes you say that?"

"I mean, I get to see Liz again, and she's one of my favorite people, but—"

"Alexis," Maddy cut in. "She has to see Alexis again. She's in the show."

"As in . . . on the runway?" Anmol asked in surprise. "I thought she only did, like, shoots."

"Yeah, she's kind of doing a tour for a designer in major cities," I explained, a sour taste forming on my tongue. "Toronto is this weekend. The next show is in Milan in two weeks."

"That's absolutely insane," Maddy commented.

"I gotta admit that girl sure knows what she is doing," Anmol said. "Modeling at eighteen? I'd drop out of university right now."

"You said the same thing about becoming a stripper," I acknowledged, remembering when she'd been complaining about school and the stress of everything.

"They can make up to two thousand dollars a day. A day! Imagine how much you can make in five days, guys!" Anmol exclaimed. "I'd be a millionaire before we knew it."

"Anmol?"

"Yeah?"

I patted her back. "Stay in school."

She laughed. "Is Maddy basically going this weekend as a barrier between you and Alexis?"

"Excuse me? Am I being used?" Maddy asked.

"You know what I mean."

"No, I'm just trying to keep a low profile the entire weekend and hopefully not have a conversation with her ever again," I insisted.

"I wish it was that easy," Anmol said, linking her arm with mine. "Don't let her get to you."

"I won't." The concerned looks on her and Maddy's faces proved that neither believed me.

"Mace, she clearly bothers you, even if you pretend she's insignificant," Maddy told me.

"Look. Sam and I have talked about this a thousand times. She's been a friend of his for years, and if I want him to accept people like Dante in my life, then I have to find a way to accept her."

"Yeah, but . . . Alexis is in love with Sam, that's the difference," Anmol said.

I rubbed my hands together, pushing my hair over my shoulders. "A part of me feels like he knows that, even though he insists it's not true, but he's hoping she'll move on. And I get that, but—"

"It's not even that, Mace," Maddy interrupted. "She's making you doubt your relationship with him. Like, as if she's better for him than you are. She's dumb as hell to even think that."

"Right," Anmol concurred.

"And if she thinks that Sam will suddenly fall for her, then she's even more stupid than I thought she was."

"Exactly," Anmol commented. She looked like she was about to stand up with the way she was agreeing with Maddy.

"You have that man wrapped around your finger; he will probably do almost anything you tell him to."

"That is the truth!" Anmol started clapping, and I took her hands, bringing them down with a smile at how crazy my two friends were.

"Was this supposed to be some motivational speech?" I asked.

"Yes," Maddy and Anmol said at the same time, and I almost grinned.

Typically, this type of speech would come from Jasmine. The lack of communication from her side was more disheartening with each day of silence that passed.

However, my friends didn't allow me to dwell on that as Maddy put a hand on my arm. "And Tanya? Trying to pull a stunt like that? Don't worry about her either. Something is incredibly wrong with her if she thought that the inaccurate pictures were going to break you guys up."

"Exactly. What we're trying to say is that when this weekend is over, we'd better see you happier than you've been since you came back," Anmol said. "Don't let a girl who doesn't understand that she doesn't have claim on your man get you down, okay?"

Her words made the corners of my lips quirk up. "Okay."

"Good." Anmol's eyes went to the field, and she squeezed my arm slightly to alert me. "They're coming out. Look."

The Hayes crowd roared as the guys walked out. I could spot the curls from miles away; he was wearing a headband that pushed them back. The headband was so ridiculous I was certain that Caleb was the one who'd gotten it for him.

Nevertheless, I held my camera up to take pictures of him walking out.

Sometimes these were the best types of pictures. The candid ones, where you would show them after and they'd be so surprised at how real it was. When it was them in their true element.

However, Sam was aware of the camera. He always had been. When I saw the curve of his lips as I zoomed in, I wasn't surprised when he turned his head to face me.

"Ooh, I see someone is looking at you," Maddy teased.

I rolled my eyes, lowering my camera to hide my smile. "Shut up."

"Derek looks so cute today," Anmol gushed.

"He didn't look cute yesterday?" Maddy asked.

"His hair wasn't like that yesterday. Now he looks extra cute."

"Never say 'extra cute' ever again, please and thank you," I told her, turning my attention back to Sam, who was still watching me. I took that moment to take another picture of him. When I put the camera down, he shook his head in disbelief, probably laughing to himself.

My hand reached up to the pendant of my necklace, and I twisted it in my fingers. I watched Sam's hand reach up and tap against his chest, right over where his heart was. I couldn't help but smile and then frown when Anmol and Maddy started teasing me.

"Me saying 'extra cute' is nowhere near as annoying as you two right now," Anmol said as Maddy laughed.

"Stop," I warned them before I held up my index finger and mouthed at Sam, *One?*

Sam looked at me in confusion before I tilted my head toward one end of the field to signal I was talking about a goal. In our first outdoor games, we had each scored a goal. Our first goals for our teams. It was exhilarating.

He shook his head, his lips curving into a smirk. *No.*

What?

I gave him my best *are you serious?* face, and I could see him laugh. He held up two fingers.

Really? I mouthed back.

Really. Someone pulled his attention back to the field.

"Does he really think that he'll be able to score two?" Anmol asked me.

Maddy and I exchanged a look. After being friends with him for months, I think Maddy knew that Sam rarely went back on his word. "We'll see," I said.

He scored two goals.

34
BURY HER ALIVE

"Caleb, can you please stop talking?" Maddy asked him as we walked into our hotel room. Liz had gotten us a room near where the fashion event was to be taking place later that day. Maddy wasn't really walking, though. She was currently getting a piggyback ride from Caleb as we all tumbled in, bags and bags of clothes in our hands from Maddy and Caleb's shopping spree that I'd somehow gotten dragged along to.

"Can't believe the first thing we did when we got here was go shopping," I mumbled.

"I needed new clothes," Caleb whined, putting Maddy down. "I have a meeting tomorrow."

"A meeting?" Maddy asked. "Important?"

"And top secret," Caleb said with a wink just as Sam came out of the bathroom. He and his aunt had been at a meeting of their own while we'd been shopping. Something about another future photo shoot for him to do. Sam glanced up from his phone and started laughing. "What the hell? Caleb, I can't see you, man."

"Wow, you're so funny," Caleb said dryly, putting the bags on one of the beds and stretching. "Remind me to never go shopping with girls again. Actually, remind me to never go shopping with Maddy."

Caleb lay down on the other bed in the room, spreading himself out on it and groaning excessively loudly. "Oh my God, there's a mini fridge in here," Maddy said, walking over to it.

"Get me a drink, would you?" Caleb yelled, his face stuffed in a pillow. "I must've lost a hundred pounds walking around Toronto with all those bags."

I sat down on Sam's lap, slinging an arm around his shoulders. "How did it go?"

"Pretty good, but I'm going to be kind of busy for most weekends outside of football."

Given the publicity that always surrounded his family, this hadn't really come out of left field. But with all that he did, how was he going to manage football and university? "How are you going to handle it?"

Sam sighed, pressing a kiss to my hand, "I'll figure it out."

"Also, if Macy asks you to feel her legs, just do it," Caleb yelled into the pillow, and Maddy laughed from the other side of the room.

"Why?" Sam asked.

I pulled up the leg of my sweatpants and grabbed Sam's hand. "Dude, feel how soft my legs are after I shave."

"Are you serious?" Sam stared at me.

He put his hand on my leg. "Feel."

"We're at the store, and what does your girlfriend say? 'Caleb, feel my leg.' We go to another store: 'Caleb, feel my leg.' We go to the restaurant, and she literally takes her leg, puts it on the damn table, and says 'Caleb, feel my leg.' You are in love with a psychopath."

"Well, they *are* really soft," Sam said, his hand running up my leg as I held in a shiver at the feel of his fingers.

"See?" I turned to Caleb, who rolled his eyes and stuffed his head back under the pillow.

"This is what you've been doing all day? Making Caleb feel your legs?" Sam asked when I pressed a kiss to his lips.

"Shut up," I told him just as there was a knock at the door and Maddy opened it to reveal Liz.

"Okay, everyone get ready." Her *don't argue with me* tone was set on High. "I have clothes for tonight in the next room. Maddy, darling, keep your shoes; they'll go well with your outfit. Samuel, no one understands how happy I am that you're finally not wearing Converse—you'll get flat feet. Okay, everyone, let's go. Places to go. People to see!"

Hours later, we were all in a building and people were taking their seats and passing through, waiting for the show to start. This was so overwhelming. Sam didn't walk down runways, and doing this seemed so daunting. The platform the models would walk on was long. If I ever did that, I knew I would fall flat on my face.

"I follow that guy on Instagram," Maddy whispered excitedly, holding on to my arm as she ogled a group of people having their pictures taken a distance away.

"That's the seventh time you've said that," said Caleb.

"It's true." Maddy took her phone out and took another photo to add to the many pictures she had already taken while being here. "I suddenly love fashion."

Liz had led us over to our seats. I took my seat, adjusting my jacket. Liz had put me in a simple dark-blue dress with a small black leather jacket on top. The fashion guru herself sat on the other side of Sam, asking him, "You spoke to Alexis?"

Sam nodded. "She's in her element. She wasn't nervous." I hadn't expected her to be. From what I could tell, she was someone who could own a runway despite how rude and demeaning she could be.

Before I knew it, Liz gasped. All our eyes went to her as she hugged a man who held a camera. The two spoke quickly and excitedly. It must have been nice to recognize so many people within your industry. To engage in conversation about their specific world.

But then I realized she was gesturing to me. Why was she pointing at me? Why was she leading him over to me with a big bright smile? "Macy!" What was she up to? "We've all come to terms with the fact that that you never want to be in front of the camera—"

"*Finally*," I exclaimed as Sam and Caleb snickered.

Maddy then gasped. "I recognize you. You're a photographer." She nudged me. "He takes photographs of bands."

The man cracked a smile, probably flattered to be recognized. "Yes." Then he turned to me. "Liz told me you're handy with the camera." Oh. "And James Cahill said so as well."

My eyebrows rose to my hairline. Sam's father had vouched for me simply based on the photos I had taken at the wedding?

The man stuck his hand out, and I shook it in a daze. "Elizabeth was saying that she'd like it if I showed you how we took photos during the show if you were interested. Maybe take a couple of shots yourself."

I had never been interested in fashion in my entire life, but this? This was cool. There were so many photographers at the event. When he gestured for me to take the camera in his hands, my eyes widened. There was no way this was happening to me. To *me*. Photography, after all, had always been a hobby for me.

"Um . . ."

"Macy, take the camera," Maddy demanded.

"But—"

"Oh, for fuck's sake." Caleb snatched the camera out of the guy's hands and put it in mine. "Go learn."

I glanced over at Sam, who was beaming, giving me an encouraging nod. I took the camera in my hands, marveling over the lens. "Whoa."

"We'll see you later, Hazel," Sam said, and suddenly I was dragged away and pulled in to something else I was sure would be out of my comfort zone. Maybe being out of my comfort zone every once in a while was needed.

~

I was backstage playing with the laminated pass as I waited for Caleb, Sam, Maddy, and Liz. The photographer I had worked with had been great. He was patient as I asked questions and did as he'd promised: he'd let me take a couple of shots as the models had walked down the runway.

It was sick.

Alexis had walked down the runway twice. One of the pictures I had taken was of her in some contraption I couldn't see her wearing outside of the show, but I thought she pulled it off. She had walked with confidence, and I was pretty sure she'd done well. Sam was right: she didn't look nervous, and if she'd seen me with the camera, she hadn't let on.

I hoped she hadn't seen me.

Currently, I was in a room glancing at a few pictures of past shows hung up on the wall when Maddy joined me. "If Sam goes to any more stuff like this then tell him to invite me if he has another ticket, okay?"

"I could tell you were having fun the entire time. You kept taking pictures."

"I want half the clothes. Some of them were bizarre, though. Like that fur coat that one girl had to wear looked like it was going to bury her alive," she said just as the door opened.

Alexis stepped inside in a halter crop top and jeans. She had a handbag on her arm and sunglasses on her head as she fixed her stare on me. I wasn't going to question why the hell she had sunglasses on her head when it was snowing and dark outside, but whatever. "Can I talk to you?"

Those words didn't sound very nice. "Sure, talk."

She didn't speak. She took the glasses off her head and put them in her handbag. After doing so, she glanced at Maddy, giving thc hint for her to leave.

Maddy looked at me, and I pleaded with my eyes, hoping that she would stay. *Please don't leave me alone with her. Please don't leave me alone with her.*

"I'm going to find Caleb," Maddy told me, walking past Alexis as she left the room.

Crap.

"What did you want to talk about? You were really good out there." I leaned against a table and put the camera on it as Alexis put her handbag on the dresser on the other side of the room.

"Why are you here?" she inquired, facing me.

"Sam invited me, then Liz kind of urged me to come."

"So, you can't leave Sam alone for five minutes?" *What?*

"I'm not with him all the time." I would think she would know that since whenever I was not in his presence, she managed to swoop in to try to get his attention.

"Sure."

Huh? "What do you mean by 'sure'? What is this about?"

"I mean, you're always there, don't you think? Kind of like his shadow."

"I'm his *girlfriend*, not his shadow. I think I have the right to be here." Where the heck was this conversation even going?

Alexis pursed her lips. "Let me just say something."

Like you weren't already, I thought as she walked closer to me.

"You need to step back." She got into my face. Well, she tried to get into my face even though I was taller than her by a couple of inches.

"No, *you* need to step back," I demanded, and she did, though not as far back as I'd hoped she would.

"You literally get everything handed to you on a silver platter," she said, and I furrowed my brows in confusion.

"No. No, I don't."

"Yes, you do. Liz offering to work with you a million times over. She says all the time how you'd be great in this industry. That she would mentor you if you said yes. I've had to work since I was a kid to even get here, but she was willing to just *hand* it to you?"

I frowned. I got it—I'd resent me if I was in her shoes, and Alexis had seen Liz ask me that question multiple times over the Christmas break. It would be like Alexis walking onto my soccer team after never playing a game in her life. "Look, I get that you're upset about that—"

"Then you just so happen to show up to your *first fashion show ever* and I walk down the runway to see you're taking professional pictures. Pictures that will end up circulating online and on various platforms. How the hell is that fair? You waltzed in here, and it was handed to you. It's like you don't even have to try and everything gets handed to you." She shook her head in disbelief, agitation evident in her voice. "Even Sam."

It always circled back to Sam. "What about him?"

Irritation grew in her face as she scowled. "I remember when you guys weren't dating. When you came to Redmond. You went out of the house in sweats. *Sweats*. You didn't even try, and before I knew it, he tells me over the phone that you're his girlfriend before I even have a chance to react."

"Alexis."

"The funny part, though, is that I remember talking to you one time before he said that. I remember you telling me you had a boyfriend." The grin on her face now was catty. "Little did I know that it was Cedric."

I didn't say anything. She was getting into my head. *And she knew it.*

"It wasn't even that you just happened to cheat on someone, but you did it with his own family."

I blinked. The reminder was something I had already dealt with. The guilt was something that had come and passed. I didn't think it needed to be brought up again, but the emphasis she placed on family made me freeze.

Alexis's eyes narrowed into slits, her lips tugging up in a smug smile. "Nothing to say? I mean, you cheated on Cedric with his own cousin. What makes you think that you won't cheat on Sam?" Wow. Had she and Tanya been separated at birth?

"I don't know what you're getting at, Alexis, but you're not getting to me," I lied.

"I'm not?" She came closer to my face. "Maybe because you already know."

"Know what?"

"That Sam doesn't belong with you. That you're going to cheat on him, or he's going to find someone better."

"Someone like you? Someone who's getting famous? Looks good with him on camera?"

"*Exactly.*"

The way she was holding herself made it seem like she was going to punch me. She was willing to physically fight with me over Sam. "You're not worth having this conversation with."

"I'm not worth it?" she scoffed. "In case you haven't noticed, I've known Sam longer than you have."

"I realize that," I said sarcastically. "Thanks."

"I've seen him at his worst, and you just so happen to walk into his life and—"

"And what?" *Say it,* I wanted to pressure her. *Say that he fell in love with me for some weird reason. That we clicked. That he's happy being with me.* But Alexis would rather have drunk poison than admit that.

"Look," she started, her gaze hard and unflinching, "you may not understand this, but Sam and I actually have something."

"Then why isn't he with you? Why is he with me?" I asked. "Why is he in love with me?"

Alexis flinched, her face paling and going tight. Clearly, I'd struck a nerve.

"I don't know," she sneered, looking me up and down with disgust. "But he's going to come to his senses one day. Besides, I can give him something he wants that you can't."

I stilled. No way was she going to throw that in my face. No way was she going to mention sex as something she could use to her advantage.

No way.

"He's going to get tired of you," she goaded me. "He's going to get sick of waiting."

"Alexis, shut up," I said quietly, trying not to let my irritation get the best of me.

"He's a *man*, Macy," she stated, her hands on her hips. "He's going to get bored of waiting around for you."

I stayed silent, clenching my fists at her words. *Don't do it. Don't do it.*

"Because unlike you, I had sex with Sam. And you can't even give him *that*." She let out a short laugh. "And when he finally gets sick of waiting, he can come to me."

And that triggered it.

I think Alexis sensed I was about to snap because before I knew it, her claw of a hand swiped against my face.

And then the next second, the two of us were on the ground.

She couldn't even make a fist, let alone punch me. Yet she managed to nick my cheekbone with her acrylics, and I hissed in pain as she continued her swatting. Alexis's hands moved wildly, but I managed to gain the advantage. I climbed on top of her, my adrenaline rushing through me. Although I could have retaliated as she continued to claw at my face, screaming and shouting, I just deflected her next moves. Finally, I managed to secure her hands down so that she wouldn't add to the cut she'd just made on my cheek.

All of a sudden, someone lifted me off Alexis, giving her the opportunity to try to kick me in the stomach with one of her stupid heels. Whoever was holding me managed to get me out of the way of her damn shoe, but due to the angle, her heel ended up hitting him in the shin instead. Another voice cursed loudly as someone held Alexis back—I immediately recognized Caleb's voice—but soon, she disappeared from my line of vision as I was dragged into another room.

"Hey, hey, calm down, it's me."

The deep breath I took was one that needed to be controlled as I got out of Sam's hold and distanced myself from him. We were currently in a closet, the smell of bleach from the cleaning products on the shelves overpowering my senses. If anything, it wasn't helping. The space was too small for everything that I couldn't contain. I tried to calm myself down, but I was getting angrier.

Angry at her for saying those things.

Angrier at myself for letting her words get inside my brain.

"What the hell happened? Why did you attack her?"

What? My head snapped up at the same time a pang settled in my chest. He had to be kidding. Why would he even say that? Why would that be the first conclusion he jumped to?

"What makes you think that *I* attacked *her*?" I asked slowly, my voice quiet in an attempt to remain still.

"You were on top of her."

I stared at him, my fists clenched by my sides. I'd been on top of her to defend myself. I'd been on top of her because she'd started hitting me first. The lack of bruises on her and the obvious scratch on my face made it rather obvious.

Then again, he only focused on what he wanted to focus on.

And right now, his focus wasn't on me. That hurt way more than the nick on my face.

Sam's eyes fell to the now-bleeding cut on my cheek, concern overcoming his curiosity. "Hazel, are you okay?"

"No," I admitted. Physically and mentally. "Your first thought was that I attacked her?"

"I didn't—" Sam shook his head. "No, I shouldn't have said that. It looked like that because you were on top of her, and we didn't see the whole thing. I'm sorry."

His sincerity made my fists loosen, but I was still aggravated. I was still tense.

"What happened?" he asked, searching me for answers, looking to see if I'd gotten hurt anywhere else. I was fine . . . on the outside.

"She provoked me," I said. "She started saying how you shouldn't be with me, and—"

"Huh?" Sam blinked several times. "Why would she say that?"

What?

"Don't you get it?" I scoffed. "It's like you can't process the idea that one of your closest friends is so in love with you! How many times do I and everyone else have to point that out to you? She loves you to the point where she has to make me doubt our relationship."

"Doubt?" He seemed puzzled. "Why would you . . . why would you have any doubt about us?"

"I think most of it has to do with her being your first, which she uses to her advantage and says to me all the time."

Sam made a face. "Why is *that* an advantage?"

"Because . . ." I let out an exasperated breath, running a hand over my face. "Because she might actually be right. I mean this time last year, you were the type of guy to go to a party and hook up with a girl. And now you don't get to do that anymore."

"I'm not like that anymore," he stated.

"I know that," I said, all my worries rushing out of me. "But now you're with me, and I—I'm just not ready to give you that yet."

"I understand that," Sam said softly, but no matter how tender his tone was, I couldn't help but think otherwise. I'd been thinking otherwise for far too long.

"Do you? Do you really? I mean, Alexis has put so many thoughts into my brain about this. Everyone around me has. Even my brother when you and I first kissed during that . . . break . . . said that. Alexis said you'll get bored of me."

"Bored?" His lips parted in surprise. "Hazel, that's not going to happen."

"But what if it does?" I asked. "What if you can't take it anymore, and you don't want to keep waiting for me to be ready? What if Alexis is there because she knows you might go to her?"

Sam seemed taken aback by my suggestion. "Why the hell would I go to her?"

"Because she'll be there to welcome you with open arms," I said. I hated it. I hated that knowledge. That fact. "Because she loves you, has always had some weird obsession with you, and wants me out of the picture."

Suddenly, my phone pinged. I ignored it as Sam processed my words, but the pinging kept going. I groaned, finally taking out my phone and looking down at the screen. *The stupid puns.*

"Who is it?" Sam asked.

I silenced my phone and shoved it back into my pocket. "It's just Dante."

His expression slackened. "*Oh.*"

I sighed, already recognizing the tone in his voice. "Dante is just my *friend*, Sam. You know this. I know this. He knows this."

"Sure he does."

What? "How many times do I have to tell you that Dante is just my friend? I know that he doesn't feel that way for me."

"How many times do I have to tell you that that is all Alexis is to me? *A friend.* There will never be anything more. I'll make sure of it."

"Yes, I know *you* think that, Sam," I repeated. I'd heard this all before, but I didn't think I wanted to hear it ever again. "But the thing is that Dante doesn't feed you constant doubts about our relationship. He has never confronted you to tell you that you're not good enough for me. He doesn't remind you that he slept with me because *I didn't sleep with Dante*."

"I was *sixteen*," he stressed, his hands running through his curls. "My sister had just died, and I found comfort where I knew I was going to get it. Her. That was at *that* time. That was forgotten. I barely remember that day. I feel *nothing* for her."

"And I feel *nothing* for Dante!" I exclaimed. "You act possessive and jealous over my friendship with him. But I can't be upset with Alexis, who says such vicious things to me when you're not in the room and has literally said out loud that she's in love with y—"

I stopped speaking at the unexpected knocking on the door.

Caleb poked his head into the room, silencing the heated conversation. His eyes flicked between Sam and me, evidently sensing the tension as he cleared his throat. "Um, Alexis is kind of asking for you, Sam."

Oh, is she?

Sam shook his head, looking as exasperated as I felt internally. But I thought I had him beat in the frustration competition.

I needed time to think. To calm down.

Caleb shut the door, but when Sam and I locked gazes, I stilled. I knew him like the back of my hand. I recognized the conflict arising in his expression even before he stammered, "I'll, um, I'm just—"

He closed his eyes for a moment, clearly deciding what to do, and the sight of him doing that only made my blood boil even further. "You what?"

The unspoken words were somehow loud and clear in the silence. He wanted to hear her side. Even after what we'd discussed. After all the conversations revolving around her, the outside perspectives . . .

He still wasn't listening.

"Go," I demanded. No, I *insisted.* "Go see her. Don't make it seem like you have to pick between staying here to fight with me when you can go and console her in the other room. Console her for something she's been meaning to start with me ever since you told her we got together."

If we kept arguing, all we would do was add fuel to the fire. I didn't have the energy to let it continue to burn so brightly.

His expression was filled with hurt, but the way I felt right now, I knew if I stayed here, we were going to say things we'd regret.

"Hazel—"

"I'm not going to be an option. Go to her. I'll talk to you when I'm ready," I mumbled, passing by him and walking out of the room.

35
A DATE?

"When was the last time you guys talked?" Anmol asked me as she tied her hair into a ponytail.

She, Maddy, and I were currently inside the four walls of Anmol's single bedroom in Farrow Hall. Anmol had been sitting at her desk, staring intensely at her laptop screen as she typed notes while Maddy was reclining on her bed, texting frantically. And I had lain on the ground, outstretched, staring at the ceiling for the past hour that we were all supposed to be doing work.

"That day," I said quietly. "Last weekend."

"It's been *that* long?" Maddy asked, her texting coming to a halt as she sat up. Even I had a hard time believing that Sam and I hadn't had any form of communication for a week.

My hands dragged down my face, a long breath leaving me; sadness and frustration had been whirling inside me all week. Perhaps the two emotions had been playing with each other for longer than I'd been willing to admit.

"I felt like I would've screamed at him or something if I didn't get away from him," I disclosed. "It was actually Caleb who had to force him not to text me or see me until I wanted him to see me."

I didn't move my gaze from the ceiling, but I knew Anmol and Maddy were peeping at each other. They probably wondered if I was going to lash out. If I was going to snap. Truthfully, I didn't have the energy.

"You know Valentine's Day is tomorrow, right?" Anmol asked.

"I'm aware," I answered, my fingers now tapping against my stomach.

"So, what the hell is going to happen with the two of you?"

"I don't know," I admitted.

"Okay, I'll cut to the chase," Maddy said, exasperated. "Is he going to stop seeing Alexis?"

"Mads, you're making it sound like Sam was seeing Alexis behind Macy's back." Anmol's lips parted, her brow furrowing in sudden anger at him and for me. "He wasn't, right? Because if he was—"

"He's not cheating on me," I interrupted.

He wouldn't have done that. After all, his own words came trailing back to me. On a night when it was just the HDF soccer pitch, a ball, our stuff, and the two of us, in a perfect bubble of just me and him, he'd said if he were to have his heart broken by someone one day, it was going to be by me.

And that was the last thing I wanted to do.

"We know that," Maddy reassured me.

"Why does he think that Dante is into you anyway?" Anmol asked, looking confused.

"I have no idea," I admitted. "It doesn't make any sense, to be honest. I have other guy friends, and he has never seen any of them like that. I understand he's upset about me being with Dante more than him because Dante and I have almost every class together and he goes here, but that's—"

"Bullshit," Anmol cut in. "He needs to trust you. He needs to trust that even if Dante does something, that you'll push him away. That you won't give in."

Exactly. And there was nothing to give in to. Dante and I had things in common, but all friends had that. The boys and I back home had soccer and video games and years of memories with everyone. Dante and I had sports and chemistry. We were friends.

But Sam and I had a lot together: we had memories, we had a connection, we had an understanding of each other. We had a possible lifetime together. Why did he not understand that? Why did he not get that Dante wasn't a factor between us at all?

"And does Sam realize that he has to cut that bitch out of his life?" Maddy mumbled.

"Maddy . . ." I trailed off.

"It's true whether you want to say it out loud or not," she snapped. "She comes in thinking that Sam is going to dump you for her. She needs a reality check. Sam doesn't love her. He doesn't care whether they had sex or not. He used her when he was completely down. He let her know that and told her that when they had sex, it meant nothing. Nothing. Nada. Zippo. Zilch. Zero."

My friends had their hands off their devices at this point. They were angry. Maybe even angrier than I was.

Maddy scowled. "He can't be friends with someone who is

trying to pull your relationship apart. He can't do that. He can't allow a toxic person in his life who is not only trying to ruin your relationship but who is also making you of all people insecure. Macy, you're not an insecure person. I knew that the second I met you."

"She's right. You don't really care about what people think about you," Anmol added.

"And the fact that this person is making you doubt yourself is so stupid." Maddy got off the bed at this point, and I was forced to look up at her irritated expression. "So what if she had sex with Sam two years ago? *Who cares?* Sam doesn't. It's irrelevant. Just because you haven't had sex with Sam doesn't mean this is a competition. What the hell?" She scoffed. "Sam has to open his eyes and see who Alexis really is. And if she really loved him, she would be happy to see him happy with someone else."

Maddy sank down on the bed, crossing her arms. Anmol twisted to face me, the two of them patiently waiting for what I had to say. At that moment, all I felt were my emotions bubbling within me; I was filled with sadness and frustration but also love for my new friends.

"I hate this situation so much."

Anmol brought herself down to lie down next to me. "We know."

Maddy joined us on the ground, her shoulder next to mine as we all stared at Anmol's ceiling. Maddy bumped my arm with hers. "Have you decided when you're going to talk to him about this?"

"I don't even know how," I told them. "I feel like the next time we talk, we're going to get into another argument. Like an actual full-sized argument with nasty words, which is where the last one would have headed if Caleb hadn't interrupted us."

"Communication," Anmol said, nudging my shoulder with hers. "It's essential, Mace."

"I know." In our few minutes of silence, Maddy slipped her hand down to link with mine while Anmol leaned her head against my shoulder. When Maddy squeezed my hand, my tornado of emotions slowed. I was grateful to have them for not only this moment but for hopefully a very long time.

Then, in the middle of the quiet, Anmol suddenly spoke up. "I can't believe Sam thinks Dante is interested in you. I always thought Dante was gay."

~

"Go to the left when you reach the hill. There's a shortcut," Andrew murmured from the speaker of my cell phone. I did as he asked, moving the joystick on my phone screen. We were both playing a multiplayer racing game on our phones.

I was lying down on my bed in the quiet of my dorm room the afternoon of Valentine's Day. Maddy was at volleyball practice. Andrew was currently in first place of the race, instructing me on the secrets within the game; I noted that he was sounding better even on a day like today. Like he and Jasmine had never happened. Like the heartbreak from the fall had just been a dream. Like they'd never broken up, and he had never gone through any pain.

Suddenly, he cleared his throat as we continued with our race. "Have you talked to him yet?"

"No. I haven't talked to him yet." Saying that out loud made my stomach twist into knots. "I've been getting that question a lot."

"Sorry, I'm just concerned. When you called me right after everything happened, you sounded really upset, Mace."

"Yeah, but . . ." I trailed off, sighing.

"I'm surprised you haven't cried or anything. Then again, it takes a lot to make you cry over something."

I cleared my throat, sucking in a deep breath as I kept my eyes on the screen. "Is there another way to get around this hill?"

"No," Andrew informed me. "You're avoiding the topic."

"Maybe I'm having a nightmare where Sam and I aren't talking," I said. "Or maybe my dorm room door opens and a bunch of bugs crawl through and eat me alive. That, my friend, would be a *nightmare*."

Andrew managed to give me a laugh. It was definitely one filled with pity. "But, Mace, it's not like you broke up, is it?"

"That's what it feels like." It felt like my heart was sinking. Deep, deep down, and I didn't think I was going to find it anymore. I took another long breath in as I kept my concentration on the screen.

"What are you going to do? Spend Valentine's Day alone?"

"I've spent every other one alone, why not this one?"

"Maybe because you have a boyfriend and you guys just aren't talking. You have to do what's right for your relationship, Mace."

"It's not that simple—"

The game cut out when another caller ID appeared on my screen. "Hold on, Caleb's calling me."

I accepted Caleb's call before putting both him and Andrew on a conference call and then back on speaker.

"Hello? Hello? Hell—"

"It's me and Drew on the line, Charming," I told him, going back to the game even though I was now bumped down a couple of places due to his interruption. "What's up?"

"Oh, hi, Drew. I might as well tell you too."

Huh? I exited the game, sitting up to give Caleb my full attention. "What's wrong?"

"Nothing's wrong," he assured me with a breathy laugh. "I, uh, you remember how in high school I wrote stuff?"

"You'd have to have been in a coma not to have noticed that, yeah," Andrew said.

"So, since last summer, I've been working with Sam's mom, Alice." The sound of his name made me freeze. *Focus on Caleb. Focus on his news.*

Drew coughed. "Nepotism."

"A *connection* to nepotism," Caleb corrected, his voice light. "Liz had given her some of my stuff to read, and she liked it. She liked it a lot, to the point where she sent my manuscript to one of her friends. And this friend is an agent. Who has decided to represent me, and I might be publishing a book in the near future."

For a second, Andrew and I didn't say anything. Caleb, someone who'd poured his heart out into countless notebooks and multiple documents on his laptop, was going to be an author.

"Charming." That was all I needed to say because he laughed at the emotion in my voice.

"Yeah, yeah, I know." I heard him clap his hands. "It's kind of a big deal."

"Not *kind of*," Andrew chimed in. "Congrats, man. It's deserved if this goes through."

"Thank you," Caleb said. "So, on that note, I'm dropping out of school."

"*What?!*" Andrew and I said at the same time.

"We all saw this coming, don't act surprised," Caleb said excitedly. "I hated college. It's not for me. I saved some money up, and after talking to my tía, she's agreed. She's going to chip in, and I'm going to go Italy to get more inspiration to make the manuscript perfect."

Italy? My heart dropped. Why Italy? Italy was so far away.

"But don't worry," he said as if he could sense what I was thinking. "You'll never get rid of me."

"Which story is it?" Andrew suddenly asked.

Caleb let out an uneasy laugh. "You see, that's kind of the issue here. One of the reasons I called Macy to begin with."

Oh my God. Realization hit me in the face. I frowned as he continued.

"Remember when you and Sam went to Redmond last year, did your thing, and we spoke on the phone, and I made a little joke about writing about you guys?"

"You *didn't,*" Andrew interjected.

"Oh, yes, I did," Caleb said with delight in his voice. "It doesn't have your names, but it's kind of obvious it's about you two."

What? "Don't tell me you gave it that dumb title: *The Bad Boy and the Tomboy.*"

"No," Caleb promised. "It's called *72 Days.* Since that's the amount of time Sam said it took for you guys to get together after you officially met."

Seventy-two days.

My heart flipped, dove, and squeezed.

"I wanted to know if it was okay," Caleb continued, "if what I was doing was okay. Sam said that he was fine with it, but he said what you wanted was what mattered the most."

What I wanted.

At those words, I wasn't upset at Caleb writing about our story. I wasn't upset that this was basically confirmation that Alice Cahill knew how Sam and I had gotten together.

Sitting here on Valentine's Day, I realized there was something I had to do. I didn't answer Caleb's question; instead, I bid both of my friends a quick goodbye and sent a short text to a number I hadn't touched for a week before grabbing my keys and heading out the door.

~

My gaze sat on the dark-gray door of the apartment. The fingers of one hand frantically tapped against my thigh while the other hand repeatedly flipped the key I held.

Why the hell am I conflicted about opening the stupid door? I asked myself.

Suddenly, the door unlocked, making my heart leap into my throat before it swung open. Peter stood on the other side, relief in his eyes. He looked the most put-together he had seemed in weeks despite his frown. "Both of you are going to drive me crazy."

"How?" I inquired.

He waved a hand to dismiss the topic, holding his jacket. "I'm going out."

"You have a date?"

"A date? On Valentine's Day? Aka Single Awareness Day?" he scoffed. "Not for the first time in years."

"You look a lot better," I commented.

"I told you I would get better," he said, giving me a soft smile.

"Now come here and give me a celebration hug for working on myself."

Peter wrapped his arms around me, and I hugged him back. Before I could say anything, he whispered, "He's stupid. Beyond stupid, and he needs to realize that what he did or what he said or whatever the hell he's been doing is dumb because looking at the two of you right now? Jesus. And it's not like you guys broke up. I can't even imagine how *that* would be."

Peter bid me good-bye, and when I closed the door behind me, the pitter-patter of soft footsteps ran toward me. Soccer panted as he approached me happily, not understanding anything that had gone on at all. The obliviousness made me smile, and I bent to cuddle him into my arms. "Hey, little guy."

"He missed you."

I glanced up at him. At Sam.

He looked off. Slightly.

It wasn't the unexpected facial hair or the way he put on a small smile for me. It wasn't the way his shirt was wrinkled at the bottom or the two different-colored socks on his feet. It was his energy. He was off.

He stared at me for a moment, and all I could do was stare right back. This conversation was bound to happen, anticipation creeping up my bones, making me nauseated the longer I stared at him. God.

Soccer shifted in my arms, and I placed him down as I slowly took off my shoes. "I missed him too," I said, watching Soccer run away toward the direction of the kitchen.

The second Soccer disappeared, I turned my attention back to Sam. Yet when we locked eyes, I held my breath in the midst of our silence. The silence stretched uncomfortably long as various emotions flickered across his face: anxiety, worry, awkwardness.

Sam and I weren't awkward. Even when we were first getting to know each other, we were comfortable. Even when we were silent or in an awkward situation, we'd glance at each other and laugh it off.

We weren't awkward.

When I opened my mouth to speak, I wasn't surprised that Sam had tried to get his words out at the same time. The two of us shut up quickly, and Sam's hand rubbed the back of his neck nervously. I gestured to let him speak first. "I know you said you wanted to talk, but—"

The small smile on his face made one appear on mine. I'd always love the way he smiled. I'd always love the warmth I felt when it was directed at me. But I'd come here to talk to him. Not to dance around the subject with soft glances and gifts. "Sam . . ."

"C'mon." He waved me over to the living room. "I . . . made you something."

The glass table in front of me made my lips part in awe. Different plates. Various Pop-Tarts. It was my food heaven. "Is that a tray of cake pops made out of Pop-Tarts?"

"There're milkshakes in there too, and I downloaded your favorite movies."

Oh my. "Sam—"

"I mean, if you want to watch one, we can do it right now," he breathed out, running a hand through his curls as he gestured to the table. "There are s'mores made out of Pop-Tarts, and I found a whole bunch of things that Lucas told me to make for you out of them because he bakes, right? Also, I looked online and made this weird thing, but I'm sure you're going to like it—"

"Sam?" I had to stop him, even though hearing him ramble was one of the most endearing things in the entire world. Even though I would have loved to see the way his eyes lit up as he explained what he had made for me, I had to stop him so I could focus on what I'd come here for.

He gave me his attention with bright, hopeful eyes that made my chest ache. "Yeah?"

"Can we talk?" I asked softly. "I came here because I wanted to talk to you."

That smile of his, the hopeful one filled with excitement, dimmed, slipping off his face as he settled into our reality. "Sure."

When we sat down on the couch, a distance apart, I felt the awkwardness again as he waited.

I hated it.

"Do you remember what we were doing a year ago today?" he suddenly asked.

"Let me guess." I perched a leg up on the couch as I got comfortable. "You were probably annoying me with your presence but didn't bother leaving me alone."

Sam chuckled. "I annoyed you for a whole month."

"Just a month?" He knew the exact timing of everything.

"Macy?"

He didn't call me Hazel. He always called me Hazel.

"Yeah?"

"Happy Valentine's Day."

"Happy Valentine's Day, Sam," I said softly.

And when he kissed me, for the first time I felt like we shouldn't. No matter what it felt like. No matter the significance of this day. Things weren't resolved. Nothing was truly fixed, and everything felt off.

I couldn't.

I pulled away, my hands sliding down his shirt. My fingers bunched the bottom of it, and he rested his forehead against mine. "Sam, I can't."

"Okay," he whispered, moving my hair out of my face, but I pulled away. I moved back, my hands still clutching his shirt. The proximity was too much. He was too much right now. No, everything felt like too much. Even my next words were too much.

They were the hardest words I'd ever had to say.

"I . . . I think we need a break."

Sam blinked. Once. Then several times.

His bottom lip rolled into his mouth as he processed my words, and he averted his gaze. "You're breaking up with me?" Sam asked in a quiet voice that was interrupted by the faint bark of Soccer in another room.

"No." I took his hands in mine. "Sam, you mean the world to me, but this, what's happening right now? We need to fix it. We need to have an understanding, and we need space."

"More space than we already have?" he asked, raising my hands to kiss the backs of them. "When you sent me that text, it had been seven days, two hours, and fourteen minutes since we last had contact. Seven days apart, and it felt like forever."

"I know," I said, blinking away the tears that were beginning to prick at my eyes. "But you need to understand that Dante is *just* my friend. That he is only and always will be my friend. You're jumping to conclusions, and the way you view Dante makes me feel like you don't trust me."

He shook his head. "But I do."

"That's what it feels like. And I need you to stop being so

rude around him so I can feel comfortable when my boyfriend and friends go out together." I paused. "The whole Alexis thing. I don't know what you're going to do."

I let him hang off that. I needed him to hear that last sentence and understand what I was getting at here.

Realization dawned on his face. "You're giving me an ultimatum."

"I don't want to, but that's what it feels like," I managed to say. "I know that you and Alexis have known each other for a long time, but—"

"You're the only person I would ever choose," he pleaded, his eyes wide and frantic and so unlike himself. "It's like you said. You're not an option. I'm in love with you, not her."

I know. I know. "But you need to understand that she loves you."

"I don't care about that, Macy."

"*I know!*" I exclaimed, my frustration reaching its breaking point. "But she loves you. No. She's *obsessed* with you because she had sex with you. Because she's *known* you for a long time. Because she thinks that every single time you have a problem or something goes wrong with us, that you'll go to her. Because of that *one* time, she thinks you will go to her. She thinks that it's bonded you or something."

How many times were we going to have this conversation?

How many times until we sounded like a broken record that was eventually going to stop the longer this kept going?

I didn't let him speak at that point as I looked him dead in the eyes. "Alexis is the kind of person who will probably do anything to get what she wants, and she wants *you*. She always has. But in order to do that, she thinks that she has to get rid of me. Since the first time I met her, she's tried to make me feel like I'm not good enough for you. Like you deserve someone who fits your standards. Who's from *your* world. *That's* who she feels should be with you. She feels like that person is herself. And if you don't believe me, then I see where our relationship stands, because I can't do this if she thinks she still has a chance with you. I *can't*, Sam."

I took a deep breath, saying my next words as carefully and as calmly as I could even though my hands were shaking. "So I think a break would probably do us some good. Talk to me when you've sorted things out. When you can trust me. When you've truly made your decision. Maybe then you'll see what I've been telling you."

Sam stared at me, dumbfounded. His eyes searched my face like I would change my mind at any second. Like this wasn't happening. Like I hadn't given him an ultimatum.

I was so sick of this. I was sick of school. I was sick of soccer. I was sick of the mistrust, the building insecurity, the jealousy, and the lack of communication in my life. This was something I had control over, and I wasn't going to change my mind until he gave me a reason. Until he stopped being so oblivious.

Without waiting for him to say another word, I leaned forward to press a kiss to his cheek. "I'll see you," I whispered against his skin, unlinking our hands and ourselves as I turned away from him and walked toward the front door.

Soccer bounced out of the kitchen, following me. As I put my shoes on, I bent low to run a hand over his fur before pressing a kiss to the top of his head. I made sure, for my sake and for the expression I knew I would see, to not look at Sam, who was watching us from the tiny hallway. "Hopefully, I'll see you soon, buddy," I whispered to the small dog.

I ran my hand over his fur one more time before I stepped out of the apartment without a backward glance.

ACKNOWLEDGMENTS

I'm going to be honest. I think writing the acknowledgments is the hardest part of any story. Nevertheless, this book, the continuation of Macy and Sam's story, could not have been completed without the support of some pretty great people.

First, thank you to my mom. Thank you for your faith in me, for answering my random calls while I was away at university, and for the constant—probably never-ending—reassurance. I owe you a steak for dealing with me. Really.

Thank you to my friends—those I've known for years and those I've met through Twitter and Wattpad. Thank you all for the strange and fascinating conversations. Thank you for making me laugh my heart out over the years. You've all unknowingly given me the inspiration to continue to write.

Thank you to Sarah. I remember you telling me to keep writing their story when we were in high school. I had dedicated that first draft to you, and numerous readers kept thanking you over the years even as we went from high school to university. Of course, I'd dedicate the finalized version to you. The future could have been so different if you hadn't said a thing.

And thank you to Lili and Ellie. Your support makes me believe I could do the impossible, even when I fail to believe I can.

To Jen Hale, thank you for helping me throughout this process. From all the time we spent breaking it all down, the plot developments, the rewrites, suggestions, and editing. I have enjoyed working with you so much.

To the team at Wattpad WEBTOON Book Group, thank you for believing in Macy and Sam's story. Thank you all for being in my corner, answering every question I had, and dealing with the moments when I could not think of a single question to ask. Thank you to Fiona Simpson's and Deanna McFadden's confidence in the future of this series (and for their reactions whenever I spoke about the cadaver course I had been taking). Thank you to Andrea Waters for being a great copy editor and to many more for all the work they have put into this story and series.

To my creator manager, Austin Tobe, thank you for your kindness, humor, and faith in me. I'm so grateful to have been managed by such a great person over the period of time we have known each other.

Finally, thank you to the readers that have followed Macy and Sam's story. My gratitude for your support is something I will never be able to put into words. I hope you've enjoyed this one and I hope you'll enjoy the next.

ABOUT THE AUTHOR

Nicole Nwosu grew up in Toronto, Canada, and she began writing online when she was fourteen. Her most popular story, the Watty Award–winning novel, *The Bad Boy and the Tomboy*, has accumulated over a hundred million reads on Wattpad and was published in October 2020. When she is not writing, Nicole spends her time catching up on binge-worthy TV shows while balancing her studies at Western University.

Check out Nicole Nwosu's debut romance novel and discover where Macy and Sam's story began!

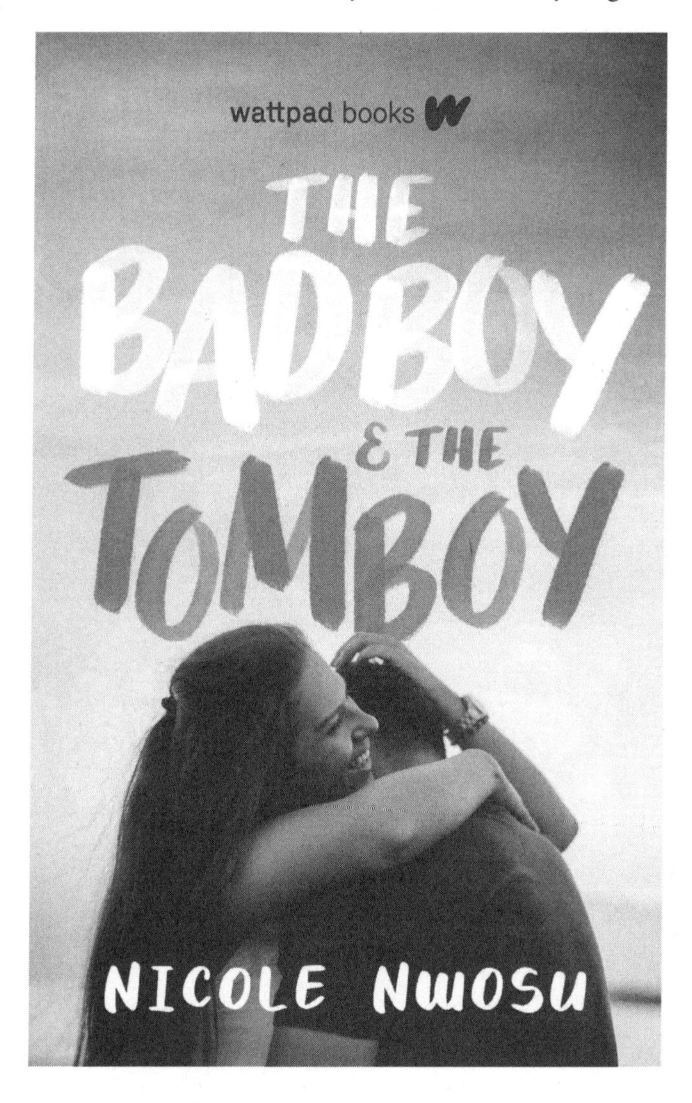

Available wherever books are sold.

1

ALMOST TOOK OFF HIS HEAD

Competition was the most consistent thing in my life. Whether it was on the soccer field against another team, video games against my fourteen-year-old brother, Justin, or a board game with my group of friends, winning was something everyone around me basked in.

Jasmine, one of my best friends, threw her arms up in the air in victory, her mouth filled with popcorn. "*Yeeffftthhh!*"

I captured her victory dance at the end of our popcorn-eating competition with my camera. Andrew, my other best friend, grimaced, "Don't get hotheaded. You won *once*."

The three of us surrounded the kitchen island at my house; empty popcorn bags littered the table. Sun rays streamed into the room through the windows, providing warmth despite the February air outside. The aroma from the multiple bags of buttered popcorn we had heated up in the microwave earlier was strong but not nauseating.

Jasmine flipped her box braids over her shoulder. “Shut up.”

Here we go. I flicked through the pictures on my camera as their argument escalated. Andrew’s blue eyes settled on Jasmine. “I’m not trying to fight with you today.”

“Then let’s not try to pick fights,” she quipped.

But, oh no. He just had to keep talking. “I know you’re having a rough time since the breakup—”

“I don’t want to talk to you about it,” she said. “I don’t want to talk to *anyone* about it.” Jasmine got up and left the kitchen, then my bedroom door slammed shut upstairs.

“I told you,” I chided. “We should give her space. Sean broke up with her only a few weeks ago.”

Andrew ran a hand through his blond hair and looked at the now-empty doorway through which Jasmine had just exited. “I’ll try to talk to her.”

“You think *you* can get through to her?” The front door opened, and I recognized the person who entered by their footsteps. *Justin.* “She doesn’t seem to favor you at the moment.”

“She doesn’t seem to favor *men* at the moment,” Andrew added. “I’ll be back.”

“Macy!” Justin entered the room, a basketball tucked under his arm, as Andrew exited. My brother unzipped his thick sweater, ears red from the cold weather as he rubbed at his rosy cheeks. “You guys ate my popcorn?”

“*I* didn’t.”

“*Liar.*”

“I said I didn’t.” As I nudged him in the ribs with my elbow he hissed, pushing my arm away.

“Anyway,” he grumbled, sticking his head in the fridge. “What’s Andrew doing?”

"Get me a ginger ale, would you?"

"No."

I gave him a look and he handed me a can as he got water for himself.

"He's talking to Jasmine upstairs."

"Is that a good idea?" Even Justin knew about the strain between Andrew and Jasmine at the moment. "To have those two in a room alone together? The other day she almost took off his head." *Good point.* I took a sip of my drink, put it on the counter, and left the room to head off the potential war.

The two of them jumped when I opened my door, Andrew springing up from my bed to stand. I wasn't sure who to question first—Andrew had a strained smile on his face and Jasmine had a sudden interest in my bedsheets. "Everything all right here?"

"I should get going," Andrew mumbled.

"Are you going to practice tomorrow?" I asked.

"Of course. I'll see you guys then." And without another word he bolted from the room.

"So . . . Andrew?" I teased.

She cringed, a predictable response. We'd all been friends for years. I couldn't even imagine what would happen if one of us got involved in a romantic relationship with another.

"No, definitely no."

Her phone beeped and her eyes scanned the message before she tossed her phone at the foot of my bed. "What's up?"

"Amy's gushing over Sam." Jasmine's friend, Amy, had a crush on *everyone*. I wasn't surprised.

The name Sam didn't ring any bells. "Who?"

"You know Sam."

"I have no idea who Sam is, dude." I raised my arms up to stretch. "Does he even go to our school?"

"Yes."

"Any teams? What grade?"

"He's in our grade."

"What does he look like?"

"He's white," she said, and shot me a look that I should've expected.

"That's literally almost everyone at school except for you."

As I searched for my cleats for tomorrow's soccer practice, she said, "You must've seen him around. He transferred from England this year."

"I know faces, not names. *Finally.*" I put my found cleats in my duffel bag.

I was just reaching to grab my soccer ball near my desk when Jasmine snapped her fingers, sitting up. "Ooh! He was in my history class in the first semester."

"You remember that I *wasn't* in your history class, right? How would I even—you know what? Never mind. Want to go to the rec center?"

"He's kind of low key." I really wasn't going to get out of this conversation. "I think he only talked to, like, three people in that class."

"Not everyone's as outgoing as you," I pointed out.

Jasmine was involved in many clubs in our school. She also played volleyball and softball, which meant she talked to *everyone.* It wasn't solely her interests—her extroverted personality also drew people to her. "I think he plays soccer too."

That got my attention. "Did he try out for the team?"

"You would have noticed if he tried out for the team, Mace."

"You sure? If he did, he could've been one of the guys who

were wondering what I was doing at tryouts. I don't think any of *those* guys made the cut."

I'd played soccer since I was a kid and every year, whenever I tried out for my school's team, I'd get the same expression from the rest of the competition. That subtle surprised look over a girl trying out for the boys' team (our school didn't have one for girls). And when I was named captain not too long ago? That surprised look was a little less subtle when people around school heard. After three years on the team, I'd become used to the guys looking at me strangely, but I didn't care—all I wanted to do was play.

Justin popped his head into my room. "Where are you headed?"

"Soccer fields are open right now at the rec center. Might attempt to get Jasmine to pass me the ball."

"No way, I've got to go," she declared. "I have a ton of things to do."

"Want to come?" My question was directed at my brother, even though I knew he had come from playing basketball there.

"Anything to get out of homework."

"Justin." Jasmine shrugged on her jacket. "You know Sam, right? In our grade?"

"How would *he* know?" I asked. "He's in grade nine."

"Curly hair?" Justin said. "Green eyes?"

"*Exactly,*" Jasmine agreed.

"Am I the only one who hasn't seen this guy?" I asked.

"You've seen him," she assured me. "You just don't know his name. See you tomorrow!"

She grabbed her things, swinging her backpack onto her shoulders as she left the house, her gesture hinting that she wasn't going to give another thought to Sam or anything school related.

~

"When does Dad get home?" Justin asked as we left the house.

"Around five." As I spoke, white air puffed in front of me. The snowfall usually stuck around until March in Port Meadow. Currently, the snow lingered in small traces on the ground, but I wanted it all gone. Canadian spring needed to come faster. I wanted to play soccer outside instead of on the indoor field. Because of the cold weather, the school's outdoor soccer season wouldn't begin until early May, and our current indoor practices focused on upcoming tournaments and exhibition games.

"Maybe he can get me popcorn since you all ate it all," Justin huffed, the tip of his nose already red from the cold. He peered over at my camera as he twisted my soccer ball in his hands, making a face at what he spotted on the screen.

"You made it a competition? And Andrew lost?" His eyes widened at the picture of Jasmine's victorious moment. He flicked through a couple more pictures. "If I was as old as you are, I'd do dumb stuff with my friends all the time to relive my youth too. I don't even blame you." As my brother continued his joking, I placed my camera in my shoulder bag. "When you leave for university, I'm turning your room into a man cave with games, a new TV, and a minifridge."

"I haven't even left yet and you're already thinking of life post-me."

I hadn't decided which school I'd be going to. Acceptance letters from potential universities' science programs were starting to come in and I didn't have to choose until the beginning of June, however, I wanted to be part of a soccer team and get a good scholarship to help with tuition fees. The potential to get scouted for a university team was slim. Scouts came to at least one off-season tournament or exhibition game before the season started, but if I didn't get the opportunity it wouldn't be the end of the world. Academically I was doing well, but soccer was my life. Securing a spot on a team and continuing my journey within the sport would be huge. Justin didn't notice that the weight of the conversation was starting to overwhelm me. *Not now.*

Justin yammered on about what he would add to his man cave during our fifteen-minute walk. We passed by a variety of houses in the quiet, residential neighborhood we'd lived in since we were kids.

This was the usual pattern. Justin would talk about anything and everything, holding the soccer ball, basketball, or both, and I would take pictures. Of the same houses I'd seen for almost the past eighteen years and the faces of people who'd recently moved in. Of two people with a child who held a tablet in their hands who passed us on the sidewalk, similarly bundled up in jackets. Of anything, really, that could capture the moment. When we grew closer to the rec center, I knocked the soccer ball out of my brother's hands, and it rolled onto the grass in front of us.

"Hey!" Justin yelled as I ran with it. I was at my best when the ball was between my feet, no matter how cold it was, the frozen grass crunching underneath my shoes, or any obstacle in my way. I handled the ball with my feet as my brother sprinted after me. "This isn't fair, I *just* played two hours of basketball!"

I slowed down so he could try to get the ball off me. He stuck his foot out to kick it away, but I rolled it back out of his reach. Dodging him, I ran with the ball, loving the feeling of it moving with me while I passed the frosted playground, the trees, and moved closer to the rec center to get away from the cold.

Throwing a look over my shoulder, I heard my brother curse as he struggled to keep up with me. For his sake, I slowed down again, and then promptly tripped over the ball and into someone's arms.

A flash of pain made me wince as the metallic zipper of their clothing collided with the side of my head. For a second, I was stunned at how distracted I had been to not notice the person in the empty park, but if they hadn't been there, my brother would've watched me fall face first into the grass. As quickly as I landed, I was equally fast to jump out of the stranger's arms. "I'm so sor—"

"Do the world a favor and watch where you're going," he muttered rudely, brushing off his leather jacket as if I'd contaminated it when my head had connected with the cold zipper. "You have working eyes. Use them."

Taking a step back, I fixed my low ponytail, glad that my brown hair hadn't gotten caught in the zipper. "Okay, jerk, relax."

"It's not my fault you don't know how to use—"

Picking up the ball with my hands, I held it under one arm. His accent gave me the impression that he'd spent a lot of time in the UK. "I know how to use this just fine."

"Doesn't look like it," he mumbled.

Justin appeared. "Aren't you Sam?"

He *did* look familiar—one of those people you'd spot in the hallway but never acknowledge. Based on my first interaction with him, it was a good thing I'd never bothered to speak to him before. It wasn't hard to see why Jasmine would think I'd have noticed him if he was at tryouts. He was tall, with curly brown hair and currently annoyed green eyes. *She* might find him attractive, but with a personality like this? *No.*

"She's your sister?" Sam said.

"I can speak for myself."

"You might want to tell her that the ball is meant to be *kicked*, not tripped over," he said to Justin. "I figured that the captain of the football team would have a much better handle on the ball."

"Justin, go long," I said, annoyed. "Soccer. We call it *soccer* over here."

Justin ran halfway across the field and I kicked the ball in his direction. It soared perfectly over Sam's head in an arc and landed in front of my brother.

"Did I offend you somehow in our fifty-four seconds of conversation?" Sam asked.

Fifty-four seconds of what? He had faint freckles on his nose and his hair looked as if he'd run his fingers through it a few times. "See something you like?"

"Not at the moment."

Sam looked amused. "It's not my fault you're having an off day with the ball. Practice helps, you know?"

"Do you mean to sound this condescending or is it just you as a person?"

"Depends. Watch where you're going next time." Sam brushed his shoulder against mine as he walked in the direction we had come from.

Justin let out a low whistle. "Sh-o-o-t."

"Jasmine didn't say he was such a—"

"Dick?"

~

Later that Sunday night, my brother and my dad surrounded the dinner table. Dad was out of the suit and tie he wore when he went to work at the law firm, and sported a T-shirt and jeans. He usually didn't work weekends but he had an important case and, even when he was tired from a long day, he liked us all sitting around the table eating dinner together. From the head of the table, he asked, "What did you guys do today?"

I shrugged, pasta in my mouth. "Nothing interesting."

Justin gave me a weird look, possibly noticing that I was still ticked off from earlier. "What happened to you, Mr. Krabs? Get any big bucks recently?"

As kids, my brother and I were obsessed with *SpongeBob SquarePants.* With our dad being a lawyer, he earned the name Mr. Krabs pretty easily. Justin's favorite character as a kid was Patrick, and I was Sandy because I had taken a month of karate lessons. My dad's expression suddenly grew serious.

"Uh-oh, what did you do, Patrick?" I teased.

"I didn't do anything! What did you do, Sandy?" my brother retorted.

"Neither of you has done anything wrong." Dad paused. "That I know of."

"Careful, Justin."

Justin feigned irritation at my words.

"What do you guys think of going to your grandmother's this spring break?" Dad asked. "You haven't seen her in a long time."

"We just saw her and Grandpa this past summer," I said.

"I mean your mom's mother."

The last time we had seen our maternal grandmother was years ago, after mom's funeral. I barely remembered the last time we saw her—everything around that time was a blur.

Mom had passed away in the early summer of 2005, when I was nine and Justin was six. She was coming home from the bookstore she owned when a drunk driver collided with her car. Even though she died when we were young, I was lucky enough to have a good memory of who she was and what she looked like outside of the pictures and old videos of us growing up. Justin had her light-brown hair but we both had her brown eyes. However, I was naturally more tanned, like she was, and Justin was more fair, like our dad.

I also shared her love of soccer. She'd played growing up, and was on her varsity college team. She'd instilled in me the foundation of the sport I loved and wanted to carry with me in the future.

As for our maternal grandmother, we hadn't seen her in years. Before Mom died, our maternal grandfather had died as well. After Mom's funeral, she didn't stay in much contact as she traveled to different places over the years, never settling down. Before then, she hadn't lived far from Port Meadow, only two towns over in Redmond. I never pressured Dad to tell us why she had left our mom's childhood home, let alone the country, but I always thought it was linked to losing her husband and her daughter. That was a lot of sadness for one person to handle.

Growing up before Grandpa had died, before Mom had died, we used to go to my grandmother's house all the time. We would meet our grandparents' friends, have nights filled with board games and great food, and hang out as a family. Last I heard, she had been in Italy, where she had lived before moving to Canada with my grandfather after Mom was born.

"I'm in," said Justin.

"Macy?" Dad asked.

He shouldn't have sounded worried. I would jump at any

chance to be reconnected with my mom in some form. My brother looked at me curiously and I cleared my throat. "Does she still live—"

"In your mom's childhood home? Yes, she moved back recently. She wants to see you guys. I figured spring break was a good time for you all to know each other."

"I'm in."

A week of the past without any thought of the future was exactly what I needed.

~

On Monday, as I shoved my duffel bag in my locker at school, Andrew approached me. "Jas said you had a little encounter with Sam."

His name was not the first one I wanted to hear this morning. "He's annoying."

"You met him once."

"*And?* I don't like him," I declared. "Besides, how do *you* know him?"

"We had history together."

"Did everyone have the same history class last semester?"

"He transferred this school year," Andrew explained as some classmates greeted us as they passed by. Wellington Secondary School was in the middle of a suburban area, not too far from my house, but a ways away from the downtown core of Port Meadow. With a big population of students, I didn't know or expect to know everyone. "You really didn't know who he was?"

"No clue," I admitted.

"Talk about timing."

Sam—scrolling through his phone—was walking down the hall with someone who was talking animatedly.

"Hey, Sam." Andrew's voice carried down the busy hallway. He and Sam did a subtle fist bump.

"Hey . . ." Sam looked at me as I scowled and closed my locker.

"Nice to see you again too," he said.

I recognized Sam's friend, Caleb. We didn't run in the same circles—he was popular, me, not so much. He had dark-brown hair, tanned skin, and his approachable nature showed in the bright smile on his face. "Caleb, right? We had math together last semester," I said.

"You're Macy. The soccer player?"

"That's her." Andrew slung his arm around me.

"You two are together?" Caleb asked.

Instantly, I gagged. "God, *no*."

Andrew pushed me away. "*Never*."

"*Ever*," I added.

"Forget I said anything." Caleb raised his hands in defense.

"It's not that—" Andrew looked nauseated. "She's like my sister." We'd known each other since preschool. He was my best friend, there was definitely no changing *that*. "The thought of—it's a no."

"A *definite* no." I shivered involuntarily. Sam stared at me. "What?"

The first warning bell cut through the air, and everyone in the hallway rushed to their first-period classes. Caleb followed suit, waving at us. "See you later."

"Bye, Hazel." Sam smirked.

What? "That's not my name."

"Make sure you don't trip on any soccer balls on the way to class." He disappeared into the passing crowd with Caleb.

"He's annoying," I muttered.

"He's playing around," Andrew said as we walked to class. "I'm surprised you didn't know him. Especially with his last name."

"What's his last name?" We got to our desks in time for the national anthem.

When the anthem ended, Andrew still didn't answer. I pinched him and he hissed, "*Fuck*."

"I'm *waiting*."

"Wait *longer*." He smirked. "Maybe I'll keep this information from you; after all, what's in it for me?"

"Would you just—"

"His last name's Cahill."

I gasped dramatically, tapping Andrew's arm frantically. "He's *Cedric's* brother?"

"He's Cedric's *cousin*," he clarified.

"*What?*"

Cedric Cahill and I met when we were in ninth-grade science class. I wasn't one to be head over heels for anyone—my friends got into relationships, broke up with people, and went through rejection to a point where I didn't want to be involved in any of that. The idea of feeling that way for anyone made me squeamish.

However, meeting Cedric changed my perspective *slightly*. He had moved here from the UK when he was younger. He played rugby, was smart, and had kind brown eyes. Eventually, as I talked to him more often, I began to have feelings for him. Feelings I'd never acted upon.

"Macy Anderson."

The loud voice coming from the front of the room forced the class into silence. My voice had carried throughout the entire classroom, interrupting announcements and violating homeroom's number one rule.

To make things worse, I was given detention, aggravating me further as I stood outside the gym after school with my friends, where practice was going to be held today.

"We'll see you at the next practice," Jon Ming said. "Don't worry about it, the team's not going to fall apart with you missing one practice."

"Cheer up." Jacob patted me on the back before he slipped inside the gym with Jon Ming. Brandon and Austin fist bumped me as they followed the other two inside.

Along with Andrew and Jasmine, Jon Ming, Austin, Brandon, and Jacob were my closest friends. I'd played soccer with them for the past four years, since we'd started high school. They were weird beyond belief, ate as much food as I did, and were the most annoying people I knew. Yet I wouldn't change any of them for the world.

"This is your fault," I snapped at Andrew as we watched our friends start to set up for drills. Where I was supposed to be.

"You're the one who yelled."

Yes, but I shouldn't have gotten detention for it. Not when we had a game next week against our biggest competitors, Crenshaw Hills. Wellington had had a huge rivalry with them for years, and soccer was a sport both schools were known for, making us the biggest competitors in the city.

My phone buzzed as Andrew slipped into the gym and I headed to the classroom to serve out my penance at detention.

Jasmine: sucks that you're in detention

Me: I can feel your sympathy from a mile away.
Please note the heavy sarcasm

Jasmine: ;)

I entered the classroom, gave the teacher who usually held detention, Mr. Malik, my pink slip, and sat down at the desk farthest away from the others who were in the room. I slouched in my chair, putting my earphones in before lifting the hood of my sweater over my head. Suddenly, my earphones were pulled from my ears.

"What are you doing here?"

Sam.

"What are *you* doing here?"

He straddled a chair backward in front of me, his elbows perched on the desk. "Got caught skipping class."

When I proceeded to put my earphones back in my ears, he hooked his fingers on the wires and pulled. "*Dude,*" I protested.

"Why are you here?" he repeated. "You should be at practice, no?"

"It's not your concern." From the look on his face I figured he wasn't going to budge until I gave him a proper response. "I may have sort of accidentally yelled during the announcements this morning."

"Which teacher?"

"Mr. Oliver."

He snorted then glanced over at the now-empty desk where a teacher *should* have been sitting. *Where the heck did he go?*

Sam stood, his chair scraping the floor, and looked at the clock. "Want to get out of here?" I must've made a face of disapproval at his suggestion because he continued. "Mr. Malik usually leaves then comes back toward the end. We're good."

"I don't know you. Why the hell would I trust you?"

"It's not a matter of trust." His green eyes were mischievous. "We're not getting caught." Sam gestured to a few other students who had started leaving the classroom. It was either here, stewing over not being at soccer practice or—"C'mon, Hazel."

"That's not my name." My earphones went back in. "And I'm not skipping detention."

Sam didn't bother me any further, settling in and taking a seat at the desk next to me. We sat in silence for the next hour and a half, him going through his phone and me doing the latest physics homework until the students who had left eventually came back into the classroom. Not long after them, Mr. Malik returned, and detention ended.

I was out the door and headed toward my locker to grab my jacket when Sam caught up to me. "Do you want to hit the diner? You've got to be hungry." He wasn't wrong. My stomach was eating itself from the long day at school. "Practice is probably over. What else do you have to do?"

A few minutes later, Sam and I were sitting at the diner a block away from school. Various people greeted Sam as they passed by, but he didn't pay attention to them. His focus for the next half an hour was annoyingly on the girl over my shoulder, as he gave her flirty eyes. He even had the nerve to send her a little wave that she returned before continuing her conversation with her friends.

"You're related to Cedric?"

Annoyance flashed across Sam's face. "Not exactly who I would like to be associated with. We aren't exactly fond of each other." He took a fry from my plate. I hated sharing. How did someone not like Cedric? Sam said, "Change the topic."

"But—"

"Change. The. Topic."

"Okay!" *Holy.* I moved the plate out of his reach. He held his hands out, stunned. "Wait, the only reason you know me is because of my cousin?"

Outside of my close friends, I didn't pay a lot of attention to anyone else. I recognized faces, but names? There was much more to focus on. Like the soccer team and picking between universities.

"*Hello?* Earth to Hazel." Sam snapped his fingers in my face.

"Not my name," I said. "Unlike you and me, Cedric and I are *actually* friends. I've seen you around but, I don't know, I never knew your name."

Sam didn't reply, his attention drifting back over my shoulder as I shoved a fry into my mouth. He reached for my plate, snagging himself another fry. "Bro, you've got to stop doing that."

"You don't like sharing?"

"Buy your own." I reached into my backpack and pulled my camera out of its bag.

"*Possessive.*" He tilted his chin at the device in my hands. "What's with the camera?"

"I like taking pictures."

"You can do that with your *phone*," he pointed out. "The captain of the football team has a hobby?"

"It's soccer."

"I'm from England. It's football."

"I'm not getting into this argument with you," I said. "I'm going home."

"Hazel, c'mon." He gestured back to my seat as I rose. "Sit, I'll stop being annoying. What kind of pictures do you have in there?"

"You sure you don't want to talk to the girl behind me?"

He reached a hand out for my camera and I gave it to him. He flicked through the pictures and I leaned over the table to get a better look. One was Andrew giving me the middle finger as we walked to his car the other day. "You and Andrew have been friends for a long time?"

"A *very* long time," I said. "What about you and Caleb? You guys seem close."

"We are." Looking at his phone, he cursed under his breath then handed me back my camera. "Shit. I got to go. Maybe I'll see you in detention again, Hazel."

"Don't count on it," I muttered as he shrugged his jacket on. "How often do you get in trouble?"

"Depends on what you consider trouble."

~

I lay on Jasmine's bed later that night, watching her fix the posters along her walls. They covered almost every inch of her room, images of all her favorite movies. I'd watched the collection grow over the years and she'd never taken a single poster down. "Did you know Sam and Cedric were related?"

"Did I know that they're cousins?" she asked. "I think *everyone* knows."

"They're so"—I tried to find the right word—"different."

Jasmine reached up to fix her *Star Wars* poster. "They're cousins, not clones."

I rolled over on her bed, resting my hands under my chin. "I mean Cedric's so *nice* and Sam's so *not*."

"Remember when you had a thing for Cedric?" Jasmine sat down on the bed next to me and grabbed my camera to look through pictures. "I'd never seen you so unlike yourself."

Had a thing for Cedric? Had it gone away? *No.* I didn't admit that out loud to anyone. Although he was a popular guy and we didn't see each other that often, it was strange that he had a cousin I didn't know about.

"Cedric's still cute, no?" Jasmine beamed, eager to hear my response.

If my face is burning up I swear—"I'm not having this conversation with you."

"Who are you going to talk to about boys? Andrew? *Please*." Jasmine held up my camera. "Mind explaining this?"

I snorted at the sight of Sam making a funny-looking face at my camera. He must've taken it when I wasn't looking. I reached for my camera with no plans of deleting the picture. "He had detention too."

"Look at you, best friends with troublemaker Sam." I grunted out a no yet Jasmine wasn't convinced. "Macy, you never know."

"It's not happening," I protested. Not with someone as irritating as he was.

© 2020 Nicole Nwosu